Praise for *Lost Along the Way*

"Duffy (*Bond Girl*) effortlessly explores complex issues, especially how much pressure women put on themselves and one another to be perfect and have everything together." —*Library Journal*

"Duffy delivers a summery novel about friendships, with both hardship and hilarity." —*Philadelphia Inquirer*

Praise for *On the Rocks*

"With its more realistic and modern ending, this engaging novel offers readers relaxing and light yet thoughtful summer escape." —*Library Journal*

"Duffy's second novel is tenderly introspective. . . . Abby's attempts to navigate the ever-changing rules of dating are infinitely relatable and will prove to be an ideal beach read for fans of Elin Hilderbrand and Sarah Pekkanen." —*Booklist*

"Alternately humorous and touching, this novel is a fast, fun read. . . . [Abby] is someone you'd want to friend, freezer full of ice cream and all." —*Romantic Times* (four stars)

Praise for *Bond Girl*

"A compelling, fun read." —*Kirkus Reviews*

"Despite financial details that may make your head spin and a workplace that will make your stomach churn, Duffy's fresh take on the single-in-the-city tale does a terrific job of reviving chick lit (not every girl works in publishing or PR, after all)." —*Library Journal* (starred review)

"*Bond Girl* is witty and very racy. . . . Trust me, you won't be bored with this Wall Street story." —*Washington Post*

Lost
Along the
Way

Lost
Along the
Way

ERIN DUFFY

WILLIAM MORROW
An Imprint of HarperCollinsPublishers

LOST ALONG THE WAY. Copyright © 2016 by Erin Duffy. All rights reserved.
Printed in the United States of America. No part of this book may be used
or reproduced in any manner whatsoever without written permission except
in the case of brief quotations embodied in critical articles and reviews. For
information, address HarperCollins Publishers, 195 Broadway, New York,
NY 10007.

HarperCollins books may be purchased for educational, business, or sales
promotional use. For information, please e-mail the Special Markets
Department at SPsales@harpercollins.com.

A hardcover edition of this book was published in 2016 by William Morrow,
an imprint of HarperCollins Publishers.

FIRST WILLIAM MORROW PAPERBACK EDITION PUBLISHED 2017.

Designed by Bonni Leon-Berman

The Library of Congress has catalogued the hardcover edition as follows:

Names: Duffy, Erin, author.
Title: Lost along the way : a novel / Erin Duffy.
Description: First Edition. | New York, NY : William Morrow, [2016]
Identifiers: LCCN 2015049964 | ISBN 9780062405890 (hardback)
Subjects: LCSH: Female friendship—Fiction. | BISAC: FICTION / Contemporary
Women. | FICTION / Humorous. | GSAFD: Humorous fiction.
Classification: LCC PS3604.U3775 L67 2016 | DDC 813/.6—dc23 LC record
available at http://lccn.loc.gov/2015049964

ISBN 978-0-06-240590-6 (pbk.)

17 18 19 20 21   OV/RRD   10 9 8 7 6 5 4 3 2 1

For D.F.

Thanks for everything

one

May 2005

Taxi!" Jane yelled, hurling herself into oncoming traffic in an attempt to slow the canary-yellow car as it came speeding down Columbus Avenue. She'd overslept and had to hurry downtown to meet the girls for brunch, leaving her husband, Doug—she loved the way that sounded—back at their apartment on West Eighty-Second Street, sleeping off the bottles of champagne they'd had after the ceremony. She was going to be late, which wasn't unusual in the slightest, but today it actually bothered her. Today she had news. Today she really would've liked to have been on time.

Jane checked her face in her compact mirror and plucked one lone false eyelash out of the corner of her eye. She tousled her blond hair, the curls from the night before now looking chicly disheveled, and dropped some Visine in each eye while her cab idled at a light on Houston Street. She pulled her phone from her bag and sent a quick text message to both Cara and Meg: *Stuck in traffic, be there in five,* even though she knew it would take her at least ten minutes to get there. They wouldn't be surprised as Jane hadn't been on time for anything in her entire life. They didn't seem to care all that much, but old friends are good like that. She loved them like sisters, and while they each had become their own women over the years, they were still best friends. She couldn't wait to tell them that she'd gotten married.

Finally, it was her turn.

When she entered the restaurant in lower Manhattan, Jane immediately spotted them sitting at a small table in the corner and waved. She was giddy, and nervous, and excited, and dying to tell them what she'd done. She'd been married less than twenty-four hours, but she already felt like a completely different person— like a legitimate adult. The day before, she'd stood in City Hall in a beautiful white cocktail dress and over the course of a ten-minute ceremony managed to redirect her entire life. Today she was a married woman. Today she was Jane Logan, the wife of a Wall Street executive, instead of Jane Parker, the unemployed actress. Today three married girls were having brunch together, instead of two married girls and their one perennially single friend. Today she was starting over.

Today was a very, very good day.

"Hey!" Meg said when she approached the table. "We ordered you a mimosa, light on the orange juice."

"Thanks!" Jane chirped, happy to have her celebration continue, even if her friends had no idea she was celebrating anything yet.

"How was your night?" Cara asked. "Do anything good? I watched a movie with Reed and went to bed at ten. I wanted to go to an early spin class before we got together."

"I did, actually!" Jane sang, secretly loving the suspense she was building without their knowing it.

"Can we tell the waiter to take the bread basket off the table?" Cara suggested, grabbing the basket of carbs and waving to get the waiter's attention. "I didn't just bike my ass off to eat these muffins, and if they sit here I will consume half the basket. You guys don't mind, do you?" she asked, though she had no intention of waiting for an answer.

"Not really," Meg said. "Although you're crazy if you think

you need to watch your weight. You look amazing." Meg was right. Cara was a poster child for natural, understated, effortless beauty, one of the only girls Jane knew who somehow managed to look good even when she was a sweaty mess. Cara always elicited quiet envy from girls who didn't know her—and loud envy from those who did.

"Thanks. You should come with me to spin sometime!" Cara said. Her chandelier earrings swayed beneath her dark hair. She looked as if she'd stepped out of a page in *InStyle* magazine instead of a locker room at the gym.

"Hey, guys!" Jane interrupted. "Not that I have a problem talking about bread baskets and spin classes, but I do want to tell you about my night." Her impatience was becoming obvious.

"Sorry!" Meg said.

"Me too," Cara added. She reached over and tucked a piece of hair behind Jane's ear. "What's up? What did you do?"

"I got married!" Jane said. "I am now a boring married lady just like the two of you. Can you believe it?" She bit her lower lip, like it would somehow contain her enthusiasm.

Meg and Cara stared at Jane with their mouths agape, their mimosas untouched and the napkins still folded in their laps. No one screamed. No one jumped up to hug her. No one grabbed her drink to offer a toast. This was not the reaction she'd been expecting.

"Did you guys hear what I just said? *I got married! Look!*" Jane held out her hand to show off the small diamond band Doug had given her, which served as a placeholder until he had the time to get her the bigger diamond he'd promised. "Say something!" she demanded, waiting for both of them to jump up and throw their arms around her neck and tell her how happy they were that she'd found someone who loved her and treated her well and had made the last five months of her life more wonderful than she ever could've imagined.

"How could you do this to us? How could you go and get married and not even include us? I've never been so mad at you in my entire life!" Meg wailed.

"Huh? What do you mean, you're mad? I think 'Congratulations' is the appropriate response when someone tells you she just got married," Jane answered.

"Are you serious?" Cara asked. "You weren't expecting us to be mad at you? Have you totally lost your mind?" Unlike Meg's high-pitched squeal, Cara's voice was reserved, if not monotone, as if she was afraid someone would overhear their conversation. Still, Jane could tell from the look on her face that she was royally pissed off. Displaying raw emotion just wasn't Cara's style. That's something that would never change.

Jane sincerely didn't understand their anger. If one of them had eloped without telling her she honestly wouldn't care. In fact, she'd be grateful for having been spared yet another bridesmaid dress. She loved both of them, and had since they were little girls sitting in the same third-grade classroom, but her wedding day didn't have anything to do with them. This was about her and what she wanted for her life with her new husband.

"Wow. I didn't mean to upset you guys. I swear I didn't see any of this coming," Jane replied, trying her best to pacify them, but at the same time resenting that she had to. Meg and Cara had been her best friends since they were kids, but they were women now, and Jane didn't feel like they needed to be attached at the hip all the time. She fidgeted with the pearl bracelet Doug had given her as a wedding present, hoping one of them would notice it and comment on how beautiful it was.

"Don't you think you rushed into this? I mean, you don't even really know this guy! I don't know him at all. I've only met him once, and he called me Mary the whole time!" Meg pointed out. "How old is he? He's a lot older than us, isn't he?" Meg bit the cuticles on her right hand until they were raw and jagged and burning bright red, which was what she always did when she got nervous.

"He's only ten years older than we are. He's forty, not sixty. I know it's been quick, you guys, but I love him, I really do. What's the difference if we've only known each other a few months? When you know, *you know*. And I know in my heart that this is what's right for me."

"Then why couldn't you at least include us? Why'd you run away and do it alone?" Cara asked. She glanced over at Meg. "Stop biting your nails!" she snapped.

"I didn't run away anywhere! I just didn't make it a big deal, that's all," Jane said, her resentment growing.

"That doesn't sound like someone who's secure in her decision. Most people share their weddings with the people who care about them. They don't hide it." Cara sighed.

"I did share it with people who care about me. My mother and brother were there. I'm sorry I didn't tell you about it, but it was a spur-of-the-moment type thing and I don't think I need to justify that decision to you guys. We are almost thirty! Aren't we a little old to be arguing over shit like this? We don't need to live in each other's back pockets all the time!"

"What did your mother say about this?" Cara asked. "She had

no problem with you eloping?" Jane immediately felt her ire rise. Cara had a way of making her feel like she needed to defend herself all the time. It wasn't that Cara was judgmental; it was just that she had everything in her life perfectly in order and had for years, and anyone who didn't do things exactly the way she did was somehow doing things wrong. If Jane had met her as an adult instead of as a little girl, she would think Cara was a snob. She wasn't. She was just perfect in a way that occasionally made it hard to be her friend.

Those occasions were starting to become more and more frequent.

"My mom had no reservations whatsoever, actually," Jane answered. "My mom and my brother are both happy that I finally have someone stable in my life." Jane's choice to have an unconventional and impromptu wedding was no surprise to anyone who knew her—except for the two people who were supposed to know her better than anyone else. "I thought you guys would be happy for me. Why are you making me feel like I did something wrong?" she asked, surprised to hear her voice crack.

"I'm sorry. I am happy for you," Meg said, finally rising from the table to give her the hug that was now about five minutes too late. "I'm just sad I didn't get to see it. That's all. I would've loved to be a part of it." She released Jane from her arms and immediately began to bite the cuticles on her right hand again. It was mind-boggling to Jane that she hadn't managed to get that habit under control by now.

"I wasn't trying to hurt you; I just, to be honest—"

"Didn't think of us at all," Cara said.

Jane shrugged. It sounded so awful when she heard it out loud.

But it was sort of true. A wedding was between a man and a woman—not a man, a woman, and her two best friends. Did they seriously not get that?

"I'm sorry. I really am," Jane said, realizing that whether or not it was intentional, she'd hurt their feelings. "I don't want to argue with you guys. Today is supposed to be a really happy day and I want you both to help me celebrate. Doug is throwing a cocktail party tonight for some of his friends and I want you guys to come. It's basically our wedding reception. It'll be fun." She was sure it would be. Doug always knew how to throw a great party, no expense spared.

"Hear that, Meg?" Cara said, dabbing her mouth with a napkin. "Jane actually wants to invite us to a cocktail party. I guess we should be honored."

"I said I was sorry, Cara," Jane said, getting tired of defending herself. She didn't need to answer to anyone anymore. It was beginning to bother her that her friends somehow felt that she owed them an explanation for why she did what she did. It was her life; what did it matter to them whether they attended the ceremony?

"Okay. I just hope you know what you're doing. Marriage is hard enough when you really know the person, and you guys have only been together a few months," Cara added. "*Trust me.*"

"I know what I'm doing. And I'm done talking about this with you guys. You've made your objections known, and now you don't need to wonder about why I didn't tell you about it beforehand. The truth is, right now, your opinions don't really matter much to me. And I'm having a hard time remembering why they ever did," Jane snapped.

"Jane, don't say that!" Meg said, obviously hurt by the tone of her voice. Meg had always been sensitive, and Jane immediately felt bad for sniping at her. "I just wish we got to see it. That's all. Please tell me you at least have pictures." Meg pushed a lock of her blond hair behind her ear. "Did anyone take any?"

"I'm sorry. I just didn't see this coming. This is supposed to be a happy time for me. Why are you guys picking a fight with me over this?" She had known they'd be surprised when she told them she'd gotten married, but she'd drastically underestimated how hurt they'd be. In fact, they were more than just hurt. They were furious.

"We're not," Meg said. "Honestly, I'm really happy for you. Where's the party tonight?"

"At the restaurant where we had our first date. Isn't that cute? He planned the whole thing. It's going to be small, but you guys have to come. It won't be the same without you."

"Of course we'll be there," Meg said, looking over at Cara, who was still trying to absorb the news and had been staring at the wall for the last few minutes. "Cara?"

"Of course," she said, finally sighing and breaking into a smile. "Jane, you never cease to amaze me, you know that?"

"Isn't that one of the things you love about me?"

"One of many," she said, though Jane wasn't entirely sure she meant it. "I hope you two will be very happy together."

"I hope that he stops calling me Mary," Meg joked.

"I think that can be arranged," Jane said with a laugh.

"So do you have any pictures? Don't make us ask again!" Cara asked.

"First, a toast. To the new Mrs. Douglas . . . ," Meg trailed off. Jane and Cara looked at each other and quickly burst out laughing.

"Oh my God. We don't know his last name," Cara said, choking slightly on her champagne. "I mean it. I have no idea what his last name is. What's your name now?"

"I can't believe we have to ask, but yeah, I don't know what his name is either!" Meg said. "I guess I won't be getting you anything with a monogram."

"It's Logan!" Jane said. "Mrs. Douglas Logan."

"It has a nice ring to it, actually," Meg said.

"Thank you. I think so, too." Jane pulled a few photos from her bag of her in her gorgeous cocktail dress and Doug in his navy suit and bright-green tie, and felt herself relax. She finally had everything she wanted. She had a wonderful new husband, lifelong friends, and a glass of champagne with a splash of orange juice.

Life was good.

two

December 2012

S o let's discuss invitations, then. I would like to take care of them this year, because in each of the last two years my name was misspelled and I would like to make sure it's done correctly this time," Christie said, more than a little annoyed by the accidental error.

"That's fine by me," Jane replied politely. She adjusted the large princess-cut diamond on her finger and hoped the other women didn't notice that it needed to be steam cleaned. She'd have to add that to her list of things to do tomorrow, though she had no idea where she'd find the time. The holidays were creeping closer and she felt totally unprepared. She hadn't even picked out the wine for the cocktail party she and Doug were hosting on Christmas Eve, and she hadn't reminded her housekeeper to polish her good silver yet. The stress of it all was really starting to get to her. She realized that she probably should schedule a massage to help relieve some of the tension in her neck before it began to really hurt—yet another thing to add to the ever-growing to-do list. The holidays could be so stressful.

"Agreed," Mindy said. "I felt so bad for you when I saw your name spelled with a Y on that invitation. You must have wanted to kill Gretchen. I mean, it's completely ridiculous that she didn't catch that."

"There's a reason she's not on the board this year!" Christie laughed, knowing full well that getting kicked off the charity board had basically ruined Gretchen's social standing for the holiday season, if not for the entire year. Jane made a mental note to never piss off Christie with an *i-e*. She had no interest in going to war with these women over a spelling error. They were ruthless.

"Well, it seems like everything is settled, then," Jane said, pushing her espresso away from her. "This was a really lovely lunch, and I'm very happy with our decisions. I think we're going to have a wonderful benefit."

"Thank you so much for organizing lunch, Jane," Christie said, albeit insincerely. "You're a wonderful addition to our little team this year. Let's chat next week." She removed her black quilted Chanel bag from the back of her chair and tied a bright-pink scarf snugly around her neck. "We're going to Saint Barts after Christmas and it can't come soon enough. This cold weather is driving me crazy."

"It was really wonderful to see you all," Jane added as she stood and waved good-bye. She checked her watch quickly and was surprised that the meeting had gone on so long. She still had a ton of things she needed to do before Doug got home from work, and while she didn't want to appear rude, it was really time for her to leave.

"You too, dear," Mindy said as she puckered her plum-colored lips and kissed the air on the side of Jane's cheek. "Let's talk next week about the catering. Everyone is so over miniature crab cakes."

"I totally agree," Heather added, still seated with her back to the windows while she used a compact to touch up her blush. Heather reminded Jane so much of Cruella de Vil that she often found it hard to look at her. Over the years, Heather's hair got blonder and blonder, her lipstick got darker and darker, and the

skin on her face got tighter and tighter. Add to that the fact that
the leopard coat she was fond of wearing was eerily reminiscent
of Dalmatian and the resemblance was striking. All she needed
was a pair of red gloves and a pack-a-day habit and children
would probably run screaming when they saw her in the street.
"If I see another one, I will lose my mind. Let's try to come up
with something a little more exciting, shall we?"

"No problem," Jane said. "I'll call you next week." She pulled
the belt on her cashmere coat tight around her waist and stepped
outside onto the snow-covered sidewalk. It was cold and she was
thankful that she'd planned ahead and called a car service to pick
her up. She pushed through the crowd to her waiting town car
and flung herself into the backseat. Christmas was barely two
weeks away, which made walking in Midtown a contact sport.
The hordes of tourists flocking to Fifth Avenue to see the store
windows and the giant tree were intolerable, as far as she was
concerned. All she wanted to do was go home to her warm apartment and finish writing out her Christmas cards.

As she rode home her mind wandered again to an upcoming
date on the calendar, though for the life of her she couldn't understand why. Cara's birthday was next month, and Jane had
come across a bright-blue ski jacket in a catalog that would look
amazing on her. She'd spent the last two weeks debating whether
she should send it to her, but she still couldn't decide. It's not
like grown women need to celebrate turning thirty-seven, and
Cara was never one to like attention anyway. Still, she'd no doubt
be spending weekends this winter skiing at Reed's family house
in Vermont, and Jane was pretty sure she'd love the coat. Then
again, what did she know anymore? *I can't believe you are spending
this much time thinking about her birthday,* she thought to herself.

You'd have to be crazy to reopen those wounds. She decided that holiday nostalgia was a dangerous thing and vowed to throw the catalog away as soon as she got home. She'd moved on with her life, and there was absolutely no reason to revisit those ghosts.

It took her driver twenty-five minutes to cross over to the West Side thanks to the unforgivable traffic, and it was almost three o'clock when Jane turned the key in the lock and stepped inside her apartment, the smell of the balsam fir they'd bought and decorated a few days ago strong enough to be detected from the foyer. She inhaled deeply. *There's nothing better than that,* she thought as she pulled off her suede boots and made her way into the den off the kitchen. She had a busy afternoon ahead of her, what with the stack of cards to address and stamp, not to mention the now crucial mission of finding exciting hors d'oeuvres to replace crab cakes. She was definitely going to need that massage.

She headed for the stack of catalogs sitting on her velvet sofa so she could rid herself of the nagging ski jacket conundrum once and for all, but was sidetracked when she unexpectedly caught sight of Doug out of the corner of her eye.

"Jeez, you scared me!" Jane said when she looked up and found him pacing the floor in front of the Christmas tree. Pine needles had already fallen off the lower branches and lay haphazardly on the carpet. "This is a nice surprise," she said as she walked over to give him a hug. They'd been married seven and a half years, but somehow Doug still managed to impress her. Some guys have the ability to fill up an entire room just by walking into it. Doug was one of those guys. She'd never stop thinking that she was the luckiest person in the world to be married to him. She inhaled the smell of his shampoo and aftershave as she clasped his hands and pulled back to look at him. "What brings you home in the middle of the day?" She felt her heart pause for a minute when she released him from her grasp and noticed the expression on his face.

"Sit down," he said quietly. Jane finally noticed that his hands were trembling slightly, and that they weren't just cool—they were clammy. Dusk was already setting over the city, and a soft gray light now filtered in through the west-facing windows of their apartment. A lamp on a timer in the corner clicked on, a small sound that seemed to echo forever. Everything else was so still.

"What's the matter?" Jane asked, prepared to hear that one of her parents had died, or that he had lost his job. She was not prepared for the bomb he was about to drop on her life.

"It's gone," he said flatly. Sweat was running down the side of his face despite the fact that it was the dead of winter and Jane had turned down the heat a bit before she left, to prevent her tree from drying out too quickly.

"What are you talking about? What's gone? Did you lose something?" she asked.

"Our money. It's all gone."

Jane stood frozen as he continued to pace back and forth in the same straight line, like he was following the pattern in the carpet. "What are you talking about?" she asked. "You're not making any sense."

"I've done some things, Jane, and I don't have time to explain them all to you. I don't think I'm going to be able to get out of this."

"What do you mean it's gone? How could it be gone? I saw our bank statement last month and there was plenty of money in our accounts. Doug, sit down and tell me what the hell is going on."

"The feds are going to be here soon, and when they're done with me, the new boobs I gave you for your birthday will be the only things we have left. I'm not entirely sure they won't try to repossess them, too. They're going to take everything."

Jane instinctively grabbed her chest. The implants had not been a present she'd wanted, but somehow she'd let Doug talk her into getting them, probably because they came with a trip to the Bahamas and a ton of new swimwear. Fine, it wasn't a traditional birthday present, but most of the women she socialized with had their boobs done, so she didn't feel like she needed to be ashamed of them.

"Are you understanding what I'm telling you? Jane, it was a scam. All of it. I'm a fraud."

Jane's mind refused to absorb what Doug was saying because it was too busy soaking up her surroundings: Christmas cards embossed with gold foil awaiting their angel-wing stamps, tree branches bending under the weight of glittering ornaments and champagne colored lights, Tiffany lamps artfully displayed on antique tables next to crystal candy dishes and sterling silver frames. She tried to memorize all of it, every relic of her privileged life, knowing that while they were sitting tangibly in front of her they were simultaneously disappearing into the mist.

"Call Gavin and ask him to loan you some money. I don't know how much longer you'll have access to anything," Doug said softly. "You'll need it."

"You want me to ask my little brother for money? Are you insane?" Gavin worked for an Internet company out in Silicon Valley and did very well for himself. Borrowing money from him wasn't the issue. The issue was that Doug had somehow managed to destroy himself, and apparently her because she'd blindly gone along for the ride.

"I'm sorry, Jane. I'm so sorry." With that, he sank down on the floor and began to cry. Jane didn't go to him. She didn't offer comfort or sympathy or empathy. The loyal-wife part of her thought about it briefly, but the fantastically angry part of her told her to stay where she was. If what he was saying was true, he didn't deserve to be comforted by her or anyone else. If what he was saying was true, her entire life was a lie. The air felt like it was slowly being sucked from the room. Her lungs began to burn and threatened to explode.

"Start at the beginning," she whispered. "What have you done to us?"

He refused to look at her.

Before he had a chance to explain anything, the FBI knocked on the door. In less than sixty seconds, Doug was cuffed and escorted out of the apartment, leaving her alone in her living room longing for the now distant time when her biggest problems were unpolished silver and crab cakes.

three

October 2013

Stop calling me! I told you for the last time, I have no comment!" Jane yelled into the phone before she slammed it on her marble kitchen counter so hard the screen splintered and cracked. *It doesn't matter,* she thought, staring at her damaged iPhone. *It's not like I need to talk to anyone.* She had stopped speaking to people months ago—or maybe more accurately, people had stopped speaking to her. It was crazy to think about how fast the people she'd thought were her friends had deserted her when Doug's crimes became public. But if she was honest with herself (something she hadn't been in a very long time), she probably would've done the same thing. Loyalty wasn't really something they cared about. Hell, half of them had husbands who were blatantly cheating on them, and they couldn't have cared less as long as their credit cards worked. She'd never heard from Mindy, Heather, or Christie with an *i-e* about the benefit, and none of them had returned her phone calls when she left messages. She hated herself for hoping that they'd still want to associate with her—that they wouldn't hold her accountable for her husband's sins. It was a completely ridiculous thought. They didn't care whether Jane was innocent or guilty. They'd disowned Gretchen because she couldn't spell.

Jane had dreamed of traveling in the higher circles of New York society her whole life, and once she'd gotten there, she'd learned that she was basically on her own. Just because people invited her and Doug to dinner didn't mean they were her friends. Then again, just because Doug was her husband didn't mean he was her friend, either. Maybe she should stop being angry at the pod people she had chosen to surround herself with over the last few years and start being mad at the people who deserved it: Cara and Meg, for not being with her when she needed them most.

Jane had been trying to figure out for years when exactly they'd started to grow apart, and how much of it was actually her fault. There was never a big fight. As far as she was concerned, no one had done anything that could've been seen as unforgivable, though she wondered now if maybe they felt differently. Their separation had been gradual and graceful. It had probably started as early as their freshman year of college, toward the end of the first semester, when Cara had called Jane and told her she was thinking of transferring from Bowdoin to NYU.

November 1994

"What do you mean, you don't like it? You've been there for one semester; you can't know if you like it or not," Jane said defensively, cringing a little at the sound of her own voice. She knew it wasn't what Cara wanted to hear, but she was unable to stop herself from saying it anyway.

"You sound like my mother. I don't care that it's only been one semester. I know enough to know that I don't like it. It's cold here."

"New York is no warmer, I assure you."

"You come to school up in Maine in the winter and tell me that. And why do I feel like you're trying to talk me out of this? I thought you'd be excited to hear that I was thinking of trans-

ferring to NYU. Why do you sound like I just ruined your day?"
Cara sounded offended, which was silly. Jane was merely trying
to point out that expecting her to serve as Cara's de facto security
blanket was a bit ridiculous. Jane loved Cara, but they needed to
learn how to live their own lives. It was as simple as that.

"That's not true. Of course I'd be happy if you came here, it's
just that you were so excited to go to school up there. I don't want
you to give up before you really give it a chance."

"If you don't want me to transfer there, why don't you
just say so?" Cara insisted. It was clear that short of Jane's
telling Cara she'd kick out her current roommate and let Cara
move in, there was no way of getting out of this conversation
without coming off as selfish. She wasn't selfish. She was just
more concerned with her own happiness than with Cara's at
the moment, which was perfectly within her rights as a newly
independent eighteen-year-old girl. Why was that such a hard
thing to understand?

"Cara, stop. That's not what I said." Which was true. She
might've been thinking it, but she never said it out loud.

"You didn't have to," Cara said quietly. She hung up the phone
before Jane had a chance to answer.

Jane put the cordless phone back on its base and stretched out on
the duvet covering her bunk bed. Cara was right. She didn't want
her to transfer, and she was angry that she felt like she needed to
apologize for it. These years at college were supposed to be her time.
All she had ever wanted was to get out of the suburbs and into the
city and be able to experience life outside the stupid small town
they'd grown up in. She wanted to do something else, she wanted
to be someone else, and she couldn't possibly do that with her past
sitting right next to her in art history class. Wasn't college supposed

to be about self-exploration and reinvention? Why didn't Cara want to do that for herself? Why didn't she get it?

Jane thought about that conversation often, wondering if she should've said something different. So what that she wanted to build her own life in college? While Meg went to school at Vanderbilt and Cara decided to brave the frigid winters in Maine, Jane had tried really hard to build her career as an actress. She'd wanted excitement and adrenaline and adventure. She'd wanted new experiences with new people.

Was that really a horrible thing for her to have thought? Did that really qualify as a friendship-altering event? Cara didn't end up transferring, and as far as Jane was concerned, things worked out for the best. Cara had met her husband (whom Jane hated with a passion) at college, and that never would've happened if she'd left and come to New York. After graduation, when Cara and Meg moved back home to look for jobs and save money, Jane decided to stay in the city so that she could continue to pursue her acting career. Plus, at that point, Meg and Cara both had serious boyfriends, and neither of them could have a conversation that didn't revolve around them. Once they got married, it only got worse.

Friendships shift and change and roll along as you move through life, and Jane was fine with all of that, but she always felt that really good friendships should be elastic—they should stretch at times but always snap back to a familiar shape and place.

She hadn't expected her friends' marriages to change anything between them, but somehow they had. All of a sudden Cara and Meg no longer had time for her or any of the things they all used to do together. Jane felt like a little kid sitting at the adult table any time they had lunch, having to listen to Cara drone on and on about the wallpaper she'd chosen to hang in the powder room of her new house in the suburbs, or Meg talk about what great meal she'd whipped up for Steve the night before. They'd been through every milestone together until then—sweet sixteens, junior proms, drivers' licenses, college graduations—but now they'd left Jane behind. Without warning, when they hit their midtwenties, the two of them set off on their own little married ladies' adventure while she was stuck on the wait list. She felt like they found her life silly or selfish or unimportant on some level. Is there anything more infuriating than your closest friends taking pity on you and your life choices because you don't have a man yet? Being single and poor in your late twenties is hard enough without having to withstand that kind of judgment over breakfast. She really didn't need it, and eventually she got tired of feeling like the odd man out. People grow up and change, and the pressure to keep up with Cara and Meg got the better of her. So she gradually decided to back out of the race entirely.

Instead, she got a little apartment down in the grimy East Village. From the beginning, though, life in Manhattan was never as grand or as shiny as Jane had imagined it to be. She'd always had such big plans, for a big life that she knew she was meant to live, but it was harder to reach than she'd originally allowed herself to believe. She was one of a million girls trying to be an actress in New York City, and so she took the odd jobs that she needed to take while she passed around head shots to anyone who would take one and performed in small plays in tiny basements in the outer boroughs that she thought were beneath her. She couldn't imagine how she'd ever be able to make enough money to live in one of the awesome apartments she saw on TV, which were somehow always occupied by characters who didn't really have proper jobs themselves. No matter how much she tried to save, she couldn't afford anything other than the tiny apartment downtown that she shared with three other girls she barely knew, despite the fact that there were only two bedrooms. Not the cool Tribeca lofts with floor-to-ceiling windows and views of the Hudson River. Not the luxurious Upper West Side condos with exposed brick walls and working fireplaces. Not the immaculately decorated East Side co-ops with thirty-foot-high ceilings and Waterford vases overflowing with calla lilies sitting on heavy mahogany tables in the foyer. There were no tasseled window treatments, no Sub-Zero refrigerators, no doormen, and no shiny parquet floors so polished they actually looked wet. None of that. Instead, she had furniture from tag sales that she tried to pass off as retro or quirky or effortlessly eclectic, but she never managed to get it right. She spent most of her twenties feeling that way about her entire life. It was exhausting.

She'd continued to try to act, but as she approached thirty, she'd accepted that she was never going to be good enough to make a living at it. As much as she hated to admit it, she wasn't talented enough. Slowly, her dreams of telling James Lipton on *Inside the Actors Studio* about how she'd struggled downtown with all the other artists until someone plucked her from obscurity and made her a millionaire began to fade away. Jane felt that life owed her more than what she was born with, but she didn't really want to work the way girls had to work to break into the business. She didn't like being a waitress and she still refused to take naked pictures, and after a certain point what else was she supposed to do? At what point would it have been okay to give up?

Then she met Doug.

She hadn't been looking to meet anyone that afternoon, which was funny because most of the time, all she was doing was looking to meet a guy who could rescue her. She was sitting in a dive bar down by the South Street Seaport, lamenting the loss of another low-paying, bullshit job (walking dogs for a spoiled bitch of a woman who didn't work but for some reason found it impossible to make time to take care of her own pets), when Doug entered. He took the stool next to her and removed a file from the leather briefcase he'd set at his feet. He glanced over at the glass of liquor in front of her and whistled.

December 2004

"What is that? Scotch?" he asked, revealing a thick British accent.

"Bourbon, actually."

"Wow. You must have had one hell of a morning to be hitting the hard stuff this early." He should've been turned off by the concept of a girl slugging hard alcohol in the middle of the day, but it seemed as if it actually intrigued him. That should've been her first clue that something was seriously wrong with him.

The truth was, she didn't even like the taste of bourbon, but she didn't have the money to buy multiple drinks, and beer wasn't strong enough. She thought one glass of the hard stuff would provide the most bang for her buck.

"Or maybe I'm just a raging alcoholic," she joked, though even then she had her concerns that if she didn't start making some changes, and soon, she might actually become just that.

"Are you?" he asked.

"No," she admitted.

"So what are you then?"

"An actress," she said. "Which means I'll probably wind up being a raging alcoholic. Just not today."

"Ah, the life of an aspiring actress in this city can't be easy. I don't blame you for drinking during the day," he said. He seemed sympathetic, which Jane liked. Usually people just rolled their eyes at her when she told them what she wanted to do with her life, but not him. Of course, there was the chance that he was humoring her, but she didn't think so. You don't have to be an aspiring actress in New York City for long before you start developing a keen sense for when people are lying through their teeth.

"That's very kind of you. I try not to make it a habit, but the truth is, it's been a really shitty day," she said, which wasn't exactly true. Lately she found herself having a few cocktails during the day on a regular basis. It was hard to find reasons not to when she had nothing else to do with her time, and since drinking wasn't keeping her from anything important, she didn't think it was that big of a deal. It didn't help that the odds of breaking into show business at twenty-nine weren't good, and the thought of being thirty, single, and a failure was more than she could handle. When she'd moved to Manhattan she had had such big plans, and none of them involved her walking dogs or going to sleep alone at nearly thirty years old. And yet somehow that was exactly what was happening. She took another sip of her drink and felt her insides warm. Maybe it was the booze, or maybe it was the man. It was hard to say.

"Not a problem. Have you done anything I might have seen you in?"

"I doubt it. You don't strike me as the type of guy who would've seen any of my stuff."

"Why do you say that?"

"We don't see a lot of Hermès ties in my audiences," Jane said, gesturing toward the bright orange tie dangling from his starched shirt collar.

"How do you know guys don't take them off and shove them in their backpacks before they enter?"

"I guess I don't," she answered. He wasn't her type. He was British, for starters, and Jane had never really been all that into foreigners, mostly because she had heard that circumcision wasn't common practice overseas. She barely knew what to do with the American dicks she was familiar with, so going international seemed unnecessary. He also had an insane amount of gel in his hair. It was slicked straight back and shellacked to the point where it almost looked like a toupee. His build was slight. He looked fit but not necessarily strong. And, like most Europeans, he wore clothes cut just a little too slim for her taste. But he was perfectly attentive and he was perfectly nice and he was perfectly interested in talking to her and, well, that made him the most perfect man she'd met since she'd moved to this crummy island.

"I do mostly Off, Off, Off-Broadway stuff," she said, trying to be coy.

"What does that mean?"

"My last play took place in a Brooklyn basement."

"I see."

"What about you?" she asked.

"I also work off Broadway."

"What does that mean?"

"Wall Street."

"So we're practically neighbors."

"And yet we've never run into each other before."

"Go figure."

He checked his watch and pushed his drink away from him. She wasn't surprised that she had scared him off. What surprised her was that he'd stuck around for as long as he had.

"I actually have to run, I just popped in here to kill some time before my meeting across the street, but I feel bad leaving a pretty girl all alone at the bar when I know she's this upset," he said, somehow managing to come off as charming and not sleazy in the slightest.

"Well, unless you want to take me to your meeting with you, I don't think you have much choice," she said. "Don't worry about it. It was nice to meet you."

"It was nice to meet you, too." He reached into the inside pocket of his suit jacket and removed a business card. He wrote his cell number on the back and slid it on the bar toward her glass. "Have dinner with me. I'll be home by about six thirty. If you'd like to meet me, call me by seven. I'll make a reservation somewhere just in case."

"You want to have dinner?" she asked.

"That's what I just said."

"I don't even know you."

"That's why I asked you to have dinner and not to marry me."

Jane could not think of a reason why she shouldn't go. He worked in finance. He was wearing an Hermès tie. He definitely wasn't an ax murderer, so what was the worst that could happen?

"Okay. I'll call you . . ." Jane flipped the card over and found his name. "Doug Logan."

"I hope you do. Although now I realize that I never even asked you your name. I'm sorry. That's very rude of me."

"Jane," she sang, now willing to flirt a little more aggressively.

"Jane Parker."

"You don't seem like a Jane."

"What do I seem like?"

"I don't know. I'll think about it and let you know tonight." He left a fifty on the bar and yelled to the bartender, *"Her drink is on me."* He nodded almost imperceptibly as he stood and grabbed his bag off the floor. *"I look forward to hearing from you, Jane. Cheer up. Things will get better."* And then he left.

She should have realized something was off with him just from the way they'd met. He was too smooth, too confident, and too eager to get to know her when it was obvious that they had nothing in common. But at that moment she was just too tired to care. She was tired of going to cheap parties in Alphabet City and pretending to think the underground scene was cool. She was tired of pretending to want to be some scrapping, struggling artist. She wanted to have dinner with a guy wearing a nice tie who carried a credit card that wouldn't be declined. Was that really too much to ask?

They had dinner at a very chic restaurant in SoHo that she would never have been able to afford on her own, and five months later, they eloped at City Hall, with Jane's mother and brother, Gavin, serving as witnesses. Just like that, Jane had everything she wanted—and a whole lot more. Meg and Cara were angry when they found out, and after that, things were never really the same. The girls didn't like Doug for reasons that Jane couldn't understand: What do you mean you don't trust him? You don't have to trust him, you're not married to him! And Doug didn't like the girls for reasons that she fully understood: they don't like him, they meddle in things they shouldn't, they don't like him. It wouldn't be the first time that a guy came between friends, and Jane was ready to deal with it if that's where it led. But it never got that far, probably because Meg was too busy tending to her perfect marriage and Cara was too busy being perfect in every way possible to care what Jane was doing with her husband in the city. They all silently agreed to let it go, and to ignore that yet another piece of their foundation had been eroded away by the passage of time. Because they loved each other they placed a patch over the tear and pretended that things were the same, every hole and rip and pull that occurred over the years continually covered by a myriad of patches made to look as if they were all supposed to be there.

Jane was ashamed to admit it, but back then she didn't care. Her feelings were too hurt and she was too insecure about how her life was evolving in comparison to theirs to ever let them know that she was devastated by how their relationship was changing. She wasn't strong enough to tell them how she really felt, and instead she got angry at them and cut them out of her life. She'd give anything to go back and do things differently.

Especially because they were right.

four

The phone rang again, forcing Jane to turn off both her current train of thought and also the ringer. Thank God she had a doorman to keep the photographers and reporters away, but she knew that the other tenants in the building wanted her to leave, and pretty soon they'd force her out. She couldn't blame them. No one paid these prices for Manhattan real estate to have to push through a bunch of screaming idiots with cameras and press passes just to get to a Starbucks for their morning latte. Jane had never understood the whole reality TV craze, and now that she was forced to live inside a fishbowl she understood it even less. Why anyone would seek out this kind of attention and scrutiny was beyond her, and Doug's story wasn't even national news. It was bad enough being hunted by every network in the tristate area. If she had to worry about reporters from CNN or *Dateline* being on her ass too, she might actually go insane. She threw herself on her king-size bed, covered in Frette linens and layers of Ralph Lauren blankets, buried her face in her pillows, and screamed. Her beautiful apartment, only a block from Central Park West, was exactly what she'd always wanted, and now it was a prison. She felt like she was living in a dream, like she couldn't figure out what was real and what had been entirely in her imagination. How could she fall in love with a criminal? How could she reconcile the fact that she loved Doug—and, if she was honest, even missed him—with the fact that he wasn't who she thought he was? Any time she felt a wave of nostalgia or found herself wishing he were still at home in the apartment with her, she became so overcome with guilt that she actually hated herself. If she were a good person, she wouldn't feel any love for him now that she knew the truth. If she did, then what did that say about her? How could she miss him and hate him at the same time? How could she hate him without hating herself for building a life with him?

Jane pulled herself together and wandered into the kitchen, knowing that the cure for her splitting headache wouldn't be found in the bottom of a wine bottle but not caring at that particular moment one way or the other. She walked past her farmhouse sink, briefly ran her finger along the copper pots that hung from brass hooks above the center island, and removed a bottle of white wine from her refrigerator. She knew she was probably drinking more lately than she should've been, but it seemed justified. She fished the wine opener out of the drawer next to the stove and gently eased the cork from the bottle, the puckering sound it made once she set it free instantly easing her stress. She removed from a cabinet one of the crystal glasses she'd received as a wedding gift and briefly thought about smashing it against the wall. Instead, she decided to fill it to the brim.

Before she could take a sip, there was a knock at her door. *Shit*, she thought as she placed the glass down on her counter, then trudged into the foyer. She looked through the peephole and saw the stern, unpleasant face of her neighbor Mrs. Cooper peering back at her. *Shit*, she thought again. *I shouldn't have left my wine in the kitchen.*

"This is getting ridiculous," Mrs. Cooper said as Jane opened the door.

"I agree. So let's stop meeting like this, and next time wait for an invitation before you come over, okay?" Jane said. Ordinarily she'd never be so rude to her neighbor, or anyone else for that matter, but these were not ordinary times.

"Jane, I feel bad for you, really I do," the wrinkled crypt keeper said.

"Thank you for your condolences." It was hard to believe that this entire nightmare had started only ten months ago. It felt more like ten years, and Jane was well aware that she was not going to be able to endure this new life much longer. She'd always thought of herself as strong, but now she had to admit that this was something she couldn't handle alone.

"However, your circumstances are making everyone else's living situations unbearable. I wish you'd stop being selfish and think about the other tenants in this building." Mrs. Cooper had a silk scarf tied around her neck like an ascot. Jane briefly wondered if that meant she'd be able to choke her out without leaving prints.

"Selfish? You're calling me *selfish*? I married a thief who stole people's money, went to prison, and left me with basically nothing except a ruined reputation, a bunch of frozen bank accounts, and, now, agoraphobia. I have no friends left in this city, no cash in the bank, and nowhere to go, but you want to come over here and tell me that the press outside is an annoyance for *you*? You're right. I must be the most selfish person alive." Jane remained defiant. Although if this were happening to someone else, she'd probably be annoyed by the disruption as well.

"I'm calling an emergency board meeting tomorrow, and we are going to vote on having you evicted from the co-op."

"You can't do that. This apartment is the only thing I have left. Without it, I'll be homeless." In what was maybe the one smart decision her husband had made in his pathetic life, he'd placed the deed to the apartment in his father's name. Legally, the government couldn't touch it, which was the only reason they hadn't sold it out from under her. But that didn't mean the co-op board couldn't evict her.

"My husband is a lawyer, and he assures me that we can," Mrs. Cooper said.

"Well, my husband was a wealth manager, and clearly he didn't know what the fuck he was doing, so I'm sorry, but that means nothing to me. It's not going to be enough to scare me out of here. Now if you'll excuse me, my wine is getting warm." Jane went to close the door, but Mrs. Cooper shoved her flabby, bespeckled arm into the door frame. Jane thought about slamming it on her, but she realized that the last thing she needed was a personal injury lawsuit brought against her by her nosy neighbor and her lawyer husband.

"Jane, it's time you find somewhere else to go. Just for a while, until things die down. Don't make us do something we don't want to do." Mrs. Cooper quickly removed her arm and clasped her hands demurely in front of her.

"Where would you like me to go?" Jane asked, finally beginning to crack.

"Don't you have anyone who can help you for a while? Give you a place to stay?"

"I told you I don't have any friends left in the city," Jane said. She rubbed the back of her neck; the knots that had been there for much of the last year were hard as rocks. She had no idea how to get rid of them. It wasn't like she could call a masseuse.

"Well, I don't know anyone who is that alone in life. If that's the case then maybe you need to reconsider some of the choices you've made."

"Yeah, tell me something I don't already know. Thanks for the pep talk."

"I mean it, Jane. Go somewhere before the board meets tomorrow. Believe it or not, I'm trying to help you."

"Thanks. As soon as the feds unfreeze my assets, I'll send you a fruit basket."

Jane closed the door and leaned against it, rubbing her shoulders as if to keep warm. Her life was not supposed to turn out like this; this was not how things were supposed to go. She was a good person, she had married a good guy, she had finally gotten everything she ever wanted, and none of it was real. Not her friends, not her fortune, not even her boobs. And the truth was, she couldn't remember the last time she had anything real to lean on.

And then she did.

She didn't want to go running to her mother or her brother. She felt like she had burdened them enough since this whole thing started, plus the press would be staking out their homes, too, in the hopes of her making an appearance. But she had another option. There were two people on earth who knew her better than anyone else, knew the *real* Jane, the Jane before the marriage and the news reports and the public embarrassment that followed. Jane's instinct to seek them out after all this time didn't really surprise her—it only surprised her that she hadn't thought of it sooner. She had waited long enough hoping that things would get better, thinking that she could somehow hold herself together without anyone's help. The truth was, she couldn't, and the only people she trusted to help her lived less than an hour away.

Jane ran into her bedroom and threw some clothes into an overnight bag. She slugged her wine in four large glugs, grabbed her large sunglasses off her bureau, snatched her purse off the floor, and walked quietly into the hallway. She half ran down the hall and exited into the stairwell, knowing that if there was one thing she could count on, it was that none of her rich neighbors would ever risk scuffing one of their Brian Atwood pumps by hoofing it on stairs when the elevator worked just fine. She descended ten flights to the thirty-first floor, which held the building's gym and laundry facilities, once again betting correctly that none of her neighbors would ever demean themselves by washing their own underwear or working out in a second-rate gym when personal trainers were available at private fitness centers all over the city. One thing she had learned was that people with money tended to be lazy, and if she wanted to be honest with herself, she'd admit it had made her lazy, too. So lazy she didn't bother to look at her bank statements, to question withdrawals and transfers and stock sales that didn't make any sense, or to wonder why the same employees seemed to work at her husband's bank for the entire time she knew him. No one new joined, and no one retired. She should've listened to the little warnings that rattled around her brain before quelling them with bottles of champagne, gold bracelets, and the convenient explanation that the firm must treat its employees really, really well.

But she hadn't, and now here she was, skulking through service elevators in a pair of Reeboks like a cat burglar in broad daylight. She turned the corner past the laundry room and found the service elevator. She pressed the button and waited, tapping her foot, for the elevator to open. Hector, the maintenance man, smiled when he saw her. Over the months since this nightmare began, the two had become friendly. He allowed her to sneak out this way when she needed to pick up wine after the store stopped delivering, and she repaid the favor by supplying him with cans of beer that he drank on the roof when he needed a break from riding up and down in his movable box all day. She entered the elevator and stood silently as she rode it to the basement level, then exited through a small metal door at the end of yet another hallway into the underground parking garage. She used to have a car there, but that had been repossessed too, so no one ever thought to look for her in the garage. Regardless, she kept her head down as she weaved her way toward the exit, reached the street, and immediately hailed a cab. She smiled to herself for winning a small personal victory: the ass clowns with the cameras were still jamming the sidewalk, annoying Mrs. Cooper, trying to further ruin her life (as if that were possible), and she was nestled in the backseat of a taxi, blissfully speeding away from her Upper West Side prison toward freedom and the Triborough Bridge.

five

Cara stood over the kitchen sink at her mother's house with a wrench in her hand, trying to figure out how to make the leaking water stop. "I know," she muttered to herself as she slammed the wrench on the faucet in frustration, the clanging sound so loud it actually made her jump. The water continued to drip, and drip, and drip. Finally she flung the wrench on the counter, admitting that she hadn't the first damn clue what to do with it, no matter how many hours of HGTV she watched, and covered her cheeks with her hands. The millionth droplet escaped from the faucet and dribbled down the basin, and she wished for the millionth time that just like the water she too could slink into the drain and disappear forever.

When her mother died, four months ago on a steamy day in June, Cara had assumed she'd have her husband, Reed, with her when it came time to dismantle her childhood home. She glanced around at the empty kitchen, the dusty shelves, the vacant cabinets, and once again stifled the ever-present urge to cry. This wasn't supposed to happen this way. She was too young to be rendered an orphan. She had taken her mother to every doctor in the Northeast looking for alternative treatments and medicines. She'd even gone to church and prayed—on her knees—and she hadn't been in a church in almost twenty years. It seemed like a waste of her too precious time, and she spent too much time on her knees washing floors and dusting baseboards and folding laundry to volunteer to do it in church. She was only thirty-seven years old and had somehow dusted away her youth, or folded it up like one of Reed's shirts, tucked neatly in a drawer next to his socks. With every shirt she folded and every dish she washed, she forgot a little more, and a little more, until she didn't remember anything about the girl she used to be. She had no idea who she was anymore, or how the hell she'd allowed any of this to happen.

She liked to think that her mother never knew how bad things were between her and Reed, but Cara was beginning to wonder if maybe she wasn't as good at hiding things as she thought she was. Not long before her mother died they'd been sitting watching daytime talk shows and chatting about a house that had recently come on the market. Her mother hadn't brought up Jane or Meg in years, but for some reason she'd decided it was time to discuss the subject that Cara had placed off-limits a long time ago.

"I think you should reach out to the girls," her mother said, seeming so frail under the blankets, the shadows under her eyes making her look impossibly pale. It had been just the two of them since Cara's father abandoned them when Cara was three. She honestly had no idea how she was going to exist in this world without her mom, either. "I don't want to even think about you being alone after I'm gone."

"What do you mean alone? I have Reed," Cara said, choking out the words.

"You do?" Her mother scoffed.

"We all have our limitations," Cara whispered. She believed that the secrets of marriage should be kept secret. Even from her mother. *Especially* from her mother.

"Hmmm. That's a good euphemism. You stick with that when you're talking to people who don't know any better. Just don't think for a minute that I'm one of them."

"Mom, we don't have to talk about this. Really. I'm fine."

"Promise me you'll try to make things right with them. I need to know that you'll reach out to them when the time comes. Don't let your anger with them overpower your love for them. It's not a good way to live. Promise me."

"Okay. I'll try. When the time comes, I promise I'll try. Now can we please talk about something else?" The truth was, Cara had been thinking about Meg and Jane both a lot lately. She tried not to wonder about how different things would be if they were still around, or if they could've helped her though this awful time. They certainly couldn't have made anything worse. Well, that wasn't exactly true. According to the news reports, Jane's life was in total chaos, and chaos was the last thing Cara needed.

They'd gone back to watching TV and Cara had tried not to think any more about her mother's request. Shortly thereafter, she was gone, and even though Cara was married, her mother had done what no mother should ever do to a child she loved.

She left her alone.

Reed went with her to the funeral, but that was the only effort he made to support her. After the public mourning period was over, he didn't lift a finger to help her get her mother's affairs in order. He didn't go with her to meet with the executor of the estate; he didn't offer to help her deal with the sale of the house or pack up her mother's clothes and personal belongings. She remembered that Jane and Meg used to be jealous of her for being an only child, and would tease her for her tendency to get whatever she wanted. Only-child syndrome, they called it. What they didn't realize was that the syndrome doesn't just mean that you get what you want; it also means that you get what you don't want—like the sole responsibility for clearing out your mother's house after she's gone.

Cara wondered if maybe she'd be able to manage her grief better if she had someone to help her though it, but her husband didn't seem to think that it was his job. In his mind, it was her responsibility to deal with her emotions and soldier on as if nothing had happened, to lock her feelings away and show a brave face to the world. That was how the people in his family dealt with hardships. It probably explained why his sister had been married three times and his mother was addicted to sleeping pills.

Cara had started selling real estate in town years ago, and her job was the only thing in her life that kept her sane. She had always loved real estate and architecture and all the promise that a new home could hold. She loved meeting people who actually listened to her and valued what she had to say. Her clients made her feel important, like she had a purpose in life other than being Reed Chase's wife. She liked making her own money, even if it all went into their joint account; she knew that she contributed, and in her mind that meant she remained independent. Of course, the job had the added benefit of keeping her busy and out of the house for a few hours every day, something that she needed more than ever now that she couldn't spend time visiting her mother. Truth be told, while she loved her job, she'd have worked for the garbage company if it meant she could get away from Reed.

If she ever told anyone that he made her feel this way, they'd think she was crazy. Everyone loved Reed and stupidly believed that he was the perfect guy, a persona that he had delicately crafted for his entire life. His leather loafers were never scuffed, his tweed blazers were impeccably tailored, his shirt collars were crisply starched. Over the years Cara realized that it was one of the things that women who didn't know the first thing about Reed found enticing: that he managed to always look like a J.Crew model. Cara saw them in the grocery store, the women who ignorantly envied her without really knowing anything about her at all. Cara wore her dark hair in a neat, even shoulder-length cut, and her pearls and white button-downs like a uniform, not because she was too lazy to get dressed in anything else in the morning but because she had learned it was the only outfit she could wear that her husband wouldn't criticize. He liked things clean, orderly, unfussy, and that included her attire. Years ago she had dared to wear patterned shirts and large dangly earrings. One particularly brazen day, she'd donned a zebra-print coat, and the ridicule that rained down on her had been so relentless it made her afraid to descend the stairs in the morning to meet him at the breakfast table. Finally she realized that this particular uniform would allow her to move about without his pulling at the small threads that were left of her self-esteem, and so now it was all she wore.

The women in town called her "classic," she knew, like she was so stylish and naturally chic that she believed all a woman needed to look her best was minimal makeup, a pair of J Brand jeans, and a stark white shirt. It amazed her how truth can differ so vastly from reality, and how utterly painful it was to be the only person in her entire life who actually knew the truth.

Cara was aware that her mother had never really approved of her being in love with Reed Chase, but when Meg and Jane first met him, they liked him. At least, Meg did. If Cara was honest with herself, she'd admit that Jane was never a fan of Reed, either. Cara had assumed Jane was jealous and ignored her friend's obvious lack of enthusiasm where her new boyfriend was concerned. In fact, Cara's assumption that Jane was jealous of her probably marked the beginning of the end of their friendship. The irony was that Cara never took Jane's opinions all that seriously, and Jane might have been the only person who had the guts to try to point out that Reed might not be the guy he was pretending to be. Back then, Cara thought she knew everything. It became clear over the years that she actually knew nothing.

She met Reed during her junior year of college, and they hit it off immediately. They had so much in common. They were both overachievers with type-A personalities, both athletes, both popular, both more mature than other kids their own age. Cara's friends at college called Reed "Mr. Wonderful," always the charmer with the big smile and the jokes and the jovial personality that made everyone want to be near him. When she was home for winter break, Reed came to visit for a weekend. Cara introduced him to Meg and Jane at a party, so happy to have a real man in her life. Jane was right. Staying at Bowdoin was definitely the right decision.

"What kind of name is Reed Chase? It sounds like some sort of rich-people sport involving mallards or racehorses or something," Jane said when they met for lunch a few days later after Reed had returned home. "He's good-looking and all, don't get me wrong, but I don't know. He seems a little off to me. He's kind of bossy, isn't he? He wouldn't let you refill your beer at the keg last night. Worse than that, you listened to him! What's that about?"

"He was doing me a favor!" Cara answered in Reed's defense. "I'd had enough at that point. The last thing I needed was another beer."

"I don't know. If you like him I'm happy for you, but he kind of comes across like one of those rich dickheads who thinks he's better than everyone else," Jane said.

"So what if his family has money? That's not why I like him!"

"Only someone who was dating a guy with money would pretend like it didn't matter," Jane said. "Just be careful with him, that's all I'm saying."

Jane was jealous, and Cara knew it, which bothered her. Friends are supposed to want the best for each other. She didn't appreciate feeling like she needed to apologize for the universe bringing her and Reed together at a keg party, and she certainly didn't need to defend him to Jane.

"He's hot," Meg chimed in. "That's what I care about. He's smoking hot. If I wasn't madly in love with Steve, I'd totally go for him. On paper he seems just about perfect."

"He is cute, isn't he?" Cara said, feeling somehow proud that she'd been fortunate enough to grab someone as good-looking as Reed. It almost validated her own vanity, reaffirmed that she was a beautiful person, too. Looking back on it, it was clear that she was already starting to define herself by him. That trend only worsened over time, and she learned the hard way that being good on paper didn't actually mean anything.

She'd been telling the truth when she said that the money had never been something she thought about. Jane was the one who was interested in meeting a guy who could buy her Chanel purses and a prewar apartment in Manhattan. All Cara ever wanted was someone to make her coffee in the morning in one of those old-school French presses and go to the movies or to brunch with her on Saturdays. She suspected that Reed's name was worth more than he was, anyway. She was pretty sure that the family's old money, allegedly stored in old vaults, had been spent by old men on young women along the way. Still, that was a subject she never dared broach. It was ironic that she had worried that he was faking his finances when she should have been worried that he was faking being something else: a normal human who didn't think that women should be silent and obedient, and not necessarily in that order.

She'd heard stories of women who got married and then claimed that their husband's entire personalities changed after the honeymoon ended, but she'd never thought she'd be one of them. When they were first married, life with Reed was more than she ever could've imagined. He was never overly sentimental or affectionate, but he was a WASP and wasn't exactly in touch with his emotions, so that was never a big deal to her. He was thoughtful in his own way: buying her jewelry or new clothes. Once he even bought her a designer bag that all the women in town were carrying, but which she'd found to be way too big of a splurge to ever buy for herself. He worked as a business manager, spending most of his time monitoring finances for his family and his boarding school buddies. His friends were constantly calling him to ask questions about their investments, or their trusts, or how to write off the expensive gifts they bought for their wives and their girlfriends. He loved his job, and at the end of the day he'd come home and they'd spend their nights having quiet dinners in restaurants in Brookville. Slowly, they settled into a routine. Wasn't that what married life was supposed to be like? Wasn't an end to chaos and the emergence of a routine one of the benefits?

After about two years of marriage, though, she began to see the jewelry and the purses not as thoughtful gifts from a loving husband, but as something else entirely. She felt like he was trying to change her, to mold her into the type of woman he wanted her to be, instead of accepting her for the woman she actually was. It was a gradual shift, so subtle she didn't even realize it at first, but eventually he developed an obsessive need to control everything in her life, including her.

He began to obsess over their own finances the way he monitored his clients', always keeping some kind of mental tabulation of payables and receivables down to the last cent. The man she lived with was not the man she'd thought she was marrying twelve years ago. She wished she'd paid more attention to the warning signs. She wished she'd paid attention to Jane and to her mother when they voiced their concerns. But she hadn't, and unfortunately, it was too late to go back and redo the past, and divorce simply wasn't an option. Even as a child, Cara had never been willing to admit that she'd made a mistake. She was thoughtful, thorough, cautious, and old-fashioned in a lot of ways. She believed in her vows and refused to advertise to people that she couldn't find a way to make her relationship work. She didn't like the thought of ditching her marriage when things got hard—she wasn't a quitter. Her father had quit her mother, and by default, her, when things got hard in her parents' marriage, and she'd sworn she'd never be like him. She wasn't a coward like he was. She'd figure out a way to make it work or die trying. There simply was no other option.

Still, she hated that she'd allowed it to go this far. Jane had seen it from the very beginning. *Why didn't I? Why didn't anyone else? Why didn't I listen to her?*, she asked herself when she lay in bed awake at night, but she hated the answer. Because she'd assumed Jane was pissed she was still single when Cara was on her way to being married. She'd thought everything Jane did back then stemmed from her being jealous, but now things looked different—how Reed had really treated her, what Jane had really seen, and how she'd responded to both of them in return. She spent a lot of time lately thinking back to the first time that the crack in Reed's perfect image showed, the first time his inner control freak surfaced and silenced her, the first time she lashed out at Jane for voicing her concerns. Ironically, it was at their engagement party.

six

"Where is she?" Cara asked Meg as she looked at her watch and wondered for the millionth time why Jane was late. Reed's uncle had been nice enough to throw them an intimate party at his apartment, and instead of enjoying the night with her family and friends, Cara was completely distracted. "The party started at seven o'clock and it's almost nine. What, is my engagement party not important enough for her to show up?"

"She'll be here! I'm sure she's stuck in traffic or something," Meg said, trying to calm her. "Don't get upset. It's your engagement party. Go mingle and I will make sure she comes right over when she gets here, I promise."

Just then, the door opened and Jane slid inside. "See, I told you she'd be here," Meg said as she waved her over.

"I'm so sorry I'm late. I had an audition that ran later than I thought it would and I couldn't find anything to wear and then I completely misjudged how long it would take me to get all the way up here. You look amazing, Cara!" Jane said as she leaned in to wrap her in a hug. Cara immediately felt herself tense because she could smell the booze on Jane's breath. Was she really running late because of an audition? Or was she late because she'd rather stop off at a bar with some of her random roommates than celebrate Cara's engagement with her?

"Were they serving wine at the audition?" Cara asked. She knew she shouldn't be picking a fight with Jane, but she'd reached her breaking point. Jane's complete lack of interest in the biggest event of Cara's life wasn't something she felt like ignoring anymore. This was as good a time as any to have it out with her.

"Huh?" Jane said. "Why would you ask that? I had a glass or two while I was getting dressed. So what?"

"The 'so what' is that you're two hours late and you had to have wine to come up here?" Cara asked. If she sounded disapproving and judgmental, it was because she meant to. She didn't think Jane deserved to be let off the hook for her behavior anymore.

"Cara, don't start an argument. She's here; that's all that matters!" Meg said. She looked around to make sure no one could overhear their conversation. "It's your engagement party. Now's not the time to do this!"

"No, Meg. I think now is the perfect time to do this. I'd like an honest answer, Jane. Did you really need to get liquored up to come support your best friend?"

"Yes," Jane said without hesitation, which surprised both Cara and Meg. "If you expect me to party with you all night and pretend that I'm happy you're going to marry this guy, then I'm going to need some wine. Lots of it, in fact."

"You're supposed to be one of my best friends."

"I am your best friend, and that's why I'm telling you the truth. If you're going to call me out for being late and insinuate that it's because I was partying downtown somewhere, then I'll be completely honest with you. I'm sorry I'm late because it's rude, but I'm not sorry that I was spared two hours of watching Reed boss you around. It's hard to stomach."

"You're shameless, and jealous, and it's sad. I'm moving on with my life, Jane. I'm sorry if that makes you feel abandoned or something, but you don't have to try to rain on my parade."

Jane laughed out loud, her eyes wide and glassy from the wine. "You think I'm jealous of you? Are you serious? Cara, I swear to God if I die alone an old shrew in a cardboard box downtown, I still will not be jealous of you. How can you say that to me? I only want what's best for you, and I'm telling you this is the worst decision in the world. I'm sorry, but I'm not going to pretend otherwise. I can't do it. I'm not that good an actress."

"No kidding," Cara said.

"Now that was just unnecessary," Jane said, looking legitimately hurt for the first time in a long time.

"I'll never forgive you for this, Jane."

"I'm sorry you feel that way, and I sincerely hope you get over it. If you're going to stay mad at me because I told you the truth, then our friendship isn't as strong as I thought it was. I thought we were supposed to be honest with each other no matter what."

"You guys, stop. You're turning this into something much bigger than it needs to be. Let it go. We can talk about it later. Jane, let's go get a glass of champagne," Meg said.

"I was also telling you the truth when I said you look amazing, Cara," Jane said as Meg tried in vain to drag her away. If the compliment was supposed to assuage her anger, it didn't.

Cara made her way through the crowd and grabbed Reed's sleeve to separate him from his friends. "Are you having a good time?" Reed asked.

"I was until Jane decided to show up drunk. Do you believe her?" Cara said. "She just waltzes in here almost two hours late and after more than a few cocktails and doesn't seem to think that's a problem? She made up some bullshit story about an audition running late, but the truth is, she's jealous that I'm getting married and she hasn't gone on a date with a guy in months.

Does she think I'm that stupid that I don't see it? She's one of my bridesmaids and she shouldn't be acting like this. What is wrong with her?" Cara's ire was evident, and she was hoping Reed would say something to soothe her.

"Honestly, Cara, the better question is what's wrong with you?"

"What's that supposed to mean?"

"I don't know why you even talk to her. She's beneath you. Even if you don't believe that, she's definitely beneath me, and I don't need my wife socializing with deadbeats like her. I don't know why you even invited her."

"How can you say that? She's one of my closest friends; of course I was going to invite her," Cara said. She found it odd that two seconds ago she had been ripping Jane apart and now she was defending her, but it was one thing for her to insult her best friend; it was another for Reed to do it.

"No. She was one of your closest friends. Now you're going to be a married woman and you need to start realizing that you're a reflection on me. We don't need people like her hanging around. It's inappropriate."

"Are you kidding? Reed, I really don't think—"

"Enough, Cara!" Reed said forcefully. His eyes darted around the room to make sure no one was listening to their conversation. He never stopped smiling or rubbing the small of her back, as if the two of them were having an intimate moment instead of an argument. "I refuse to spend one more second of this party talking about this. This is not how we are going to act in public. Now, get over it, pull yourself together, and go mingle with our guests. Don't bother me with this stupid stuff again."

Cara was stunned by what he said, not to mention the way in which he said it, but she didn't want to ruin her own engagement *party by fighting with Reed over anything, especially not Jane. This was supposed to be a night of celebration, and she'd already had an argument with one person; adding Reed to the list didn't seem like a good idea. "You're right," she said, forcing a smile. "It's our night. I don't know why I care what anyone else is doing."*

"Exactly," Reed said. He planted a quick kiss on her cheek and ambled over to a group of his friends on the other side of the room as if the entire conversation had never happened. At the time, Cara chalked his mood swing up to nerves and convinced herself that he wasn't entirely wrong. She wasn't going to let Jane's behavior ruin her and Reed's party, so she shrugged it off. It simply wasn't worth making an issue over. If this was how Jane felt about Cara's marriage, then she didn't need to be a big part of Cara's life anymore.

She pushed the memory from her mind and forced herself to focus on the task at hand. She took one last look around her childhood home before she locked up and drove back to her own house, wanting nothing more than to climb into a hot shower and then go to bed. She was hoping that Reed would be working late, so she wouldn't have to talk to him when she arrived home around 5:00, but she found him sitting at the kitchen table with a book and a glass of wine. She wiped her hand across her face to dry her cheeks, but there was no hiding the fact that she'd been crying. Her eyes were burning and swollen and she hadn't slept well in weeks, which wasn't strange considering everything she was going through. What was incredibly strange was that her husband didn't seem to understand her grief. Not only did he not understand it, it actually seemed to bother him immensely.

"What's wrong with you?" Reed asked, as if crying were some

sort of mortal sin that she should repent for instead of a normal human emotion that comes from grieving the loss of her mother, the loss of her marriage, the loss of herself. She wasn't sure which loss was responsible for these particular tears.

"I just need a minute. Today was hard. I put my mother's entire life into boxes and threw them in storage, and the house I grew up in is no longer mine. I shouldn't have to explain to you why I'm upset. Why won't you let me process this my way?" She had been married twelve years, but in retrospect, twenty-five had been too young for her to get married.

"Your sulking isn't helping this marriage any. Your mother died. That's life. Dwelling on it isn't helping you, and it isn't helping me. Don't forget, we have dinner with Cody and Tabitha tonight," he added, tossing his copy of the *New York Post* on the counter and looking at her as if daring her to say she wasn't going to go. She didn't answer, somehow still stunned by his complete lack of compassion. He grabbed his jacket off the back of the kitchen chair. "I'm going down to the club to work out and take a steam before we go, but I'll come by and pick you up for dinner at eight. Try to pull it together by then. No one wants to spend a night with a weepy woman. Put on some makeup. It will make you feel better." With that he grabbed his sport coat and exited out the back door, into the driveway that abutted the patio at the back of their house.

The words should've stung. They should've ripped her soul out so that she was wearing it around her neck like a scarf. But they didn't. If she had felt anything for him anymore, his words would've caused her to hide under her duvet for days and come out only for showers and glasses of water so that she didn't dehydrate and die. But she didn't. The only things she felt these days were empty and alone.

That fucking club, she thought as she watched him back his Jeep out of the driveway. She'd never understand the draw of this men's club, which of course was by design, as women weren't allowed on the premises. It wasn't the fact that the club excluded women that bothered her, it was the fact that it was where men went to get away from them. The only places she could go to get away from Reed were the grocery store or the dry cleaner, and neither of them provided much solace or helped her deal with her problems. Where was she supposed to go?

She ran into the bathroom and closed the door behind her, pushing in the silver button next to the doorknob to lock it. She stared at herself in the mirror, rested her hands on the ledge of the sink, and exhaled deeply enough to make her entire upper body cave in. *What happened to you?* she asked herself. *What the hell happened to you?*

When she looked up, she glanced out the window, past the flowers that lined her front walk, past the lamppost with the bulb that burned out weeks ago that she hadn't gotten around to fixing, to the woman standing at the curb in front of her house. Her breath caught and she felt her insides churn in shock as the woman approached her front door. Cara wondered if her eyes were betraying her, or her grief was causing her to conjure ghosts. All she'd been doing lately was thinking about why Jane really pulled away. More important, she'd done a lot of thinking about how she'd not only let her go, but encouraged it, because she knew Reed didn't like her. She suddenly remembered what her mother had said to her, asking her to reconcile with her friends, as if knowing this was going to happen. It was no apparition. For some reason that she couldn't understand, Jane was about to ring her doorbell.

seven

Jane glanced around the immaculate grounds of her friend's suburban home. The bays and harbors of the North Shore of Long Island were packed with boats and yachts, old money families mingling with financiers and lawyers who looked after the old money and became rich from it themselves. Cara's house was exactly as Jane remembered it from years ago—a large brick colonial that was both classic and comfortable-looking. White shutters encased large windows across the entire façade in perfect symmetry on either side of the red front door. Hedges ran along the perimeter of the property to separate the house from the neighbors, something that Jane had a hard time understanding. No matter how large a Manhattan apartment is, you're still sharing walls with your neighbors. So hedges for a property that was already acres wide seemed redundant. Jane paused at the bottom of the walkway that led from the sidewalk to the front door as she watched the cab pull away and head back to the concrete jungle that was intent on eating her alive. She felt herself struggle to take her first step, knowing she wouldn't be welcomed with open arms, and worse, knowing that she didn't deserve to be. She listened to the birds in the trees and watched the kids down the block riding their bicycles in wobbly circles in the road, and didn't miss the irony that Cara was living the exact life Jane had spent the last twenty years trying to avoid. She had barely pressed the doorbell before the door opened and Cara stood in front of her, slack jawed and bewildered.

"Hey," Jane said with a weak wave. It had been years. She had no idea where to start, but hello seemed as good a place as any.

"'Hey'?" Cara repeated, staring at her like she was an alien and not someone who used to borrow her bathing suits. "That's what you have to say to me?" She peered at Jane again, and Jane knew immediately what she was thinking. Cara had been one of the prettiest girls in school (though she either truly didn't know it or truly didn't care), with hazel eyes that flecked gold or green or auburn depending on what color shirt she wore, bouncy hair that didn't require a straightening iron, and skin that never needed makeup. She was the quintessential all-American, natural girl who never needed any help enhancing what she was born with, whereas Jane now had so many fillers in her face she basically looked like a wax figure. She was sure Cara was horrified by the implants and wondered how long it would take her to ask about them. In fact, she was surprised it had already taken this long.

"I always found it to be a good ice breaker," Jane joked. There had been a time when Cara had loved Jane's ability to laugh at any situation. She realized that that was probably no longer the case, but falling back into her old role made her feel less uncomfortable about seeking refuge in a friend she hadn't seen in years.

"What are you doing here? You haven't been here since before you eloped. Eight years ago."

"I know. It hasn't changed a bit. Neither have you," Jane said. She meant it, but she was afraid she came off as insincere.

"I wish I could say the same," Cara answered. She stepped out onto the porch and closed the door behind her. Jane didn't expect to be welcomed with a bottle of champagne, but the icy insult caught her off guard.

"How have you been?" Jane asked. She couldn't believe how

nervous she felt—how this woman had become a stranger. For a second she wondered if maybe she was wrong to assume that her old friend would want to help. Maybe too much had happened between them. Jane's heart ached as she tried to prepare herself for the possibility that Cara, like everyone else in her life, might turn her back on her.

"Spare me the pleasantries, Jane. Why are you here? What, did your elitist friends in the city ditch you when they discovered that your husband is a white-collar criminal?"

"Basically." It seemed silly to lie, especially since she'd just paid seventy dollars she didn't have on cab fare to get here. Still, it wasn't easy to announce how pathetic she'd become, especially not to Cara. The last thing Jane needed was to give Cara yet another reason to say her four favorite words: *I told you so.*

"Gee, couldn't have seen that one coming."

"You don't have to look like you're enjoying watching my life implode on the news, Cara. I've paid plenty for my husband's sins. I don't have any money. I don't have any friends. And I'm about to be evicted from my apartment. I've begged the feds to give me access to something so that I can get out of there and start over, but they weren't interested in helping me. I feel like I'm drowning and I don't know what to do." Jane choked on her words. Asking for help wasn't easy, and having her oldest friend look at her like she didn't recognize her wasn't making anything easier. If someone had told her this would happen to their relationship, she never would've believed it. Not ever. Not for anything.

"You asked the feds for a favor and were denied? I wish I could've seen the temper tantrum you threw when you heard the word 'no.' You always had a way of throwing your toys out of the pram in spectacular fashion when you didn't get your way."

Jane was trying to remain calm and keep her temper in check. It wasn't unreasonable for Cara to be angry with her for showing up at her house, but she had underestimated just how angry she'd be. It was becoming very clear that this visit was just the latest in a very long list of bad decisions Jane had made lately.

"Look, I'm not saying that I've done everything right, and quite honestly, if that's how high the bar is to stay friends with you then I was never going to clear it anyway. You don't have to be a bitch about it."

"You still haven't told me why you're here."

"I'm here because I've been trapped in my apartment. If I go outside I'm literally chased by paparazzi with cameras who think that splattering the image of the moron wife who didn't know any better across the front page will sell papers. I'm here because I'm afraid my lungs are starting to shrivel up due to lack of fresh air, and I'm here because I need to see someone who knew me before I was *his* wife. I need to get out of the city, Cara. I'm afraid I'm going to literally lose my mind if I don't. I'm here because I need to be around people who know me—who really know me."

"You're here because you need something. Some things never change."

"Fine. Forget it. I thought maybe you'd be willing to help me."

"You're unbelievable. All these years go by without a word from you and you show up here and expect me to jump for joy? You have no idea what's going on in my life, and you don't even care. You still think that everything is about you. The sheer fact that you came here expecting me to feel *bad* for you, to feel *pity* for you, is just another sign of how completely out of touch you are with reality."

"Fine, Cara. I'm sorry I bothered you," Jane said, surprised at her own tone of voice. She'd had enough of people insulting her. She'd rather wrestle Mrs. Cooper and the entire co-op board than put up with this shit. She was alone in this. She'd have to figure out a way to go on relying on no one but herself.

Jane spun around and started to walk down the block. It was probably a mile into town, where she'd have to wait at the train station for the next westbound train to shuttle her back into the city. She hadn't reached the curb yet when she heard Cara clear her throat.

"Jane, wait," Cara called after her.

Jane slowly turned around to stare at Cara, standing in the doorway of her beautiful, probably unmortgaged home wearing jeans and a white shirt, and swallowed a lump in her throat.

"What?" Jane shot back, regretting her decision to show her vulnerability.

Cara fidgeted with the strand of pearls at her neck. "Where will you go?"

Jane hesitated a moment, then shrugged. "I don't know. I'll figure it out."

"Stay here. For tonight at least. It's getting late and it's cold, and . . . I can still be mad at you without turning you out on the street."

"Don't do me any favors," Jane said, knowing full well that this was exactly the favor she'd sought in the first place.

"Please, Jane. Just come inside. You can crash in the spare bedroom." Cara opened the door and stepped to the side, giving Jane room to enter. Jane trudged up the walk, hoping Cara could somehow hear her say *thank you* and *I'm sorry* to herself without actually having to say them out loud. Her dislike of Reed had ultimately been what had come between them, but she was willing to admit she'd been wrong. Years later, they were still happily married, they had a beautiful home, and as far as she knew, Reed was on the right side of the law. Jane had misjudged him. When the time was right, she'd tell Cara that. She'd tell her that she was just trying to protect her, but she had gone about it all wrong. She'd tell her that she should've kept her mouth shut and been on time for her engagement party and been supportive and happy for her back then. She'd tell her all of it—if Cara would only give her the chance.

She dropped her bag on the floor next to the console table just inside the foyer. The spindled staircase circled up from the right of the entry, a grandfather clock ticking away quietly in the corner.

"Come with me," Cara said. "We can put your bag in the spare room." Jane followed Cara up the stairs, and tried very hard not to be shocked at how strange it all felt. When they were little they used to walk in and out of each other's houses without even ringing the doorbell. Now she felt like she was standing in a museum or something, afraid to touch the grass cloth on the wall, nothing feeling familiar. They walked past the master bedroom, and Jane peeked her head in and saw the large leather headboard and stark white sheets, a huge flat-screen TV, and two pairs of men's lace-up dress shoes sitting in the corner next to a StairMaster. They continued down the hall and passed another bedroom, the bed once again covered in white linens, with a large overstuffed chair sitting in the corner. It wasn't the color palette that made Jane look twice, it was the assortment of objects on the bureau under the window: a bottle of perfume, a hairbrush, a porcelain dish holding bangle bracelets, and next to it all, in a large silver frame, the old black-and-white picture of Cara's mother that she recognized from Cara's childhood home. She also noticed a pair of slippers sitting neatly next to the bed and a book on the nightstand, next to the alarm clock.

When they got to the end of the hallway, Cara opened a door and ushered Jane into a third white bedroom. This room had a four-poster bed with a white duvet, white curtains on the windows, and a small bureau with a lamp resting on it.

Before Jane opened her mouth to ask Cara if someone else was staying in the second bedroom, she caught herself. There were no other guests.

Cara and Reed were sleeping in separate bedrooms.

It hadn't occurred to Jane when she decided to parachute into Cara's life that things might be anything other than perfect. Now she felt like she had stumbled into something Cara didn't want her to be a part of, and she understood, a little bit at least, why Cara was so angry when she showed up unannounced. *I was right!* Jane thought. *I was right, I was right, I was right!* She realized that she shouldn't feel vindicated by discovering that her friend's marriage wasn't perfect, but she couldn't help it. Oh man, it felt good to know that her instincts weren't completely wrong. She may have drastically misjudged her own husband, but she had Reed right all along.

Jane pretended she hadn't noticed anything. "Thank you so much for this," she said as she gazed out the window at the backyard. There was a large oak tree in the corner of the property, and for a second, Jane inadvertently smiled. A long time ago, in a life now far, far away, Jane used to climb trees like that in her own backyard. She'd swing from the lower branches and scrape her legs on the bark as she shinnied up the trunk, trying to climb higher than the squirrels running along the limbs with abandon. She'd loved the view—the tops of the houses across the street, the giant hill that led down to the brook running behind the train tracks. It had been a very long time since she'd thought about that.

"It's not a problem. Maybe a good night's sleep will help you find a way out of this mess," Cara said.

"I doubt it, but it will probably help the bags under my eyes. That'll have to be enough for now."

"Come downstairs, I'll make us some tea."

Jane was hoping for something slightly stronger than tea, but she had a feeling the only other options would be decaf coffee or orange juice. She felt around in her bag for her bottle of Xanax, relieved that she never left home without it.

Downstairs, Jane sat at the kitchen table and watched as Cara filled the kettle with water. From the cabinet above the microwave, Cara removed a box of Entenmann's crumb cake and cut two fat squares from the slab before carefully closing the box and returning it to the shelf. She placed the cake on white china plates and dropped two herbal tea bags into matching mugs. When the water boiled, she filled the mugs and brought the snack over to the table. It was as if she were doing ballet, a choreographed routine she performed all the time, silently, efficiently, dutifully. When she finally sat down next to Jane and stopped fidgeting with her pearls, Jane decided it was time to at least try to bridge the canyon-sized gap between them.

"I'm so sorry about your mom, Cara. She was a really great lady. And she made some mean chocolate chip cookies. How are you holding up?"

Tears welled in Cara's eyes. "You heard?" she whispered.

"My mom told me. She called me as soon as she heard."

"And you didn't come to the funeral? I assumed when you didn't show, it was because you hadn't heard. My mother always loved you, Jane. You and Meg both." Hearing the pain in Cara's voice hurt her, but before she could speak, Cara continued.

"I'm sorry, I don't know why I'm surprised. You were one of my bridesmaids, but you showed up late to my engagement party and then left my wedding early to go hang out in a bar somewhere. I shouldn't expect anything else. At some point, allowing you to continuously disappoint me is my own fault."

Jane felt her anger grow at the mention of her leaving the wedding early. It wasn't that she hadn't wanted to celebrate Cara's marriage; it was that she couldn't celebrate Cara's marriage to *him*. By the time Cara and Reed got engaged, Jane had no doubt whatsoever that Reed wasn't the nice guy he pretended to be. The more carefully she'd watched him, the more sure she'd been that he was really a huge asshole. She'd tried to keep her feelings to herself, but it had become harder and harder to keep her mouth shut, and by the time the engagement party rolled around she'd felt like she was going to explode. Jane saw the way he treated Cara. He ordered for her at restaurants, answered questions directed to her in conversations, started to buy her expensive clothes so he could control what she wore. Reed didn't want a wife. He wanted a German shepherd that would obey his commands, and it was so obvious to Jane that she couldn't understand how Cara didn't see it, too. After their fight at the engagement party it had seemed totally ridiculous for her to stay and watch them dance and celebrate at the wedding with a huge fake smile plastered on her face. So she'd left. She told herself it wouldn't have mattered anyway, but her early exit had probably severed the last real thread holding their friendship together. It was something she regretted. Maybe she should have just sucked it up, tucked her venom for Reed away in her clutch, and pretended to be thrilled for her friend. But she couldn't. Jane had never been good at keeping her true feelings hidden. She was well aware that she had made more than her fair share of mistakes, but she wasn't going to let Cara criticize her for things she hadn't done. "I did show," she said softly.

"What?" Cara asked. "What do you mean you did show? To the funeral? No you didn't."

"Yes I did. I stood in the back and left before the recessional because I didn't know if you'd want me there, and I was worried that my showing up might somehow upset you even more than you already were. Maybe I should have stayed. I swear, I thought I was doing the right thing. If I'd known that you'd wanted me there, I would've stayed to talk to you. You gave a beautiful eulogy."

"Thanks," Cara said, tears welling in her eyes again. "She couldn't believe that our friendship had devolved into this."

"Me neither. I can't believe what life has done to us."

"Before she died, she begged me to reconcile with you."

"You're kidding," Jane said. She stared out the window, wondering if Cara's mother had orchestrated this entire thing, and if she'd somehow sent Jane to this house to fill the void she'd left in Cara's life. "It's like she knew this was going to happen. She always had answers for everything."

"Maybe."

"It's just so weird because I've been thinking so much about you lately. Last year I found a ski jacket I thought you'd really like. I almost sent it to you for your birthday, but I wimped out. I didn't think you'd want to hear from me."

Jane's confession was met with a silent shrug and a raised eyebrow. She was saddened to realize she couldn't interpret Cara's nonverbal cues anymore.

"You believe me, don't you?" Jane asked. It was a silly question to ask, but she suddenly felt she needed to be sure.

"I don't know what to believe anymore. I don't know you, Jane. I knew the girl buried inside you. I haven't seen her in a long time."

"Neither have I," Jane admitted with a sigh.

"Do you miss her?" Cara asked the question Jane had been asking herself a lot lately.

"I'm starting to."

"I'm sorry, but I have to ask. What's with the boobs?" Cara asked, cracking a slight smile. "They're so . . . huge!"

"Birthday present," Jane answered, looking down at the D-cup silicone sacs attached to her rib cage. She hated them, not just because they were too big for her body, not just because they made sleeping on her stomach impossible, but also because they reminded her of Doug and everything that was wrong with her life.

"Your husband bought you boobs for your birthday?"

"Yup."

"They look . . . uncomfortable," Cara said. "You don't have the frame to carry them."

"Last winter I walked out of the gym with my shirt wide open and I had no idea. I couldn't even feel the cold air hitting them. *That* was uncomfortable, let me tell you."

Cara laughed. "I so wish I could've seen that."

"It was mortifying."

"You look tired. No amount of Botox can cover that up."

"So I've learned." She sighed.

Jane looked around the room. It was perfectly neat, which wasn't surprising. Cara had always been a stickler for cleanliness and order. What surprised her was that everything was colorless. Cara used to love color: bold patterns, bright nail polish. This home was beautiful, but it was sterile. Two white couches were covered with white and beige pillows, and camel-colored cashmere blankets were neatly folded over their backs, begging someone to curl up under them with a book or a cup of tea or a glass of wine. The carpet covering the hardwood floor was cream with a tan diamond pattern and looked like no one had ever stepped foot on it. Polished end tables supported the weight of heavy crystal lamps and antique lacquered boxes. Other than their wedding photo, there wasn't a single picture of Cara or Reed in this room. In fact, so far, she hadn't seen a single picture of either of them in the entire house. Jane had a feeling that Cara was probably able to convince people that Reed didn't like pictures, or that age had made them camera shy. They wouldn't be the first people approaching middle age who decided to steer clear of high-definition lenses, but Jane knew Cara too well to ever believe that.

"I hate to do this to you, but I have to go out to dinner tonight. Reed is picking me up here at eight," Cara said, shifting in her chair.

"Don't apologize. It's not like you knew I was coming. You don't sound too happy about it, though," Jane said. She'd hoped they would stay up and talk. She'd hoped Cara would explain the bedrooms and the lack of photos. She'd hoped Cara would tell her that she had been right all along.

"I haven't felt much like socializing lately, to be honest. I have to get in the shower and start getting ready. You should go to bed early, and we can pick this up in the morning. Make yourself at home while I'm gone."

"That actually sounds pretty amazing. I remember when I didn't even go out until eleven. All I want to do is sleep, to be honest," Jane said, not realizing how absolutely pathetic that was until she heard herself say it out loud. It was almost like a confession. "I have pills to help take the edge off."

"Sleeping pills are addictive. You shouldn't rely on them too much."

"I know, but I don't really care right now. I have bigger problems to deal with and I feel safe in bed. I know once I get out of it, I have to contend with the press, and the rumors, and the accusations, and the overwhelming self-hatred for being inadvertently involved in something that hurt so many people."

"This must be hard for you," Cara said. Jane looked up to see if she was being sarcastic, but she wasn't. Cara now seemed understanding, even sympathetic. It had been a long time since anyone had been either of those things toward her.

"The hardest part is being alone. I don't mean without a husband. That, I could handle. I mean just alone. The only person who will even speak to me without wanting to spit in my face is Hector, the maintenance man in the building. Once they evict me, I won't even have him."

"I'm speaking with you now."

"Yeah, but you looked like you wanted to spit at me when I first showed up, too."

"I'm over it."

"Thank God," Jane said. She reached out and grabbed Cara's hand. It felt cold. "Thank you for letting me stay here tonight."

"You're welcome."

"What time will you guys be home?" Jane asked.

"Not late if I can help it, but it's hard to say," Cara said. "We won't leave until Reed has had enough scotch and small talk and not a moment before."

"Well, I hope Reed doesn't mind my staying over," she said.

Jane tried to ignore the uneasy look that crossed Cara's face.

eight

Cara hated socializing with the people who traveled in Reed's circle. Especially the women. They all had names like Bitsy, Buttons, Tiffy, or some other ridiculous moniker that made it impossible to take them seriously, which wasn't actually much of a problem as they rarely had anything serious to say. Tonight, she and Reed were having dinner with Cody Miller, Reed's squash buddy, drinking comrade, and oldest friend from his boarding school days at Exeter, and Cody's wife, Tabitha. The thought of it was almost as horrid as the idea of having to somehow explain to Reed that Jane was sleeping in their guest room. She felt like the ceiling and the floor were compressing like a vise and trying to flatten her, but there was no way around it. *This is the life I built,* she reminded herself. *It is what it is.*

They rode most of the way in silence. By the time they valeted the car, Cara was no closer to telling Reed, but maybe that was for the best. Maybe the news would go over better after he'd had a few drinks and relaxed.

"I don't want this to be a late night," Cara said as they entered the restaurant, even though she knew it was pointless. She couldn't think of any seamless way to tell Reed that Jane was at their house, and the anxiety was making her jittery.

"Stop fidgeting," Reed snapped. He was already annoyed with her, and they hadn't even sat down. Reed pushed his way through the crowd and ordered them both drinks at the bar. When he handed her a glass of white wine, she had to hold it with both hands to keep the glass from shaking.

"What is the matter with you?" Reed asked. "Why can't you hold still?"

"I'm sorry. I'm just not really up for this," Cara answered.

"You're never up for doing anything!" Reed said. She didn't feel like explaining to him for the millionth time that she wasn't ready to be social yet, that she was still very much mourning her mother and wanted to stay home, alone. "Here they come," he said as he caught sight of Cody and Tabitha entering the restaurant. "Smile, and pretend you're happy to be here, would you please?"

Cody waved as he pushed his way toward the bar, Tabitha scurrying after him, glancing around the room to see who else was in attendance. Cody's hair was still wet from a shower, and he wore khakis, a cashmere sweater, and his usual Stubbs and Wootton shoes. The initials *CM* were monogrammed in yellow thread on the black slippers, so that no one would ever again mistake Cody's Stubbs and Woottons for their own and accidentally take off with them. That had happened once, at the annual Fourth of July beach barbecue down on the Sound, and for months afterward he'd inspected the footwear of every man at the club in an attempt to identify the thief and have his membership revoked. The slippers were never recovered, but Cody swore he would never be the victim again, and it would be a brave man who'd steal shoes that were emblazoned with someone else's monogram.

"Hey there, guys," he said, tugging at the cuff of his shirtsleeve until it matched the length of his sweater. "I'm sorry we're late. Tabitha couldn't find anything to wear, despite the fact that she has a walk-in closet larger than a New York City apartment. Explain that to me!"

"No problem at all!" Reed said, showing more affection for his buddy than he had for his wife in years.

"It's nice to see you," Cara lied as she leaned in so he could kiss her cheek.

"Another good day at the office?" Cody asked after the hostess had escorted them to their usual table in the back corner of the room. "Stock market was up again. If this keeps up it will be a banner year."

"I know. I reallocated some money into a few riskier assets. I'm liking the returns I'm seeing, but I think there are some better opportunities out there. It never pays to be conservative," Reed replied, loving any conversation that had to do with money and his acumen for making it.

"Tabitha seems to think we need to start worrying about our retirement. Do you believe that? I'm thirty-eight years old. Maybe she's planning on me retiring at fifty but I sure as hell am not. I have a long career in front of me—unless, of course, she kills me in my sleep. Maybe that's her master plan." Cody laughed. "She'll probably dress me in a suit and push me down the stairs so she can collect double indemnity on my life insurance or something."

"I love when you talk about me like I'm not here even though I'm sitting right next to you," Tabitha joked, though Cara didn't think that it actually bothered her at all. "It was just a suggestion. I don't know anything about *business*. I saw something about it on a talk show and thought I should mention it—that's all! Cara, do you think I'm being ridiculous?"

Reed smiled and sipped his scotch. Cara knew that Reed

thought Cody was a fool for letting his wife weigh in on business decisions. Reed had once told her that he suspected Cody's willingness to include Tabitha on financial matters when she knew nothing about numbers was exactly why his trust fund wasn't what it should've been. Reed would be damned if he was going to make the same mistake. No one would ever be in charge of his finances except him.

"Cara doesn't care much about the finances," Reed answered for her. "She lets me handle the money and she handles the household. That's how it is in our marriage."

"Ours too. But that doesn't mean I can't have an opinion!" Tabitha added. "I called you yesterday, Cara. I haven't seen much of you lately."

"I'm sorry! I've been so busy. I'm dealing with my mother's estate, and I haven't had much spare time." The truth was, Cara wouldn't have called Tabitha back no matter what was going on in her personal life, because all Tabitha ever wanted to do was gossip about the women around town. She considered knowing exactly what was going on with people to be some kind of neighborly responsibility.

"It's no problem at all! Listen, you know how I don't like to spread gossip, but I drove by your house on my way home from the gym today and I could've sworn that I saw you outside on the front lawn talking to . . ." Tabitha glanced furtively around the room to make sure no one was listening, and then motioned for her and Reed to lean in closer. Cody could barely lean over at all because he had a potbelly so large it made bending at the waist nearly impossible. "Jane Logan," she whispered.

Cara's smile froze on her face. It had never occurred to her that in the few minutes she and Jane were outside, someone might have seen them. Reed tried very hard to seem unfazed, but she could tell that his insides were roiling at the mention of Jane's name. "That's ridiculous," Reed said, forcing a tight smile and shooting Cara a look that meant she was supposed to play along. "Cara doesn't know Jane Logan. That woman is holed up in Manhattan somewhere until the feds can figure out how to exile her from the island. I assure you that whoever you saw Cara speaking to, it wasn't Jane Logan."

"It was just someone asking for directions. I didn't get her name, but I don't think it was the woman from the papers, no. Sorry to disappoint you, but my life's not that interesting!" Cara joked, praying that her act was convincing. Reed was obsessed with what the men at his stupid club thought of him. If Cody caught on that he had the wife of a felon hanging out at his house, Cara would never hear the end of it.

"I didn't think so!" Cody added. "I told Tabitha she was being crazy. Her brain is so saturated with images of that woman from reading every tabloid in the supermarket that she now thinks she's seeing her in real life."

"I guess you're right," Tabitha said. "She really did look like her, though. It was uncanny!"

"Tabitha, I promise you that my wife is not cavorting around town with criminals," Reed said firmly.

"Anyway, what else is new with you guys?" Cara asked, well aware that Reed was all but glaring at her from across the table.

"Not too much," Tabitha said. "What time do you want us to pick you up next Friday? I think a party is just what you need to lift your spirits, Cara."

"Friday?" Cara had no idea what Tabitha was talking about, but that wasn't surprising. Reed kept the social calendar. He told her where she needed to be and at what time and she'd show up. "I'm sorry, what's next Friday?"

"Neal Booker's fiftieth birthday party! You're coming, aren't you?"

Cara stayed quiet as she watched Reed purse his lips in a tight smile. Neal Booker was the club president, and one of the most influential board members of the golf club Reed was hoping to join down in Palm Beach. His birthday party was likely to be the event of the season, if not the year. Missing it would be akin to social suicide. The only thing worse would be for Reed to show up alone.

Cara thought back to a cocktail party she'd attended a few years ago, where she'd had the misfortune of having to listen to Neal Booker share his views on the current attitude of young men at Yale, where his son was a sophomore.

"We drove up to New Haven last weekend to take Tuck and his friends out to dinner," he'd said as he'd sipped his Tom Collins. "Not a single one of them is dating anyone seriously, and none of them seem to care. None of these kids are concerned with their futures or understand that the good women are going to be snatched up quickly. They only care about the next piece of ass that walks in front of them. I don't get it." Cara distinctly remembered wondering how she was going to make it through the entire party listening to guys like this spew such nonsense all night long.

"I don't have kids, so I can't really say," Reed answered. "But they're still young. They have plenty of time."

"That's the problem. They *don't* have plenty of time. Because other, smarter young men will realize that they need to get the quality women before they're taken. He's at Yale, for God's sake.

The girls there are smart, well-bred, and beautiful. Why would you waste the opportunity to nail one down? Do they think they'll have better luck with some twenty-six-year-old who's probably contracted a venereal disease at community college who they'll meet in a bar somewhere?" Neal's features were rigid, the grooves in his forehead deep enough to swipe credit cards. Cara found him to be a serious man who worried an awful lot about things that didn't matter. Still, to Cara's horror, Reed wanted to befriend him. Neal's connections were wide and vast, and Cara knew that Reed hoped to benefit from them.

"I don't disagree with you. I met my beautiful wife in college in Maine. I knew enough to snatch her up before anyone else got to her. Best decision I ever made," Reed said as he wrapped his arm around her waist. It drove Cara crazy that he always referred to her in the possessive, and never introduced her to anyone by her name. It was a subtle way of asserting his ownership of her. Reed knew she hated it, and continued to do it anyway.

Cara never forgot that conversation. It was the perfect example of why Reed was so obsessed with making sure that Cara kept up appearances. He wanted to be viewed as a certain type of man, and that man had to be married to a certain type of woman, and showing up without her at the birthday party was the fastest way to remove himself from Neal's good graces. Not an option. He was planning on applying to the Palm Beach golf club next year, and he would need Neal's recommendation to ensure his acceptance.

"I'm sorry, of course we'll be there," Cara said. She heard the word *we* come out of her mouth and once again felt as if she were drowning. There hadn't been a true *we* for a very long time.

She stopped listening as Cody began to drone on about the gift he and Tabitha had gotten for Neal. He mentioned something about a new putter or maybe private golf lessons, about some exotic bottle of scotch he'd had imported from some distillery overseas, about the new blazer he'd purchased from Barneys in the city just for this specific occasion, and about how he was debating getting a new pair of Woottons because the thread on the initial C had begun to fray. Cara nodded politely as Cody, Reed, and Tabitha continued their pointless banter, hearing the rest of their conversation as clearly as Charlie Brown would hear his teacher.

"We'll pick you guys up at seven. Be ready! We don't want to miss the cocktail reception. I hate when people arrive late for parties. Punctuality is a gentleman's calling card. Don't you think?" Cody asked.

"Cody, sometimes it's perfectly acceptable to be fashionably late. After all, it takes time for us ladies to get ready for a big event. Isn't that right, Cara?" Tabitha teased.

Her last statement cleared Cara's ears quickly. "Of course! It takes some of us longer than others," she joked.

"Oh, please. You always look fabulous! It will be fun. I think a night out will be good for you; don't you think so, Reed?"

Cara didn't know anyone whose mourning period had been shortened by a birthday party. Instead of finding Tabitha's suggestion friendly, she found it insensitive and irritating. Tabitha should be giving her an out, saying that it was perfectly acceptable if she wasn't up to attending the party, not encouraging her to put on a happy face for the fiftieth birthday of a man she hardly knew. Tabitha was one of those women who thought that every problem in life could be solved with a pretty dress or a new shade of lipstick.

"I do. I think a night out among friends is exactly what she needs," Reed answered.

"Great!" Cody said. "We have a car service grabbing the four of us. No sense pretending we all aren't going to get more than a little inebriated at the party."

"Good thinking," Tabitha added, already on her way to being more than a little drunk tonight as well.

"Last time I drove home after having a few, I dinged the mailbox pulling into the driveway. Tabitha let me have it for a week. Lesson learned on that one."

"Don't even get me started!" Tabitha laughed.

"So seven o'clock?" Reed offered, placing his hand on top of Cara's and giving it a squeeze. Cody and Tabitha would think he was being affectionate. She knew that he was encouraging her to slap a smile on her face and work on her performance of loving wife. Cara noticed that Reed's ears were starting to turn red and felt her insides tense. Red ears the color of clown paint were Reed's tell, one of the reasons that he'd never been a good poker player. He had gotten very good at being steady and calm in any situation over the years, but his ears always betrayed him.

"Perfect." She flashed a smile. Reed finished off the rest of his scotch, ordered another, and watched as Cara continued to dance, slipping back into her role of perfect wife.

The car ride home would be another story.

nine

Jane woke at nine in the morning to the sound of a chainsaw operating on a tree branch somewhere in the near vicinity, and remembered immediately why she'd opted to live in the city. She had to admit that she had slept soundly, though, more soundly than she had in a long time. Her conscience hadn't let her feel at ease in her home once she'd discovered that almost everything she owned was bought with stolen money. Maybe being evicted wouldn't be the worst thing. It was time for her to start over, and it might be better if her new life didn't involve that apartment. Problem was, she had no money and no job, and that would make finding anything to rent, even a flea-infested rat hole in the East Village, impossible. Maybe she could have her breast implants removed and sell them on eBay. There were all sorts of sick freaks out there who would probably pay good money for them.

She trudged into the attached guest bathroom, took a quick shower and dried off with an impossibly soft white towel before getting dressed in a pair of jeans so worn they felt like suede and a light green sweater. She made the bed, hung her wet towel on the hook on the back of the bathroom door, and repacked her short cotton nightgown in an effort to eradicate her footprint from the room entirely. She walked barefoot down the hallway and slowly descended the stairs to the foyer. Halfway down, she froze, overhearing the heated conversation taking place in the kitchen. More specifically, she heard Reed's voice—that condescending, controlling asshole—the sound of it still eliciting the same quiet, visceral rage it always had. What Cara ever saw in him, Jane swore she'd never understand.

"I don't know why you bought two of them when we only need one," Reed said. His voice wasn't raised at all, but it was laced with condescension, as if he were talking to a child and not his wife.

"I bought two of them because they were on sale and it's not a big deal to have an extra box of rice lying around," Cara answered in a hushed tone.

"Really? This receipt doesn't indicate that they were on sale. This looks like they were full price to me," he insisted.

"Where did you even get that? I threw it out yesterday. Did you dig through the garbage to find it? Are you afraid that I'm spending thousands of dollars on chicken cutlets and toothpaste at the grocery store?"

"I'm getting really tired of you mindlessly spending money on things we don't need. You don't need to plan for a nuclear attack. We're only two people, and you should be watching your portions anyway. Carbs are no friend to a middle-aged woman."

Jane bit the inside of her lip to keep from screaming. Getting involved in their argument was probably not the hallmark of a good houseguest.

"Middle-aged? I'm thirty-seven. And so are you, I might add."

"In Hollywood that's geriatric," he said.

"Good thing I live in New York. If you want to go out and find someone younger, be my guest."

"Spare me the false permissions and just start following the grocery list that I give you when you go to the store. I don't know why you have such a hard time following directions, Cara, I really don't. All I want you to do is take the list and buy exactly what's on it, and nothing else. And don't try to be cute by thinking you can hide things in the back of the cabinets and I won't notice. From now on you will show me the receipts when you get back. It's really too bad that I can't even trust my wife to shop correctly."

Jane had to grip the banister until her hands turned white to not go storming into the kitchen and tell Reed what he could do with his fucking list. She should've said something before the wedding, instead of just staying quiet and leaving early. She should've objected at the church, or done something, anything, to prevent this blessed nightmare from happening in the first place. She wondered if Cara had been dealing with this kind of criticism for their entire marriage.

"Fine. I'm sorry I overspent," Cara replied. Jane almost choked listening to her once strong, opinionated, smart friend submit so willingly to the pointless criticism of her slimeball husband. *What the hell happened to her?*

"Good. I can't even get into how angry I am about this whole Jane thing. I don't know what you were thinking and I don't really care. All I know is that I don't want her in this house. You get her out of here, today. Discreetly. Do you know what people will say if they find out we're harboring a fugitive? Do you know what that will do to my reputation?"

"She's not a fugitive, she's my friend. And she didn't do anything wrong."

"Jesus, do you not understand the concept of guilt by association? Spouses reflect on one another. *Why don't you understand that?* Do you think the guys at the club or at my firm are going to differentiate between her husband and her? They are both lying, thieving, pathetic excuses for human beings and she is not welcome in this house. What were you thinking when you told her she could stay?" he asked.

"I was thinking she was an old friend who needed help."

"She's no friend of mine, and I told you that years ago. Why don't you start caring about what I want and about how you can help me? That should be your concern. I'm your husband, Cara. I'm your number one priority."

"Okay. I don't want to fight about this anymore," Cara said.

"Good. I'm going to work. It's nine thirty in the morning, and I'm already aggravated. Honestly, other men have no idea how lucky they are to be able to get out of the house without having to solve a million different problems first. I don't know why I can't be one of them. Also, don't forget it's Friday. I want the sheets on my bed changed today. Don't think I didn't realize you didn't get around to doing it until Saturday last week. I hate starting the weekend with dirty sheets. You know that. And grab my shirts at the dry cleaner this afternoon, too. They've been ready since Wednesday."

"Okay," Cara said quietly. She sounded defeated.

The Cara Jane remembered wouldn't have ever put up with this. The Cara she knew was so much stronger than this. The Cara she knew was someone different entirely.

June 1994

"We shouldn't be here!" Meg whispered, even though there was no one around to hear her.

"That's why it's fun. If we were allowed to be here, this wouldn't be worth doing!" Jane said as she pulled out a pair of bolt cutters she'd managed to borrow from one of the maintenance

men at school—neither Cara nor Meg wanted to know how—from the large duffel bag she had thrown over her shoulder.

"What if we get in trouble?" Meg asked again.

"We graduate tomorrow. What are they going to do to us? Give us detention?" Jane answered. She was really going to miss Meg and her rule-abiding, scaredy-cat ways. She wondered if Meg would loosen up at all when she went to Vanderbilt in August or if she would spend the next four years of her life in college drinking sodas and turning papers in early. "Besides, Cara needs this."

"I still don't know why we're here!" Cara said. "I'm not much in the mood for a midnight stroll."

"Why?" Jane asked sarcastically. "Because you just discovered that your boyfriend is cheating on you with a sophomore on the cheerleading team?"

"Yes," Cara said through gritted teeth. "There are too many things wrong with that sentence to even count."

"I can't believe him," Meg said. "If I ever see him again I'm going to smack him."

"Thanks, Meg," Cara said. "I seriously can't believe that I am only a few hours away from graduating high school at the ripe age of eighteen, and I've already been ditched for a younger girl with a set of pom-poms. Thinking about it makes me so mad I could hurt someone. Like I might lose my mind."

Jane watched as Cara squeezed her hands into fists so tightly her thumbnail actually broke the skin and drew blood. "Good! Channel your anger. That's exactly what I want you to do," Jane cheered, despite the fact that there was nothing happy about this entire situation.

"Why are we here, Jane? Seriously, tell me," Cara ordered.

"We're here because I am a genius and I refuse to let your last memories of high school be of that asshole and the fact that he ruined the best thing that ever happened to him." With one click, Jane used the bolt cutters to break the lock on the gate of the school tennis courts. "Come on! This will make you feel better, Cara, I promise."

Jane hurried over to the electrical box located at the far end of the court and flicked a switch. The lights above the court blazed, forcing the three girls to shield their eyes for a minute while they adjusted from the darkness. She dropped the duffel bag on the court and removed a tennis racket. She promptly tossed it to Cara, yelling, "Catch!"

Cara always used her athleticism as a way to relieve stress and tension in her life. Whenever she needed to clear her head she went running, or golfing, or skiing, or swimming, depending on the weather and the circumstance. Jane knew that in this case, nothing in the world would make Cara feel better than to blast tennis balls flying at her into oblivion. She'd be picturing Mark's face with every swing. He should be very happy that Jane had the brilliant idea to break into the tennis courts so his scorned girlfriend could work off her rage. Otherwise he'd probably be sporting a broken nose or a black eye tomorrow with his cap and gown.

"We're going to hit tennis balls? Seriously?" Cara asked as she crossed to the far side of the court.

"No. We aren't hitting anything. I want you to hit tennis balls. Meg and I are just going to man this ball machine thing." Jane ran to the corner and pulled out the ball machine. She plugged it into the small electrical socket and turned it on. She fished two dozen tennis balls out of the duffel bag and loaded them into the ball machine.

"How do you work this thing? I've never used one of these before in my life," Meg said, biting her cuticles as usual.

"That's because you've been too busy making muffins," Cara replied, never missing the opportunity to jab her best friend for her love of home economics and her general apathy toward any and all athletic endeavors.

"You never mind eating the muffins!" Meg reminded her, still biting her cuticles.

"That's true," Jane said. "You make a mean chocolate chip muffin. Don't ever let anyone tell you differently. Now, let's focus and stop biting your nails. Cara, I think you need to work out some of your aggression toward Mark."

"Don't even say his name to me. I hate him so much it hurts. I mean, do you believe this guy? He's going to cheat on me with a sophomore? Seriously?"

"Gross," Meg said. "He's a pig."

"I want to slash his tires or something."

"I believe you. That's why you're going to take your anger out on the tennis balls. It'll feel great!"

"You think it's that simple, huh?" Cara asked.

"I think it's a pretty good place to start. Pretend the ball is Mark. Tell him what you really think of him and then nail these tennis balls! Really hit them, Cara!"

Cara laughed as she twirled the racket in her hand. "I've played on this court thousands of times, but for some reason it's a lot more fun when we're not allowed to be here!"

"Everything is more fun when you're not allowed to do it. Have I taught you nothing?"

"Seriously, Jane, I will never understand how your brain works. You couldn't come up with a better way to let her burn off some steam?" Meg asked, constantly looking over her shoulder to make sure no one was coming to arrest them.

"I had a lot of ideas, but I decided that breaking onto the tennis courts was the best one!" Jane answered with a shrug.

"Oh jeez," Meg moaned.

"Okay, ready? I'm going to let this one fly," Jane said as she took her position behind the ball machine.

"Bring it!" Cara said, her knees bent, her back straight, and her racket poised squarely in front of her.

"Okay, Cara, here it comes! Crack it!" Jane yelled as she hit the button and started the balls flying.

"You stupid asshole!" Cara yelled as she slammed the ball with such force that Meg had to duck to avoid getting pelted by it.

"Watch it!" Meg yelled as she ducked. "You're going to hit me by accident!"

"You think she's better than me? You think you can cheat on me with some cheerleading slut?" Cara screamed, the tennis ball once again serving as a wonderful proxy for Mark's head.

"I will kill you!" Cara screeched as she slammed a ball over the net.

"I will destroy you!" she cried, knocking the next ball so hard it became trapped between the links of the fence surrounding the court.

"I will make you wish you never met me!" Pop! She smashed another one, the sound of the racket on the ball reminiscent of a champagne cork being freed from its bottle.

"You stupid, arrogant, asshole!" she shouted as she nailed the ball with a powerful backhand that unfortunately went a bit wayward and hit the machine—which promptly stopped working. Man, Jane *thought. No matter how many times she watched Cara in action, she'd never stop being impressed by her strength or agility.*

"Uh-oh," Jane said as she heard the machine sputter and the motor slowly wind down.

"What just happened?" Meg asked. She went over and began pushing buttons on the back of the machine. "Oh my God, she broke it! What are we going to do?"

"What's going on?" Cara yelled from the other side of the net, flushed and out of breath but energized. "Come on, I'm just getting warmed up! Turn up the speed! Let them fly! I can do better than this!"

"It's not broken—it's just . . . not working at the moment," Jane said, trying very hard not to panic.

"What if we broke it?" Meg whispered to Jane as they blindly banged on the machine, trying to bring it back to life. It was pointless. It had flatlined.

"Well, what do we care? Cara won't be on the tennis team next year, and I'm pretty sure they'll replace it by then."

"But that means we damaged school property! We can get in a lot of trouble for this! What if someone saw us? What if they dust the tennis balls for prints and find out it was us? Can they keep us from graduating?"

"You really need to stop watching Court TV. No one is going to dust tennis balls for prints, you lunatic. You're overreacting! Who's going to find us anyway? There's no one here!"

"Hey! Who's over there?" a security guard called from the far perimeter of the court, waving a flashlight in their direction.

"Oh shit! Run!" Jane said, grabbing the duffel bag off the ground but leaving the bolt cutters and tennis balls behind.

"Oh my God!" Meg squealed for the millionth time as she took off for the gate, her strides somewhat inhibited by the skirt she was wearing. "I can't go to jail! I want to go to Vanderbilt!"

"Shut up and run, Meg!" Cara yelled as she tore through the gate ahead of the others and made her way to the parking lot. Jane had insisted that Cara park her car a block away from school, which at the time had seemed totally unnecessary, but now made perfect sense. No middle-aged security guard was going to catch three teenage girls running at a full sprint, and by the time he got to the street they'd be long gone. Once again, Jane had thought it all out.

Jane heard Meg's footsteps behind her, and off in the distance saw the dim glow of the guard's flashlight as they ran from the courts. Then, a cry from Meg.

"Owwww!" she yelled. Cara turned to see what happened but never broke stride.

"Are you okay? Come on, Meg! Run! If we get caught they might not let us graduate tomorrow!" Jane said.

"You said I was overreacting to worry about that!"

"I lied!"

"I'm going to kill you, Jane! And I think I just ripped off part of my skirt!"

"What?" Jane asked as they continued to sprint toward the car.

"How the hell did you do that?" Cara called.

"It got stuck on a spike on the fence! I hurt my butt!"

Cara and Jane burst out laughing as they reached the car, both of them exhausted from running and the adrenaline of the last caper they'd ever pull together in high school. All three climbed into the car and they sped off, Cara driving with Jane beside her in the passenger seat and Meg nestled in the back, the same seats they'd always sat in since they'd learned how to drive. Jane had gotten her driver's license first, but for some reason even though Cara had turned seventeen a few months after her, she still was the de facto chauffeur. No one asked where Cara was headed because they already knew. They'd made this drive down toward the beach multiple times a week, using the time in the car to talk about boys or school or anything else that they needed to discuss without worrying about their mothers overhearing the conversation. Jane exhaled loudly as she stared at the dirt that disappeared into underbrush and darkness just a few feet in front of her. Cara pulled her car over onto the shoulder of the road, put it in park, and turned off the headlights. Jane realized she'd be nervous sitting in the dark on these back roads if she hadn't done it thousands of times before.

"Okay, let's see it," Jane said as she turned from the passenger seat to get a look at Meg's injury.

Meg leaned to her left in the backseat to reveal a huge tear in the back of her skirt and a large red scratch on the bottom of her ass.

"Is it bad?" Meg asked.

"Oh my God," Jane squealed. "Only you would manage to hurt your butt on a fence you weren't even climbing over. How does that happen?"

Cara was near hysterics. "You're right, Meg. You should stay in the kitchen. I love you but you are not meant to be outdoors."

"You guys!" Meg giggled. "This isn't funny! What am I going to tell my mom? What if I get tetanus?"

"How is your mom going to know that you have a giant cut on your ass?" Jane asked.

"She won't! But she's definitely going to ask why my skirt is ripped! I told her we were going for frozen yogurt!"

"Tell her the truth. That you snagged it on a fence at school. The fact that it occurred while we were trespassing, breaking and entering, damaging private property, and then fleeing from security are details that she probably doesn't need."

"You left the bolt cutters on the court, you know," Meg said. "The poor man who gave them to you is probably going to get into a lot of trouble."

"I'm sure he'll talk his way out of it. Besides, it's not like we did anything terrible. We hit a few tennis balls after hours. So what?" Jane said.

"And broke the lock on the gate," Cara added.

"And then broke the ball machine," Meg said.

"Right. And we broke a few things," Jane admitted. "So what? It's not like we hurt anyone."

"How do you feel?" Meg asked Cara. "Was it worth it?"

"I feel better," Cara said.

"When you think about it, being angry over losing a boyfriend is stupid. You'll meet someone better at college and would have broken up with Mark anyway, so really all he did was speed up your timeline by a few months," Jane said.

"Totally," Meg agreed.

"Whatever. I'm not going to let that loser embarrass me like that. I am way too good for him anyway," Cara said.

"Totally!" Meg said again.

"Thanks, guys. I really did need that." Cara sighed. She reached over and tucked the piece of hair that for some reason refused to grow long enough to fit in Jane's ponytail behind her ear. "What am I going to do without you guys at school?"

"You'll probably commit fewer crimes without Jane around," Meg teased.

"If that was supposed to hurt my feelings, it didn't."

"I'm just kidding," Meg reassured her.

"Anyway, I guess we can check breaking into school off our list of things to do before we graduate, right?" Cara asked. *"So we have that going for us."*

"Exactly!" Jane said. She laughed and felt so proud of herself for being able to change Cara's entire mood. *"And we can thank Mark for being such a moron that he made that little outing necessary. Without him we wouldn't have that awesome memory to look back on now."*

"I still really wish I could just break his nose," Cara said.

"Maybe next time," Jane promised. *"For now, breaking the ball machine will have to be sufficient."*

ten

Jane heard the back door close and the car start in the driveway, which snapped her mind back to the present. She entered the kitchen and found Cara leaning against the refrigerator with her arms wrapped around her middle, staring at the ceiling. Jane had no doubt that if she had slept in five minutes later, she'd have come down to the kitchen and found Cara toasting English muffins. Five more minutes, and Cara might have been able to hide this from her entirely.

"Good morning. What day is today?" Jane asked, trying to figure out if she should let Cara know she had overheard everything.

"Friday," Cara said, forcing a smile.

"I have my days all mixed up. They became harder to keep straight once I started sleeping through them, you know?"

"I could see how that'd be a problem. Do you want coffee? I made some earlier." Cara opened a cabinet, reaching for a coffee mug on the top shelf.

"I'd love some. But please be careful, I'd hate to see what happens if you break a mug or something," Jane said casually, deciding that in this new phase of her life, honesty would always be the best policy—even if that meant intruding on things that had absolutely nothing to do with her.

"You heard that?"

"Hard not to."

"Please, Jane, I don't need a lecture. I let you stay here because you had nowhere to go, not because I wanted you to get involved. Just stay out of it."

"Stay out of it? Are you joking? Cara, what are you doing listening to this crap? How long has this been going on? Please, please don't tell me since you got married or I swear to God I'll scream."

"It's none of your business, Jane."

"Yes, it is. You're my friend and I love you, and that makes it my business whether you like it or not."

"How can you think you have a right to say anything when we haven't spoken in years?"

"I'm invoking a grandfather clause. And I may not have seen you for a long time, but I'd never, ever speak to you like that."

"Well, doesn't that just make you friend of the year. Should I go try to find my half of the 'best friends forever' necklace we had in fifth grade? I'll put it back on to commemorate this special moment between us." If Cara was hoping her comment would get Jane to back off, she was wasting her time. Jane knew her moves better than anyone, and sarcasm was not going to be a strong enough weapon to make her drop the topic.

"Cara, you don't have to be defensive. None of this is your fault."

"I'm sorry," Cara said, rubbing her brow. "I'm just so tired of being put down all the time. I shouldn't take my anger out on you. At least not for this. There are other things I can be mad at you for, but you have nothing to do with this."

"I meant what I said. It's not your fault."

"That's not entirely true. I married him. *That's* my fault."

"Well yeah, that was your fault. Now you see why I couldn't bring myself to stay at your wedding. Your husband is a fucking asshole! Who gets that upset over a box of rice?"

"He's gotten worse over the years. I don't know what happened. It's like he's just become more and more controlling and now it's to the point where I'm afraid to get dressed. I'm afraid to go to the store. I can't get out of bed in the morning without him telling me that I'm doing something wrong. I feel like the air is being sucked out of my lungs."

"Is that why you're sleeping in the second bedroom?"

"You noticed?"

"Once again, hard not to."

"Thanks for not saying anything yesterday."

"I wasn't sure how much longer I was going to be able to stay quiet."

"You haven't even been here for a day."

"Yes, well, I never could keep my mouth shut."

Jane took Cara by the elbow and led her over to the kitchen table. They sat in silence for a minute while Cara fidgeted with the cuffs of her shirt and Jane stared at the clock on the wall, searching for words. There was a time when she wouldn't have had to censor what she said, but those days were gone, and the woman sitting in front of her didn't seem to want to talk. Jane figured she'd wait her out. It wasn't like she had anywhere to be.

"I'm so ashamed," Cara finally said. "Everyone in town thinks he's this great guy. That we're a perfect couple. They're like fucking lemmings who just follow along behind Reed and the bullshit act he puts on every time he leaves this house. The other women think I wear these pearls every day because I'm trying to make some kind of Audrey Hepburn fashion statement, and I wear them because he bought them for me for our anniversary a few years ago and told me that he never wanted me to take them off. I thought he was kidding, you know? The next day I came down for breakfast without them on, and he berated me for an hour about how I take him for granted, how I'm unappreciative of everything he does for me, how I'm spoiled and assume that I deserve nice things when I haven't done anything to earn them. It was so awful that I just kept them on after that. I mean, it's not like they're ugly or anything. I figured if it would keep him happy, and he'd leave me alone, I'd wear them. No big deal. That was five years ago. I'd have hanged myself with them by now if they were long enough."

"I guess neither one of us were the best judges of character, were we?"

"No. And we thought we had it all figured out when we got married. We were young and stupid," Cara said.

"Maybe you can claim being young and stupid. I was almost thirty. I should've known better. I clearly remember feeling like I'd won the lottery when I walked out of City Hall on Doug's arm. Why couldn't I see that he was a phony?"

"I saw it. You rushed into it, but you weren't going to listen to anyone, and I wasn't going to try to stop you. I knew it would've been a complete waste of time. You always do things on your own terms, for better or for worse."

"This is very clearly for worse."

"Yeah. I guess it's always harder to look at your own life the way you look at your friends' lives."

"That's why you didn't see what I saw in Reed. Nothing I did was out of jealousy, Cara. I swear. I wanted to be happy for you, but it just made me ill to see you guys together. I knew you could do better. I don't know how I knew, but I knew."

"It's too bad you didn't have the same feelings for yourself."

"Tell me about it. Maybe I felt pressure to keep up with you and Meg. I hated feeling like you guys were moving on with your lives, and I was just standing still. I hated feeling like you guys pitied me. I don't think it's why I got married, but I think it contributed to how quickly I said yes. If I'd waited, maybe I would've seen something. Now I've gone and fucked up my entire life. I'm in no position to give advice to anyone."

"I know there's not much of a bright side for you, but at least now you can start over. Doug's gone, but Reed's coming home. I don't know what I'm going to do," Cara said. She suddenly seemed so small and vulnerable. It astounded Jane to think that she'd bought into Cara's act and actually believed that everything was going well in her life. She should've known better . . .

"Why can't you?"

"What are you talking about? I've been married for twelve years. There's no starting over for me."

Jane had an idea. This was not how she'd thought this was going to end up when she made her wildly impetuous decision to come out to Long Island, but circumstances had changed. There was a reason things happened this way—timing, fate, cosmic intervention, whatever you want to call it—and she wasn't going to miss the opportunity. This time, she wasn't going to disappoint her friend. "Let's get out of here," she said.

"What are you talking about?"

"You and me. Let's leave. I'm hiding from everyone anyway, and you can't stay here. Not with him. Not anymore."

"I can't just walk out on my marriage, Jane," Cara said. "It's not that simple."

"This isn't a marriage anymore. I'm not saying never come back, but let's just get out of here together. Let's do some soul searching, reconnect, get some distance from our problems. Maybe it will help us both figure out what we need to do from here."

"I have a job, too." Cara reminded her.

"Your job is flexible and you know it. Do you have any standing appointments?"

"No," Cara admitted. "I don't."

"Then that's not a reason to stay."

"I think you're having a midlife crisis," Cara said.

"Did your darling husband tell you that when he called you *middle-aged*?"

"That makes you middle-aged, too," she quipped.

"Exactly. Come on, I can't go without you."

"Yes, you can," Cara said.

"No, seriously, I can't. I don't have a car. Or money. I spent it all on cab fare."

"Where do you suggest we go? If I check into a hotel somewhere and put it on our credit card, he'll throw a fit. Not to mention the fact that you're media bait and the last thing I need is my picture in the newspaper because I'm standing next to you. No. This will only make everything worse."

"Cara, your mother would want nothing more than for you to get the hell out of this house, and you know it. I never supported your marriage, and now look, I'm back and your mother is gone. I'm sure you'd rather have it the other way around and I don't blame you. But if you think that she'd be okay with what just happened here this morning, with what's been happening for the last decade, you're kidding yourself. So if you don't want to do it for me, do it for her. And let me help you."

The mention of her mother made Cara burst into tears. "That

was a cheap shot," she said as she dabbed at her eyes with a tissue she pulled from her pocket.

"I'm sorry. But it's true," Jane said.

"I know it is. I shouldn't have to live like this. I shouldn't have to be a guest in my own home, and I shouldn't have to buy one box of rice at a time if I don't want to."

"No, you shouldn't. You should be able to buy every fucking box of rice in the grocery store if you feel like it."

"I can't keep going on like this," Cara said.

"Does that mean you'll come?" Jane asked.

"Come where? Where exactly are we going to go?"

"I don't know. There has to be somewhere. Let's call Meg. Maybe she'll have an idea," Jane said.

"Meg and Steve bought a summer house in Montauk a few years ago," Cara stammered. "But I don't know if involving her in any of this is the best idea."

"They did?" Jane asked, instantly feeling like things were falling into place. "That's perfect! Why don't we call Meg and ask her if we can go out there for a few days and regroup? Maybe we can even convince her to come out and stay with us. It's perfect, Cara. It's empty out there this time of year. I haven't seen her in way too long, and I really would like for us all to be together. Will you call and ask her?"

"No," Cara said firmly. "Forget I said anything. I'm not calling her and we're not going there."

"Why not? You can't tell me that she has no idea any of this is going on. Even if she hasn't said anything to you about it, I promise you she knows. You don't need to hide what's going on from either of us."

"It's not that. It's just that things between us are complicated. I don't really want to get into it right now, just trust me when I tell you that I think it's probably best to leave Meg alone."

It had never occurred to Jane that Cara and Meg would've encountered problems of their own, but she tried not to let the shock register on her face. Right now, it was more important for them both to leave town than for her to hear the details of their issues. "We can talk about whatever happened between the two of you later. I promise you, we can work it out. Hey, yesterday you never thought that you and I would be on good terms, and here we are, about to go all Thelma and Louise on our husbands."

"You say that like it's a good thing," Cara said.

"It's better than the alternative."

"That's what Thelma and Louise thought, too," Cara said. "They both ended up dead."

"Come on. You won't call her and ask her if we can use her house? You know what? I'll call her."

"She changed her number," Cara said. "I don't know how to get hold of her. She doesn't answer my e-mails. It's not that I don't want to call her. It's that I can't."

"Seriously?" Jane asked, stunned.

"Yes."

"Jeez. Here I thought I was the only one having problems."

"Not exactly."

"Okay. I have an idea. We can talk about it in the car, but I really think we should get going. Stop stalling," Jane said.

"Just give me a few minutes to pack, okay?" Cara said.

Jane felt like she was having an out-of-body experience. Had she really just convinced Cara to run away?

"Just don't bring those pearls. Actually, wait. I'm coming with you. We can leave Reed a note."

Upstairs in the second bedroom, Jane watched as Cara packed pajamas, a few pairs of jeans, a pair of sneakers, three sweaters (none of them white), every pair of underwear she owned, and her toiletries. She placed everything in the tote bag she kept tucked in the back of her closet behind her heavy winter coats and walked back to the master bedroom she had been evicted from. "Where do you keep your stationery?" Jane asked, following behind her. Jane grabbed a pen out of her purse.

Cara opened the drawer in the nightstand next to the bed and removed a small white box. "Here. This is what Reed uses to send thank-you notes."

"Such a good WASP. What is he saying thank you for? The latest round of golf or bottle of scotch or fucking carved wooden mallard to add to the shelf in his library?"

"Basically."

"God, I could puke all over this," Jane said. She pulled Cara down on the duvet next to her and handed her the pen. "Are you ready to do this?"

"I don't know what to say," Cara admitted.

"Just write what I tell you," Jane ordered. "I'd do it myself, but he'll know it's not your handwriting."

"I don't think this is a good idea, either."

"Yes it is. Now write."

Cara silently shrugged again as Jane dictated her letter.

Dear Reed,

I know that you will think it's cowardly for me to write this letter, but I realize that caring about what you think is all

I've been doing for years, and it's time that it stops. I married you because I loved you and I thought you loved me. Maybe you once did—I don't know—but this is no longer a marriage, as evidenced by the fact that I fear you coming home right now and yelling at me for sitting on your bed. I need to tell you how sorry I am for everything. I'm sorry for making you put up with such an incompetent wife for as long as you have. I'm sorry that I don't work out as much as I should, that sometimes I don't change the sheets on time, and that I buy too many boxes of rice. I've done so many silly things over the years they're impossible to count. But out of all of those stupid things, I've finally realized that the stupidest thing I've ever done is wait this long to leave.

Now THAT was stupid.

    Yours truly,

    Cara

"Give me your necklace," Jane said.

Cara stared at the note. "I'd never have the guts to say this stuff to him," she said.

"Really? The old you never had a hard time sticking up for herself. The old you would have taken a tennis racket to his face and knocked him across the room. Maybe you don't think you'd have the guts to say it, but I promise you, once upon a time you did. That's the Cara I just channeled. Now give me the necklace."

Jane took the pearls from Cara's hand and placed them next to the letter on the nightstand. "Let's go," she said. Jane grabbed Cara's bag off the floor, and before Cara could panic and change her mind, she got her the hell out of the house.

eleven

Meg decided to take the scenic route home and drive along the water. She was letting her mind wander as she went down the dark road that circled around the bend and along the ocean's edge when suddenly an old song came on the radio. Out of nowhere she felt the bile rise in her throat and her insides begin to buck and heave. She had no choice but to pull over or risk driving her car into a pylon. It really was amazing how hearing certain songs transported her back in time to a place she really didn't like to revisit. Whenever she heard Counting Crows's album *August and Everything After*, a sound track to her adolescent life, her mind immediately snapped back to the drives she used to take with Cara and Jane, where they'd obsess over the huge issues they had in their lives: whether the frozen yogurt place had failed to put sprinkles in the bottoms of their cones, whether the football team would make the playoffs, whether they should take the SAT *again*. They never would've predicted that things would turn out like this.

She lowered the passenger-side window so she could stare unobstructed at the fishing boat lights as they headed out to sea and listen to the boats still on their moorings, bobbing back and forth and side to side. She looked at her reflection in the mirror and saw herself the way she used to be—tangled hair, an unlined forehead, and the sparkle in her eye that signaled a spirit that had yet to be broken. She had taken all of it for granted because she was too naïve to realize that her beauty would eventually fade.

Jane and Cara used to tease her for looking like a little girl—but now she felt old and worn. The world had changed so much since then, and so had she. They had been friends in a world where you didn't have to take off your shoes at the airport and had to use pay phones to call home. It was a lifetime ago. She was so tired of treading water and drifting nowhere, alone. Just like the boats in the water in front of her, bobbing back and forth, and side to side.

When Meg left home for Vanderbilt University, her mother had told her to always act like a lady, to send letters home to her parents, to study hard, and to find a nice southern boy to marry. One of the main reasons Meg had wanted to go to school down south was to reconnect with her roots. While Meg had grown up on Long Island, her mother was a born-and-bred Virginia girl who was not at all happy when Meg's father's job relocated the family to New York. Meg's mom fought hard to maintain the traditions that were important to her, like church on Sundays, homemade peach pie in the summertime, and daughters who knew how to write a proper thank-you note. When Meg decided to go to school down south, her mother was beside herself with happiness. The idea of a southern boy intrigued Meg not because she had a problem with the northern guys she'd grown up with, but because the way her mother told it, a southern man was more refined and more gentlemanly than his northern brothers. Who didn't want a guy with good manners who would hold doors open and pull out her chair?

She remembered the first time she laid eyes on Steve, in the lobby of their freshman dorm. Right away she knew he was someone special. He was muscular and fit, with scruffy blond hair and bright blue eyes that were slightly afraid to look at her. He wore a navy-blue T-shirt and flip-flops, and had a notebook tucked under his arm. Somehow she knew that he'd be loyal and loving and everything she could ever have hoped for in a boyfriend. They stood next to each other as they waited for the elevator, and she remembered so clearly thinking that she had to get to know him. She resisted the urge to nervously bite her cuticles while she said a silent prayer that he would say something, *anything* to her.

"Do you have the time?" he asked, which Meg quickly realized was a stupid question for someone who was wearing a watch to ask someone whose wrist was bare.

"I'm sorry. I don't," she said with a shrug as they stepped on the elevator. "Hi," she added, because it was all she could think of to say.

"Hi," he said. "I'm Steve."

"Meg," she said. Then before she could say anything else, the elevator door opened on her floor and she stepped off into the hallway. As the doors began to close on his face, Meg did something that completely surprised her. She jammed her notebook in the quickly shrinking slice of space between them. "I was going to listen to some music for a while. Do you want to join me?" she asked, shocking herself with her courage.

"Oh yeah, sure. Why not?"

They married two years after graduation, but somehow no one worried that they were rushing into it. They very clearly were made for each other. No one ever had any doubts about that.

With some much-needed financial support from Steve's parents, they rented a little condo and Meg went to work testing recipes for a popular cooking magazine while Steve set about teaching poetry and going to school to get his Ph.D. They spent their early years of marriage saving money and dreaming of the future, trying to decide how many kids to have. How would they know when there were enough little people in enough little chairs at the kitchen table?

Meg found out she was pregnant a few months after they were married and moved back north. Those first few weeks of her pregnancy had been a true honeymoon period, and the love she felt for Steve grew stronger and stronger. She couldn't wait to tell her friends that she was going to have a child. When they were in junior high Meg had been the president of the town babysitters' club. She spent most Saturdays playing with children in the park, or taking them for ice cream in the afternoons while their mothers got manicures. She used to tote Jane's brother, Gavin, around like he was her very own living Cabbage Patch Kid. Now it was her turn to have her own child, and she knew she'd never forget the look on Jane's and Cara's faces when she told them: surprise, love, and in some ways, shock that it was happening so fast. It killed her to keep the news to herself for as long as she did, but she was superstitious. When she looked back, she realized that should've been her first sign that something was wrong. Things shouldn't have been so easy.

Meg, Cara, and Jane were all still so close at that point, and pregnancy was the first real journey she wouldn't be able to travel with them. She'd be going through the next phase of her life alone.

July 2000

"Does this mean you won't hang out with us anymore?" Jane asked, her mouth still hanging open in shock. "Don't get me wrong. I'm pumped for you, I really am! But this kind of sucks for us. Who's going to come with me to happy hour now? Cara never

shows up for early drinks because she refuses to skip the gym."

"That's what you're worried about? Happy hour?" Cara asked. "Ignore her, Meg! We're thrilled for you. Do you feel okay?"

Their reactions didn't surprise her—Jane worried about how this would affect their social life, and Cara worried about how it would affect Meg's health.

"I feel great! I don't have any morning sickness. I don't have any real cravings for anything, either. I'm tired, but I feel fine other than that!" she said.

"I read somewhere that pregnant women have really bad gas. If that's true, you can stop sitting next to me at the movies," Jane quipped before reaching over to give Meg a huge congratulatory hug. "I think I'm going to love being an aunt. I will buy it really cute clothes and sneak it into R-rated movies when it's only fourteen."

"Please stop calling my baby 'it'!" Meg said.

"This is so great. I only wish we could do it together. Wouldn't it be fun to be pregnant at the same time? Now I feel like you're going forward in time or something and are going to have to report back to the rest of us what it's like on the other side," Cara said.

It was exactly how Meg felt. The second she peed on the stick and it came up positive, she'd stopped living in the present and thought only of her future. She lived more in her head than she did in the actual world, dreaming about what would happen when Cara and Jane had kids of their own, how all of their offspring would be friends, maybe date each other. How Cara, Jane, and Meg would attend school functions, carpool, bake cupcakes for birthday parties, chaperone class trips, and watch their kids graduate from the chairs set up on the lawn of the high school. It

would be like living through the best years of life all over again,
this time without the acne and braces.

"I promise I'll tell you everything," Meg said. "All the things
that no one ever talks about. I swear I will tell you, as long as you
guys reassure me that I look skinny even when I've gained thirty
pounds. I'll tell you the truth as long as you lie to me."

"Seems fair," Jane said as she looked at Cara.

"Totally," Cara said.

Meg miscarried at the end of her first trimester. Women's intuition is a powerful thing, and one morning she woke up and knew
something was wrong. She waited two days before she made an
appointment because she couldn't bring herself to face it. Steve
thought she was being crazy. They'd had their twelve-week ultrasound the week before and everything had been fine; there was
no reason for her to worry that something had changed. But she
knew. When her suspicions were confirmed there was stunned
silence, then tears, then shock, then sadness, then anger, then
acceptance. All the phases of the grieving process dutifully followed as she mourned the loss of the family she thought she had.
Meg had dreamed of names and what the baby would look like,
clothes she would buy from catalogs, and the rocking chair her
mother had used when she was a baby, tucked away in the corner
of the basement, patiently waiting until it could be refurbished
so she could rock her own baby to sleep. What bothered Meg the
most was that Cara and Jane tried to assuage her pain by promising that there would be other babies, that the best way to move
on was to get pregnant again, to put the whole thing behind her.
Look forward, they said to her one night while they sat on her
couch together, as if a new baby would be a substitute for the one

she'd lost, like it was as replaceable as a bracelet, or an earring, or a set of car keys. She knew they didn't understand, and she didn't blame them, at least not then. That was when she believed that things happened for a reason.

When she got pregnant again she was cautious, but once again the girls were there to help quiet her nerves.

June 2001

"I knew it would happen again, see?" Cara said. "Your angel was coming. You just had to wait a little while for it."

"Don't you guys think it's ironic that you spend your whole adult life worrying that one day you'll find out that you're pregnant, and then when you want to be, you spend all of your time worrying that you won't be? I mean, don't you think that's strange? Is God just fucking with us or what?" Jane asked, smearing blue cheese on an apple wedge. Meg wasn't even comfortable being in the presence of blue cheese, as it's high on the list of foods a pregnant woman is supposed to avoid. She had already lost one pregnancy. She wasn't about to risk losing another due to some bizarre incident involving cross-contamination with unpasteurized dairy products.

"I think I read somewhere that a woman can increase her chances of becoming pregnant if she eats broccoli rabe and shoves a pillow under her ass when she has sex. Is that what you guys did?" Jane joked.

"What the hell are you reading?" Cara asked. "It sounds like something your crazy Sicilian grandmother spewed out years ago that you somehow remembered. That's ridiculous."

"Entirely possible. Then again, my crazy Sicilian grandmother had seven kids, so maybe she was onto something," Jane said.

"Just don't stress out," Cara ordered, trying to add some reasonable advice to the conversation. "You and Steve will get through this. Lord knows you aren't the first couple to endure some bumps in the fertility road."

"I know. You're right," Meg said. She believed it.

After the fourth miscarriage, Meg decided that she would embrace the very best the world had to offer in an East-meets-West attempt to conceive a healthy baby that she could carry to term. She endured countless blood tests, genetic tests, shots, and prenatal vitamins; acupuncture; diets that embraced gluten-free, dairy-free, sugar-free, antibiotic-free, hormone-free, pesticide-free, preservative-free, and taste-free food; green tea, meditation, yoga, and decaf coffees. She had ultrasounds to check her ovaries, and her uterus, and her tubes, and anything else they could possibly check. She visited fertility specialists and tried Clomid, but even after all that, none of the doctors could explain why she couldn't seem to carry a baby to term. Meg put herself through two rounds of IVF, hoping that if the doctors selected only the strongest embryos, her chances would increase. Both rounds failed before her heart was ready to accept what her body had been trying to tell her for the better part of ten years: she wasn't meant to be a mother. The doctors weren't optimistic that the results would be different if they tried the procedure again, or that surrogacy would offer a solution. She and Steve had dipped their toes into the adoption waters but quickly discovered the hard way that there were no guarantees there, either. She was too tired to fight anymore, and it was then that she decided that if she wasn't going to be a mother, then she wasn't meant to be a wife.

Having children was all that she wanted, and her body had failed her. It had failed both of them. Why bother with the lipstick and the blowouts and the heels and the lacy lingerie if she wasn't a woman when it really mattered? She couldn't apologize to Steve for tricking him when she hadn't known. She couldn't apologize for all the years she'd wasted. All Meg could do was let her husband go and pray that he was able to find someone who could give him the family he deserved. She'd allow someone else to resurrect his dreams of coaching Little League and drinking out of WORLD'S BEST DAD coffee mugs. She'd allow him to find someone else to love—the second-best gift she could give him. It was horrifying for her to accept, but there was no way to ignore it anymore.

A year ago she'd sat at the kitchen table and looked around her cozy Long Island home—specifically at the walls, which would never be decorated with family portraits or covered with scribbles drawn in crayon. She'd waited for Steve to get home from work. Whether or not he sensed it was coming, she'd never know.

"I think it's time for us to admit this isn't working," Meg said. She refused to look at him, choosing instead to focus on a tree branch in the backyard that rocked in the wind. "You've done the best you could, and so have I, but we don't work. Not like this."

He dropped his briefcase on the floor at the back door and hung his car keys on the small hook on the wall. He opened the fridge and removed a can of beer, then decided against it and returned it to the shelf. He sat next to her and took her hand.

"We can try adoption again. The last one just wasn't meant to be, but there are plenty of kids who need good parents. Don't give up because you're frustrated. I'm frustrated too, but we need to keep trying," Steve pleaded.

"I wish I was strong enough to go through it again, but I'm not. I've accepted that this is my life, and that for whatever reason, it's what God wants for me. I can't take any more disappointments. It will break me. I need to start looking forward. You should, too."

"I'm not giving up on us. I want to make us work. I don't know why we can't move on from this," he said, looking so very tired.

"I can move on from this, but I won't take you with me. You can have a different life. You can have a different future. The only thing holding you back is me, and I haven't been a wife to you in a very long time."

"That's not true," he whispered.

"Do you remember that night not long after we were married, when I got all dressed up and wore that beautiful necklace you bought me for my birthday? We went to dinner and then walked around talking about all of the things we were going to do and all of the things we wanted for our life together?"

"How could I forget it? Your heel got stuck in a subway grate and broke in half. You had to hobble the last five blocks home," he said, rubbing his thumb across the veins in the back of her hand.

"That was right before I found out I was pregnant for the first time. And after that everything just went off in a different direction. We never did any of the things we said we were going to do. I never got to be the wife I wanted to be. I never took care of you the way you deserved. It's like this little hole started to grow inside me, and over the years I've just crawled further and further inside it. The only thing I can do now is let you go."

"I don't want a divorce," he said, sighing deeply and fighting to hold back a lone tear that was brimming in his left eye. She reached up and brushed it away with her thumb, tracing his jaw with her finger before returning her hand to her lap. "If you want to separate while we figure out how to go forward, just the two of us, how to make just the two of us enough, we can do that, but I won't divorce you. I'm not giving up on us."

"That defeats the purpose," Meg said, having a hard time believing this conversation was happening. She looked over at the framed picture taken at Jane's twenty-fourth birthday party, right after she and Steve had returned home from their honeymoon in Mexico. They were two people so very much in love. This wasn't how things were supposed to go. "I want you to give up. I need you to give up, for me. I'll go to a hotel until I figure out what I'm going to do."

"No. I won't let you move to a hotel. I want you to stay here. Let me at least do that for you."

Once Steve had packed a bag and left for a friend's house, Meg sat alone with a glass of wine on the leather couch in his office that he'd kept from his bachelor days. She didn't want to call her parents or her sisters or anyone else, because no one would understand what she was going through. She wasn't as bothered by her isolation as she'd thought she'd be.

The way she saw it, she was going to have to get used to being alone.

twelve

really don't think that this is a good idea," Cara said to Jane as they made their way through the halls of North Shore High School, looking for the classroom where they'd been told Steve taught his last-period English class.

"I can't think of a better way to find her, can you? Besides, I always liked Steve and he always liked us. Why would he mind a little surprise visit?"

"No. I certainly don't have a better idea, but that doesn't mean I have to like this one."

The women climbed the four flights of stairs to his classroom, which overlooked the athletic fields out front. Jane stopped for a minute and gazed out a window, vividly remembering her own days in high school and how eager she'd been to get out of there. It'd been twenty years since their graduation, but the after-school scene still looked exactly the same. She watched the jocks in their football pads trying to impress the popular girls as they made their way to their practice field, and caught sight of a group of outsiders who would no doubt spend the afternoon sitting in parked cars somewhere smoking cigarettes and joints, discussing their latest tattoos or piercings or whatever new and inventive way they'd come up with to piss off their parents. God she missed school.

They paused when they got to Steve's classroom and nodded silently at each other before Jane knocked softly on the open door.

"Hi, Dr. Steve," Jane said. She was trying to keep it casual, to act like it was a completely normal thing for Meg's estranged friends to show up at his school. Cara stood next to her and seemed to be even more uncomfortable than she was, which didn't really make any sense. Jane knew that Meg was mad at her for disappearing from her life, but she still had no idea why she had a problem with Cara. At some point, someone was going to tell her what happened between them, even if she had to beat it out of her.

Steve was sitting behind his desk, reading and mindlessly twirling a red pen when Jane knocked. When he looked up, he dropped the pen on the floor and stared at them like they'd risen from the dead. Jane would have understood his being surprised, but the emotion he was registering wasn't surprise; it was something much closer to horror. Slowly he stood, knocking a copy of *Jane Eyre* off his desk in the process. He ran his hands over his corduroy pants as he desperately blinked back tears. He swallowed hard, his Adam's apple almost getting stuck in his throat as his breathing became more labored. "She's dead," he said, choking out the words.

"Meg's dead?" Jane screamed. The inside of her throat began to burn, and she could actually feel her brain stuttering in her skull, every thought she had bouncing off the others, causing one loud, buzzing, crash.

"What?" Cara asked. She dropped her purse, causing her wallet, car keys, and a lipstick to scatter all over the floor.

"Why didn't you tell us?" Jane wailed.

How could this have happened? she thought. *How could we not have known?*

"Wait. That's not why you're here?" Steve asked. "I thought you were here to tell me that!"

"Why would you think that?" Jane asked.

"Then why are you here?" Steve answered.

"Not to tell you anyone's dead, for Christ's sake!" Cara said.

"Meg isn't dead?" he asked, noticeably calmer.

"Not that I know of, but I haven't seen her in years. You're her husband; wouldn't you know if she were dead? Jesus Christ, what the hell is going on?" Jane asked. She was beginning to realize that the perfect lives she'd imagined for her friends were, in fact, imaginary.

"Oh, thank God," Steve said.

Jane felt herself relax, just a little. "Okay. Let's try this again. We came here to tell you that we wanted to talk to Meg. We had no idea where you live anymore, but we found out you were still teaching here, and this seemed like the best way to find you and thereby her."

"We separated," he said. "I haven't talked to her in a while."

"When?" Jane asked in utter disbelief. If Meg and Steve couldn't make it work, then there was no hope for anyone.

"About a year ago."

"*Why*? You guys were perfect. Why would you split up?" Jane asked.

"I'd rather not get into it," Steve said.

Cara picked her things up off the floor and shoved them back into her purse, as if she didn't want to be a part of this conversation anymore. It struck Jane as odd that Cara didn't think the lipstick that had rolled under the radiator could wait.

"Cara, did you hear that? Would you get up off the floor and listen to Steve?" Jane asked.

"I'm sorry," she replied, standing up and tossing the lipstick back in her purse. "What happened?" Jane noticed that Cara stared at the floor when she asked the question, as if she already knew the answer.

"It's personal," he said quietly. "I'd rather not get into it."

"Oh, Steve, I'm so sorry," Jane said. "I don't know what to say."

"I'm sorry, too," Cara added.

"Anyway, she's been withdrawn and depressed for much longer than we've been separated. She won't let me help her. I've tried to help her. I want to, but she pushes me away."

"I know the feeling," Cara said, finally looking up to meet Steve's eyes.

"Okay. I wasn't expecting this at all. I'm sorry we barged in on you here," Jane said, the realization that Meg's marriage was also a mess somehow making her feel better about her own—which totally disgusted her. What kind of woman used a friend's disaster as a reason to feel good about her own shortcomings? She really needed a shrink.

"Why are you two looking for her?" Steve rightfully asked. "What are you two even doing together?"

"Looking for someplace to hide," Jane answered.

Steve smiled. "Jane, you were always one of those people who never had a problem telling it like it is. I like that about you. It's nice to see that you haven't changed that much over the years."

"Except for the fact that I'm now tabloid fodder on the run on Long Island because I couldn't find a place to hide in a city of ten million people. Other than that, yeah. I'm exactly the same."

"I've seen the news. I'm sorry you've had to deal with this nightmare. Did you really not know? I mean, is that really true?" Steve asked. "I don't mean to sound like a jerk and I don't mean to pry, but you did just track me down in my classroom and scare the life out of me. So I'm hoping it's okay to ask."

"No. Believe it or not, I really did not know," Jane said. "Yes, I actually am that stupid."

"I'm sorry, Jane. I really am. I guess you can't win at this point, right? You're either an idiot for not knowing or a thief for being part of it. Having those as your only two options must suck big time."

"Yes, it does. So that's my story. Cara over here, she's—" Jane started, but Cara cut her off.

"Just along for the ride. I thought maybe Jane should have some company and we were thinking maybe it's time the three of us should get together and talk."

Jane wasn't sure what to think of the bizarre interaction between Cara and Steve. Cara prided herself on being strong. She always kept part of herself hidden, afraid that if she showed some vulnerability it would somehow be used against her. That was just her personality. She was the polar opposite of Meg, who trusted everyone and wore her heart on her sleeve. Back in the day Cara had served as Meg's de facto bodyguard, making sure that no one hurt her. No wonder Steve was so worried about her—without either of them, Meg didn't have anyone watching over her.

"Right," Jane said. "Along for the ride. Listen, Steve, I'm sure that Meg is in need of some friends and maybe we are the worst people in the world to show up and try to help her, but maybe it makes perfect sense. Maybe we can help. Do you know where we can find her? Cara said she changed her phone number."

"Yeah, she did. We also sold the house. I live in an apartment over by the train station now, and Meg has been spending most of her time out at the place by the beach. She likes it. You know how she always loved those farm stands."

"She's in Montauk?" Jane asked, surprised. "That's amazing!

This is fate. We were going to ask her if we could hide out there for a few days while I figure out what I'm going to do with my life. I was planning on calling her and asking her to join us. It never occurred to me she'd be living out there."

"It never occurred to me, either," Steve said, obviously heartbroken that the love of his life had found a place that made her happy but didn't include him.

"In the summer I get it, but she likes it out there now all by herself? It's October! It's desolate out there in the off-season, which is exactly why I thought it would be the perfect place to hide. What does she do out there all winter by herself?" Jane asked. As soon as she heard the words she knew that Steve was probably wondering the same thing, and worrying that maybe she wasn't by herself at all. Maybe she'd found someone else.

"Spending a long, cold winter alone in a deserted town doesn't sound like a way to improve her mood," Cara said. "She must be lonely."

"She's still working. She's writing a blog for a gourmet magazine. She comes up with new recipes and posts them online, and I think there's some question-and-answer thing she's involved in. A lot of cooking and blogging and yeah, a lot of time alone in her head. Unless she's started dating someone else. Maybe I'm sitting over here alone and worried about her and she's actually shacked up with a fisherman. I don't know anymore. She's made it pretty clear that she wants to be alone, so I've been trying to respect her wishes," Steve said, vocalizing what Jane had already been thinking.

"Do you think she'll freak out if we show up?" Jane asked. "Cara, I assume you know where it is, right?"

"Yeah. Meg showed it to me not long after you guys bought it three years ago."

"She hasn't seen either of you in a long time and you're going to just show up unannounced? Yeah, I think she'll freak out." He tapped his pen on his desk. "You know what? I don't know if this will make things better or worse, but I have to try something. How much worse could things possibly get at this point?"

"Does that mean you'll help us?" Jane asked.

"Yeah. Here," he said. He ripped a piece of paper off his pad and wrote down the address and phone number of the cottage. "This is the landline. I don't know if she'll answer if you call, and I don't know if she'll be there when you get there, and I don't know if she'll want to see you. Hell, I don't know if she'll let you in the front door. But if I give you this, do you promise that you'll do one thing for me?"

"Anything," Jane said.

"We'll try," Cara hedged.

"Tell her I love her. Tell her I miss her. Tell her . . ." He stopped. "There's way too much I want to tell her to even try to encapsulate it in a single sentiment to send along with the two of you."

"Take your time," Cara said.

"Just tell her that I'm waiting for her. I want her to know that."

"You're a good man, Steve," Jane said. She walked slowly toward him and wrapped her arms around his neck. She didn't realize it would hurt this much to see Meg's husband. She missed her friend more than she'd ever realized.

"We'll tell her that, too," Cara said from where she stood in the doorway.

"Then go," he said as he pulled from Jane's grasp and pressed the paper with the address into her hand. "At least you won't have to worry about the paparazzi finding you out there. There's not much action in Montauk this time of year."

"No, there's not," Jane said, a familiar glint returning to her eye. "But I have a feeling there's about to be."

Jane and Cara headed east on the Long Island Expressway for the two-hour drive to the tip of Long Island. It took three hours to drive from Manhattan to Montauk if there was no traffic, and while it wasn't quite as far as Jane would have liked to get from the city, it was a pretty good start. She lowered the window and let the cool air hit her face before she started fiddling with the radio, just like she used to when she rode shotgun in Cara's car. The only difference was that now she struggled to find things to talk about. It seemed as good a time as any to try to get some answers.

"I know that I disappeared on you guys and everything, but now that I'm here, can you please tell me what the hell is going on?" Jane asked.

"What do you mean?" Cara replied.

"I know you know what happened between them. You have no poker face whatsoever. I can't think of any reason on earth why the two of them would separate. None. She loved him more than anything in the world. Tell me what happened."

"I don't want to get into it."

"Okay," Jane said, tired of playing the will-you-or-won't-you-tell-me game when they both knew Jane would make her crack. "This is stupid. I know you, and I know that part of you probably feels like you're betraying Meg's confidence by discussing it with me, but we're on our way to her house and keeping secrets isn't going to help anyone. Haven't you learned that by now?"

"Fine," Cara said. She paused briefly and then said quietly, "Meg can't have children." Jane was struck by her blunt delivery, but then figured that some things are impossible to sugarcoat.

"What do you mean? I remember she had two miscarriages, which is awful, but lots of women have a couple of them. Are you saying there're more than the two I know about?"

"Yes. As far as I know, there's nothing they can do to help her. Maybe things have changed . . . I don't know . . . but I doubt it, if she left Steve. She tried everything, but nothing worked. My best guess is that the stress of it all became too much for her. It's been chipping away at her for years. She wasn't the same anymore. It broke my heart, to be honest."

"I don't even know what to say. Meg's wanted kids for as long as I can remember. I can't imagine what it's been like for her to accept that it won't ever happen." Jane stared out the window for a minute and then fiddled with the radio again while she tried to process the information Cara had just given her. If her guess was accurate, then Meg would be devastated. It would explain why she left her marriage, but Jane still couldn't figure out what it had to do with Cara. Finally, she asked. "I still don't really understand why you guys aren't talking anymore, though. What does that have to do with you?"

"I don't want to talk about it, Jane. I really don't," Cara answered, a bit too aggressively.

"At some point you're going to have to tell me. You can trust me. What did you fight about?"

"Everything and nothing."

"Well, that's specific. Thanks for clearing that up for me."

"It's complicated. Anyway, I've blocked out most of it."

"Come on. Just tell me."

"I don't want to tell you. I'm not the one who started this pilgrimage for friendship atonement, you are. You're too smart to have gotten wrapped up in a criminal investigation. I don't understand how you let him drag you into his mess," Cara said.

"Says the woman who's explaining buying too much Uncle Ben's to her husband. Do you really think you're in a position to judge?"

"No, I guess not."

"Me neither. If you don't want to tell me what happened, do you want to talk about Reed?" she asked.

"Not even a little," Cara answered.

"Okay then. I give up . . . for now."

Jane turned up the volume on the stereo, and they rode the rest of the way in silence.

thirteen

Meg couldn't remember when she'd started baking bread. She'd always enjoyed cooking and baking, much preferring to spend her time in the kitchen than anywhere else. In college she had a part-time job at a specialty foods store near campus where she learned about different kinds of cheese and imported coffee beans, and soon she discovered that food was her passion. She took an internship at a gourmet magazine the summer between her junior and senior years of college and immediately knew she never wanted to leave.

She started out as an editorial assistant and went to culinary school at night right after graduation. Now she spent most of her time testing recipes for the magazine, tweaking the spices or cooking time so that it worked best for home cooks. At some point over the past year, she'd begun to find the specific tactile nature of bread baking cathartic, and had asked her boss if she could focus on bread recipes that even a novice baker could master. She enjoyed the smell of the yeast as it fermented and worked its magic on the flour and water and sugar in a bowl, coming alive. It was chemistry that worked the way it should. She appreciated that dough required patience, time to rise, a warm environment, and a gentle hand to punch it down and reshape it and let it rise again. She loved that when it finally went into the oven it filled her entire house with comforting aromas that made her nostalgic for friendship and company. She hadn't actually had company in a very long time, but somehow baking made her feel a little less alone.

When she and Steve had bought the house back in 2010, they knew they had their work cut out for them. It was a fixer-upper in every sense of the word—a neglected, outdated beach shack that they just knew could be a perfect spot to spend summers and holidays over the next sixty years if they took the time needed to fix it up. Steve's uncle had left him a little bit of money when he died, and they decided to take advantage of the real estate market collapse and invest in a second property they'd otherwise never be able to afford. It took about two years, but they accomplished exactly what they had set out to do. They'd gutted the inside, ripping out ancient fixtures, broken tiles, and linoleum flooring in favor of farmhouse sinks, bamboo floors, and white subway tiles. The parochial green paint in the kitchen had been stripped off and the space redone with white cabinets and butcher-block counters. There was an old office on the right side of the first floor that Meg had hoped would be a playroom one day, and they managed to furnish the entire home with items they found at flea markets and tag sales all over the Hamptons. She had scoured *Coastal Living* magazine for more than a year looking for inspiration, knickknacks, and new uses for refurbished wood. The old aluminum siding had been replaced with gray clapboard shingles, the dead plants had been dug up and carted away, and new cherry trees and rhododendrons were brought in to redo the landscaping in the front. When they were finished, she and Steve sat on the porch out back with glasses of wine and talked about how lucky they were to have everything. At that point, Meg was still hopeful that things would work out for them. She hadn't given up yet.

Now she was living in the house alone, separated from her husband, and that office on the first floor was still an office. It's a sad day when you accept that all of your childhood dreams are dead. *I've made my peace with it,* she told anyone who knew anything about her and had the indecency to ask. Then she went home and baked bread, and soothed her soul with the rhythmic pulses of her kneading.

She was waiting for the timer on the oven to count down the final ten minutes of cooking time on her Pullman loaf when there was a knock at her front door. She wiped her hands on a striped kitchen towel, threw it on the counter, and casually opened the door. She couldn't have been more surprised to see the ghosts of her past standing there next to her potted plants.

"Hey, Meg," Jane said.

She had seen pictures of Jane on the news and in the tabloids over the last few months, and she more or less looked the same in person. Truth be told, Meg had thought about reaching out to her. She wasn't sure why they had stopped speaking. It was more like Jane had just decided that she didn't want to be friends with Meg and Cara anymore and simply disappeared. Meg couldn't possibly understand how they could've been as close as sisters and then just have her walk away for no reason. She'd felt abandoned, and it was something that she hadn't ever really gotten over. The part of her that still loved Jane had wanted to call her and tell her that she was sorry her husband did what he did to her, that she knew without a doubt Jane had nothing to do with it, and that she would be there for her, whatever she needed. She never called. The scab that had formed over the part of her heart that loved Jane wouldn't let her dial.

"Hi," she said back. "It's good to see you."

"It's good to see you, too," Cara answered.

"No," Meg answered, turning an icy glare in Cara's direction.

"I wasn't talking to you. I told you I never wanted to see you again, and I meant it."

"I . . . I knew this was a bad idea. I'm sorry, I shouldn't have come," Cara said quickly as she walked back to the car and got in the driver's seat. Her white button-down nipped in at the waist, her jeans were perfectly cropped, her driving loafers were immaculately clean. Meg felt rage begin to build as she realized that Cara hadn't changed at all. She was still pretending to be some perfect Stepford something or other when they both knew that wasn't the case. The fact that Cara had the nerve to come anywhere near her made her so angry that she had to quell an urge to stomp her feet on her own doorstep.

She hadn't seen Cara since her last miscarriage, three years ago. The pregnancy had been progressing perfectly, and Meg had finally let her guard down, believing that this time, things would be different. She was thirty-four and had been through it enough times to know better, but still, she'd made herself believe that she'd paid her dues. When she found out that she'd lost the baby, she didn't have the heart to call Steve at work and ruin the tenuous happiness he'd allowed himself to feel over the past few weeks. Instead, she just got in her car and drove. She wound up at Cara's house, without any recollection at all of getting there.

June 2010

Meg knocked softly on the back door and entered the kitchen, finding Cara sitting at the table staring out the window. She walked over and sat down next to her, not really stepping outside of herself long enough to notice that Cara uncharacteristically looked like shit.

"It's gone," Meg said. She followed Cara's gaze out the window, but there was nothing there. It was like she was staring at the wind.

"What?" Cara asked, turning to look at her. For the first time, Meg noticed that Cara was very pale, and her eyes were vacant. Still, there she was, in her white shirt and jeans, her hair brushed, her nails done. Just once Meg wanted to feel like Cara wasn't an android—like she was capable of sitting around the house all day in her pajamas or going out without a full face of makeup and a strand of pearls. Just once Meg wanted to know that Cara knew what it felt like to unravel. She knew that her anger was misguided, that lashing out at Cara for anything when she had shown up at her house unannounced wasn't fair.

Until it turned out that it was.

"I lost the baby. Again. I'm never going to be a mother," Meg said quietly. There weren't even any tears left.

"Oh my God, Meg," Cara said. She was struggling to look at her, but Meg didn't know why. Cara reached over to grab Meg's hand and when she did, the cuff of her shirt nudged a piece of paper out from the stack of mail on the table. A magazine had been thrown on top of it, but Meg saw the headline. WHAT TO DO FOLLOWING YOUR PROCEDURE. Meg pulled the paper from the stack and began to read, her brain computing only a few words on every line: sporadic bleeding, no exercise for seventy-two hours, doxycycline. Meg would be handed a similar sheet after her next doctor's appointment, she knew, because the same instructions were given every time a surgical procedure was necessary to finish off what nature had started. But Cara had never told her she was pregnant. Meg saw her all the time and she never mentioned it, plus she still had glasses of wine with dinner and steams at the gym. There was only one explanation, but Meg's brain was having a hard time processing it.

"Why do you have this?" she asked. Cara looked at the paper and the little color she had in her face quickly drained. "Why do you have this, Cara? Answer me."

"It's nothing," Cara said, snatching the paper out of her hand.

"It's not nothing. I know what this is. If there is anyone on earth who knows what this is it's me. What did you do?"

"Nothing, Meg. Leave it alone."

"You had an abortion," Meg said, stunned that the sentence had come out of her mouth. Never in a million years would she have thought it was possible.

"Meg, please," Cara said, as if Meg was annoying her by asking the question. What did she expect her to do? Ignore it?

"Oh my God. Why? How could you do that? You've seen what I've been going through for years. You have a normal pregnancy, and just end it? You just give that away? How could you be so selfish?"

"This has nothing to do with you, Meg. What I choose to do with my personal life is none of your business. I'm sorry that you saw this. I never meant for you to know. And I'm sorry that this happened to you again. But our situations are different. Our lives are different, and the last time I checked, I don't have to consult you or anyone else before I make decisions concerning my body and my life."

"You didn't even tell me you were pregnant! Why? I don't keep anything from you! Why would you hide this from me?" Meg was shouting, but she couldn't help herself. She and Cara never fought; in fact, she couldn't remember the last time they'd disagreed over anything.

"Because I didn't want to have this conversation, that's why! And you know what, Meg? Just because you can't keep your mouth shut and tell everyone everything there is to know about your reproductive system doesn't mean that I'm the same way. I'm allowed to have a private life."

"I do not!" Meg said.

"Oh, please! You tell me when you have fucking yeast infections, Meg! Why does anyone need to know that?"

The words hurt Meg. She'd always thought that best friends shared everything, and now Cara was making her feel like she'd been boring her with the details of her life. Or worse, that she'd been a burden.

"What does that have to do with anything? You've never once mentioned not wanting kids, and it's not like the topic of conversation has never come up between us. How is it possible that through all of these years, you never once said anything about it? How could you have an abortion? How could you do that?"

"What, are you political now? Why are you choosing this moment to pick a side?"

Meg couldn't believe that she was insinuating this argument was at all academic. It was emotional, pure and simple, and if Cara were better attuned to her feelings, she'd get that. "I don't give a damn about the politics of it! I care that it hurts me. I'd give anything, anything, to be able to carry a normal, healthy baby, and you just gave your chance away? Why, Cara? You're in your thirties, you're married, and you have money. There's no reason for you to have an abortion. You've seen firsthand what this whole experience has done to me, and that's the decision you made? I don't know how to handle that. I don't."

"There's nothing for you to handle! It's not the right time for me, and that's all you need to know!"

"Are you kidding? That's all you're going to say? It's not the right time?"

"Look, Meg, you came to my house to talk about your problems, not to quiz me on the decisions I make for myself. You don't have an all-access pass into my personal life just by virtue of being my friend. You've been like this your whole life, you know that? You have no filter, and you expect me to be the same way. I'm not. You're not entitled to know everything. I'm sorry if that hurts you or if you don't understand it, but it's true, and if you want to stay friends with me, you're going to have to accept that there are parts of my life that I'm not going to discuss with you or anyone else. This is one of them. You can either be okay with that or not. Either way, this conversation is over."

It was crazy. How could Cara possibly think that they'd just go back to pretending everything was normal? It was like all the advice and sympathy Cara had been giving her over the years was tainted, like she'd never cared at all. Meg was enraged, and maybe jealous in some way, that Cara could have what she wanted so badly and not value it at all. She looked at Cara sitting across from her at the table and somehow felt like she didn't know her. There was no longer a reason for her to stay there that afternoon, and as it turned out, no reason for her to ever go back.

"I don't have anything to say to you. This is unforgivable," Meg said.

"I don't know, Meg. There's nothing I can do about it now. And even if I could, I wouldn't. So you're going to have to find some way to forgive me. I'm sorry. I really am. I didn't want you to find out this way."

"How'd you want me to find out?"

"I didn't want you to find out at all," Cara admitted.

The words stung. She was insulted that after years of telling Cara everything about her struggles, her friend had kept this secret from her.

"I have to go," Meg whispered as she stood and grabbed her purse off the back of her chair.

"Meg, wait," Cara said as she watched Meg scurry toward the door. "Don't leave like this!"

Meg closed the door behind her, climbed into her car, and headed home. When she got there she curled into a ball on the couch and waited for Steve to come home from work. Her phone rang two different times, but she never got up to answer it. Over the next few weeks she received multiple calls and at least a dozen e-mails from Cara, but she didn't answer any of them. What was there for her to say? She was jealous, and angry, and hurt, and depressed, and felt like she'd been betrayed. There were no words left. After a while the calls stopped coming, and they both understood that the friendship was over.

Slowly, Meg got used to having lost her dream of having children, her best friend, and eventually her husband. She was learning to live this new life alone with her walks on the beach and her bread making and trying really hard to be okay with everything that she had lost along the way.

And then Cara had the nerve to selfishly show up on Meg's doorstep without ever wondering if Meg had any interest in seeing her.

"Cara, wait!" Jane yelled, but Cara ignored her. "Meg, please. We didn't come here to fight."

"Then you shouldn't have come," Meg whispered, all the emotions she'd felt at that kitchen table years ago flooding her again.

"I'm sorry I was an asshole. I know I was. I know I owe you an explanation, and I will give it to you, but can't we just come in? I need you guys right now. Please. Let's just talk about whatever happened between you two. I think it's time all of us sit down and figure this out. It's been too long, and we'll never get the time back. Let's not make this worse than it already is. Please, Meg. Say something. We just drove over two hours to get here."

Beep. The oven sounded. Finally, her bread was ready.

fourteen

Cara stifled tears as she sat behind the wheel of her car. She knew she shouldn't have come here. She knew that she should've just told Jane to figure out her problems on her own. By trying to help her, Cara would be opening up the old wounds that she'd let heal years ago. But how was she supposed to let Jane go through all of this alone, especially when she was looking for a way out herself? She'd stupidly believed that maybe this was her chance to fix the friendship that she'd so desperately missed. She should've known that things couldn't be that easy.

Cara was surprised at how different Meg looked, how much she'd changed over the past three years. She had the same hair, a short blond bob with a piece tucked behind her right ear, and the same sprinkling of freckles across the bridge of her nose. She had the same pale skin and the same blue eyes, but she looked nothing like her former self. Her eyes seemed vacant, her skin was sallow, her energy was gone. She looked like she'd aged ten years over the course of three. Most people probably wouldn't notice the subtle way her shoulders slumped forward, or the few extra pounds she was carrying on her hips, or the dark hollows under her eyes—but to Cara, she looked as worn as the faded green cardigan hanging loosely off her body. She wasn't over anything. If anything, time had only made things worse.

Deciding to end her pregnancy hadn't been easy, especially since she'd been thirty-four, and well aware that time was no longer on her side. One morning she was in the shower getting ready to show a four-bedroom Tudor on the other side of town when nausea overwhelmed her. After the appointment, she stopped at the drugstore and bought a test, but she knew she was pregnant before she ever peed on the stick. She had stopped taking her birth control because it seemed unnecessary. Her husband hadn't touched her in months, and she thought pumping herself full of hormones was stupid. Meg had gone through hell trying to get pregnant, and all Cara ever heard women talking about was the innumerable problems they were having trying to conceive. What were the odds that one night, after her husband had had too much whiskey with his buddies, he would get lost in the hallway and wander into her room when he got home, and that she would actually let him stay? What were the odds that one night was all it would take?

Reed had become particularly insufferable at that point in their marriage. One morning he woke her up by throwing a pair of gym shorts at her head.

April 2010

"Get up. It's six A.M.—I've already run five miles and you're still in bed like some lazy housewife."

"What?" she asked, still pulling herself out of a deep sleep. It was still dark outside—she was hardly oversleeping, and even if she had been, why should he care? If she spent more time in bed lately it was because it was the only place in the house she could count on him leaving her alone.

"You should care about how you look. I don't understand it. Why don't you go for a run or something? You used to work out all the time."

"I weigh the exact same as I did the day we got married. I don't feel the need to run five miles before the sun comes up. Just add it to the list of things on which we don't agree."

Still, Reed was right. Cara used to exercise all the time. She was the captain of the tennis team, the basketball team, and the soccer team in high school. She used to love to spend her weekends skiing, kayaking, hiking, or spinning—the tougher the workout, the better. But then Reed started grilling her about the women she played tennis with, constantly asking her questions about their conversations, specifically what she told them about her marriage. Somewhere along the way, Reed had become completely paranoid that Cara was airing their personal problems to anyone who would listen, and forced her to stop playing with her foursome every week. After that, he began to question her relationship with her spin instructor, and the clothes she wore to the gym, and the amount of time she was gone. Eventually, he'd somehow managed to take something she'd always enjoyed and ruin it. She was tired of dealing with the reprimands that came every time she left the house to go to an early exercise class. She was tired of answering detailed questions about every conversation she had with every woman she encountered. She was tired in general.

And now he had the nerve to wonder why she didn't work out anymore?

I can't win, Cara said to herself. No matter what I do, I'll never win with him.

"That's how you're going to talk to me?" He grabbed her duvet and ripped it off the bed, exposing her to the cool fall air that leaked through the poorly insulated windows.

"It's freezing in here. Stop it!" she yelled, already feeling assaulted despite having been awake for a total of two minutes.

Another start to another beautiful day as Mrs. Reed Chase, *she thought.* "*Can we please get someone in here to redo the windows? I shouldn't have to wear mittens in my own home. We're both going to get pneumonia.*"

"*You know, the kitchen is the warmest room in the house. Why don't you try using it sometime? The stove gives off heat.*"

"*The last time I cooked for you, you told me you hated it. You told me I overcooked everything and that I should take cooking classes in town. Do you remember that? So which is it, Reed? Do you want me to cook for you or not? I can't keep up with your constant demands anymore. They change daily.*"

"*I've given you everything you could want, Cara. You should just say thank you for the roof over your head and the clothes you buy with my credit card and maybe for once try to do something that you think might make me happy. Why is my happiness never a concern of yours?*"

"*I'm sorry,*" *she whispered as she sat up and shoved her feet into the pair of slippers she kept at the foot of the bed in case she needed to go to the bathroom in the middle of the night.* "*I'm trying my best to make you happy. You don't make it easy.*" *Cara realized that fighting with him was a waste of her time. She would never win. It would be easier to just do what he wanted and hope that he'd leave her alone. Over time, he'd slowly sucked the fight out of her, and now there was very little left.*

"*Start by getting up. That will make me happy.*" *He left the room and went down the hall to the master bath. These were the moments, after his tirades, when she sat and tried to think of all the things she'd like to point out to him if she only had the nerve. He had no problem telling her when she had a blemish on her cheek, or when her gray hairs were showing, or that cellulite was now visible on the backs of her thighs. She never pointed out that he needed to start trimming the hair that was beginning to sprout from his ears, which would soon be long enough to braid. She didn't point out that she could see the skin on his scalp when his hair was wet from the shower. She didn't dare mention that despite the push-ups and the chest presses and the bench presses, his pecs were beginning to sag and soon he'd be able to fill out one of her bras. She never said any of these things. She was too much of a wimp to handle the consequences.*

She exhaled when she heard the door close and the water start to run. She already felt attached to the baby she thought she was carrying, and at the same time resented it, because without meaning to, it was binding her to him forever. She wished she could be one of those women who had no problem admitting her marriage was a disaster. She wished she weren't so stubborn. She wished she weren't such a perfectionist.

She wished she weren't pregnant.

After the test confirmed her suspicions she lay on her bed for hours feeling alone and helpless. There was no one for her to call. She knew she couldn't confide in her mother—how could she admit that she was going to deny her only chance at being a grandmother? She couldn't call Meg, knowing how insensitive it would be to involve her in a decision that was inherently at odds with where she was in her own life. The feeling of isolation was the main reason why she finally worked up the nerve to call her doctor and schedule an appointment: she didn't want to be responsible for bringing a child into a home with a man who was incapable of feeling love for anyone but himself. In her heart, she knew that if she did have the baby, he'd somehow manage to use it against her. That was no way for a life to begin.

It had haunted her ever since, but she still didn't think that it was any of Meg's business, or anyone else's for that matter. Some things you just had to go through alone.

A month later she'd driven herself to her appointment, despite the doctor's insistence that she have someone with her to drive her home. How was she supposed to tell him that as a grown, married woman, she had no one who could escort her home when everything was over? She'd lain in a recovery room for a half hour, eating saltines and drinking orange juice in an effort to appease the nurses and reassure them that she was able to drive. Then she slinked back to her house with a super-plus maxi pad between her legs and a sheet of paper that detailed how she should take care of herself following the procedure. When she got home she made herself a cup of tea. She was sitting alone in her kitchen, trying to figure out how the young girl with the freckles and the tennis racket ended up a lonely, middle-aged woman who decided she shouldn't have children, when Meg burst through her back door. It never occurred to her that Meg might see the letter from the doctor until it was too late.

Cara hoped that maybe Meg had stopped feeling so sorry for herself by now, and that she would be able to see Cara's side of things. She had imagined them reconciling thousands of times, convincing herself that if they could just sit down and talk, everything would be okay. She'd been wrong. The years had done nothing to dull Meg's misguided feelings that Cara had somehow intentionally hurt her, which was always Meg's problem. Cara wasn't going to let Meg play the martyr and continue to make her feel like she was a horrible person who had somehow taken her friendship for granted. She was over paying for things she never asked to have happen to her in the first place. She had paid more than enough.

Cara glanced at Jane and Meg still standing on the stoop and was struck by how different they now all were from each other. Back in high school they'd tried their hardest to look exactly alike. They'd had the same anoraks and the same sweaters from J.Crew. When they went to flea markets on the weekends they bought the same bracelets and enamel earrings and wore the same Dr. Martens to school and the same Nike sneakers during after-school sports. They had the same dancing bear bumper stickers on their cars and listened to the same CDs—Pearl Jam and Counting Crows and Tracy Chapman—as if having all of the same things would somehow bring them closer together. Those girls were long gone, and the women who replaced them didn't seem to have anything in common. Cara decided it was time to admit that and let the past stay where it belonged.

She put the car into reverse, backed out of the driveway, and pulled away. She didn't feel bad about leaving. Jane may have asked her to bring her here, but she never said anything about taking her home.

fifteen

Was she your ride back to Manhattan?" Meg asked. She stood next to Jane on the porch and happily watched Cara's car turn right out of the driveway and speed off.

"I hadn't thought that far ahead. But yeah, I guess so. Now what am I supposed to do?"

"If you still want a ride just go stand in the middle of the road. She'll be back in one minute," Meg said.

"Why do you say that?"

"Because she went the wrong way. The road dead-ends that way. She's going to have to turn around and pass us again." Before Jane could answer, they heard a car approaching and watched Cara speed by them again in the opposite direction. "That probably wasn't the grand dramatic exit she'd been hoping for."

"Get your keys. We're going after her," Jane ordered, pointing Meg back into the house.

"I most certainly am not. I have recipes to test, then I'm going to go out back and water my herb garden, which is exactly what I was planning on doing before you rang my doorbell and ruined my day."

"Do you hear yourself? You just threw her off your doorstep and you don't even know why we came to begin with. You're too old to be acting like this, and honestly it's not like you. You can be pissed all you want, but I'm going after her. You can either give me your keys with the knowledge that I live in Manhattan and haven't driven a car in about eight years, or you can drive and take me with you. Either way, your car is leaving this driveway. Do you understand?"

Meg didn't appreciate being bossed around in her own house, but there was something in Jane's voice that made her reconsider her initial reaction. It wasn't that Jane was being her typical bossy, brazen, obnoxious self, it was that she looked legitimately panicked. She was acting like Meg had just done something much worse than deny Cara entry into her home. If something bad happened to Cara after she made her leave without ever knowing why she was there to begin with, Meg would never forgive herself.

Meg spun on her heel, went directly into the kitchen, and removed the loaf of bread from the oven with the striped oven mitts she'd bought in town on Memorial Day weekend. Then she turned off the oven, grabbed her car keys from a rattan basket on the kitchen counter, walked past Jane, and climbed into the driver's seat of her car.

"I didn't ask for any of this," Meg said as she drove west down Montauk Highway. "You guys just show up on my doorstep and barge into my life, and now I'm chasing Cara down the highway why, exactly?"

"Because my phone died and I don't have a better idea. Do you?" Jane answered.

"That's not what I meant. I don't understand why any of this is *my problem*. You don't need her to get back to the city. I could've dropped you at the train station. We should just let her go," Meg said, trying to sound completely detached, which was nearly impossible for her.

"You know what, Meg? It's not your problem, okay? Does that make you feel better? You've never done anything wrong and we are just horrible, evil people for driving all the way out here to check up on you. Did it ever occur to you that we were worried about *you*?"

"Why would you be worried about me? Don't you have enough going on in your own life right now to worry about?" Meg asked.

"Well, when your husband told us that you've been out here alone for the better part of a year and won't talk to him anymore, we found that to be cause for concern. I don't know, I guess we're just crazy overprotective or something."

"He told you that?" Meg asked, the color draining from her already too pale face. "He really said that?"

"You should've seen the look on his face when we walked into his classroom. He thought we were there to tell him that something awful happened to you. What the hell is going on with you that that is the impression your husband has of your mental state?"

"Nothing's going on with me. I've just decided that he's better off without me," Meg said, still trying to sound unaffected—and failing miserably because she was intrinsically one of the most sensitive people on the planet.

"That's a nice decision that you made for him, but I don't think he agrees with you. He's a nervous wreck. To be honest, now I am, too. We came here hoping that maybe we could help."

"You guys came here because you need something. Don't make it sound like it's all about me. Nothing has ever been all about me. Stop pretending that you're here out of the goodness of your heart, because I've known you too long for that. Just tell me the truth."

"You're right," Jane said, her frustrations overflowing. "I need some help, and I realized that I've made some very, very bad decisions in my life. I turned my back on everyone who really cared about me and surrounded myself with vapid, selfish people. I guess you don't really learn those things about yourself when times are good and the champagne is flowing. I went to Cara's to escape the camera brigade set up outside my soon-to-be-repossessed apartment, and she let me crash there for the night. It turns out that things aren't all that great for her, either. Of course, you would know that, if you had given either of us a chance to talk to you before you ripped our heads off. That said, it seems like you could maybe use some friends too, so why don't you stop being so fucking stubborn and admit that you're happy to see us!"

"What's wrong with her?" Meg asked. "Did one of her pearls get scratched?"

"No, Meg. Actually, for starters, her jackass husband is abusing her," Jane said. "Is that statement enough to force you out of your tough-girl act? It's starting to annoy me."

"What? Reed hits her? There's no way," Meg said. She squeezed the wheel so tightly her knuckles turned white.

"No, at least not that she's admitted. I heard him talking to her, though. It's psychological. He tells her what to wear, who to see, what she's allowed to buy at the store. I think it's been going on for years. You can pretend you don't care anymore, but I know it's complete bullshit. You care. A lot. And you know her mother died, right?" Jane asked.

"I didn't. No," Meg said, surprised at how quickly sadness overcame her. Cara's mom had always been a second mother to both of them. She was the one who made sure they had the good ice cream at sleep-overs, and the one who picked them up from

parties when they drank too much and couldn't drive home. Cara
and her mother were extraordinarily close, and losing her must
have been outrageously painful. It must have been even harder
for her to go through it without a husband who supported her or
friends who even knew enough to send a card.

"I went to the funeral. I thought maybe I'd see you there. I was
surprised when I didn't."

"I haven't talked to Cara in years. I didn't know any of this was
going on. I never thought Reed was the fuzziest guy in the world,
but I didn't know things had gotten that bad."

"Believe me, they have. He's been awful to her, Meg, and
she's been all alone. She just had to sell her mother's house. She
cleaned out the whole thing with no help whatsoever. I don't
know why you guys are so angry at each other, and right now, I
don't care. Well, that's not true. I'm actually really curious about
it, but I've accepted that this is something that I'm going to have
to pry out of one of you over time and probably after a few glasses
of wine. Anyway, the point is, she has nowhere to go now except
right back to Reed. She doesn't deserve that. I don't care what
she's done to you. Unless she slept with Steve. She didn't sleep
with Steve, did she?" Jane asked.

"No, Jane. She didn't sleep with my husband. You're the only
one living out a soap opera."

"I'm so glad we had this talk. I see you've been reading the
tabloids. I don't need to be reminded of the drama surrounding
my life. I'm living it, remember?"

"I'm sorry. I shouldn't have said that."

"It sucks bad enough to be judged by strangers who don't know
any better. It's excruciating to be judged by friends who should

know that I'm not a criminal. Christ, I'm aware that no one is offering me up for sainthood, but is it really too hard to believe that I wouldn't knowingly steal? Why are you even reading those stupid tabloid stories? You know they're all garbage."

"I had to keep tabs on you somehow," Meg joked.

"I think it's too early for humor in all of this."

"I'm sorry. You're right. I'm just trying to make you laugh a little, I guess."

"Can we try to figure out a way to help each other here? No one is free from blame in how our relationship disintegrated over the years. You can either try to make it better, or you can cling to the anger that you've let overtake your life and remain a hermit on the far reaches of the island. Those are your options. All things considered, I think it's a pretty easy choice, but what do I know? I'm just living out my own little soap opera over here."

"I don't know if there's any way for us to help each other. We don't even know each other anymore."

"Well, then try to get to know us. Honestly, you need to chill the hell out. The mood in this car is not exactly Zen, and if I'm supposed to be the glue that holds this group together, then we are all completely fucked. Mediation was never my strong suit."

"Is that her car?" Meg asked, pointing to the side of the road across the street from Jack's Coffee House. Meg wasn't surprised that Cara had noticed the small clapboard coffeehouse on the side of the highway, as it was undeniably cute and comforting— just the kind of place she'd like.

"Yes. She must've stopped for coffee. This place looks adorable, actually. Do you ever come here?"

"Not really. Twenty minutes is too far away to travel just for a cup of coffee, and in the summer the crowds descend on it with such fury you'd think they were giving away gold bricks with the lattes."

"Gotcha. Well, are you ready to play nice with her, or what?"

"It's not that simple, Jane. If I were her I wouldn't be in a rush to come back. You're going to have to run this show."

"I've been running this show since the beginning of time. Don't forget that."

"How'd that work out for you?" Meg asked.

"Fair point. I didn't say I was good at it."

They crossed the street and pushed through the rickety wooden door into the coffeehouse. Meg was immediately overwhelmed by the smell of cedar and arabica beans. The chalkboard behind the counter listed elaborate drinks with cute names that enthralled the Hamptons summer set who liked extremely expensive specialized java. These days, Meg was a simple girl who took her coffee with a splash of whatever kind of milk was available and two packets of sugar. This new trend of half-caf, skinny, low-fat, vanilla, mochaccino nonsense aggravated her. She'd just as soon make it at home in her French press and call it a day—one less reason to leave the house.

She saw Cara talking to the barista with the green apron behind the counter.

"This herbal tea is decaffeinated, right?" Cara asked, examining the tag from the tea bag that was hanging over the rim of her drink.

"I don't know for sure, but I think so," the barista answered, not seeming to care one way or the other.

"What do you mean, you think so? You work here, shouldn't you know?"

"I think it is, but I'm not one hundred percent sure," the girl behind the counter said again.

"I see. If you went to buy a car and asked the sales guy if the brakes worked and he said 'I think so,' would you still drive it? If you went to a drugstore to pick up a prescription and the pharmacist told you that he thinks it's penicillin, but he's really not sure, would that be okay with you?" Cara yelled.

"It's not a narcotic, lady. It's just tea."

"I'll have you know that caffeine is a drug. Why do you think high school kids spend half their free time sucking down cans of Red Bull?"

"Ma'am, there's a line, so if you could please just step aside . . ."

Meg waited for Cara to turn around and notice the two of them standing in the corner, stifling their laughter, which Meg felt bad about. No one should find humor in someone else's mental breakdown, but it was just so hard to see Cara lose her marbles over an herbal tea and not laugh.

"I get that pouring coffee is one step removed from nuclear physics, but you should care that you're giving your customers life-altering chemicals, instead of being preoccupied waiting for some casting agent to call and tell you that you got your big break jogging down the street in white shorts for a tampon commercial. Things matter. So you really should start thinking about how your carelessness can affect others," Cara reached over and snatched a comment card off the stack, then began scribbling on it furiously. "Yes, I'd like to leave a comment. You suck at your job." Cara grabbed her tea and a muffin as the barista continued to wait, immobile behind the counter as if she was afraid to make any sudden movements. When Cara spun around, she smashed into Jane, who had moved toward the line and was about to tap her on the shoulder, spilling her tea all over Jane's cashmere sweater.

"Oh my God, that's hot!" Jane said, delicately pulling her soaking-wet sweater away from her skin.

"What are you doing here?" Cara yelled before turning back to the barista. "Nice job putting the lid on my cup! Can you do anything right today?"

"Cara, pull it together! You should be more concerned with the fact that my boobs now have third-degree burns!"

"Oh please, you can't feel those things and you know it. You already told me that, remember?"

"The skin on my stomach and arms is real! Of course I can feel it!"

"Hey, aren't you Jane Logan?" the barista asked.

"I thought the Hamptons were known for being discreet. Can you please keep your voice down?" Jane begged.

"Wow. You really do get recognized, huh?" Cara asked, slapping at Jane's sweater with small white napkins in a completely unproductive attempt to dry her off.

"I told you. I know you think that I was exaggerating, but in this case, I assure you, I'm not."

"What are you doing here anyway? I'm leaving. All I wanted to do was get tea and something to eat for the road."

"We don't want you to leave," Jane said.

"What *we*?" Cara asked. "I'm sorry I left you there, but Meg made it very clear that we were not a welcome surprise. I shouldn't have come. I should never have let you talk me into any of this, and now I have to go home and try to explain the note I left for Reed. Do you have any idea how he's going to react when he sees that? I don't know what I'm going to say to him, but this was a colossal mistake."

"You shouldn't have to deal with him," Meg said quietly. Cara turned and finally noticed Meg standing in the corner. Meg quickly bit her upper lip, trying to keep herself from saying something else she'd regret. They'd done enough of that for a lifetime. She fidgeted with the lavender scarf wrapped around her neck and shoved her hands inside her back pockets.

"I didn't see you there," Cara said.

"How'd you think I got here?" Jane asked. "You were supposed to be my ride and you ditched me. It's like being at the homecoming party in eleventh grade all over again. I'm still mad about that, by the way."

Cara ignored Jane and spoke to Meg instead. "I'm sorry to just show up out here and expect that you'd want to see me. I thought . . . I don't know what I thought. I don't know that I was thinking at all. I'm sorry."

"Jane told me what's going on," Meg said. She removed her hands from her pockets and chewed her nails.

"She always did have a big mouth," Cara said. "Stop biting your nails."

"In my defense there were extenuating circumstances that allowed me to spill your secrets. Primarily that I basically forgot how to drive and needed a ride to come find your ass. But if it will make everyone feel better to hear me say it, fine. I have a big mouth. Is that why no one will tell me what is going on with you two?" Jane asked.

"I didn't know about your mom, either," Meg said. "I'm really sorry you've been dealing with all of this. I liked to think that everything was perfect with you, you know? I always thought that you had everything you ever wanted. It made it easier to stay away."

"I have exactly zero of what I really want. But in all the years of wondering how both of you've been, not once did I expect to hear that you left Steve and secluded yourself on the tip of Long Island. And I never thought that the white-collar division of the FBI would target Doug or that Jane would need to be medicated to leave the house. So things didn't turn out how any of us expected them to, I guess."

"Hey. I don't *need* to be medicated. I just prefer it that way," Jane said. "There's a difference. I want to be clear on that."

"I don't want you to go back home, Cara," Meg said. "At least not tonight. Jane is going to stay with me—"

"I thought you were going to make me take the train?" Jane asked.

"Enough, Jane!" Meg snapped, which she instantly felt bad about. She glanced at the girl behind the coffee counter, who was staring at Jane with morbid curiosity, and smiled apologetically for raising her voice.

"Anyway, I'd like for you to stay too, Cara. We could all catch up a little. Maybe it'll be fun."

"Sure, it's been a barrel of monkeys so far," Jane added. She removed a bottle of pills from her bag, popped two into her palm, and swallowed them dry.

"Are you sure? Because I'll be okay if you want me to leave," Cara said.

"I'm sure. Come back to the house. Please," Meg said. She meant it.

"Maybe just for the night," Cara said.

"Do you have wine at your house? If not, there's a liquor store across the street, and we are so absolutely going to need booze for this. I'll run and get some as long as one of you gives me money. My funds are a little low these days," Jane said. "This will be fun. It's long overdue."

"I have some, but I'd have bought more if I knew you were going to be there, Jane," Meg teased.

"So I take it you guys know each other?" the barista asked. Meg didn't like that the barista was so interested in their conversation, and she kept her fingers crossed that she wasn't going to call the press two seconds after they left to relay the entire conversation she'd just overheard. If anything deserved to be kept private, this was it, but then again, they probably shouldn't have had the conversation at a coffeehouse in the Hamptons to begin with. Meg should've just let them into the house and talked to them in private.

"No, I guess we don't," Meg answered. "But I think it's time that changed."

sixteen

Jane purchased wine at the liquor store across the street and climbed into the front seat of Cara's car. They made an illegal U-turn on Montauk Highway—something you could do only in the fall when the traffic was nonexistent—and followed Meg back to her house. Jane didn't even bother to turn on the radio to kill the awkward silence. If they were all going to shack up together for the night, then she was going to have to get comfortable with awkward moments, and quick.

"Why'd you guys come and get me?" Cara finally asked. Jane was staring out the window, catching brief glimpses of the ocean on the other side of the bluffs. In the summer, the foliage made it impossible to see the water from the highway, but with the bare trees you could see the dunes and the white-capped swells of the Atlantic. Jane had figured it would take Cara about five minutes before she probed into how she'd gotten Meg to agree to look for her. Jane glanced at the clock on the dash and discovered it had taken about seven. Not bad, she figured. She was a little rusty, but she could still predict Cara's behavior with uncanny accuracy.

"I couldn't let you go back to him. I assume that was where you were headed?"

"Since it's my home, yeah. To be honest, I thought about taking your keys and crashing at your apartment in the city, but if some random picture of me ended up in the paper, Reed would go berserk. Going home and dealing with it seemed like the better option."

"Both of those options blow."

"Don't sugarcoat it, Jane, really. Just tell me what you honestly think."

"Well, they do. This might only be a short-term fix for right now, but it's a fix and that's all I care about."

"And Meg? Is she going to make me sleep in a tent in the backyard?"

"No. She wants to help you, too. She was surprised when I told her what was going on with you and Reed," Jane said.

"I wish you hadn't done that," Cara said. A single tear rolled down her cheek, and she wiped it away with the back of her hand. "She won't understand. She never understood me."

"Well, I had to if I was going to stop you from going back there. And you're wrong about her. She understood. You two may have your problems, but she'd have to be a pretty evil bitch to think that you deserve to have your husband shred you on a daily basis. There might be a lot of anger there, but there's a lot of love, too. Don't forget that."

"I haven't forgotten. That's part of the problem. If I didn't love her it wouldn't hurt so bad. They say that best friends make the worst enemies. It's true."

"Really? That's what you're going to say to me? This enemy right here let you pour scalding-hot tea on her and is now riding shotgun in your car. You've got a screwed-up definition of enemies if that's what you think we are."

"This is only for tonight. I just need a place to stay for one night while I figure things out. I typically would've gone to my mom's . . ." Cara's eyes welled again and she exhaled loudly. "I don't know how to go on from here."

Jane reached over and rubbed her arm. "I know. But he

would've gone to look for you there. He will never in a million years think you're out here with us."

"With you in the picture, he won't know what to think. He never liked you, you know."

"I know. I don't care. Never did. And he knows it."

"What *do* you care about?" Cara asked.

"You. Meg. Getting the paparazzi off the sidewalk outside my apartment building. Other than that, nothing. I'm a very simple girl these days."

"Simple? Somehow I doubt that. One thing you've never been is simple. Need I remind you of the freshman-year dance? Oh wait, I can't, because we weren't allowed to go!"

Jane felt a smile creep across her face.

March 1991

"Bye, Mom! I'm heading to Cara's, but don't wait up. I might be late. The test is going to be brutal!" Jane said to her mom as she headed toward the front door with her backpack slung over her shoulder.

"Okay. Don't study too hard," Jane's mom said as she finished giving Gavin a bath. "Call if you need anything!"

"I will, Mom. See you later," Jane answered. She hopped down the stairs and crept into the backyard. She glanced over her shoulder to make sure her mother wasn't looking out the window— when she was sure she wasn't, she hissed as quietly as she possibly could, "Are you there?"

"Over here," Cara answered, popping her head out from behind a tree a few yards away. "Are you sure this is a good idea?" she asked as she and Jane changed into baggy jeans and midriff tops in Jane's backyard.

"Are you serious? It's a great idea. It's foolproof. There's no way we're going to get caught. It's going to be so fun! I can't believe we're going to see Janet Jackson! What did you tell your mom?"

"That I was studying at your house. What if our moms talk to each other?"

"Why would they talk to each other? There's no reason for that to happen! Relax. Everything is going to be fine. We're going to have the best time. You're beginning to sound like Meg."

"Oh, come on. I'm not as bad as Meg and you know it. I'm here, aren't I?"

"Then stop worrying about everything and have some fun, for God's sake."

"I am having fun! I'm going to completely freak out when I see her. I've never been to a concert at Madison Square Garden," Cara said.

"Me neither! We just have to make sure we stick together and don't get lost once we get off the train."

"How'd you get these tickets again?"

"A girl who worked with me gift wrapping at the Gap over the Christmas season had a few extra seats and I bought them from her. She's eighteen and very cool. She's going to meet us there. You'll like her."

"I still wish Meg would've come."

"She was too much of a chicken to sneak out on a school night. It's her loss. Come on, we have to hurry if we're going to catch our train." Sneaking into the city to see a concert unchaperoned when they were only fifteen was one thing, but sneaking into the city on a school night to see a concert unchaperoned when they were only fifteen was another. In Jane's opinion, that's what made it all the more fun. Jane was never one to take no for an answer, so after her parents told her she was forbidden from going, she'd decided she'd do the logical thing: lie. It was an easy answer to a stupid problem as far as she was concerned.

One hour later they were getting smashed in between thousands of people trying to get a better look at Janet and her dancers. The music was so loud Jane couldn't hear herself think.

"Isn't this amazing?" she shouted as she leaned over to Cara, who was dancing in a circle and singing along to "Miss You Much." Her striped tube top and baggy jeans would look ridiculous on most people, but with Cara's perfectly flat stomach and muscular physique they looked totally cool. She couldn't remember the last time they'd had so much fun. Meg was crazy for opting out of this.

The dancers immediately broke into yet another routine. Jane was mesmerized by the way they could move their bodies in perfect sync, the choreography so detailed she marveled at how they possibly remembered it all.

"I will never forget this night as long as I live!" Cara said. "How do people dance like that? It's crazy!"

"Ms. Janet is the best!" Jane said, feeling somehow proud that she was able to supply the tickets for such an epic night. The older girls kept knocking into her, drunk or high or both, but Jane didn't need anything else to help her enjoy this show. The music and the dancing were enough to keep her going.

"Totally!" Cara echoed.

Jane checked her watch and nearly had a panic attack when she saw the time. She couldn't believe the night had gone by so fast. "We're going to have to go soon if we're going to make the train.

If we miss it we have to wait a long time for the next one and we'll get home way too late."

"Who cares?" Cara said as she continued to dance and sing and soak up the energy that was blazing through the Garden.

"We need to go!" Jane said, grabbing Cara by the wrist and leading her out of the arena. The LIRR was located directly downstairs. If they ran they'd be able to catch the train. If not, they were going to be stuck in Penn Station for another hour and blow their cover. She checked her watch again. The train was going to leave in five minutes. They would have to run fast. "Let's go, Cara! Hurry!"

They took off in a full sprint toward the escalator, Jane's heart pumping so loudly she could barely hear the voice over the loudspeaker announcing last call.

"Jane, slow down! I can't run in these shoes!"

"I thought you were the athlete! Run, Cara, or our moms will kill us!"

"I should've worn a sports bra. Damn it!" Cara yelled as she ran faster and pulled ahead of Jane. "I'll hold the train doors!"

They ran past the newsstands and down a flight of stairs. The voice over the loudspeaker said the track number one final time, and Jane watched as Cara sprinted down the stairs to track eighteen, leaving Jane heaving and panting behind her. Jane hit the staircase hard and had to brace herself against the railing to keep from falling down the entire flight and onto the train platform below. "Cara, don't let the train leave!"

Jane looked up just as Cara jammed her leg in between the closing train doors and watched as they ricocheted open again. Cara braced her body in between them and held them open just *wide enough for Jane to squeak through . . . and fall directly on the train floor.*

"Oh my God!" Cara yelled as the two girls lay next to each other, gasping for breath. "I've never run that fast in my entire life!"

"I find that hard to believe," Jane said, worried that her chest might actually explode. "I, on the other hand, might have a heart attack. Oh my God, we are so lucky we made this train!"

"I had so much fun, Jane. Thank you for convincing me to come."

"It didn't take much convincing!" Jane reminded her. "I'm glad you came, too. This is the stuff we'll remember when we're old and married and boring."

"You'll never be boring, Jane. I'd bet money on it."

An hour later they returned home, and Jane was surprised when she noticed the kitchen lights blazing. Uh-oh.

Jane hid behind the tree in her backyard while she changed out of her concert attire and put on her normal clothes. She left her jeans and tube top tied up nicely in a black garbage bag, where they'd stay until she retrieved them tomorrow, and slinked through the back door. "How was the concert?" her mother asked from the armchair in the corner of the living room.

"What are you talking about?" Jane said, even though she was completely busted.

"Jane, I swear to God I am not in the mood to play this game with you," her mother said. There was a magazine on the small circular table next to the chair, but Jane was fairly certain her mother hadn't even opened it. She'd seen this look on her mom's face often. It never ended well for her. Jane stared at the floor.

For some reason, holding her mother's disappointed gaze was basically impossible.

"Why are you waiting up for me anyway?" Jane asked. Usually her parents went to bed at eleven o'clock—it was one of the things she'd been counting on when she decided that sneaking into the city was a good idea.

"Because Gavin fell off the kitchen counter in his footie pajamas trying to reach a box of sugar cones and broke his collarbone. We needed to take him to the emergency room, so I stopped by Cara's house to pick you up while your father drove him to the ER. Imagine our surprise when her mother informed me that not only were you not there, but that Cara was supposed to be at our house. Now what on earth would make two teenage girls lie to their parents about where they were for the night?"

"We decided to go to Meg's," Jane lied without thinking. Dragging Meg into this was completely unfair and she knew it. Meg had wanted nothing to do with this from the very beginning. Still, it was a last-ditch effort.

"It scares me how easily you lie! We called Meg to find out where you were. Janet Jackson, huh? Didn't I specifically tell you you couldn't go to that concert? And you dragged Cara into this mess now with you! I hope you're happy with yourself."

"Meg told you?" Jane squealed. She was going to kill her. Unless they'd threatened to physically hurt her, she should've kept her mouth shut.

"Of course she told us. We have been worried sick! Do you have any idea how much trouble you're in? Do you have any idea what can happen to young girls in Madison Square Garden? What were you thinking going into the city like that? Not to mention I specifically told you no Janet Jackson concert on a school night, no

Janet Jackson concert without an adult, no Janet Jackson concert, period! I don't understand why you have no respect for authority, Jane!"

"Where's Gavin? Is he okay?" Jane asked, pausing for a minute to stop thinking about herself and start thinking about her poor little brother and his broken bone. Once it healed, she was going to torture him for choosing tonight to break something and ruin her fun.

"He's sleeping, and you're grounded for a month."

"Mom! What about the freshman dance? It's in two weeks and I already have a dress!" Missing this dance was not an option. Everyone was going and she would be the social misfit of the entire class if she wasn't there.

"You should've thought about that before you did something so stupid. And while we're talking about clothes, why don't you go back outside and bring in the outfit you changed out of before you came back in here."

"How did you know that?"

"Because you're not as good a liar as you think you are."

Damn.

"I'm sorry. Is Cara's mom really angry?"

"I don't think Cara will be at the dance, either. I have no doubt that this was all your idea. Now you can deal with the fact that you ruined the dance for the both of you."

"I still feel bad that we got caught, but come on! Are you telling me that if we had to do it all over again you'd have made a different choice? That concert was awesome!" Jane looked over at Cara, who was trying to suppress a smile. "Yeah, I didn't think so."

They pulled into the driveway and Cara clenched the steering wheel before turning off the car. Jane knew Cara didn't want to be here, but she also didn't want to be home. Knowing that there is no place in the world that you fit in is a feeling that's hard to explain. But Cara didn't have to—Jane had felt the same way for most of the last year. If there was anyone anywhere who understood how all-consuming that sense of solitude could be, it was her. And that was exactly why they needed each other.

"Come on," Jane said. "Let's go inside."

Meg's home was as bright as a tanning bed, courtesy of enormous windows that would be a peeping Tom's wet dream, the entire expanse of the first floor visible from the backyard. Candles covered every surface and the air was saturated with the smell of fresh bread. The sign over the small console table on the wall read LIVE A GOOD LIFE. Lincoln said that, if Jane's memory served her correctly. She liked the sentiment, but Lincoln really should have been more specific. What the hell defined a "good life"? Damned if she knew, and if she had to guess, she'd bet that Meg didn't know, either. But admittedly it read a lot better than "Fuck up your life," which was exactly what it seemed like all of them had done. Hanging *that* sign on the wall probably wasn't the welcoming that Meg wanted to give her guests, though, so Lincoln's abstract statement would have to do.

Jane glanced past the white walls of the den into the red-walled library in the back of the house. She caught sight of a fireplace with more candles adorning the mantel, throw pillows covering the couch, and a bookcase jammed with books. Jane had no problem picturing Steve curled up on the couch in front of the fire reading while Meg cooked in the kitchen. At one time, this house must've made both of them so happy.

"Make yourself at home," Meg said.

"It's really beautiful," Jane said as she pulled four wine bottles from the shopping bag and popped three of them in the fridge. "You guys were really smart to buy this when you did. You'll probably make a fortune on it if you ever go to sell it."

"I don't know that I'll ever sell it," Meg said quietly. "It's the only home I have now."

Jane began opening Meg's cabinets in search of wineglasses, as if it were perfectly normal for her to be rifling through the kitchen in a home she'd never been to. She didn't care. The only way the three of them were going to get back to a place where they could be in the same room without it being weird was to pretend that it wasn't weird for them to be in the same room. So she found no sensible reason whatsoever why she shouldn't make herself feel right at home, and in her home, she drank wine.

She found dusty wineglasses in a small cupboard above the sink, difficult for her to reach, and she was a few inches taller than Meg. Clearly Meg wasn't drinking her problems away. Jane opened the freezer to retrieve ice cubes to help chill down the wine and discovered countless loaves of bread, all of them meticulously wrapped and labeled, stacked on top of one another in the freezer like little tinfoil bricks. The sight of the carbohydrate carnival made Jane feel better about herself: Meg might not use wine as a crutch, but she, too, was seeking comfort in consumable items, and Jane liked discovering that they still had things in common.

It was a start.

seventeen

They'd enjoyed a simple dinner of grilled fish and salad and did their best to only discuss topics that no one really cared about: the weather, music, new movies that were about to hit the theaters. It somehow seemed like a better idea than discussing anything personal. When they'd finished cleaning the dishes, Meg showed them to their rooms; Cara turned left at the top of the stairs and placed her bag in a small but comfortable bedroom with a large bay window and soft yellow walls, while Jane took the guest room next to Meg's at the opposite end of the hall. Jane threw her bag on the floor and ran her hand over the soft cream-colored sheets on the bed. The gauzy linen curtains that hung on the lone window blew softly in the breeze. She couldn't remember the last time she'd been anywhere so tranquil, and couldn't wait until she could climb under the duvet and go to sleep.

But first they were all going to head back to the den for a nightcap.

Ten minutes later, Jane took a seat on the couch and sipped her drink. She didn't want to discuss neutral topics anymore, and she figured the best way to break the ice was to pretend that nothing about this evening was strange. "So, what's everyone been up to? Have you guys seen anyone from back home? I'm so out of the loop," she said.

" 'Out of the loop'?" Cara asked, cracking a slight smile. "That's a nice way to put it!"

"I know, but in fairness, I really am out of the loop. Everybody knows what's been going on in my life, but I have no idea what's going on in anyone else's. When you think about it, it hardly seems fair," Jane joked. Making fun of her situation was a tricky thing to do. She didn't want to seem like she wasn't horrified by what her husband had done, but at the same time, she had to be able to laugh at least a little bit.

"It must be hard," Cara said. "Unfortunately I can't help you. I haven't exactly kept in touch with anyone, either. I'm not on Facebook and I missed the ten-year reunion."

"Did anyone go to that?" Meg asked. "I didn't think anyone went to those things. At least, I never had any intention of going. I didn't want to play the 'who has a better life' game with people I haven't seen since the nineties. I like to think I left some of that teenage-girl competitive nonsense in my past."

"I don't think girls ever really outgrow it, do you?" Jane asked.

"Seriously?" Cara asked, surprised to hear Jane actually admit something so silly out loud. "You find yourself competing with other women? At our age?"

Jane sighed. "Sometimes. I feel ridiculous saying it, but it's true. It's basically impossible to keep up with the women I hung out with in the city. It used to drive me crazy."

"What do you mean?" Meg asked.

"I don't know. Sometimes we'd go to lunch at this French place on the Upper East Side, and these women would sit around and order French food, and wear French designers, and talk about their trips to Paris or Saint-Tropez. The hysterical part was that none of them could actually speak a lick of French. They're all phonies. But the crazy thing is that I wanted them to accept me so badly that I set about building a life that was full of material things, but completely empty, just so that they'd think I was one of them. In retrospect I can't believe I cared about what they thought, but at the time, yeah, I felt like I was constantly struggling to keep up with them. For the record, it's exhausting."

"That's how you know you never really belonged in that world," Cara said. "You just need to take some time and reflect on what's really important to you. Once you do that I think things will start to fall into place again."

"The only things that have been important to me for the last few years are my age, my weight, and the number of calories in a glass of sauvignon blanc."

"You probably should add your checking account balance to that list now, too," Meg suggested.

"Good point. It's all pretty ironic, since I've never been good at math and yet numbers now seem to define me."

"Your real friends would love you for who you are. The sad thing is, these new friends you made never even got to know the real you," Cara said.

"Why do you say that?" Jane asked.

"The Jane I knew would never have spent her free time focused on all this silly stuff. The old you would've thought they were annoying. She was pretty great, you know. At least, from what I remember," Cara said. "You used to care about real things. Sure, you always wanted to be a star, but you were never shallow. You were just . . . ambitious. There's nothing wrong with that."

"Thanks, Cara," Jane said, genuinely touched. "It means a lot to hear you say that." Jane had been worried that there was an epic argument brewing under the polite conversation, but maybe she'd been wrong. Maybe everyone was ready to let the past stay in the past and start again.

"That said, pretending to be stupid has kind of been your modus operandi for as long as I can remember, and I guess it finally caught up with you."

Or maybe not.

"What's that supposed to mean?" Jane asked. "I'm not stupid. Why would you say that?"

"I didn't say you *were* stupid. I said you've been *pretending* to be stupid."

"Cara, that's not a nice thing to say," Meg protested, in a half-hearted attempt to defend Jane.

"Come on, Jane. You just said you knew those women were a bunch of fakes. How could you not have known that Doug was, too? You chose to ignore the signs. That's all. You're like one of those women who knows that something's wrong with her body but won't go to the doctor because she's afraid to hear the diagnosis. It was easier for you to just ignore the warning signs, so that's what you decided to do. That's all I'm saying. I'm sure a lot of people do the same thing."

"Thank you for sharing your opinions, Cara. I would take them to heart a little if you weren't living in the biggest glass house I've ever seen." Jane knew she was going to have to answer for her behavior, but she'd hoped to delay that for as long as possible. Apparently, as long as possible meant right now.

"I don't even know what that means. I never did anything to you. You're the one who just woke up one day and decided to abandon your oldest friends. Don't get mad at me for bringing it up."

"You know what? I'm really tired of you telling me that I abandoned you. You two always had your own thing going. You made me feel like the third wheel every time I was around you. Do you know that when I found out that you asked Meg to be your maid of honor and only made me a bridesmaid I cried for hours? Do you have any idea how that made me feel? It was always Cara and Meg with Jane on the side. And you know what? I got tired of it. And now you want to be mad at me for pulling away? You pushed me away, Cara. So why don't you take some ownership for your role in this?"

Cara's eyes bulged in their sockets, and Jane remembered why the kids at school used to call her Bug Face behind her back. It was really unfortunate she hadn't grown out of that. "Wow. I always knew that you lived in a world where you never did anything wrong and were always the victim. How could you possibly expect me to make you maid of honor when you hated, and I mean, *hated*, the guy I was marrying? You wouldn't even speak to him! That makes it kind of hard to ask you to stand next to me at the altar."

"That's not true! I tried to be a good friend to you. I tried to be happy for you despite the fact that I hated Reed. And, clearly, I had every reason to! You seem to be forgetting the fact that my instincts were totally right!"

"You sent me a card right after I got engaged that said 'I'm happy you're finally happy.' What the hell was that even supposed to mean?"

"It wasn't supposed to mean anything! I sent you a card! How is that a sign of my not being happy for you? What did you want me to do? Hire a twelve-piece band to play on your doorstep? See, this is the type of stupid stuff I wanted to avoid by eloping. There's so much pressure on women and their weddings, it makes everyone crazy. I wasn't being passive-aggressive. The better question is, why were you trying to find problems with everything I did?"

"And at the shower, when people gave speeches, did you or did you not sit there and roll your eyes when everyone spoke? You made it clear you didn't agree with anything people were saying. I was sitting next to you. Did you honestly think I couldn't see you?"

"I thought the speeches were stupid. Why did we all need to sit around and talk about how wonderful you are just because you were getting married? It's redundant. The people at that shower were supposed to be your close friends and family. Of course we thought you were wonderful. We wouldn't have been there if we didn't. Forgive me if by the fifth speech I was a little tired of hearing about what a good person you are and what a great wife you were going to make. I was over it. I don't apologize for that, either. Besides, I gave you a *very* nice shower gift. And you never wrote me a thank-you note, by the way. If I'd done that to you, you probably would've taken it as a sign that I didn't like your gift or something and been offended by that! There's no winning with you sometimes."

"And did you or did you not say that you thought I looked fat in my wedding dress? How can you possibly call yourself a friend and then say something like that?"

"How do you even know that I . . . ?" Jane asked as she flashed back to the events surrounding Cara's wedding. She could not believe that she was being forced to defend things that she may or may not have said more than a decade ago. Jane had commented on the dress after Cara had sent her a picture of it, but only to one person, and only in confidence. She should've known that Meg would tell Cara.

"I never said that! All I said was that your hips were your problem area, and I was surprised you were going with a mermaid gown. I simply thought you'd have looked better if you had worn something that flared at the waist. And I would've told you that to your face if you had ever bothered to ask me to go dress shopping with you. But you never did. All I had to go by were the pictures you showed me."

"I went with my mother! Don't make it sound like I was running around Manhattan with an entourage looking at dresses and left you out. And how is that a defense to what you said about me? Is that why you couldn't bother to stay for the entire wedding? Because I didn't ask you to go shopping?"

"Why did you tell her that, Meg?" Jane asked, angry at herself for being surprised to discover that Meg had broken her trust. "To hurt her feelings or to make her mad at me? I'd like to know exactly why you decided to betray me like that."

"You're mad at *me* now?" Meg yelled. Her voice was high-pitched and whiny. Jane had forgotten how annoying it could be. "You were the one backstabbing her at every turn and you expected me to just keep my mouth shut? Honestly, Jane, I was so disgusted by the way you were acting that I thought Cara should know. If you said those things, then own up to them. Admit it and stop blaming other people for the things that you said and did."

"Are you happy now? Was this what you wanted? For Cara to resent me? Well, congrats. But don't either of you sit there and tell me how upset you were when I decided to pull away from you. This is exactly the reason why I did. I was so fucking sick of always feeling like you didn't want me around but I was grand-fathered in so you didn't have a choice. And you know what, Cara? I wanted to be happy for you, I really did. I tried, even though I thought then, and I still think now, that your husband is a loser. So yeah, I left early because I couldn't stand pretending for one more second to be pumped that you attached yourself to an asshole. I was the only one willing to at least be honest. Besides, it's not like you ever made any effort after that. All I heard from you after you got back from your honeymoon was a Christmas card with a preprinted note on it. You didn't even sign it. Did you ever think about how that made me feel? That maybe I was hurting, too?"

"You can't say you're sorry, can you?" Cara asked. "All these years later and you're still making excuses for everything you did. And now that all the bad decisions you've made over the years have caught up with you, you're playing the poor-me song you've played your whole life, and the reality is, you're complicit in what happened to you. You are no one's victim."

Jane's breath caught in her throat. She had been prepared for some painfully honest arguing, but she was not prepared for this. "You want to know what a good friend is, Cara? Someone who is willing to fight for you. When I pulled away, you didn't even bother to come after me. You never tried to fix the rift between us. You just let it go, like our friendship meant nothing. Like I meant nothing."

"I e-mailed you. You never wrote me back. Your version of revisionist history won't work on me. I was there. Remember? I know exactly what happened."

"And if I'd known that that was all it took for you to just give up on me, I would've cut our ties long before I did. You guys always thought you were better than me. Always."

"That's not true," Meg said. Jane couldn't even look at her, knowing that she'd betrayed her confidence. She wasn't sure why she was surprised. One thing she'd learned since leaving for college was that most girls were bitches, and the idea of a real friendship existing among any of them anywhere was utterly ridiculous. Maybe it was better that she didn't have any friends anymore.

"Oh, really? You guys don't think I know that you looked down on me all those years I was trying to get acting jobs? That you thought I was being silly, and vain, and unrealistic? You never thought I was as smart as you. You never thought I would amount to anything. Once you guys got married you looked down on me because I was still single and you thought I was pathetic. I know you did."

"I never said that. Not once," Meg said.

"You didn't have to. You never said otherwise, either."

"Still waiting on that apology," Cara said.

"What do you want me to say? Okay, Cara. I'm sorry. I'm sorry that I said you'd have looked better in a different style dress. Shoot me for disagreeing with your fashion sense. But you owe me an apology, too."

"For what? I didn't do anything!"

"There was a time when we did everything together. Not a single day went by where we didn't talk multiple times a day, and then all of a sudden, you were too busy for me. You don't think you owe me an apology for that?"

"It's called growing up, Jane. Grown women don't sit around and gossip all day on e-mail. I'm sorry that I got married and had a husband, and a life, and a job to tend to, and that I didn't have time to listen to you debate the merits of liquid over pencil eyeliner for hours on end. Your problem was that you never wanted to grow into an adult, and you didn't want anyone else to, either. You never loved anyone as much as you loved yourself. I'm sorry, I'm not sorry."

"That's absurd! I loved you enough to get you out of that fucking house when I saw how you were being treated. I loved you enough to tell you that I knew it was a terrible idea before it happened, and you turned it around and made me out to be a jealous, petty person. This bitch was the one who convinced Meg to come look for you after you took off. You're right. I'm the worst friend in the world."

"You were probably just worried about how you were going to get home."

"I would've found a way. Or I would've just stayed here."

"No, you wouldn't have," Meg said. Jane realized that she had been very selective about when she spoke up during this entire argument. Cara had always been Meg's mouthpiece, fighting her battles for her whenever things got tough and poor little Meg couldn't muster the energy to defend herself.

"Gee, thanks," Jane said, growing so tired of this argument.

"What do you guys want from me?" Meg asked, tears welling in her eyes. "I didn't ask for either of you to come here. I didn't ask for you to start fighting with each other, and I didn't ask either of you for help. I don't want it, and I don't need it."

"Steve seems to think differently," Jane said.

The mention of her husband made Meg stand perfectly straight. "Don't you dare say a word about Steve. You have no idea what's going on with us."

"Whatever," Jane said. "I don't care what's going on with you guys anymore. You want to blow up your marriage, go right ahead. Hey, maybe that will be the one thing the three of us still have in common. Maybe we can all use the same divorce lawyer, and get a group rate or something."

"Screw you, Jane," Cara said.

"Screw me? Screw you! I should have left you to deal with your abusive husband and your fucking guest bedroom and your fucking grocery receipts!" Before Jane knew what she was doing, she picked up her wineglass and whipped it at the fireplace. It exploded as it hit the mantel. What was left of her wine (which thankfully was white, so at least she didn't ruin the furniture) sprayed anything in reach with a grapey mist. Jane was stunned, not expecting her own reaction.

"I want you both to leave," Meg said. Jane looked at Cara, who seemed equally surprised. They'd all had some wine. Forcing them to drive home drunk in the dark didn't seem like the responsible thing to do, regardless of how much they may have hated each other at the moment.

"Now?" Cara asked. Jane could tell she was trying to count the glasses of wine she'd had since before dinner to see if she was in any way fit to drive. Cara wouldn't get behind the wheel after a single drink, never mind three, so Jane knew she wasn't going anywhere.

"Tomorrow morning. I don't care where you go, I don't care what you do, and it hurts me to say that. It hurts even more to know that I mean it. We aren't the same people we used to be, and we never will be. The people we are now have no business hanging out with each other. This is my home and you're not welcome here. So I will say this once, and only once. I want you both to go to bed, and in the morning, I want you to get the hell out of my house," Meg said.

She turned and went upstairs, slamming a door behind her. Ten seconds later, Cara stomped upstairs after her, and Jane heard another door slam. Jane wasn't finished drinking yet, but she went into the bathroom on the main floor and slammed the door behind her so hard that one of the sailboat pictures on the wall fell off and the glass shattered on the floor. Jane slinked down the wall, pulled her knees to her chest, and once again started to cry.

eighteen

Two hours later Meg still couldn't sleep. She was angry, and hurt, and tormented by the blowup earlier, but now something else was keeping her awake: the sound of bottles rattling downstairs. She got out of bed and tied her cashmere robe around her waist, then descended the stairs, oddly hoping that she was being robbed and that the source of the clamor wasn't what she thought it was. When she reached the bottom of the stairs, she found Jane sitting under a blanket on the couch, a glass in her hand so full of wine she could have drowned in it. Meg was still angry, and was planning on yelling at Jane to go back to bed, but the look in her eyes made her stop. Slowly, pity began to creep in and replace some of the anger. She sat down on the floor at the foot of the couch and watched her friend stare blankly at the LIVE A GOOD LIFE sign hanging on her wall.

"Why aren't you sleeping?" Meg asked. "It's almost one o'clock in the morning."

"There was a time when one o'clock was early."

"That was a long time ago. Now if I see the ten o'clock news it's a late night."

"I guess we're getting old. I'm sorry about your wineglass. I shouldn't have done that," Jane said, tipsy and groggy and so clearly lost.

"It doesn't matter, Jane. Just go to bed."

"I tried, but I can't sleep. I'm too busy thinking about how much I suck at life." Jane held her wineglass to her face and peered through the pale yellow liquid at the fire on the other side. "I made a new fire. I hope that's okay."

"It's fine," Meg said, though she was less than thrilled at the thought of a drunk Jane literally playing with fire in her house.

"This looks so weird. I feel like I'm tripping."

"You don't suck at life," Meg said. Jane glanced over at her quickly, then decided to stare at the ceiling instead. "You just fell in love for the wrong reasons. You loved him for his money, and that's why you're in this mess."

"I didn't just love him for his money. I loved him for his willingness to spend it on me. It's not the same. That's the thing, though. I thought it was *his* money. I didn't know I was hurting anyone. You believe me, right? I'd never steal from people. But I should've known something was wrong, and I didn't. I lived my entire adult life at two extremes. I spent most of it chasing the life I *thought* I wanted. Then once I got it, I spent all my time trying to figure out how to live in it and not lose my mind. I didn't realize that I didn't love him. I thought, 'Well, Jane, you're not sixteen anymore, love isn't necessarily what you thought it was. Just because you don't hear "Dream Weaver" in your head every time he walks in the room doesn't mean you don't love him.' Do you believe that? I'm such a moron."

"You're not a moron. And I repeat, you don't suck at life."

"Who sucks at life?" a voice asked from behind Meg. It shouldn't have surprised her that Cara couldn't sleep, either. Meg was suddenly reminded of the slumber parties they used to have in junior high. She wondered how those little girls would feel knowing that the future versions of themselves would be reduced to strangers who had no problem tearing each other to shreds and then locking themselves in separate rooms, cursing each other in the silence.

Cara sat on the floor and crossed her legs under her. "You guys couldn't sleep either, huh?"

"I was trying. But Keith Richards over here felt like having a nightcap," Meg said. "Now I'm trying to convince her she doesn't suck at life in the middle of the night, and honestly I am too old for all of this." She turned her attention back to Jane, her wineglass empty already. How Jane managed to drink so much and still stay coherent was beyond her. If Meg had more than two glasses in the course of one night she felt unsteady on her feet and unable to control her chaotic emotions. It was one of the reasons she didn't drink a lot anymore. "Anyway, can we please go back to bed now?" she asked. A yawn began to rise up in her throat, escaping her mouth like a growl.

"I'm a horrible person. I am, and it's okay to say it," Jane said, her eyes heavy with fatigue and alcohol. "The tabloids have all basically said it. My neighbors say it. My former *friends* think it. The coffee chick in Amagansett thinks it; I could tell by the way she was looking at me. She didn't even offer me a napkin when the tea spilled all over me. Did you notice that? She probably wanted me to burn. She was probably chanting 'Burn, bitch, burn' in her head, because she thought that that's what I deserved. You guys don't need to feel bad saying it to my face. My husband stole from pension funds and retirement funds that good, honest people had worked their whole lives to build. He stole from them, and unapologetically spent their money on frivolous things that nobody needs—like these boobs. I was too damn stupid to put the puzzle pieces together. I suck at life bad."

"I suck at life more," Cara said.

"No, you don't. Why is everything always a competition with you?" Jane asked. "You can't even let me be the worst at something."

"I'm just saying I'm no better than you are. Neither one of us picked the right guy. Neither one of us listened to ourselves when we knew something wasn't right. Now we're both hiding out in Meg's house and she doesn't like either of us. If you suck at life, then so do I."

"That's not true," Meg said. "I like you guys."

"No, you love us. You don't like us. It's not the same thing," Jane replied. "It's okay. I know, I deserve it. I've been a shitty friend to you guys. Did you hear that, Cara? That would be the sound of me apologizing."

"Yes, I heard you. And I forgive you," Cara said.

"Do you really? Do you mean that?" Jane asked. "Or are you just trying to placate me because I'm smashed and you want me to go to sleep?"

"I do. And I'm sorry that I said such nasty things to you. I guess I still harbor a lot of anger over losing you as a friend. I had to let the anger out before I could deal with any of my other emotions. I regretted the words as soon as I said them."

"It's okay. I've been thinking a lot lately about what happened between us," Jane said, the alcohol making her more honest than she'd ever have been without it. "I think it's time I come clean about a few things. If I'd done it years ago, maybe we'd all have very different lives."

"We don't need to get into it all again now," Cara said. "It's late."

"No, I want to. I want to tell you guys something. I really have thought a lot about why I felt the way I did and when it all started, and as much as I hate to admit it, I think a lot of it began around the time that Meg got married."

"What?" Meg said. "What did my getting married have to do

with anything? I had a wonderful time at my wedding. I thought you did, too."

"I did. I swear, I really did. But still, it was hard for me, too. I'm not proud to admit that."

"Hard how?" Cara asked.

"I think that after Meg's wedding I kind of started to gradually withdraw. I was foundering in the city by myself. I didn't have a boyfriend, or a job, or the grand life I'd imagined when we were younger, and I stupidly believed that I was going to make something of myself. I was barely getting by, and it was kind of hard to watch you pass by me in life, with a great guy and everything you'd ever wanted laid in front of you, while I struggled to hold myself together. I wasn't strong enough, I guess. When Cara got engaged it made everything worse. It sucked. It sucked really bad."

"I never knew you felt that way," Meg said. "I never felt like you were the third wheel. I wish you'd have said something to me. We could've talked about it."

"I know. It's a hard thing to talk about. Especially when you're in your twenties and an insecure mess. I guess I didn't have the guts to talk about it, and I didn't want you to know that I was actually lonely."

"I knew you were lonely," Cara said. "We were young, and there were millions of other single people running around the city. We weren't racing each other. It wasn't a contest."

"That's where you're wrong, though. It *was* a contest. In my mind, at least. It's hard responding to wedding invitations without a date. It's hard being at a couples dinner and having the reservation be for five people instead of six. I feel silly saying it, but it is. I felt like there was something wrong with me because you guys were able to find people who loved you and I couldn't. You were checking all the items off life's to-do list without me: Get engaged, check. Get married, check. Leave the city and buy houses on Long Island, check. You guys were off in a whole new world that I couldn't be a part of, and I felt like I was stuck and going nowhere."

"You took it personally?" Meg asked. "I guess I never thought about it that way. I was never alone after college. I never had to deal with that kind of pressure. It never occurred to me."

"Exactly."

"It doesn't mean I wouldn't have understood if you told me how you were feeling. The funny thing is, I understand it now. How's that for ironic."

"You're married. And approaching forty. How could you possibly understand it now?"

"Just because we're older doesn't mean those things go away. New Year's Eve never used to bother me. Now I swear to God I want to go to sleep on the thirtieth of December and wake up on January second. It's torture not having someone to kiss at midnight or go to a party with. Starting off the year like a walking advertisement for loneliness isn't uplifting. I certainly don't think it's cause for celebration. This year I'm staying home alone."

"Oh my God, exactly. That's exactly it. That's how I felt for the better part of a decade. Every holiday, every event—anytime something came in the mail with a response card. Every time you guys wanted to go to dinner or told me that the four of you were going to a movie or something. I felt like I was being punched every time. The happier you guys seemed in your marriages, the worse I felt about myself. I should've seen a shrink, but I didn't have the self-awareness at the time to realize I needed one."

"Or the money to pay for one," Cara added. She reached over and gently squeezed Jane's foot. The familiar gesture made Meg smile.

"Good point. Instead I decided to deal with it by pretending that I was too busy being fabulous to keep in touch, and fading away. Pretty stupid, huh?"

"Yeah. Pretty stupid," Meg said. "But even dumber that I didn't think of that. I probably would've seen it if I'd stopped focusing on Steve and my marriage for two minutes and devoted any time to thinking about how you felt. I'm sorry I didn't try to understand where you were coming from. I'm sorry I ignored you. I didn't mean to."

"Better you just ignored her than accused her of being jealous of you," Cara admitted.

"I was jealous, though. There, I said it out loud. I hate myself." Jane said.

"Don't say that," Meg said. "Stop beating yourself up over everything."

"You know, I thought I'd feel better getting the truth off my chest after all of these years, but saying it out loud hurt more than I expected. My self-loathing right now is epic."

"Why is it so hard to talk about things like this?" Cara asked. "The pressure we women put on ourselves and each other to have everything together at all times is ridiculous. No one wants to admit when things go badly. Seriously, look at the three of us. We're all imploding and doing it silently. Until now, none of us has confided in *anyone*. We are making the same mistakes all over again. Why couldn't I tell anyone that my marriage was a disaster? Why do I continue to smile and show up at dinners and parties and pretend like I'm happy to be there? I feel like I don't want to admit to anyone that I'm not good at it. Like being 'good' at marriage is a skill you can improve."

"It's not. Not if it's broken to begin with. Some things can't be fixed," Meg replied.

"I don't want anyone to know my life is broken," Cara said, the sadness in her voice so hard for Meg to hear.

"I know the feeling," Meg said.

"Yeah, well, your broken lives aren't on the news. So you can feel good about that. And for once, I win! All of our marriages might be in disarray, but no one has it worse than me. Finally, I'm in first place. I thought it would feel different," Jane joked, trying to add some levity to the conversation.

"If we had each other to talk to this entire time, maybe we would've made different decisions. Keeping everything quiet didn't do us any favors," Cara said. "I wish I'd have reached out to you guys."

"You can't think about things like that," Meg said.

"What do you think about, then? When you look back on the choices you made that led you here?" Jane asked.

"I guess the best any of us can do is to make the decisions that make you happy when things are good so that you have nice memories to fall back on when times get hard. I think that's the end game for everyone," Meg said. "I have some really great memories. They help. Not enough, but a little."

"Are you happy being away from Steve and hunkered down in this admittedly adorable beach house alone? Is this the decision that makes you happy?" Jane asked.

Meg pushed herself up off the floor and teetered over to the small leather bar cart she had parked in the corner. The bar cart had been her grandfather's, and her father's after that. Now it belonged to her. She traced the soft edge of the leather before she grabbed the wine bottle and filled her glass. She wondered how many of her ancestors had drunk away their problems with the help of this bar.

"Of course not. But it's for the best," Meg said, hoping that they believed her, but knowing them both better.

"Why don't you let him decide what's best? He's a big boy. Do you really think you should be making those decisions for him?" Jane asked.

"She's right," Cara answered. "You got one of the good ones. You shouldn't give him away just because you won't be able to have children. You can adopt. There are other ways. I'm sure it's been awful and I'm not trying to downplay it at all, but leaving him isn't the answer."

Meg eyed the black lacquered box on top of her bookshelf. She hesitated before removing it and carrying it over to the coffee table in the middle of the room. She crossed her legs under her and placed the box on the table. It had been so long since she'd opened it. She couldn't for the life of her understand why she felt the need to show them, but she didn't fight it. She was tired of fighting.

"What's in the box?" Cara asked.

"Is there a bowl or some rolling papers in there? Do you smoke pot?" Jane asked.

"What are you, fifteen?" Meg said.

"Oh please. Like you haven't smoked since high school," Jane said.

"I haven't!" Meg said. "I didn't smoke pot *in* high school."

"Well, that's an entirely different issue we should probably address," Jane said.

"Jane, I've got news for you: most grown women don't sit around in their apartments smoking weed by themselves."

"Who said I was alone? Sometimes I invite the maintenance man over, too."

"Sometimes I feel like you haven't changed a bit, and sometimes I feel like I don't know you at all," Cara said.

"I am a paradox, aren't I?"

"What's in the box, Meg?" Cara asked again. Her voice was timid—their cease-fire was tenuous and she knew it.

"Is it a Ouija board? Because I swore off those after it told me I was going to die at twenty-five. It completely screwed me up for a while," Jane said, remembering that awful slumber party and pretending to shiver.

"They're letters, actually," Meg said. She rubbed the top of the box gently, like she was petting a kitten.

"What kind of letters?" Jane asked. "The only letters I've gotten are hate mail telling me how I deserve to die. I found it's not good for my self-esteem to keep them around. Throws off my inner chi."

"They're letters from Steve. He sends me one a week. I haven't written back, but I keep them. It makes me feel close to him just knowing they're around. Don't laugh at me."

"You mean to tell me that you have an entire box full of love letters?" Jane asked. She was incredulous, as if Meg had just told them she had a million dollars in cash stashed under the couch cushions in the living room. "Listen, Meg, I realize that I'm in no position to tell you what to do with your life, but if you've got a guy who actually writes you love letters, you'd be a complete idiot to throw that away. I didn't know Steve was a romantic. I just thought he was a sap."

"He's not a sap. He's old-fashioned in that way. He used to say how no one ever writes love letters anymore and how everything is so impersonal. He hated how the kids in his classes thought that an appropriate sign-off to an e-mail was 'TTYL.' He doesn't think that anyone really knows how to communicate with one another anymore."

"That's for sure," Jane said. "My husband's idea of communicating with me these days is a monitored two-minute phone call asking for a conjugal visit. I don't go, in case you're wondering."

"Sometimes, when it's late and quiet and I feel lonely, I take them out and read them. They're not as good as being with him, but it makes me feel like he's still part of my life, like we still have something special. It isn't fair, what happened to us."

"What do you mean by 'fair'?" Cara asked. "Fair has nothing to do with life. I think we all should've learned that by now."

"It isn't fair that there are women out there who have no problem staying pregnant and take it for granted. I used to see women eating fast food on the train while they were nine months pregnant and toting toddlers on their hips and it used to make me so angry I couldn't even see. I had to stop reading magazines because every one I picked up had some story about a celebrity who was pregnant at like forty-seven years old, or a story about how someone else got her body back two weeks after having twins, or how some celebutante whose idea of a meaningful life is discovering a new way to prevent her lip gloss from wearing off on her martini glass accidentally got knocked up and how her life was changed. It's not fair. It's not fair that they don't seem to even care that they're pregnant. I did everything right, and God wouldn't let me keep any of mine. I know I sound silly and bitter, but I just can't understand it. How is it fair, huh? Tell me."

"It's not," Jane said. "It's not even remotely fair."

"No, it's not," Cara echoed. She stared at the floor.

"And you wonder why I had a hard time staying friends with you when I found out that you just opted out," Meg said, finally addressing the elephant between her and Cara. "You didn't even realize the gift you had, or you didn't care. I don't know which, and at this point it doesn't matter. You basically decided you didn't want to be pregnant anymore, and just like that, you weren't. How am I supposed to forgive you for that? I'm sorry, but to me it just seemed so selfish."

"Wait . . . what are we talking about?" Jane asked. "I'm confused."

"Cara's abortion," Meg said flatly.

"Whoa. I need more wine. And weed, if you have it. Are you sure there's no weed in this house?" Jane asked. She stared at Cara and at Meg, neither one of them willing to look at the other.

"I told you it was complicated," Cara said.

"I can't believe I didn't know," Meg muttered. "How could you not tell me?"

"I never wanted you to know. Do you think I felt good about it? That it was an easy decision? It wasn't. The entire thing was excruciating. I couldn't possibly have a child with Reed. I wasn't strong enough to handle it. I've second-guessed that decision every day since. And I probably will for the rest of my life, but there's nothing I can do about it. I may not forgive myself for that, but I don't think that I need to answer to you. I don't mean that to be harsh, but it's just the truth."

"I had no idea, Cara. When?" Jane asked.

"Three years ago."

"I'm really sorry. For both of you," Jane said. "Wow."

"What was it you said, Meg?" Cara asked. "Make decisions that make you happy, so that you have good memories to fall back on? If I had made a different decision, I wouldn't have the option to leave. I'd be tied to him for the rest of my life. You didn't know what I was dealing with, and you never bothered to ask. You just disappeared from my life. You didn't answer my calls, my e-mails, nothing. You abandoned me. And the truth is, I needed a friend then more than ever. I'd always been there for you. And when I needed you, you walked out on me."

Meg was silent. "I didn't walk out on you. I walked away from everything. I'm sorry, but I just wasn't able to see your side of things. To be honest, I'm still having a hard time with it. I know it seems selfish, but it's complicated for me, too. I thought about calling you, but what was I supposed to say? It was too hard to talk to you. I wasn't able to untangle everything."

"You could've tried. I should've meant enough to you that you'd at least try."

"I know that. I'm not proud of myself, but somehow it just seemed easier to be alone. I'm sorry, Cara. I never meant to hurt you."

"Well, you did."

"I'm sorry."

"If you had called and said that years ago, we could've moved on from our argument and been there to help each other. There was no reason for both of us to be alone all this time."

"I know. Do you forgive me?"

"Yeah, I do. Still, what are we supposed to do now? Group hug and pretend that none of this ever happened? I don't think we can just rewind time and start over like nothing ever happened," Cara said.

"I disagree," Jane said. "Women can totally do that because we are just better at accepting our own shortcomings and asking for forgiveness. None of us are free from blame, but that doesn't mean that we can't forgive each other. I don't want to lose another ten years with you guys."

"I don't know how," Cara said. "I don't know how to start over."

"I do," Jane said. She hopped off the couch and grabbed the last bottle of wine from the bar cart. She opened it and returned to her seat, filling each glass with a healthy slug of white. "Let's toast."

"To what? How much we all suck at life?" Cara asked.

"No—to friendships that are worth more than any argument. And to women who may be in pretty fucked-up predicaments at the moment, but who nonetheless are trying to pull themselves together. I think it's time we start over without having to pretend. I'd like you both to know that I am a complete mess. I'm totally and completely fucked up."

"So I heard," Cara said.

"I read that in a magazine, actually," Meg added.

"Good. All cards on the table. What do you guys say?" Jane asked.

Meg and Cara stayed silent, each of them waiting for some sign from the other that sins would be forgiven. Finally, Cara spoke. "I'd like that," she said.

"Okay," Meg said. "Maybe you're right. I guess it's time we leave the past in the past."

They clinked their glasses together and took a sip, and then sat in silence for a minute.

"Am I the only one who'd like to see some of these letters?" Cara asked, reaching for the box.

"I'd love to. I always liked Steve. It makes me happy to know that he at least is as good as he seemed," Jane added.

"Yeah," Meg said quietly. "He really is." She removed a letter from the box and without hesitation began to read.

nineteen

Meg woke early in the morning despite barely sleeping and slipped down into the kitchen to make muffins for breakfast. It felt strange having houseguests, but so good to have a reason to get out of bed on a Saturday morning. She scooped coffee out of the bag and poured the grinds into the large old-fashioned coffeepot she kept stored in the hall closet but hadn't used in years. She removed the canisters of flour and sugar from the cabinet and began measuring ingredients for muffins. Soon the smell of coffee began to waft through the house, and as she expected, Jane appeared in the kitchen in search of a cure for her hangover.

"That is the biggest coffeepot I've ever seen in my life," Jane said. She grabbed a mug from the kitchen cabinet and stood in front of the percolator, inhaling the aroma.

"It comes in handy when you have houseguests. I haven't used it in a while," Meg admitted.

"And you're making muffins now? If I had your job, I'd weigh two hundred pounds. How do you stay so thin?"

"I don't know. I give a lot of this stuff away, or stash it in the freezer. Anyway, I wouldn't worry about the calories. When was the last time someone made you breakfast?"

"I can't remember." Jane reached over and squeezed her shoulder. "I can't remember the last time I breathed this much fresh air."

"That's sad."

"Lots of things in my life are sad. That said, I'm really happy we're here. Thanks again for letting us stay. I don't know where we would have gone without you."

"It's nothing. Really."

"What's nothing?" Cara asked. She appeared in the doorway in her pajamas looking well rested and much more relaxed than she had seemed when she'd arrived the day before. Meg wasn't surprised. Ocean air had a way of sucking the stress out of you without your even knowing it. It was one of the things she loved most about the beach. Meg pulled another coffee mug from the cabinet and filled it, then handed it to Cara.

"So you made us breakfast, too? You didn't have to do that," she said. She took a long sip from her mug. "God, this tastes good."

"Don't look a gift muffin in the mouth," Jane joked.

"Are you helping?" Cara playfully asked Jane. "Because if you're involved in the making of these muffins, I think I'll go to town and get bagels."

"Hey! I think maybe you forgot what happened the last time you made a comment like that."

"You wouldn't dare," Cara challenged.

"Oh my God. No. I just cleaned in here!" Meg said.

"Wouldn't I?" Jane asked, a glint that had disappeared a long time ago returning to her eye. She plunged her hand into the canister of flour. "Admit those brownies were good. Admit it!" she ordered.

"Jane, we aren't kids anymore. We are too old for this kind of stuff!" Cara said.

"Admit it or I swear to God I'll do it. I am nowhere near too old for this stuff and you know it."

"Okay! They were awesome," Cara agreed. "Even if you forgot the marshmallows."

January 1997

"Come on in. She's sleeping on the couch," Cara's mother said when she opened the front door. "It's so sweet of you guys to do this."

"How's she doing?" Jane asked as they stood in the foyer, speaking in hushed voices.

"She's hanging in there. The doctor said it will be six weeks until she can start rehab, and the drugs he gave her are helping with the pain. I think more than anything she's just depressed she's stuck on the couch for a while."

"It's got to be torturous for her," Meg agreed. "Cara can't sit still to save her life."

"I think I'd like it," Jane said, trying to make everyone laugh. "Assuming I had a butler to bring me things and a really big TV."

"I don't think she'd agree with you!" Meg said as she elbowed Jane in the side. "Can we go in? Are you sure you don't mind if I take over your kitchen for a while?" She held up two huge shopping bags.

"Not at all. You girls are really great friends. She's lucky to have you both."

They smiled as they made their way into the kitchen and glanced into the family room at Cara lying on the couch with her leg in a massive brace. "She should sleep for another hour or so, so make yourself at home. I'm sure she'll be thrilled to see you when she wakes up."

Cara's mom went upstairs and left Meg and Jane to unload boxes of butter, a carton of eggs, and bags of flour, sugar, and chocolate chips onto the counter. Meg had packed an entire baker's kit to bring over to Cara's house, complete with wooden spoons, measuring cups, and in true Meg fashion, aprons for them to wear while they tried to bake Cara back to good health. Meg set up mixing bowls while Jane stared at the groceries they now had spread out all over the countertops.

"I don't know how I let you talk me into this. I don't like to cook," Jane said as she held up a box of unsweetened chocolate. "Why is this chocolate unsweetened? Don't we like the kind with sugar in it?"

"This isn't cooking, it's baking," Meg corrected. "And we're going to add our own sugar to sweeten it. That's called baking chocolate."

"The fact that I didn't know that such a chocolate exists should prove to you that I am not the one to help you with this kind of stuff. Are you sure we can't just go buy her a whole bunch of stuff from the bakery?"

"Come on! It's fun. Besides, it's for Cara. Don't you want to help cheer her up? Anyone can buy her something from the store. We're her best friends, so we're going to bake for her. Don't you think that's nicer?"

"You're right. I'm sorry; I think I'm just overwhelmed by all of this stuff. I don't want to mess it up."

"You won't mess anything up. Just do what I tell you to do and it will smell amazing in here in twenty minutes."

"Okay, Betty Crocker. I know better than to question your authority in the kitchen. What can I do to help?"

"I'm going to make her brownies. Where are the marshmallows I told you to bring?"

"Oh, shit," Jane said. "I knew I forgot something!"

"You forgot the marshmallows? You had one job!" Meg cried, as if Jane were supposed to bail her out of jail and forgot to bring her checkbook instead of forgetting to pick up a bag of mini marshmallows.

"I'm sorry! I can go get some now. I'll be back in twenty minutes. You just make the batter. Crisis averted," Jane said, trying to keep calm. This was not a big deal in the slightest.

"Forget it. I'd rather you stay and help in case she wakes up. We'll just make regular brownies. Maybe if I have time we can make some peanut butter cookies, too."

"This is how you say 'sorry you hurt your knee'? Peanut butter cookies and marshmallow-less brownies? I think I'd rather you guys buy me a sweater or something," Jane said.

"Yes. This, and we are going to spend a lot of time at her house watching movies with her until we have to go back to school. She's going to go crazy being forced to stay inactive. We need to help take her mind off it."

"Okay. But if we decide to bake again at some point, can I put in a request for chocolate cupcakes?"

"Deal."

The truth was, Cara didn't just hurt her knee; she ripped two ligaments skiing with her new boyfriend from Bowdoin at his family's house in Vermont over Christmas break and needed surgery. She had to wear a huge leg brace and was going to be laid up for a while, which would've been bad for anyone. For someone who couldn't go more than two days without doing some kind of activity it was excruciating both physically and mentally.

"I feel so bad for her," Meg said. "I mean, she's going to be in a lot of pain for a while. I wish there was something more we could do for her, but making her baked goods is kind of all I can think of."

"What exactly happened? Cara's an amazing athlete, I can't believe she took such a bad fall."

"I know. I don't really know any of the details. I just hope she's not in too much pain."

"They can give her pills for that. What's really going to upset her is that she embarrassed herself in front of Reed's family, too. I mean, did the ski patrol have to bring her down the mountain? Do you think she cried in front of him?"

"Oh, there's no way she cried in front of him."

"She ripped ligaments. I've seen professional basketball players cry on the court when that happens," Jane said.

"They're not as tough as Cara is," Meg reminded her.

"You're right."

"You guys are very funny. I'd laugh if the painkillers hadn't made me so groggy I can barely see straight," Cara said, propping herself up on the couch. She winced a bit when she tried to shift her weight.

"She's awake!" Meg said.

"Are you going to come in here and talk to me or are you going to make me hobble out there on my crutches?"

"I'm so sorry, Cara. What happened?" Jane asked as they scurried into the den. She leaned over to kiss Cara's cheek while Meg gently tucked a blanket around Cara's legs.

"I'm so mad at myself. I don't know what happened. One minute I was fine and the next minute my edge caught some ice or something and my ski flew out from under me. I'm so embarrassed I could die."

"Why are you embarrassed? Who was with you?" Meg asked.

"No one. Just Reed. But now I look like an unathletic girl who can't keep up with the family activities."

"That's ridiculous. You had an accident. It could happen to anyone," Jane said.

"I don't want him to think I can't keep up."

"He should be worried about keeping up with you. Not the other way around," Meg said.

"Seriously! Since when are you insecure about your athletic abilities? That's absurd."

"I don't know. I just want to impress him." Cara sighed.

"He's already your boyfriend. I think you've already impressed him. Your ego is just a little bruised because the mountain kicked your ass. Don't worry about it!" Jane chirped in an effort to cheer her up.

"You're right. It is. I'm just so mad at myself. We go back to school in two weeks and I'm going to have to spend the entire winter hobbling around on crutches and doing rehab. It's not exactly how I wanted to begin my semester."

"You'll do the rehab and be good as new before you know it. Until we go back to school we will come over every day and hang out with you as much as you want," Meg reassured her. "It'll go fast, you'll see!"

"What are you guys doing in there?"

"Baking. Why don't you come sit in the kitchen? Do you need help with the crutches?"

"No, I can do it. It will feel good to get up off the couch. Even if I only move to a kitchen chair." Cara grabbed the crutches that were lying on the floor next to the couch and Meg and Jane helped her stand up.

"Are you sure you're okay to move?" Meg asked.

"Definitely. I'm allowed to hobble around. I'd rather sit in there with you guys." The two girls flanked Cara as she slowly made her way thirty feet into the kitchen and collapsed in a kitchen chair. Jane dragged over the footstool from the den and helped slowly prop Cara's leg on the cushion. She winced, which for Cara was a pretty clear indication that she was in pain.

"So, what am I getting? Thank you guys so much for doing this. You're the best, by the way."

"Brownies," Meg answered. "And you're welcome. It's our pleasure. I wish we could do something else to help you feel better."

"With marshmallows?" Cara asked. "I love those!"

"Don't say it, Meg!" Jane begged. "Don't do it!"

Meg didn't blink before she answered. "They were supposed to have marshmallows. But Jane forgot to bring them. Even though it was the only thing I asked her to do."

Cara smiled. "It's okay, Jane."

"I offered to go get some now, but Meg said no because she'd rather I stay here and help."

"You want Jane to help? Seriously?" Cara asked, as if assisting in mixing brownie batter were somehow akin to neurosurgery.

"Hey! I resent that."

"No seriously, are you helping?" Cara asked Jane.

"Yes, I am. I've already learned about unsweetened chocolate. You should know that I wouldn't do this for just anyone."

"I know. I really wish that there were marshmallows, though. You know they're my favorite. Oh well," Cara joked. "I'll live."

"Fine. If you don't want me to help, I won't help," Jane said. "I'd much rather keep my clothes clean anyway. Too bad yours are already a mess." Jane dunked her hand in the bag of flour and flung a small amount at Cara, knowing full well that she couldn't get up from her chair.

"Oh my God. You did not just do that. I'm an invalid. You

can't throw flour at me!" Cara said, shocked that Jane would have the audacity to attack her when she was immobile.

"Except, I think I can," Jane said, flinging another handful of flour in her direction. "Oops, I think I got some on your pants now, too."

"I'm going to kill you!" Cara said, cracking a groggy smile.

"I think that's going to be difficult, seeing as you can't move."

"Here!" Meg said as she grabbed the bowl she'd poured flour in and brought it over to Cara. "Use this!"

"You're arming her? Whose side are you on?" Jane asked.

"Every man for himself. And next time I ask you to bring something, you better not forget!"

"Fine, then! This is war!" Jane stuck both her hands in the flour and threw it at Meg, causing white powder to cover the kitchen counters, floors, and appliances. They'd turned Cara's kitchen into the PG version of Scarface.

"What is going on in here?" Cara's mom asked as she stood in the doorway of the kitchen. She stared in bewilderment at her previously clean kitchen and three college-aged women in the midst of a flour fight more appropriate for twelve-year-olds. "I thought you were going to bake brownies!"

"We were. And then . . . we weren't," Jane said, shrugging her shoulders but still smiling.

"I'm so sorry," Meg said, already on her hands and knees trying to clean flour off the floor with a kitchen sponge. All it did was turn the powder to paste. It was going to take forever to get this place clean. "We're so sorry. I promise I will clean the entire kitchen."

"In our defense, this seemed like a good idea a few minutes ago," Jane said with a smile, hoping Cara's mom would appreciate *that while they'd wrecked her house, they'd made her daughter laugh.*

"I hope you know how to work the vacuum as well as you know how to work the oven," she said to Meg, coughing from flour she'd accidentally inhaled.

"Jane started it!" Meg cried, always the obedient rule follower. Meg knew that she didn't need to tell Cara's mom that Jane was the one who spearheaded the destruction of her kitchen. Any time something went wrong, people assumed Jane was the ringleader, which would really bug her if they weren't right.

"Hey!" Jane said, momentarily offended. "Okay, fine. I did, actually. But she deserved it."

"Your mom was so mad," Meg remembered. "We tried to do something nice and I think it took her months to get all the flour out of the grout in her kitchen tiles."

"I think she was happy that I was happy, to be honest. She could never stay mad at you guys anyway. It was nice of you to come help take care of me. It gave her a break, you know?"

"I was happy to do it then, and I'm happy to do it now. And anyway, it's my job to cook. Don't forget that. I'll post this recipe on the blog later this morning."

Cara and Jane smiled but said nothing. Instead, Jane flung flour in Meg's direction.

"For old time's sake," she said.

"I was in a lot of pain but I had a good time," Cara said.

"You were so loopy I'm surprised you remember it."

"I remember the brownies." Cara walked over and stuck her hand in the flour and flicked a little at Jane. "That was for attacking an invalid. I've been waiting almost twenty years to do that."

"I had no idea you were holding a grudge. This explains a lot. It all started with the flour."

Cara smiled. "Maybe it did!"

"Are we even now?" Jane asked, dusting flour off her hairline.

"Even."

"Good."

"Now that I think about it, I was so upset after I hurt my knee. Not just because of the accident, which sucked in a big way, but because I was worried about what Reed would think of me. He was my boyfriend. He should've cared that I was hurt and that's it. Why was I worried about how I would look to his family?"

"I thought it was a little weird at the time," Meg admitted.

"So did I. But I thought it was the drugs talking," Jane added. "Besides, we were kids. We worried about stupid things."

"Yeah, but I already wasn't acting like myself, you know? He was already making me feel insecure."

"Probably because he felt inadequate around you. Not to play psychiatrist, but just guessing."

"I think he was trying to undermine me. He's always trying to undermine me. Still. I wish I'd seen it then."

"You'll drive yourself crazy pinpointing moments where you could've done something differently. They don't matter. What matters is that you did something now. The past is the past, and there's not a person in this room who would do things over the same way if given the option," Jane said forcefully.

"I guess that's true," Cara admitted.

"So, what do you guys want to do today?" Meg asked, the potentially awkward moment thankfully passing. "Besides start a flour fight in my kitchen."

"Well, if you're going to ruin all of our fun, I'm up for doing something outside. It looks really nice out," Jane said. "I rarely get fresh air anymore since I've been afraid to leave my apartment. Do you think we could go for a walk or something?"

"Why don't we go down to the beach? I have a few travel mugs; we can bring our coffee with us," Meg answered.

"I'd like that. I haven't been to the beach in ages," Jane said.

"It hasn't changed much," Meg assured her.

Jane smiled. "The best things in life never do."

twenty

They ate their muffins, filled their travel mugs, and drove the two miles to the beach with the windows down and the radio up. Jane stuck her arm out the window and spread her fingers wide, feeling the wind blow against her hand. In the summer, the parking lot would be full by nine A.M., but since it was October it was completely empty. They rolled up their pant legs, kicked off their shoes, and wandered down the sand toward the water. Meg adjusted her sunglasses and stared at the surfers in their wetsuits—the only people crazy enough to swim this time of year—and an elderly couple holding hands as they strolled toward them. Meg felt her insides begin to ache. She would've bet every dollar she had that would've been her and Steve one day—older, kids grown and out of the house, retired at the beach, just happy to have each other for company. Instead she had two crazy ladies from elementary school using her for shelter as they hid from their own lives. But she'd take it. It was certainly better than nothing.

"God, it's really beautiful out here. Do you come down here a lot, Meg?" Cara asked.

"I do, actually. It's tranquil. I come here when I need time to think," Meg said, meaning she came here daily, even when it was cold or raining. She found there was something therapeutic about having the beach all to herself in bad weather.

"Why do you need to come here for that? You live alone. You can think all day at your house, can't you?" Jane asked, blunt as ever.

"I think she likes the change of scene and the sound of the waves and the fresh air. What's the point of being out here if you can't enjoy it?" Cara countered.

"Exactly," Meg said. "I can't smell the ocean from the house."

They continued to stroll down the beach, the bluffs and the dunes punctuating the vast sky and the sounds of seagulls and crashing waves the only discernible noises for miles. As they walked, Meg caught sight of a man sitting on the sand a hundred yards in front of them reading a newspaper. His baseball hat was pulled low over his eyes, but the large Labrador retriever lying quietly next to him was a sure sign that it was Nick, her only friend in Montauk. She waved as she approached and veered over to where he was sitting.

"Good morning!" Meg said. "How are you?"

"Hey!" he said. He folded his newspaper and tucked it under his backpack. "I thought that was you, but I wasn't sure. You don't usually come down here with an entourage." He stood and brushed his hands against his jeans, causing grains of sand to scatter in every direction. He hugged Meg and planted a quick kiss on her cheek.

"These are old friends of mine," Meg said. "This is Cara and Jane. We grew up together. They came out here yesterday to spend a few days with me. I figured I'd show them why fall is the best time of year out here."

"Nice to meet you, I'm Nick," he said. He shook both their hands, and Jane bent over to pet his dog behind the ears. "You guys grew up together, huh? That's great. I don't know too many people who are still tight with their childhood friends. It's really cool, actually."

Meg smiled, because sometimes it was better to just smile and play along than to tell the actual truth.

"We like to think so," Jane said. She left the dog alone and slyly wiped drool off her hand.

"Do you live out here all year?" Cara asked.

"I do. I'm a Realtor. I have listings mostly in Montauk, but a few in Amagansett also. It's been slow for a while, obviously, but things are picking back up a bit, which is great. My buddy Sebastian and I were getting bored out here with no buyers poking around. Hopefully the market has turned for the long term. Fingers crossed," he said, Sebastian wagging his tail at the mention of his name.

"I'm a Realtor, too," Cara said. "I feel the exact same way. I really love selling a family a new home. It's like I'm able to play a small part in creating a lot of happy memories for them. It's a sappy way of looking at it, I guess."

"I don't think it's sappy at all. Except for when I have spoiled clients who have no grip on reality or what their money can buy them. I'd like to drown those people. Fortunately, I haven't had to deal with too many of them as of late. What do you do, Jane?" he asked.

"Oh, I'm a housewife, I guess," Jane said. It occurred to Meg that no one had probably asked Jane that in forever, and she seemed caught off guard by the question.

"Well, it's nice to meet both of you. Any friend of Meg's is a friend of mine. This girl makes a mean muffin. I hope you enjoy the rest of your time out here."

Suddenly Meg had an idea. This was perfect. She'd been anxious all morning about how the three of them were going to stay at her house for another night without fighting again. Meg didn't want to spend the night screaming at them, or worse, throwing them out of her house a second time. Nick would keep them all on their best behavior, give them neutral territory to talk about, and force them to stay away from painful topics that would erupt into an argument. "Nick, are you busy later?" she asked.

"No, not really. I was going to maybe do some surfing this afternoon, and then head over to the Dock for dinner. I'm a sucker for the clams there."

"Why don't you join us for dinner at my place?"

"Really?" Nick asked.

"Really?" Cara and Jane answered simultaneously.

"Why not?" Meg said. "I was going to go down to the fish market and get something for dinner, and Jane bought some wine . . ."

"Actually, we drank all of it last night."

"And we're going to buy some more wine," Meg corrected herself.

"Sounds good to me," Jane said with a shrug.

"It won't be anything fancy, and you're more than welcome to bring Sebastian, of course. What do you say? We'd like the company."

"Are you sure I won't be intruding?" Nick asked, though Meg could tell he'd love to join them.

"Absolutely not," Cara said. "It'd be nice to get to know you better. Besides, like you said, any friend of Meg's is a friend of ours."

"Great! We'll be there. I'll bring some wine, too, Jane. So don't buy too much."

"No such thing!" Jane replied. She was trying to sound breezy, but Meg thought she sounded more like a raging alcoholic. When she thought about it, and she hadn't until just now, Jane had basically had a glass in her hand since she showed up, and she'd popped two pills with her morning coffee. *Great*, Meg thought. She was probably going to end up dragged into an episode of *D-List Celebrity Rehab* before the week was over.

Every group of kids growing up had a wild child: the one who always pushed the envelope, defied authority, and seemed to be present whenever something went wrong. Jane's parents had tried to control her, but she'd somehow managed to find ways around their rules. She'd throw parties in her basement whenever they were away, change out of her clothes into something short or skin-tight in her backyard before going to parties, and sneak out of her house after her curfew on a regular basis. It was Jane who got Meg to smoke her first (and last) cigarette in ninth grade, Jane who tried to convince her (unsuccessfully, thank God) that she should get a dolphin tattoo on her ankle junior year, and Jane who forged Meg's doctor's notes to get her out of class so they could go shopping when she had a date with a cute senior and wanted a new sweater to wear. Meg's parents had always thought that Jane was a bad influence, that Meg was just a timid mouse following the Pied Piper. They were thankful for Cara, for balancing out the group. Meg never thought this was true, and loved that Jane kept her from being boring and bookish. Now, as an adult, she realized that Jane might not have grown out of that reckless teenage laissez-faire attitude. She was such a wonderful person and had such a big heart, but Jane had always been her own worst enemy. It was becoming more and more evident that she still was.

"Great then, say seven o'clock?" Meg asked.

"See you then! Enjoy the rest of the day, ladies. I'm going to take Sebastian home and grab my board. Looking forward to it! Thanks a lot, Meg."

"It's my pleasure," Meg said with a wave.

Nick called the dog, and they headed toward the parking lot as the girls continued down the beach. Meg breathed a sigh of relief. Running into him had been a fantastic twist of fate. Nick somehow always made her feel at ease.

"He's cute! Too bad none of us are single," Cara joked. "There was a time we would've fought over him."

"I am!" Jane said.

"No. Your husband is incarcerated, but he's still your husband," Cara said.

"Are you seeing him?" Jane asked Meg, which horrified her. How could Jane possibly think she'd be seeing someone behind Steve's back?

"Of course not! Why would you ever ask me that?"

"Don't get offended! I know how much you love Steve, so I figured he must be just a friend, but since I myself have never had a male friend I wasn't interested in sleeping with, I figured I should at least ask."

"We're just friends, that's all."

"Okay, fine. Cara, you should go for him. Maybe a little fling with a nice guy with a cool dog and a great butt is exactly what you need," Jane said.

"I hate to burst both of your bubbles, but he's gay," Meg said with a laugh.

"I should've known," Jane said. "He was too good-looking to be straight. Oh well. Cara, don't worry. We'll find you someone else to have an affair with while we're out here. Maybe we should go hang out at a sports bar or something!"

"I'm not even going to justify that with a response. I still can't even believe I'm here. I'm going to have to call Reed at some point. What if he calls the police and reports me missing?"

"You wrote a note. You aren't missing. You left him. They're not the same thing. And it's only been twenty-four hours. No offense, but I hardly think Reed is going to go into panic mode and call the cops because you didn't come home for dinner one night."

"Still. I know he's freaking out most about what people will think if they find out I left him. He's going to be so pissed off. We're supposed to go to a birthday party next weekend and if I don't go with him he'll have a conniption."

"He's always pissed off! You sleep in separate bedrooms anyway. What's the difference if you're there or not?" Jane asked, as if she was mildly irritated by talking about what else might make Reed angry. "It's a beautiful day at the beach, and we've been enjoying the walk. Let's not talk about him. I'm declaring this beach a Reed-free zone for the duration of our stay out here."

"Wait. You sleep in separate bedrooms?" Meg asked.

"Thanks, Jane," Cara said.

"I think it's time we stop keeping secrets from each other. You're staying at her house. She deserves to know what you're hiding from."

"Yes. I sleep in the guest room."

"How'd he get the master anyway?" Jane asked.

Cara flinched. "He said my name wasn't on the deed to the house, so I'm not the master of anything."

"Oh, give me a break," Meg said.

"He is such an asshole!" Jane yelled. "I didn't think I could hate this guy any more than I already do, but I was wrong. I want to kill him. I swear to God, I think I could."

"It sounds like maybe a few days away isn't the worst idea. Stop worrying about him, and let's worry about you," Meg suggested, trying to calm Cara and ignore Jane's mini meltdown.

"That's good advice. You know, when Doug made me get these new boobs, I didn't really want them. I mean, the old ones weren't anything great, but they were fine. Then I thought, you know how many women in Manhattan would love for their husbands to spring for a little maintenance now and then? Every woman I hung out with had something nipped or tucked or sucked or augmented, so really, what was the big deal? I figured that I should consider myself lucky that we could afford to buy these things. So I went along with it. Now he's gone, and I'm stuck looking like I'm hiding cantaloupes under my sweater. Do you have any idea what that feels like?"

"I can't imagine it's comfortable!" Meg laughed. "Can you sleep on your stomach without worrying that you're going to pop them?"

"Feel them," Jane ordered, pulling her sweater up to expose her overstuffed bra. "You need to see what this is like. They're awful. I can't tell you how much I hate them."

"Jane, put your shirt down! Someone will see you!" Meg squealed, the same way she always had when Jane did something that shocked or embarrassed her.

"Relax! We're at the beach. Pretend it's a bikini top," Jane said.

"You wear purple lace bikini tops?" Meg asked. "Actually, don't answer that. I don't even want to know."

"Come on, just feel them."

"I don't want to feel them," Meg insisted, even though now she kind of did.

"Seriously, I want you to. Feel them or I'm going to take off my sweater. You think it'll hurt or something? You could squeeze them into oblivion and I wouldn't even notice. I have no feeling in these things whatsoever. I'm terrified I'm going to pop one in my sleep and die from silicone poisoning without even knowing it. That's not a good way to live, let me tell you. Or die, now that I think about it." Cara and Meg started to giggle, and then the giggling grew to uninhibited, gasping-for-air laughing. "Fine. Laugh away. If I die in my sleep tonight you guys will feel bad about this. Know that."

Meg reached over and grabbed Jane's right boob, squeezing it hard, but it didn't give at all. Jane wasn't kidding. It was the most unnatural thing she'd ever felt in her life. "Whoa. He actually liked this?" Meg asked, so in awe at the weight of it that she reached out with her other hand and fully felt up Jane for anyone to see.

"Yup. Now do you feel sorry for me?" Jane asked as she pulled her sweater down and folded her arms protectively in front of her. "Just a little?"

Neither Cara nor Meg answered, because they were sitting on the sand laughing. It had been a long time since the two of them had laughed like that, and before long Jane joined in. If there was one thing they could always count on Jane for, it was a laugh.

Dinner would be easy, as dinners at the beach should be. Meg went down to the docks, where the fishermen dropped off their catch daily. She purchased some bass fillets, two dozen clams she'd douse with lemon and bread crumbs and bake in the oven, some local lettuces for salad, a loaf of crusty bread, and berries she planned to macerate in sugar and serve over a pound cake she'd baked and frozen weeks earlier. Twenty minutes in the kitchen and Meg could have the entire dinner ready—plus, she could write an article for her blog about creating easy suppers for last-minute guests. She was happy the girls were there and she could exercise her hostess skills. Maybe it was time she stopped trying to plan everything, and let life take her where it was going to take her. She hated to admit it, but the truth was, she could learn a thing or two from Jane in that regard. Well, sort of.

As Meg made dinner, she thought back to her wedding day. Not the ceremony itself, which she thought about all the time, especially now that she and Steve were separated, but the hours leading up to it. She was sure that she'd obsessed over every single detail of that day, but now she couldn't remember any of that. For some reason, she found herself accessing snippets of her memory that had been tucked away. She'd worn her mother's pearl earrings, and her hair in a bun, and she remembered smiling so broadly for so many hours that her face actually began to ache. Cara and Jane had been co–maids of honor while three friends from college quietly assumed the role of bridesmaids. As per usual, Cara and Jane ran the show. That was exactly how Meg wanted it.

April 2000

"Don't you love the noise these dresses make when we walk?" Jane asked as she and Cara swished around the kitchen in Meg's house, nibbling on wrap sandwiches.

"I know. Is it weird that part of me wishes crinolines would come back in style?" Cara answered. "I feel like a million bucks in this thing."

"If I eat one more bite I'm going to explode. I don't need to eat anything before the ceremony. I don't want to look fat."

"I heard that, Jane!" Meg's mother called as she entered the kitchen in her burgundy suit, a white rose corsage pinned to the lapel. "I won't let you guys have any champagne while we take pictures if you don't eat. The last thing we need today is tipsy bridesmaids!"

"We're the maids of honor, to be exact," Cara corrected her as she took another small bite of her grilled chicken wrap.

"I'm sorry. You're right. The maids of honor, then. Either way, eat the wraps!"

"Meg, aren't you going to eat anything?" Jane asked as she returned to the platter centered on the kitchen table and grabbed a small plastic plate. "There are still plenty left."

"Oh my God, no way. I'm too nervous to eat, and I don't want my lipstick rubbing off on my teeth. I'm not eating or drinking anything until the cocktail hour."

"That's like, four hours from now!" Cara protested. "Are you sure that's a good idea?"

"Nothing is going to ruin this day for me—especially not a smudge on my dress from a vinaigrette. Keep those sandwiches away from me!"

"Fair enough," Jane said. "Point taken."

"You guys really look gorgeous!" Meg said. "I'm so happy you like the dresses." Meg stared at her friends in their matching navy-blue satin dresses and felt like her insides were going to burst. They were so happy for her. She couldn't wait until it was their turn and she could do for them what they'd done for her. She'd make sure they'd feel exactly how she felt right now—like life was perfect.

"They're fabulous," Jane said. "And navy looks good on everyone. Thank you for giving us such a great color."

"Not that it even matters," Cara added. "No one is going to

be looking at us after you walk in the room. You're stunning. You honestly have never looked better."

"You look like a porcelain doll. You're so perfect I'm almost afraid to touch you," Jane said, letting out a deep sigh.

"Thank you! Do you think Steve will like the dress?" Meg asked, even though she knew he would. Steve thought she looked beautiful in her pajamas. She had no doubts that he would love the way she looked in her gown.

"He'll love it. It's perfect."

"Okay, while it's just the three of us, I wanted to do a quick toast."

"Without the other bridesmaids?" Cara asked.

"Yes. Just the maids of honor and the bride for this one."

Cara and Jane held up their glasses as Meg cleared her throat. "I know you guys think I'm sentimental," Meg said.

"Oh, you're the worst!" Cara laughed. "You cry at long-distance phone call commercials."

"You define 'sap,'" Jane said with a laugh.

"Fine. I don't care if I'm sappy. I like that about me."

"So do we," Jane said.

"I just want you to know how happy I am. I'm so happy that I have the two most important people in my life up until this point with me in this kitchen, and I have my entire future waiting for me in a tux a few miles away. I don't know what I did to deserve you guys, but in case I forget to tell you later, I love you more than anything and I don't know what I'd do without you."

"Okay, now you're making me cry!" Cara said, waving her hands in front of her eyes so the makeshift wind could dry her impending tears. "You're going to ruin my mascara!"

"I want a group hug but I'm afraid I'll get wrinkled," Meg said sadly.

"Screw it," Cara said.

"Totally!" Jane added.

They flanked Meg and wrapped their arms tightly around her waist. Suddenly, Meg heard a small click and saw a quick flash.

"That's going to be one great picture," the photographer said as he adjusted the lens on his camera. "Gorgeous!"

Meg wondered if they ever thought about that day, or how when Cara got married, Jane didn't stay for the whole reception, or how when Jane got married, neither Meg nor Cara was there. Meg had been first, before their rope had frayed so much that it broke. She'd been the only one who was able to have that kind of moment with them. She was sorry they'd been denied that.

"You need help?" Cara asked as she sauntered into the kitchen, snapping Meg out of her nostalgia and back to the present, where the person who stood before her wasn't the girl in the navy-blue dress, but a woman in jeans whom she no longer really knew.

"You want to slice the bread for me? There are knives in the drawer next to the stove." Cara removed a bread knife and began to saw the baguette, the crust splintering into shards that scattered all over the countertop. "How are you doing?" Meg asked.

"Honestly, I don't know. I feel like I'm sleepwalking. I don't know how I ended up here. Here in this house, here with you guys, here with my life. I didn't really think any of this through. Running away isn't going to solve anything. Eventually I have to go back. Jane made such a good argument for why I should leave, and the next thing I knew, we were on the expressway."

"That's Jane for you. She has a way of making really rash decisions sound like fantastic ideas."

"Like when she told me I should get bangs," Cara laughed.

"Or date that guy you met at the Blind Melon concert! What was his name?"

"George. What a loser that guy was! I never did have good taste in guys. Neither does Jane," Cara said sadly. "We should have looked to you for that."

"None of this is your fault. I'm sure you don't need me to tell you that, especially since I don't even know what's been going on, but it doesn't matter. You didn't do anything to deserve this. Don't let him tell you differently."

"Yeah, well maybe at some point that was true. At the same time, I'm a grown woman and I'm at least partially to blame. I could've stood up for myself from the start, and I didn't. I don't know if I was too scared or too worried about what people would think. I guess the reality is that I didn't want to admit I'd made a mistake. I'm stubborn, and I refuse to quit because it makes me feel like a failure. I figured if I stuck with it, maybe he'd change."

"Quitting a marriage isn't like quitting the tennis team. The bottom line is, you can't change people. Even I know that," Meg said.

"You never had to."

"I guess."

"Listen, it's none of my business, and I don't pretend to know what you've been through, or how much it hurts, but Steve loves you and it's pretty clear you're not out here because you don't love him anymore. If I had what you have, I'd fight for it forever. Don't give up on him. Don't give up on anyone. You deserve to be happy."

"This is what's best for me," Meg said, even though it was blatantly obvious to both of them that she didn't mean it.

"Best for you? Or what you think is best for him? Either way you're wrong, Meg."

"Can we talk about something else, please?" Meg asked. She'd had enough forced reflection for one evening.

"Sure," Cara said. "Do you have any plans this week?"

"Not really. I'm going to a spin class tomorrow morning, but that's about it."

"Really?" Cara asked. "Would you mind if maybe I tagged along with you? Would that be okay? I totally understand if you'd rather go alone."

"Of course it would be! Remember when we used to go to the Equinox together and then get sushi after? I loved that."

"Me too."

"I think you'll like this one."

"If it doesn't kill me. I haven't worked out in a long time."

"You don't look it."

"Haven't we all learned that looks can be deceiving?"

"Fair," Meg said. "Do you need to borrow clothes?"

"If you don't mind. I didn't pack any exercise clothes. I don't even know where most of mine are anymore."

"It's not a problem. It'll be nice to do something together again."

A knock on the door ended their conversation. Nick and Sebastian were right on time for dinner.

twenty-one

Jane popped a Xanax. It was seven P.M., and she found she enjoyed twilight with a tranquilizer. She was relieved that Nick's disinterest in her on the beach hadn't been because he didn't find her attractive, but because he had no interest in women whatsoever. As much as she hated to admit it, she didn't have quite the same impact on men as she'd had when she was younger. She wasn't sure how the signs of aging had crept onto her face without her even knowing it, but when she looked in the mirror in the morning, they were undeniably there: crêpey skin under her eyes, an uneven skin tone, and since she no longer could afford the luxury of regular highlights, wispy strands of gray scattered throughout her once golden-blond hair. Anyway, it didn't really matter whether anyone was interested in her, because as the girls had so nicely pointed out, she was still married. To a felon.

The Xanax helped with that, too.

"Can I get you a drink, Nick?" she asked. Meg was in the kitchen with Cara, making Jane the head entertainer, which was fine by her. She could pour wine with the best of them. Truth be told, her drinking habits were probably not doing anything to help her appearance, but these days she'd take a cheap bottle of wine over expensive highlights to help her mood without question.

"I'd love one, Jane. Thanks! It smells great in here," Nick said. Sebastian had scurried over to the carpet in the living room and curled into a tight little ball. Jane thought about the furry, happy golden retriever named Biscuit she'd had growing up. She'd talked to Doug a few times about getting a dog in the city, as she missed the companionship, but he'd emphatically said no. He thought it was cruel to keep an animal confined in a New York City apartment. Her home wasn't small by New York apartment standards, not even close, but the dog would never get to be outside to run and play the way dogs should. Funny how he thought it would be mean to keep an animal confined to an apartment, but not her. She walked over to Sebastian and gently petted his soft, furry head. For a moment, she envied him. He had a man who loved him, a cozy place on the carpet to nap without worrying about anything, and a home in the Hamptons to boot. The dog had a better fucking life than she did.

Jane poured wine for the four of them, grabbed glasses for herself and Nick, and walked into the den. Nick threw newspaper into the fireplace and then loaded wood from the pounded copper bucket in the corner on top of it. He pulled a book of matches from the back pocket of his jeans and held the flame to the paper. He seemed comfortable in Meg's house, and he clearly knew where everything was. Jane realized that Nick was quite at home here, and for a second wondered if maybe he was the person keeping Meg sane.

"How did you and Meg meet?" Jane asked as she sat down on one of the couches and curled her legs under her. She glanced back at the kitchen to make sure that Cara and Meg were still busy with dinner before she spoke. If she was going to have a few minutes alone with Nick, then she was going to try to find out what she could about what Meg had been up to out here by herself all these months.

"I actually sold her and Steve this house," he said.

"Oh, wow. So you've known her for a few years? That's nice.

I'm sure she loves having a friend out here to keep her company. I hate to think of her as being lonely."

Satisfied that the fire had sufficient traction, Nick grabbed his wine off the mantel and sat down on the couch opposite Jane. His eyes searched her, as if he was trying to decide whether he could trust her. She couldn't blame him. She was pretty sure that until today, he'd never heard of her. "I think she's doing some real soul searching. It's best to do that somewhere quiet. We've all been there, I guess."

"Yeah, I guess we have," Jane said. It didn't seem like Nick had any idea who she was, which was wildly refreshing. She figured she'd enjoy these moments for as long as possible, because once he placed her, he'd probably never talk to her again. That was the way things had been lately.

"It's really great to put a name with the face. Meg's told me about you—about both of you, actually. I didn't mention it this afternoon when we met because I was caught off guard. I was surprised she didn't tell me that you were coming for a visit."

"Well, that's not her fault," Jane said with a shrug. "She didn't know we were coming. We kind of ambushed her."

He laughed. "How'd that go over?"

"Not well. But she came around. She's agreed to let us hang out here for a bit. We have to make up for a lot of lost time."

"Do you think you can do that? With everything that's happened?"

Immediately, Jane went on the defensive. "Why do you ask that? What did she tell you?"

"Relax," he said. His shirtsleeves were rolled up, exposing hairy arms and some kind of sport watch that probably worked thirty feet under water. "It wasn't like that."

"How could it not be like that?" Jane asked.

"Here. Let me show you something." Jane watched as Nick
got up and went to the bookcase in the corner of the room by a
large bay window. He bent down and scanned the leather spines
of books that looked like they had been tucked away and left to
collect dust. Jane was struck by the number of books Meg had
managed to cram onto that bookshelf. Jane had never been much
of a reader herself, enjoying the random romance novel or spy
thriller or roman à clef when she was afforded the time. She used
to say that her busy social calendar and charity obligations prevented her from indulging in the kind of escapism books could
provide. Now that she had nothing but time on her hands and
needed to escape more than ever, it occurred to her that she still
hadn't bothered to crack open any of the books in her apartment.

Nick removed an album from the lower shelf, a thick, leather-
bound mammoth, and for a second, Jane thought about telling
him to stop. She assumed the book contained photographic relics
of their childhoods—of happier times that were now just distant
memories—and she didn't know if she was ready to see them.
She worried that they'd give her yet another reason to pop Xanax
like Pez candies, but the intrigue of what he was going to show
her prevented her from speaking up.

He placed the album on the coffee table and moved over, mo-
tioning for her to come sit next to him. Jane obediently nestled
in and watched as he opened it. It was Meg's wedding album, a
monument to the happiest day of her life, neatly organized and
immaculately cared for. The leather wasn't cracked, the pages
weren't yellowed, and unlike Jane's own visage, the cover was
no worse for years of wear. Meg's wedding was the last time that
the three of them had all been together and totally happy, and

the flood of memories that suddenly came back to Jane made it hard for her to breathe. The girls in these pictures had their whole lives in front of them, and believed that life would be good to them. The girls in these pictures hadn't yet been damaged by miscarriages, bad marriages, deception, or despair. If the girls in these pictures had had any idea of what was in store for them, they wouldn't have been smiling so broadly.

"I can't believe she has this out here. I actually don't think I've even seen a lot of these pictures."

"Really? You girls were a good-looking group. How come you never saw them?"

"I don't know," Jane lied. "I just never did."

He began to leaf through the pages. "Meg has shown this to me a few times. She looks at it often."

"That's nice. I don't even have a wedding album. I eloped, and didn't bother to hire a photographer. Not that it matters now. It wouldn't really be appropriate to have a large framed photo of my husband and me hanging on the wall at this point, you know?"

"Yeah, I could see how that could be awkward," he said. *So much for his not knowing who I am,* Jane thought. She quickly realized that she liked Nick even more than she thought she did, for having the decency to know and not say a word. It really was too bad he was gay.

He turned the page again and stopped at a picture of the three of them, Meg in the center with Cara and Jane flanking her like navy-clad bodyguards. Jane's eyes went blurry as she stared at the picture. She remembered the day so clearly: how Meg's mother force-fed them sandwiches, despite Jane's insistence that runway models and celebrities *never* ate before events and that it was ridiculous that they were expected to shove down turkey wraps while wearing gowns and expertly applied lip gloss. When Jane thought about it now it was even more ridiculous, as this picture was taken in the pre-Spanx era. Jane hadn't thought about how the flowers in her bouquet had started to prematurely wilt and how she had choked up on the stems and basically strangled them at the nape to keep them upright. She hadn't thought about how by the end of the night she and Cara were so drunk that they actually tried to get onstage at the reception and sing with the band. And now here it was: proof that they hadn't imagined how close they once were. She wiped her hand across her eyes to dry the tears.

"She told me all about you guys. All of it good," he added, as if reading her mind. "I know how much she misses you."

"I had no idea that she thought about us at all," Jane said. "I hate to admit it, but I really thought she didn't care anymore."

"Just because she never said she misses you doesn't mean she doesn't," Nick said. Jane was impressed that Nick was comfortable enough to get even marginally involved in their relationship. Most men would rather kill themselves than get anywhere near women fighting.

"And just because someone doesn't say she's sorry doesn't mean she isn't," Jane answered.

"Have you told her that?" he asked.

"Did she tell you why we haven't seen each other?"

"No. But I'd like to hear the stories now that the infamous friends are sitting here in the living room," Nick admitted.

"Not on the first date, Nick," she said. She wasn't flirting, just trying to let him know nicely that these were not questions any of them was willing to answer just yet. Instead, she thought this was the perfect opportunity to get some answers of her own.

"Does she talk about Steve?" Jane asked.

"She used to. Not so much anymore. I know she misses him, too. She stares at that photo on the mantel all the time."

They turned to look at the framed photo of Meg and Steve sitting in the backseat of the Rolls-Royce they'd rented to take them from the ceremony to the reception. They held champagne flutes and laughed as if that car were the most wonderful place in the world. Jane had only been in the backseat of a Rolls with a guy once, and she sincerely hoped there were no pictures.

"We stopped by to see him before we drove out here. He's worried about her. So am I," Jane said.

"Do you want to know a secret?" Nick asked.

"Are you sure you can trust me to keep my mouth shut?" Jane said. Jane had never been all that good a secret keeper, but since she was intent on trying to improve herself, she decided that no matter what Nick told her, she'd take it to her grave—unless it was something just way too big to keep to herself.

"I'm willing to take a gamble."

"Sure," Jane answered. "What is it?"

"Steve and I talk once a month. I told him I'd check in on her every now and then. I think he sleeps better at night knowing that someone out here is keeping an eye on her."

"You're spying on her?" Jane joked. The soft spot she had for Steve grew even bigger. She found it adorable that he loved Meg enough to let her go out there alone. So much, in fact, that he'd enlisted Nick to check up on her.

"I don't like to think of it as spying," Nick said. "I'm her friend, and I'm Steve's friend. I just want to make sure that she's doing okay. And he deserves to know that, too. That's all."

"How did that happen? Did he actually call you up and ask you to hang out with Meg as some kind of charity case or something?

She trusts you. She thinks of you as an actual friend, and if you're only spending time with her because Steve asked you to, you're going to break her heart. I don't know that lying to her is helping her in any way," Jane said.

"It's not like that. I swear."

"What's it like, then?"

"Steve called me and asked me if I would mind doing him a favor. I assumed that he was going to ask me to stop over and collect the mail, or water the plants, or make sure none of the windows had broken if we were hit with a storm. It turned out he wanted me to spend time with Meg while she's out here. I could tell it was a tough call for Steve to make. He kept coughing, which I'm pretty sure was his macho attempt to disguise the strain in his voice."

"I don't get it. Why would he want you to spend time with her?"

"He was worried that she was really depressed because she wouldn't talk to him. The way he made it sound, she wouldn't talk to anyone. At first I didn't really feel like it was fair of him to ask me to do it, but he didn't know what else to do. He needed to know that Meg wasn't going to be sitting in the house alone all the time, and he didn't want me to tell her because then she'd feel like she was being chaperoned."

"Isn't that what you're doing, though?"

"Only because I love her too much to let her just waste away any more than she already has. Steve was clearly desperate. He wouldn't have asked if he wasn't. I couldn't say no to him."

"They're separated. Don't you think she'd like to know that Steve is worried about her? Isn't it worse if she thinks he doesn't care?"

"I thought the same thing. Steve seemed to think that Meg would be angrier if she knew that he blatantly disregarded her request for space. He needed her to know that he loved her enough to leave her alone. At least, that's what he said. To be honest, I didn't really think it made any sense," Nick said.

"It does, actually," Jane answered.

"Women are complicated."

"Men aren't much better."

"If it makes a difference, I don't give him progress reports or anything. Not that he asked me to. It just made him feel better to know that I was around."

"I get it. You're a good guy, Nick."

"I don't know. At the time I really believed that I was doing the right thing, but now that I'm trying to convince you of it, I'm not entirely sure."

"I think it's really sweet," Jane said. "It makes me feel better, too. I won't say anything to her."

Just then she heard a cork pop and Cara call out, "Dinner's ready!"

"You promise you won't say anything? If you tell her she's going to question my motives for hanging out with her, and the reality is, I'd be doing it anyway. It makes me feel better to know that I'm giving Steve some peace of mind in the process. Plus, she's an awesome cook and I'd be heartbroken if she stopped having me over for dinner," he joked. "We will keep this between us?"

"I promise, I won't say a word."

"Thanks, Jane."

Nick put the album back on the shelf and linked his arm through Jane's, and together they walked into the kitchen.

twenty-two

A re you going to give up? Are you going to let the fact that you're tired and sore get the better of you? No, you're not! You're going to keep pushing because it's your time and it's your body and you're going to give it one hundred and ten percent!" The spin instructor screamed into her headset from her bike at the center of the room as the class spun furiously on the stationary bikes surrounding her. Meg listened to the music blare from the speakers, pop tunes that the college kids probably knew all the words to and she only marginally recognized. Just another sign that she was getting old. Was it OneRepublic, then 50 Cent? Or 50 Republic and then One Cent? She had no idea. All she knew was that her shirt was sticking to her and sweat was dripping from her forehead, and she had no idea how she was going to last another twenty minutes without keeling over. She looked at Cara, who had a puddle of sweat on the floor beneath her bike and was pedaling so fast she was starting to turn purple. Meg smiled. It was nice to see that side of her again.

Meg loved her Sunday-morning spin class, not only because it kept her body in shape but because she found it helped to clear her mind. Today she kept thinking back to a day she hadn't thought of in ages, and despite the screaming instructor and the loud music, she could hear the entire conversation in her head.

December 1997

"*There are too many candles on this cake,*" Meg said at dinner on the night of her twenty-first birthday. Meg's birthday was right after Christmas, which was really annoying because people either forgot about it in the midst of the holiday chaos or tried to lump it in with Christmas, thereby reducing her number of gifts. In college, however, the fact that her birthday coincided with winter break ended up coming in handy because it meant she was able to celebrate it with her friends at home. She'd treated herself to a manicure and wore the new earrings her parents had given her earlier in the day, and had felt pretty as they'd sat through dinner. But even though she'd been adamant that she didn't want a birthday spectacle in the restaurant, she found herself staring at a birthday cake Cara had picked up from the bakery in town. She'd had the hostess stash it in the kitchen, covered in candles, a giant wax 21 dripping all over the fudge frosting. "*You should not have done this!*" Meg said to Cara, blushing as everyone in the restaurant turned to stare at them while Jane and Cara sang and clapped as if they were the only people in the room. "*I'm too old for cake.*"

"*Stop being stupid. You're never too old for cake!*" Cara said. "*Jeez, Capricorns. You guys are never happy. Besides it's about time you turned twenty-one. That's worth celebrating.*"

"*Seriously!*" Jane added. "*It took you long enough!*"

Meg laughed. Cara and Jane never missed the opportunity to remind her that she was the youngest person in their class, almost a full year younger than both of them.

"*You'll be jealous when you guys turn forty and I'm barely thirty-nine!*" Meg joked. She caught a group of middle-aged women sitting at the table next to them rolling their eyes as they listened to them discuss how old they were. In fact, the women had been listening to their conversation the entire night, and if they were trying to be discreet they were failing badly. They'd scoffed at Meg when she'd proudly produced her driver's license to prove she was finally able to drink legally—in public! They rolled their eyes as the girls talked about who had better grades (Cara), who had a better boyfriend (Meg), who had managed to avoid college weight gain for yet another semester (Jane), and whose parents were more annoying and out of touch with reality (three-way tie). The women didn't try to hide their disdain of the table of girls with their parents' credit cards and their whole lives in front of them, complaining about such stupid things.

"Do you have any big birthday plans with Steve once you get back to school?" Cara asked in between bites of cake. "Is he going to take you somewhere special or what?"

"Yeah, what are you two going to do? One of the perks of having a boyfriend is that you should at least get a really good dinner and a nice bracelet or something from the deal. Otherwise what's the point?"

"I have something planned, actually," Meg said slyly.

"You're planning your own birthday present?" Jane asked, oddly impressed by Meg's taking the initiative. "Good idea. The last thing you want is to end up with something heinous that you're forced to wear so you don't hurt his feelings. What are you going to get?"

"It's not what I'm going to get. It's what I'm going to give away."

"I don't follow," Jane said.

"I'm going to lose my virginity," she whispered, not wanting the nosy ladies at the neighboring table to overhear her and actually laugh out loud.

"You're joking," Jane said. Her forkful of cake hung suspended in midair.

"What? Do you think it's too soon?" Meg asked. She'd been thinking about finally giving in to Steve's persistent attempts to get her to sleep with him, and after months of careful consideration had decided it was finally time. She was now twenty-one, and if she was old enough to drink wine in a restaurant, she was old enough to have sex. It made perfect sense as far as she was concerned.

"Too soon? I can't believe this. You've been dating this guy for two and a half years, and you're still a virgin? Why?" Jane asked, like Meg had just admitted that she had never shaved her legs or something. "How did we not know this?"

"I didn't want to talk about him like he's just a random guy. He's special and our relationship is special and I didn't want to gossip about what we have. It's private."

"That's the most ridiculous thing I've ever heard," Jane said. "Best friends discuss this stuff! I tell you guys everything. I just assumed you were being a prude and not wanting to talk about it. It never occurred to me that you hadn't actually done it yet!"

"Jane, stop it!" Cara scolded. "If she wants to wait, she wants to wait. What's the rush anyways? She has her whole life to have sex."

"I just can't believe that you've been living on a college campus, unsupervised, with alcohol and no curfew, and you're not sleeping with your boyfriend. Is there something wrong with him?"

"There's nothing wrong with him! He's been great. I shouldn't have said anything, except, well, I have a question." Meg didn't like having to admit that she still had questions where sex was concerned. The last thing she wanted was for Jane to make fun of her for being inexperienced. Jane might be one of her best friends but they had very different attitudes about how to deal with members of the opposite sex. Actually, they had very different attitudes on a lot of things.

"Ask me, not Cara," Jane instructed. "No offense, but there are some things you come to me for, and some things you go to her for, and on this topic, I'm your girl."

"I went to the doctor last week for my checkup and I mentioned it to her. She gave me a prescription for the pill, but I'm a little afraid to take it. I heard that it makes some girls fat."

"Oh, stop," Jane said. "That's totally not true. It won't make you fat, but it may make your boobs bigger, which is a total bonus. Steve will have a girlfriend with better boobs who's sleeping with him. He won't care if you pack on a few pounds. Most guys don't even notice that stuff unless you gain like thirty pounds and start wearing sweatpants every day anyway."

"I just want to make sure I'm careful. I need to take the pills for a month before they'll work and I want to start taking them this week if I'm going to do this. Do you think they're safe? The doctor says they are, but they don't protect against diseases."

"Is Steve diseased?" Jane asked.

"Of course not!" Meg said, offended that Jane would ever say something about a guy who was about as perfect as a person could possibly be.

"Then what's the big deal? Pop the pills, have sex, drink booze. Welcome to twenty-one."

"That's it? That's all there is to it?" Meg asked. It seemed like a very simple answer to a very complicated issue.

"I'll be happy to answer any questions you have. Consider me your emergency hotline. I'm open twenty-four hours a day. I still can't believe you're a virgin. Wow."

"Not everyone gave it up at sixteen, Jane," Cara said. They had finished eating their slices and were now picking at the remainder of the cake from the platter in the center of the table.

"That's hurtful. I was two weeks from being seventeen. Big difference."

"I see," Cara said, knowing full well that Jane was only pretending to be offended.

"Are you sure you're ready? There's no rush. If you want to wait until you're sure, he'll understand," Cara said.

"Or he'll start banging a freshman. One or the other," Jane added.

"Don't say that! He'd never cheat on me!" Meg squealed, suddenly feeling very sorry that she'd brought up this topic in the first place. Especially in public. There was no way the other women weren't listening to them.

"Jane, that really is awful," Cara said.

"All I'm saying is that it's time. You love him, he loves you—clearly, as evidenced by the fact that he's still dating you even though you won't sleep with him—you have protection so you don't need to worry about getting pregnant. What else is there to talk about? If you ask me, girls make this a bigger deal than it is because they talk about it too much. Less talking, more doing."

"Most people like to talk things through, Jane. Not everyone lives in the moment the way you do," Cara said.

"It's worked all right for me so far."

"One day it's going to catch up with you," Cara warned.

"I'll worry about that day when it comes. Of course, I'll be too busy enjoying myself to notice, soooo . . ."

A waiter appeared at the table with a bottle of champagne. "Excuse me, ladies, this was sent to you by someone named Steve. He says happy birthday to the most beautiful girl in the world. Which one of you is Meg?" he asked. Meg shyly raised her hand and blushed, knowing that the hags at the neighboring table were staring at her. "Shall I pour it?"

"Please do!" Jane said as the waiter placed crystal flutes on the table. "Maybe Steve sensed that we were talking about getting him laid and this is his way of saying thank you."

"Stop it!" Cara said. She reached over and grabbed Meg's hand. "I don't know him very well, obviously, but he seems like a great guy. I can't wait to get to know him better."

"Me too," Jane said. "To be honest, I'm a little jealous."

"What, you want to lose your virginity again?" Cara teased.

"No! Are you crazy? My first time sucked," Jane said. "I'm jealous that Meg has someone who treats her so well. I've dated a few guys, but everyone I meet at school is constantly looking over my shoulder to see if a prettier girl is going to walk into the party. No one has cared about me yet the way that Steve cares about Meg. What does it feel like?"

"What does what feel like?" Meg asked.

Jane paused, as if her question was even more embarrassing than the one Meg had asked. "What does it feel like to be in love?"

"I don't know if I love him," Meg admitted. "I think I do. But *what if that's not what this is? What if it's just infatuation or something stupid? What if one day I look back on this and want to kick myself for buying into all of it?"*

"You're just a wimp. You don't want to admit that you love him because then you'll be afraid if he fucks you over you'll look stupid. You love him. If you didn't you wouldn't be taking birth control pills," Jane said. "This champagne is good. We're going to have to call someone to come pick us up. I don't think any of us will be driving after this."

"I know that he makes me happy. Every day when I wake up I can't wait to see him. I want to call him in between every class. I want to sit on the couch and watch TV with him even if all my friends at school are going out. When my phone rings I get excited, even now. He brings me breakfast in the morning, and sometimes he writes little notes that he tucks in my wallet or in one of my notebooks. We can talk about anything. I don't think I've ever been closer to anyone in my life. Well, except for you guys."

"Of course. We don't count," Jane said. Her eyes were starting to glass over, the wine and champagne making her giddy.

"I think that sounds awesome," Cara said. "It must make life so much nicer. You never have to worry about being alone."

"But I do worry about that. I worry about him breaking up with me. I think I would die, you guys, I really do. I don't know how I'd ever get over that."

"Why do you think he'd break up with you?" Cara asked.

"Because he can do better than me," she whispered. Cara and Jane seemed surprised to discover that Meg's insecurities were still very much intact. She had everything: looks, brains, person-

ality, and now, it seemed, a good guy who loved her, and still she couldn't see it.

"Maybe he's worried about you leaving him," Cara said. "Did you ever think of that?"

"I'd never leave him. If things stay the way they are now, I think maybe we could get married. I swear I think we could. That's another reason why I haven't wanted to talk about this stuff. If we end up getting married I don't want to betray him by talking too much about our private life, you know?"

No one spoke. When did they become old enough to even have this kind of conversation?

"Wow," Jane said. "If you're thinking of marrying him at some point after college, then you really should just sleep with him and get it over with."

"You really think you might get married?" Cara asked, unable to hide the shock in her voice.

"Maybe, yeah. And I think that I'd regret saying too much to you about our relationship if we do. Does that make sense?"

"I guess it does," Cara said.

"Not even a little bit," Jane countered.

"Well, I'm sorry! You guys are just going to have to deal with the fact that I'm not going to share every detail where he's concerned. There are some things that should be kept just between the two of us."

"Then stop worrying about him leaving you and trust yourself!" Cara advised. "Though I have no idea what I'm talking about. I'm no expert."

"And if that doesn't work, just get really drunk. That always helps," Jane said.

"Do you think it's crazy to marry your college boyfriend?" Meg asked, looking for reassurance from the people whose opinions mattered the most.

"Not if he's the right guy; what difference does it make? You meet him when you meet him. You're not an idiot, you'll know it if it's right," Cara said, though Meg wasn't sure that she actually believed it.

"I hope so. All I know is that I can't imagine my life without him, and I don't ever want to find out what that would be like."

"Then don't fuck it up," Jane said.

"I won't. I would never do anything to ruin this. Unless he breaks up with me, I plan on being with him forever."

Meg remembered thinking that the women at the table next to them that night were just jealous because they were old—middle-aged, with crow's-feet around their eyes, lackluster hair, and fat rolling over the tops of their pants. Now she realized those women hadn't been middle-aged at all. They were probably the age that she was now. Her younger self had thought they were just a table full of bitter bitches, but that probably wasn't the case. They were likely just a table full of women who, like them now, had lived through marriages, children, jobs, loss, love, and everything in between, and found it impossibly hard to listen to little girls discuss how they felt old because they were turning twenty-one. God, if she had been sitting at that table, she probably would've smacked her younger self in the face. In retrospect, she admired the older women's restraint.

Meg snapped out of her daydream as the music was turned up a notch and the whole class started counting down the last ten seconds before they crossed the imaginary finish line. She glanced over at Cara and forced herself to refocus on the here and now instead of remembering the life she used to have. When the class ended she unclipped her spin shoes from the spikes on the pedals and made her way to the hallway to change back into her sneakers. Cara soon trailed after her.

"Oh my God, that was amazing! I forgot how good it feels to work out like that."

"It's a great class," Meg said, trying to shake the memory. "You were riding pretty fast for someone who hasn't worked out in a while."

"Are you kidding? You kicked my butt! I looked over at you at one point and you were pedaling like a million miles an hour. You're fired up this morning, huh?"

"I guess so. I just spaced out there for a bit," Meg said with a shrug.

"What were you thinking about?" Cara asked.

"Nothing," Meg lied.

"Okay," Cara answered. "You don't have to tell me."

They dragged themselves to Meg's car, parked a block away on the side of the road, and Meg tried desperately to understand why she'd given up on Steve so easily—why her younger self had been so willing to fight, but the adult version had somehow allowed forever to have an expiration date.

twenty-three

ook at you guys! You look like you had an awesome work-out. I'm a little jealous," Jane said when they returned sweaty and reinvigorated. She was sitting cross-legged on the floor in front of the TV with one of Meg's photo albums in front of her. "I was thinking of making myself a Bloody Mary. Do you guys want to join me? You worked hard, you deserve a midmorning cocktail."

"I don't think I'm ready to break into the alcohol this early in the day," Meg said. "I'm going to shower and then I actually need to run into town to get a new pie plate."

"What's wrong with the five that you have?" Jane asked, only partially teasing.

"I want to make a deep-dish apple pie, and I don't think any of the ones I have are big enough to hold the filling properly."

"I don't know how you sleep at night knowing that," Jane joked. "It would keep me up for sure."

"Do you mind if I tag along?" Cara asked. "I'd like to get some fresh air and maybe a new pair of sneakers in town. I'm thinking I might want to go for a run while I'm out here. It's so beautiful and the weather is perfect. I think it's time I lace up again."

"You guys are starting to make me feel bad that I don't have any desire to exercise," Jane said.

"Do you want to come to spin tomorrow?" Meg asked. "I think I'm going to go again."

"I don't feel *that* bad," Jane replied. "I'm happy right here for now!"

"Good!" Meg said. "Cara, do you really want to come?"

"Yeah, I'll take a quick shower and then let's go."

"Sounds good!" Meg said as she turned and made her way to the bathroom to strip off her sweaty clothes. It wasn't lost on her that in less than forty-eight hours, Cara was starting to get her energy for workouts back and Jane's sense of humor was returning. They were both starting to heal, but after a full year out there Meg felt no closer to finding her old self than she had been when she arrived. *Maybe that Meg is never coming back,* she thought as she turned on the hot water and let steam fill her bathroom. *Maybe this is as good as it's ever going to get.*

She stepped into the shower and disappeared into the fog.

"Are you sure it's okay to leave her there? What if we come home and she's passed out drunk on the floor or something?" Meg asked Cara as they drove through town toward the hardware store.

"She'll be fine. You know her, she doesn't believe in moderation. Anyway, we should cut her some slack. If I were her I'd be drinking a little more these days, too."

"I just don't want to enable her. It's not the best way to solve her problems."

"We're not. Anyway, Nick seems like a nice guy. Do you guys spend a lot of time together?" Cara asked, changing the subject.

"I guess we do, yeah. He's become a very good friend of mine."

"I'm glad you have someone to spend time with out here. How'd you meet him?"

"House hunting, actually," she said. "We were just looking for a house."

November 2009

"See anything you like?" a strange voice asked. Meg looked up from the photos of homes for sale in the window of a real estate office. She was surprised to see a tall, dark, and handsome man standing next to her on the sidewalk, drinking a coffee. She wasn't sure whether he was referring to the houses or to himself. She in no way wanted this man to think she was even remotely interested in him; she made a show of waving her diamond rings in front of him so that he would see she was married.

"I'm sorry?" Meg asked. "My husband and I are interested in houses. That's all I'm interested in," she added coolly.

"Great! Hopefully I can help you. I'm Nick. This is my firm."

"Oh," Meg said, feeling more than a little embarrassed that she'd mistaken his sales pitch for a come-on. "Then, yes! There are a few things here that look interesting! I'm Meg, and this is Steve," she said as her husband returned from parking the car in a lot across the street.

"Hey, Steve. I'm Nick. Meg tells me you guys are looking at houses."

"We are!" Steve said as he shook his hand firmly. "Do you think you have a little vacation home for us in your inventory somewhere?"

"Why don't you come inside so we can talk? I'm sure we can find something that might interest you. Do you have kids, or is it just the two of you?"

"No kids . . . yet," Meg said. "But hopefully one day we will, so we want a four-bedroom."

"Yeah," Steve agreed, albeit half-heartedly. "And we'd like something with a yard."

"You got it. Let's see what we can do."

Over the next two months Meg and Steve made the drive to Montauk almost every weekend so that Nick could show them properties that fit their needs. One Saturday in January he drove them to a quaint house tucked in the woods. The mailbox was dented and the pavement on the driveway had cracked like uneven slabs of layer cake. The front yard was covered with dead trees and plants that had long since surrendered to the cold, and one of the shutters on a second-floor window was hanging on for dear life. From the outside it looked like a house little kids in the neighborhood would be afraid to visit on Halloween.

"This is what you wanted to show us?" Meg asked, more than a little confused at how Nick had come to the conclusion that this would be a good vacation home for them.

"I know what you're thinking. It's scary."

"It looks like it belongs in a Stephen King movie," Steve said.

"This house needs work, but it has great bones and it's in a good part of town. If you're willing to invest a little money in renovations and cleanup, you can buy it cheap and turn it into something really great. You'll be able to make a nice profit down the road. It has character," he said, looking at the sad structure and somehow managing to keep a straight face.

"It looks like it has ghosts," Meg joked.

"Let's keep an open mind," Steve suggested as they climbed out of Nick's car and stood in the front yard. "He makes a good point. We have the time to do some work, so we don't need to pay for something that's totally finished. If we buy a fixer-upper we can do whatever we want with it. I kind of think it could be nice."

"Maybe," Meg said. "It does have a nice front yard, and this is a quiet street."

"There's a huge rental market in the summer for this part of town. If you choose to rent the house, even just for the month of August, you can make a nice amount of money. The house will basically pay for itself. It's a really smart investment if you have the patience to do the work."

Meg wasn't sure how, but somehow Nick was starting to change her mind.

They climbed the rickety porch stairs and Nick opened the door. The appliances in the kitchen were twenty years old and were surrounded by cheap pink Formica counters on a diamond-patterned linoleum floor. The window in the living area was broken and a light fixture dangled precariously from the ceiling, but Meg still felt something tug at her heart. The second she stepped inside she began to play a home movie of her future in her head. She heard her kids laughing; she heard Sinatra playing on a stereo; she heard herself calling them all for dinner. She could see everything. It all just seemed to make sense.

"I can kind of see us living here," Meg said.

"I can, too. How weird is that? This house is a mess, but it's the first one we've seen where I feel like we belong."

"I told you there was something about this place," Nick said. "It has so much potential. Not everyone can see it, but it really does."

"It just seems like a nice family home," Meg said as she wandered into a bathroom off the kitchen and imagined pairs of sandy flip-flops tossed in the corner and tiny bathing suits hanging on a wall hook to dry. She knew she would most likely never have children, but she wasn't ready to fully abandon her dream.

"I'm glad you aren't totally against it," Steve said. Meg turned to look at him and saw that he was falling in love with it, too.

"It could be a great house," she said as she grabbed his hand and dragged him into a small bedroom tucked in the corner. "For now it could be an office, but this room would make a nice size nursery." Meg's eyes glazed over as she squeezed Steve's hand and got lost in a daydream where there was a mobile hanging from the ceiling, a crib tucked in front of the window, and a rocking chair in the corner. "What do you think?" Meg asked.

"I think we'd like to make an offer," Steve said as he pulled her toward him. Meg tried not to let the fact that he blatantly avoided her question bother her.

"Fantastic!" Nick said. "You guys will be very happy here. I can sense it. Plus, I think you'll be able to get it for a steal."

One month later they owned the house and soon after began renovations. They left the closing and Meg reached over and hugged Nick, unable to squash her bubbling enthusiasm for this major milestone in their life. "Thank you so much, Nick."

"It's my pleasure. I hope you guys are very happy here. Oh, I almost forgot!" he said. He walked over to his car parked on the side of the road, and removed a bottle of champagne from the front seat. He handed it to Meg. "Congratulations, guys. If every client was as easy to work with as you were, this would be a very different job," he joked.

"Why don't you let us take you to lunch before we head back?" Steve asked. "We're going to be doing a lot of work out here, and I'd love your recommendations on who we should use. Would you mind if we picked your brain a little bit over lunch?"

"Are you guys sure?"

"Of course!" Meg said. "We insist."

Two hours later they were still at lunch, more than a little happy from celebratory drinks and the fact that it was Friday and no one had to go to work the next morning.

"Are you married?" Meg asked as Nick sipped his beer and popped fried clams into his mouth.

"Nope! I'm just a lonely bachelor. It's tragic, isn't it?" he joked. "I have a dog named Sebastian. He's the only man I have in my life at the moment."

"Oh, you're gay?" Meg asked. "I was going to try to set you up with a friend of mine from work. Damn."

"I'd love to meet your friend one day, but yeah, I won't be interested in her," Nick said.

"I teach with a very cool guy, actually. I don't want to play matchmaker, but if you're ever interested in meeting someone, let me know. I'll set it up!"

"We can double date!" Meg added.

"Do you think that's a fair trade? I find you a house, you find me a boyfriend?" Nick joked. "Most people just send flowers or bottles of wine. You guys are really awesome."

"Just happy," Meg said. "So we like to see other people happy, too. We'll set it up. I promise."

The date never happened.

Lots of things didn't.

"He was our Realtor, that's all," Meg answered. "When we met him I was just hoping he'd be able to sell us a house. I never in a million years would've guessed that he'd become one of my

closest friends—my only friend for a while, actually—or that I'd
end up living in the house alone. It's crazy the way things turn
out sometimes," she added sadly. She couldn't shake the mel-
ancholy that had descended on her since spin class. For some
reason, today was one of those days when the memories refused
to leave her the hell alone.

They entered the hardware store and Meg waved to the stock
boy, Tyler, who was busy trying to fit a coiled-up garden hose
onto one of the shelves.

"God, I love the way hardware stores smell, don't you?" Cara
asked as she followed Meg through the aisles.

"What? You do? I never knew that! They kind of smell like
dirt, don't they?" Meg asked, surprised.

"Not at all! It smells like rubber and sawdust and testosterone.
You know, when I was younger I always thought that hardware
stores were a great place to meet guys."

"Name one guy you ever met in a hardware store!" Meg
laughed.

"I'm not saying I ever met one, I'm just saying it's a good place
to look around."

Meg glanced over and noticed the two burly men perusing the
barbecue tools. Maybe Cara was right.

"If we were young and single, I'd come back here before I went
to a bar, that's all I'm saying."

"Good to know."

They made their way toward the back of the store, where the
kitchen equipment was located. Meg was fishing through the
pans when Cara grabbed her arm.

"Oh, speak of the devil! Look, there's Nick. Who's he talking
to? She looks familiar."

Meg glanced over at the girl with her arms wrapped around Nick's neck and sighed. "That's the girl from the coffeehouse. The one you threatened to sue."

"That *is* her!" Cara said, stifling a laugh. "I'd rather not have to see her again—can we just stand back here until she's gone? That was not one of my finer moments."

Meg allowed Cara to pull her behind a rack of paint cans. Nick was at the register, buying new dog bowls for Sebastian.

"Hey, Sheila," he said, throwing the bowls on the counter and trying to remove himself from her grasp.

Sheila released her arms from around his neck and inhaled deeply. "You smell great—what is that?"

"Soap. And maybe some salt water. I was down at the beach earlier. I went surfing this morning."

"You always smell so good. How come straight guys don't ever smell the way you do?"

"I have no idea," Nick answered. It was obvious he wasn't all that interested in talking to Sheila, either.

"How'd the waves treat you?"

"Pretty good, actually. Sebastian and I had a nice time down there. What's new with you?" He eyed the middle-aged woman working the cash register as if trying to encourage her to ring him up faster. Meg giggled, watching Nick make small talk.

"Nothing much," she said. "We're in the usual post–Labor Day slump at the coffeehouse. It's funny, by the end of the summer we're all so sick of the crowds, we just want them to leave. Then, when they do, we remember all the money they spend. Now I'm complaining that I don't make tips, and the workday seems to stretch on for six years."

"The grass is always greener, I guess."

"I guess so," she agreed.

"Say hello to your parents for me. I have to run," Nick said, trying to get away from her as fast as his good manners would allow.

"Will do. Oh, wait, I forgot! You'll never guess who I saw the other day in the coffeehouse!"

"Gwyneth Paltrow?" Nick guessed, though he was clearly running out of patience. "She has a house out here, Sheila. At some point that specific celebrity sighting has got to get old."

"No. Not her. Jane Logan!" she hissed, like saying the name left a bitter taste in her mouth. "Do you believe that? What do you think she's doing out here? Her husband ruins people and she comes out to the Hamptons to relax in some beachfront mansion somewhere? That woman is even more evil than I thought."

Meg held her breath. She'd never particularly liked Sheila, and now she was pretty sure she hated her. She gripped Cara's hand, and Cara firmly squeezed it back.

"I don't know who that is," Nick lied. "Anyway, I've never been much into celebrity sightings. They bore me. Sorry." Nick turned to walk away, but Sheila kept talking.

"You do too know who she is! She's the wife of that Wall Street asshole who stole from all those people. She's all over the papers. Don't you watch the news? She came in with two other women. One of them looked familiar—I've definitely seen her around before. The other one actually spilled hot tea all over Jane. She claimed it was an accident, but it probably wasn't. I'm sure more than a few people would love the chance to inflict physical pain on that woman."

"Sheila, do yourself a favor and stop spying on people. One day you're going to find yourself overhearing things you don't want to know. Trust me. Besides, it probably wasn't even her."

"It was her! Here, look!" Sheila removed her cell phone from her purse and clicked on a picture. She showed it to him.

"You took a picture of her?"

"Oh shit," Cara said as they watched Nick snatch the phone from Sheila's hand and stare at whatever picture she'd snapped while they were arguing.

"We have to do something," Cara whispered. "What if she sells it to the newspapers?"

"She's not going to sell it to the papers," Meg whispered back. "She probably just wants to show it to her friends. She's an idiot, but she's harmless. Trust me."

"You're right, I guess that is her," Nick said, pretending to look closer at the picture.

"I told you so! I haven't showed it to anyone yet, but I was thinking of calling the *New York Post*. I could probably make some good money off this, right? She doesn't deserve any discretion. It's not like I'm taking pictures of Martha Stewart and throwing them on Facebook or anything. This is legit news. People have been trying to get shots of her for weeks! How much do you think I could get?"

"Okay, I might have been wrong," Meg whispered.

"I don't know. Is this the only one you have?" Nick asked casually.

"Yeah. Maybe I can send it to more than one place and get into some kind of bidding war for it. Wouldn't that be amazing? Who else should I call?"

"How do you zoom in on this?" Nick asked as he began to hit

buttons on her phone. "I want a closer look at her. I'm terrible with iPhones."

"Wait, that's not the zoom! Don't hit that!" Sheila screamed, but she was unable to stop him.

"Oops," he said. "I'm so sorry! Did I just delete that?"

"Please tell me you didn't just do that!" she moaned. From the look of horror on her face you'd have thought he'd just deleted her wedding photos, or the last picture she had of her grandmother before she passed away.

"It was an accident."

"Now what am I going to do?"

"I guess go to work, and hope that they'll come back for another cup of tea," Nick said.

He waved as he grabbed his bag off the counter and left.

"That was awesome!" Cara said. She and Meg watched in amazement as Sheila futilely punched buttons on her phone. "I love him. I officially love him."

"I told you. Nick is the absolute best," Meg agreed.

"Okay, come on, we need to get out of here before that girl sees us and follows us home like a stray cat."

"What about my pie plate?" Meg asked as they slowly made their way out from behind the rack of paint cans.

"It will have to wait. We have bigger problems," Cara said. She grabbed Meg's sleeve and the two of them inched quietly toward the back door, leaving Sheila standing alone, violently cursing Nick.

twenty-four

Jane figured she'd hang on the deck at the house and have a few cocktails in peace, but something stopped her. If she was going to sit and drink by herself all day, she might as well have stayed in her apartment in Manhattan. In Montauk she was free. Free to go outside without worrying that people would throw rocks at her. Free to be seen in public without needing to hide behind sunglasses and a baseball hat. Most important, she was free to drive. Jane decided that if she had to choose between a glass of wine and the open road, this time she'd choose the road. She remembered passing some farm stands on the side of the highway about thirty minutes west of Montauk, and she thought it'd be a really nice gesture to pick up some things for Meg. She grabbed Cara's keys off the console and headed out to the driveway, feeling like a teenager who'd just gotten her license. She hadn't been this excited to run an errand in her entire life.

Jane never shopped at farmers' markets, though. Supporting local farmers seemed to be the cool thing to do these days and, because Jane had never been much for trends, she never stepped foot inside any of the markets in the city. She had no interest in mingling with the hippies who drove down from upstate on the weekends to force organic produce on people who probably washed down their meals with wine and cigarettes. She didn't see the need for it. Her delivery menus had served her just fine, and that was how she liked it.

Out in Montauk, it didn't seem like people frequented farm stands because it was cool or trendy or politically correct. It was just part of life. And, since Jane was now part of life on the East End, she didn't mind driving the thirty minutes to visit one of the various stands scattered along the side of the highway. It seemed silly to go to the one grocery store in town to buy things when it was less expensive to watch them be pulled from the ground immediately before they were purchased. Plus, it felt nice to be in a car with the windows open, the radio on, and clean air making her hair blow in tangles. It felt nice to be free, unencumbered, and better yet, not tailed by anyone with a camera, a notepad, and a misplaced vendetta against her.

Jane finally felt at ease. She remembered driving out to Long Beach with her boyfriend from high school one summer. They'd talked about how things would be when they went off to college, how they couldn't wait to get out of their small town, how they were going to do great things with their lives. She'd sat in the passenger seat with her sunglasses on, her charm bracelet clanging against the outside of the car, and her head bobbing slightly, keeping time with the music. She couldn't remember where Cara or Meg had been that afternoon. Maybe they were busy, or maybe Jane had decided that she wanted to spend the afternoon without them. Maybe those were the first small steps she took to separate herself from the group. She thought she knew everything back then, that she was making all the right decisions, that there would be a million other boys after she broke up with the one driving her down the Meadowbrook Parkway. She glanced at Cara's passenger seat, half expecting to see the dark-haired boy in the green baseball hat sitting next to her. Instead, there were two brown paper bags overflowing with lettuces, potatoes, squash, and apples that she'd purchased with some of the little money she had left.

When she returned to the house, Cara was lying down in her room and Meg was baking her seventh batch of muffins in three days. Jane knew Meg was using the muffins as some kind of weird Steve substitute, but she really needed to get it under control, as three grown women did not need to eat a dozen muffins a day. That said, if she did take on the Meg diet of blueberry, banana nut, and cranberry oatmeal muffins, she'd probably put on enough weight that no one at home would recognize her, and she could hide in plain sight. It wasn't the worst idea. Carbo-loading did offer its own special brand of comfort.

"Smells good in here!" Jane sang as she dropped the bags on the floor by the refrigerator and began to unload them. "I went to the farm stand and picked up a few things. I'm sorry I couldn't buy more, but it's the best thank-you gift I could get you under the circumstances."

"That's so nice of you!" Meg said, fishing through one of Jane's bags and placing the apples in a large ceramic bowl on the counter. "We were a little nervous when we got home and saw the car was gone. We weren't sure you even remembered how to drive!"

"It was actually really nice. I didn't realize how much I missed driving until I did it. I hope Cara doesn't mind. I thought getting out of the house was a better alternative than drinking by myself."

"Definitely. And it was really nice of you to bring back groceries. Do you want me to teach you to cook something? Maybe you'd find it de-stresses you the way it does me!"

"Maybe I'll light the house on fire and burn your refuge to the ground."

"Always the optimist."

"Just my luck lately, that's all."

"Your luck will change, Jane. It will," Meg said.

"I know. I just need to chill the hell out and relax. I'm three hours away from midtown Manhattan and anyone who knows me. There's no reason on earth for me to be so tightly wound at this point."

"Come on," Meg said. She handed her a small china plate with a warm muffin on it and a mug of coffee. "Let's watch the news. I feel like I have no idea what's going on in the world."

"Isn't that the whole point of being out here?" Jane asked. "I don't want to know."

"Relax. No one is out to get you," Meg said.

"I know. I know. I know. *I think*."

Ten minutes later Jane sat in front of the TV with Meg nestled next to her on the couch and Cara sitting quietly in an armchair, watching the news. One of the myriad of smug reporters with whom Jane had become very familiar was standing in front of the courthouse in lower Manhattan, using her best "on camera" voice to update the American public on Doug's affairs. Their life, now in ruins, was the day's lead story. Jane shuddered to think about how many people whom she'd never even met were rooting for her husband to go to jail for the rest of his life and for her to suffer some equally tragic fate.

They watched in silence as men in dark suits escorted Doug past the throngs of cameras and microphones, hairy hands in polyester suit sleeves reaching across her husband, begging for a sound bite. *What do they want him to say?*, she wondered. What made them think that this time he would finally open up and explain his actions? She knew he didn't have an explanation, at least not one that was acceptable to her or anyone else. Their questions were pointless. If they were waiting for some sort of epic confession, they'd have to wait forever. And they'd have to wait in line behind her.

"Doug Logan is back in court today as prosecutors prepare to bring their case against him for the financial scheme he masterminded in an attempt to steal from countless investors. What's most interesting today is that his wife, Jane Parker Logan, was not in attendance in the courtroom, as she has been for previous court appearances. In fact, sources at her Upper East Side apartment building say that they have not seen her in days, and her whereabouts are currently unknown. Sources tell us that Jane recently had an argument with another tenant in her building, and that the co-op board has been in discussions to evict her from her home. It's possible that this was too much for her to bear in light of the stress that she's currently under, and we are now forced to wonder if Jane has left town entirely and gone into hiding, *or worse*. Only time will tell. We will of course update you as this story develops, but right now it seems as if Jane Logan is missing. This is Alecia Sparks, Channel Four News."

Jane gripped her mug, wishing that it contained whiskey. She tried to speak but instead sipped her coffee until it caught in her throat and she coughed it back up all over her jeans and the white slipcovered sofa. *Great,* she thought. *Two more things that are now probably ruined. Just like my husband, just like my marriage . . . just like me.*

They stared at the newscast, now reporting on a lost dog that had been reunited with its owner four years after running away. The dog turned up thanks to an embedded tracker in its ear. Instinctively, Jane pushed her hair behind her own ears, wondering if she should consider herself lucky that she didn't have a chip of herself so people could locate her. She picked at the muffin Meg had given her but couldn't taste it. Her mouth had suddenly gone very dry and some kind of sticky film coated her tongue. With her luck she'd probably picked up a rare fungus at the farm stand and now had mouth scabies. Finally she was ready to speak. " 'Or worse'?" she asked, repeating the reporter's words. "What exactly is she implying?"

"That's ridiculous! It's irresponsible journalism!" Meg said, placing her hand protectively on Jane's leg. "So what if no one has seen you? Maybe you went to visit your parents in Florida, or your brother out west! Maybe you're holed up in your apartment! Maybe you went to visit a friend in Montauk!"

" 'Or worse' makes for a better news story. What difference does it make? No one cares if I'm dead or alive anyway," Jane said, a dull pain beginning to throb inside her skull. She'd been having such a nice day, and now it was ruined. She should've just sat at the house and drank like she'd originally planned. Maybe if she were buzzed, this latest broadcast wouldn't hurt as much. "All they care about is that they lost the chance to shoot the long-suffering spouse sitting in the courtroom while her husband pled not guilty. Supposing I'm dead keeps people from turning the channel. God forbid I decide I'm tired of pretending to care what happens to him anymore. I want my own fucking life back."

"What are you going to do?" Cara asked. She picked up the remote control and turned off the TV. It didn't matter. It wasn't like they could unwatch the news just because the TV was off. If there were a way to rewind life and do it all over, she'd have known about it and done it by now. Many, many times.

"Order a tombstone? Buy a casket? Actually, now that I think about it, I don't have a plot. I was supposed to be buried next to

Doug, but lying next to him for all eternity seems a bit awkward considering he's the reason I'm dead. I mean, what would we talk about, you know?"

"I'm serious, Jane!" Cara said, a somewhat inappropriate giggle escaping her lips.

"Are you laughing? I can't believe you're laughing!" Jane said, surprised that a small laugh grew in her belly, too.

"I'm sorry, I know that this isn't funny. Except it kind of is," Cara said. "Just a little."

"You two are sick. There is nothing funny about this!" Meg said. Jane smiled in spite of everything at the ferocity of Meg's reaction. Jane loved that Meg would never laugh at something so sadistic. She was too nice a person. Plus, she was hugely superstitious and probably thought that laughing about Jane's death would somehow make it a reality. There weren't enough muffins on earth to bring her back from that if Jane were to suddenly drop dead in the living room. "Honestly, Jane. What are you going to do about this? Can you call the news yourself and issue a statement?"

"I don't know. I probably should call my doorman and make sure that my crazy-ass neighbors haven't tried to sell my apartment out from under me by enacting some death clause in the co-op bylaws, and I should probably call my parents and make sure that they know I'm fine in case word travels down south. My brother, too. He will just love this."

"You should probably call Alecia what's-her-name and tell her that she should eat her microphone before she goes on the news again and says something that ridiculous," Meg added—harsh words, coming from her.

"They're probably trying to draw you out and force you to issue a statement. I think the fact that you've said nothing is driving them crazy," Cara suggested.

"What makes you think that?" Jane asked. She wasn't trying to antagonize the press; she was just trying to pretend they weren't there.

"I don't know," Cara answered, though the look on her face made it quite clear that this was not the first time the thought had crossed her mind.

"Except, I think you do," Jane responded, demanding an answer. "Tell me."

"It's just that every time I saw something about this on the news and you refused to comment, it made me wonder if you knew more than you were saying. I'm sorry, but I wondered. And if I wondered, then you can bet other people are wondering, too."

"Cara!" Meg gasped. "How could you say that?"

"Oh, come on! Don't tell me you didn't think it! I'm sorry, Jane, if I'd been privy to anything that was going on I wouldn't have doubted you for a minute. But I knew as much about this as anyone else who read the paper, and I was curious! So are other people. That's all I'm saying. People are dying to hear you tell a different side of the story, any side. And you're not giving it to them. So now the press is just beating the drapes to see what falls out."

"I never thought about it that way," Jane admitted. It hurt to hear Cara say she had doubted her, but Jane understood it. Most women know their husbands; most women have intuition that tells them when something isn't right. She didn't. That made her hard for people to understand. It made it really hard for her to understand herself. "I always felt like it wasn't my fight because it wasn't my crime, and I shouldn't be forced to speak out about anything. People who say there's no such thing as bad press have clearly never had any. They've tormented me for so long under the bullshit First Amendment crap that saying nothing seemed like the only option I had. I just never thought any of it would go on this long. I thought they'd get bored chasing the woman who never said anything and would leave me alone. I underestimated them."

"Why don't you release a statement?" Meg asked. "You must have a PR firm you can contact. Aren't there crisis people who handle this stuff? Do you know anyone who knows Justin Bieber? His people have been busy. Maybe they could help?"

"No, I don't know anyone who knows Justin Bieber. After just seeing my possible death reported on the news, that's the second strangest thing I've heard someone say today."

A quick knock on the door interrupted their conversation, and Nick and Sebastian entered. The screen door slammed shut and Sebastian barked a high-pitched yelp, his tail wagging so vigorously that when he ran by the console table, he actually rattled a picture frame. He scurried up to Meg and thrust his furry head into her lap, begging for some attention. *If only that technique worked as well for humans,* Jane thought.

"Well, ladies, it seems we have a problem," Nick said, pulling a beer out of the fridge and popping the top with a bottle opener attached to his key chain. He might have been the straightest gay man in America.

"Did you see the news, too?" Meg asked.

"No. Why, what's on the news?" Nick responded.

"Jane may be dead," Cara answered.

"They never actually said that," Meg pointed out.

"It was implied. So I guess that means we're in the middle of a séance. Does anyone have any questions they want answered from the great beyond?" Jane asked. "I'll do my best."

"They said you were dead?" Nick asked, a grin creeping over his stubbled face.

"Yup," Jane answered.

"I repeat, they never actually said that!" Meg said again.

"Whatever. Maybe it was wishful thinking on their part."

"Well, I don't mean to kick you when you're down, but I ran into the girl who took your coffee orders the other day in town this morning. She recognized you, Jane," Nick added.

"Tell her I don't give autographs."

"I don't think that's what she was after. She took a picture of you guys in the coffee shop on her phone. She was planning on selling it to the tabloids."

"Are you kidding me?" Jane asked as she jumped off the couch, having had enough of people attacking her for one day. "This is the Hamptons. There are famous people—legitimate celebrities— all over the place. Why would anyone care that I was out here in a coffeehouse?"

"Because Sheila is bored and not making as much money in tips as she was during the summer, that's why," Meg answered.

"Anyway, I deleted the photo, so you have nothing to worry about on that front. That said, she's onto you, and she has a big mouth. If you were looking to hide out I'm afraid your days are numbered."

"How much money do you think a photo of me in a coffee-house would go for?" Jane asked.

"Less than a photo of you naked, I'd imagine," Cara answered.

"Depends on who you're naked with," Nick offered.

"True. But since no guy with any concern for his reputation

would be caught anywhere near me, naked pictures are probably not in my future. Unless you're offering, Nick?"

"Sorry, I'm not. But I swear, it has nothing to do with your husband being a criminal. It's because girls have cooties."

"Right."

"Look, I just wanted you to know that you're not entirely off the radar. Maybe, considering this news report bullshit, that's a good thing. What do I know? But if you don't want to give Sheila a second chance at a snapshot, maybe steer clear of the coffeehouse."

"Meg's coffee is better anyway," Jane said.

"I think you need something stronger after this," Meg added.

"You're right, Meg. I deserve to have a few drinks after this. We all do. I deserve an A for effort for not having one earlier in the day, but circumstances have changed. Wine. We need wine. Pronto."

"I stopped and picked some up on my way over, but I left it in my car. I'll go grab it," Nick offered.

"This is kind of like my funeral. If I'm going to be present for it, I want a drink," Jane joked.

"Seems like a reasonable request," Nick answered.

"I'll start lunch," Meg said, fishing some of the vegetables Jane had brought home out of the drawer in the refrigerator.

"I'm not that hungry," Jane said. "I think maybe I'll just have a liquid lunch."

"What about all the things you bought from the farm stand? You don't want to try anything?" Meg asked, hoping she'd be able to guilt Jane into eating something.

"No thanks," Jane said, once again feeling lost in a way she hadn't since she'd left the city three days ago. "I just lost my appetite."

twenty-five

D id I ever tell you guys about the time Doug took me to the opera?" Jane asked a few hours later, after Nick had left and she'd drunk a few glasses of wine. They had decided to get away from the TV and were sitting outside on the back deck, enjoying the last of the afternoon sun, hoping that some fresh air would make Jane feel a little better. Jane knew that Cara and Meg were racking their brains for something helpful to say but were coming up empty. So Jane figured it was better if they just listened. "It was probably two or three months after we'd started dating."

"I don't think so," Meg said. "You never really talked about him all that much."

"Until you told us you'd married him," Cara added. "Is it too soon to joke about that?"

"Nah. I deserve that. I guess I didn't really talk about him much, but it wasn't because I didn't want you to know about him. I think I was afraid to let people know how much I loved him. I knew it made me vulnerable and I hated that. I guess I figured if you never knew about him, you'd never know it if he left me. That was my biggest fear back then, that one day he'd call me up and tell me he wanted to break up with me. I was so insecure that I remember thinking I'd just die if that happened, that it would be the absolute worst thing in the world. Guess I underestimated that one, huh?"

"Tell us about the date," Cara encouraged her.

"It was really nice. We went to dinner uptown at an Italian place in his neighborhood. He knew the maître d' and they treated him like a king. You know the drill, the small table in the back corner, after-dinner drinks on the house, the whole bit. I felt special just being there with him. I think about that night a lot, and I wonder if he was already crooked at that point. I like to think that something was real. At least in the beginning, you know? I like to think that I fell in love with a good man and that he wasn't just playing me. Otherwise my whole relationship was just one big con, right? Just like everything else in his life. Did I imagine *everything*? Is it possible that I was so lonely and desperate for attention at that point that I made our relationship up? Was I just a trophy wife the entire time? Someone to hang off his arm at business functions?"

"Don't even think that," Meg said. "He was a rich, handsome guy. He could've dated and married a million different girls. He picked you."

"Maybe he picked me because I was the only one who couldn't see who he really was. Maybe he picked me because I was too stupid to see the truth," Jane whispered as she began to cry. Crying had never been her thing. She was the one who got angry, the one who yelled and screamed and cursed. Crying was something she did rarely and only in the privacy of her own home, but she couldn't keep the tears at bay. She was just too tired to even try.

"Thinking like that will drive you crazy," Cara said. "You were vulnerable when you met him, and maybe he preyed on that a little. Who knows? But you're not stupid. Not even close."

"I can't be sure anymore. I can't be sure of anything anymore. I don't even recognize myself," Jane said.

Her mind wandered back to the night at Lincoln Center. It was the night she knew that she wanted to marry Doug. It was a night that now haunted her.

March 2005

"Are you excited?" he asked as he removed the tickets from the pocket of his suit jacket. "I'm by no means an expert, but I really like going to the opera every now and then. This is New York, right? It'd be silly to not take advantage of this kind of thing."

"Very," she said as they made their way through the plaza and into Lincoln Center. "I've always been curious about it, but I've never had a guy offer to take me before." She looked up at the massive chandeliers glittering overhead and had to catch her breath.

"You haven't been hanging out with the right guy," he said with a smile.

No arguments there, Jane thought as she took his arm and let him guide her through the crowds. It was one of only a few times she'd ever had reason to get dressed up to go out on a date, and she'd loved being able to leave her jeans and boots at home. When she'd first moved to Manhattan she'd thought that she'd be like the girls in Sex and the City, constantly dressed to the nines and dripping in sequins or feathers to hit the bars on a Tuesday night. She'd quickly realized that the only women running around town dressed like that were either high-priced escorts or Rockettes, and she'd sadly tucked her little black dress away in the back of her closet, where it had stayed for a very long time. But now here she was, all dressed up and heading to the opera, and wondering if maybe there was an entirely different life ahead of her.

"No, I haven't. That's for damn sure," she said with a wink.

"If you like it we can come back another time and have dinner at the restaurant here. It's really very good and it overlooks the plaza. It's one of those things that you have to do at least once. We can order soufflés before the first act and they'll have them waiting on the table for us during the intermission."

"It sounds amazing," she gushed, unsure that she'd ever go on another date that would top this one.

"I think it is. I hope you like it."

"I already do. I love it."

He'd led her to their seats, and Jane glanced around the room at the other patrons, all of them sophisticated, well-dressed, and cultured—and she was sitting right there next to them. She might as well have been one of them. She looked over at Doug and it was as if something inside her clicked. Even if she never saw another opera for as long as she lived, she knew she never wanted to date anyone else ever again. It had only been three months, but she knew.

"Did you enjoy it?" he asked a few hours later. They exited Lincoln Center and walked a few blocks over to Central Park West. They turned uptown toward his apartment, the music still ringing in her ears and the taste of the wine still on her tongue, and she felt like she was swimming.

"It was amazing. You're right. You'd be crazy to live here and never experience that. I'm blown away by how talented some people are. I'd kill to be able to sing like that," Jane said, clutching his arm tightly. She never wanted to let him go.

"I've heard you singing in the shower. I think you'd better stick to acting," Doug joked.

"Hey! Maybe if I had some voice lessons I'd be good. You never know! What would you do if you weren't in finance?" she asked.

"What do you mean?"

"If you had to do another job, what would you do? When you were little, did you want to be a fireman or a fisherman or a cowboy? What did you want to be when you grew up?" she asked, fully expecting him to say something adorable that would help give her some insight into Doug Logan the five-year-old boy.

"I don't know, actually," he'd said flatly. "I don't think I ever wanted to be anything specifically. I just knew I wanted to be rich."

Jane laughed. "Really, that was it, huh? So if being an acrobat in the circus meant you'd be rich, that's what you would've wanted to do with your life?"

"Maybe. Lucky for me that wasn't the only option I had. I don't think I'd have liked wearing tights to work every day."

"No, probably not. That's not very romantic, though, is it? Clearly I didn't want to be an actress for the money or I'd have given up on it by now. It'd be a nice bonus, don't get me wrong, but it's not what I like about it."

"What do you like about it?" he asked. They slowed so Jane could adjust the strap on her heel.

"I like that I have the chance to be a different person. I like trying to get inside the minds of women from different eras or cultures or walks of life and figure out what it would've been like to live their lives. It's a lot more interesting pretending to be other people than just being me. I'm pretty boring." She hoped that Doug wouldn't find her silly or flighty. He didn't seem like he was much of a dreamer, and she wasn't sure he was going to understand where she was coming from. A lot of people didn't.

"I don't think so at all. In fact, I think you're one of the most intriguing people I've ever met," he said, flashing her a smile that immediately put her at ease.

"You do?" They found a bench and sat, watching the traffic barrel up Central Park West and giving Jane's feet a much-needed break.

"I do. I admire you for sticking with your dream for as long as you have. Like you said, a lot of people would've given up on it by now, but you haven't. That tells me you're passionate, and committed. I love that you loved the opera and were really looking forward to experiencing something new, but that you don't need to be wined and dined all the time to be happy. You would've been just as comfortable at home on the couch with a movie. You're grounded. And I love that you had the nerve to call me that first day we met. I was just a random guy in a bar. You didn't know anything about me, but you still called because you're adventurous. I don't know why you think you're boring, but I assure you that that's very far from the truth."

"That might be the nicest thing that anyone has ever said to me. And that includes more than one seedy casting director who tried to get me on his couch. You're a special guy, Doug Logan. I think I knew that the day we met. That's why I called you."

"I've worked hard for a long time to get where I am. I worked hard in college, then I worked hard in business school, and then I worked hard at my job. And now I finally have most of what I've wanted from my career. The one thing I've never really had time to focus on was my personal life. But then you appeared, and now everything seems to be falling into place. Which is crazy, isn't it? People always told me that that would happen, but I thought it was bullshit. Now I'm beginning to see that it can actually happen that way. I'm forty and I'm just beginning to realize that you can have everything at the same time. I always thought I'd have to sacrifice one for the other. You make it so easy to not have to choose."

"Thank you," Jane said, still swimming in the compliments he'd just given her.

"You've taught me that you can always find a way to get what you want," he said.

"If you're resourceful and smart, that's probably true," she agreed.

"And creative. Never underestimate the power of creativity."

With that he pulled her up from the bench and hailed a cab. They nestled in the backseat and continued uptown, Jane wondering the whole ride how she possibly got so lucky.

Jane's daydream was interrupted when a raindrop fell squarely on her nose. She opened her eyes and saw clouds rolling in overhead, the first bad weather they'd experienced since they'd been at the beach. "I guess it's time to go inside," she said. She tried very hard to not think about the beginning of her relationship with Doug. For a while she'd gone over every conversation, every minute they'd spent together, trying to figure out whether she could've seen any of this coming. Eventually Jane had accepted that beating herself up for allowing him to fool her wasn't going to get her anywhere. Sure, she had her regrets, probably more than most people, but there was no point in dwelling on them. Somehow she had to find a way to leave it in the past and move on. She just hadn't figured out how to do that yet.

"I'll grab the wine. I'm getting hungry anyway. Jane, you need to eat something. I don't care if you're not hungry. At least let me make you a snack," Meg said as she grabbed the bottle off the table and opened the sliding glass door.

"Okay. I guess it won't kill me to have some cheese and crackers. Especially since I'm dead already."

"Good girl," Cara said as they got up from the chairs on the deck and headed back inside. "Besides, it's probably going to be nasty for the rest of the night anyway. A nice cozy fire sounds pretty dreamy. Don't you think?"

"Sure. Why not?" Jane answered. "It's Sunday night. What else do we have to do with ourselves?"

An hour later they sat in the den with a fire roaring and a plate of cheese, crackers, and dried apricots on the coffee table in front of them. "You know what the crazy thing is?" Jane asked.

"There's only one thing? Really?" Cara teased.

"That he didn't trust me enough to tell me the truth from the beginning. The whole time he was doing whatever it was he was doing he never told me about it. Why do you think that is?"

"That's kind of a hard conversation to have with your wife," Cara offered. "Don't get me wrong, I agree with you. He should never have allowed you to be blindsided the way you were. But what was he supposed to say? 'Hi, honey, I'm home, and by the way I'm going to jail for fraud'? He probably didn't want to admit it to himself."

"Maybe he didn't want to hurt you," Meg suggested. "Maybe he was hoping he'd find a way out."

"But I'm his wife. We're supposed to tell each other everything."

"You didn't tell him you didn't want the boobs," Cara said.

"It's not exactly the same thing."

"No, but maybe he was hoping he'd be able to protect you or something. Maybe he thought what you didn't know couldn't hurt you."

"Well, he did hurt me. He hurt me more than I ever would've thought possible. I didn't get out of bed for more than a week after this whole mess became public. I thought I was in a loving marriage with a guy who was maybe a little superficial, but so what? I thought he loved me. I thought we wanted the same things out of life, and I thought he had scruples. I really did."

"I know that," Meg said. She hesitated before she continued. "Can I tell you something?"

"Sure. What?"

"The day after your wedding, when we were all at the cocktail party, I overheard Doug talking to someone. One of his buddies, I guess."

"Oh God. Please don't tell me you knew he was a crook the day after I married him and never told me. Please don't tell me that. There's not enough wine on this island for me to handle that."

"No! Relax. I overheard him telling his friend how lucky he was, and how you were the best thing that ever happened to him. He was watching you from across the room, and I remember thinking that maybe I was wrong to assume you rushed into things. I remember thinking that he was really in love with you. I could tell just by looking at him. I remember thinking that I was happy you'd found your right person. So he conned me, too. Either way, he wasn't faking his feelings for you. What you guys had was real, even if nothing else was."

"Does that make things better or worse?" Jane asked.

"Neither. It doesn't change anything. But maybe you can sleep a little better at night knowing that your marriage wasn't based on a lie. At the very least, Jane, I don't think you should be taking those pills anymore. You don't need them. They're only making things worse."

"I know." Jane sighed. "I've become even more of a cliché than I already was. I've devoted the last few years of my life to giving an award-winning performance of the role I'd been offered to play: trophy wife. I got so damn good at playing one I didn't even know I was doing it, and now I'm a blond bimbo with a border-line substance abuse problem. If they ever turn my life story into a movie, the actress who gets to play me will probably win an Oscar. It would take quite a talented lady to pretend to be this tortured. That will be ironic, won't it?"

"Meg's right," Cara added. "Don't get me wrong, I'd be drinking a lot too, but I think you should probably keep an eye on it before it becomes something you can't control."

"I know. Thanks for mentioning it, though. It helps to know that now at least I have people looking out for me."

"I'm sure Doug still cares about you, too. If that's worth anything," Meg offered.

"It's not. Why didn't you ever tell me that you overheard that conversation at the party?"

"Why would I have? Under normal circumstances it wouldn't have needed mentioning. Everyone should feel that way on their wedding day, right?" Meg asked.

"I did," Jane said. "I know you guys weren't on board with how I got married, but I really did feel lucky."

"I did, too," Cara said.

"I still think it," Meg added.

"So what does that tell us? That we're all idiots?" Jane asked as she slowly began to laugh. "I mean, it's comical that this happened to us."

"No. It means we made the decisions we made for the right reasons. So did you."

"Yeah. Well, it's over now, so I guess there's no use harping on it." Jane sighed again. "I can't change the past, or my role in it. So I'd better get used to it."

"You have to figure out what you're going to do, Jane," Cara said. She reached over and rubbed her arm. "There are a lot of moving parts, but you need to start focusing on something. I think you should start with making sure your co-op board knows you're still alive. At the very least, call the building."

"I'll do it tomorrow. Tonight is my night to fall apart a little bit. Tomorrow I'll put myself back together and figure out what I'm going to do. I promise."

"You've earned the right to wallow," Cara said. She reached over and topped off Jane's wineglass, then her own.

"Thanks," Jane said. She'd forgotten what it was like to be in a room with people who didn't pass judgment. "Thanks for listening. And for not getting on me about drinking too much."

"That's what friends are for," Meg said. "I don't condone all of your coping mechanisms, but tonight you deserve to unwind any way you want to. I'm just happy that this time you don't have to do it alone."

twenty-six

"Hangovers never used to hurt like this," Cara announced the following morning to an empty house. Meg had somehow found the energy to attend her spin class. Jane had walked into town in an enormous pair of sunglasses and a baseball hat, insisting that power walking was an integral part of rebuilding her life. Cara could barely find the energy to brush her hair, so she took on the responsibility of making coffee and cleaning up the glasses and the cheese board from the night before. She didn't mind the quiet. She felt the cool floor under her bare feet and listened to the birds in the trees. Jane wasn't the only one who had some long-overdue soul searching to endure, and as much as she was enjoying her time with her friends, she was all too aware that this was just a small reprieve. Her life waited for her a few hours west, and she was going to have to return to it at some point. Neither she nor Jane could hide forever.

She took the morning paper and her coffee to an armchair in the living room and curled up under a fuzzy throw blanket that was tossed on the couch. She hadn't made it so far as the end of the first page when she heard barking outside, and moments later, a perfunctory knock before Nick and Sebastian plowed through the front door. *So much for silence,* she thought.

"Good morning, Cara!" Nick said, throwing a bag of bagels on the counter. One thing she particularly liked about Nick was that he never showed up to the house empty-handed, and he always arrived in a good mood. It was no wonder Meg and Steve took to him so quickly. Some people just have a way of making you happy whenever they're around. It was too bad that this was a quality she hadn't learned to appreciate in a man until later in life. If she had, she probably would have realized that her husband entered the room with all the alacrity of the grim reaper. She never would've decided to move in with him in the first place.

"Good morning. I see you brought breakfast," Cara said as she put down the newspaper and pushed herself up from her chair. She followed Nick into the kitchen and poured him a cup of coffee. "What's new?"

"Not too much. I was in town and thought maybe you guys could use some bagels to soak up your liquid dinner, which in retrospect was probably silly since Meg has enough muffins in the freezer to feed the entire town for months."

"It was sweet of you to bring breakfast. Thanks so much. I'll have one a little later."

"Where is everyone? I was fully prepared to find you guys passed out on the couches in the den or something."

"We may have been drunk, but we did make it to our beds last night, so that's a win! Meg also somehow managed to drag herself to her spin class this morning, and Jane went for a walk. I think she wants to enjoy the time she has out here, you know? It's good for her to get out. I'm just hanging out. Pretty boring morning for me!" Cara wished she'd had the energy or the stamina to go to spin with Meg again, but the truth was, she was out of shape. She made a vow to get back into working out again, but she'd do it slowly. She was almost forty. She needed to take care of her knees and didn't want to risk getting injured. She'd go to another class with Meg while they were out here, but as much as she hated to admit it, back-to-back classes were a bit too much for her at this point.

"Ah. I forgot about Meg's spin class. She goes to that thing religiously."

"We all should have such aerobic coping mechanisms, right?" Cara said. "Anyway, what are you up to today? Are you heading down to the beach?"

"Actually, no. I have some new clients in town who are looking to buy a bungalow. I'm going to show them a few properties today. Fingers crossed I can get them to bid on something."

"Oh, that sounds like fun! It must be great to see all the new houses that come on the market out here. Some of them are absolutely spectacular. It's really fascinating, isn't it? How different people can have such different visions for the same four-walled structure? It's almost like a sociology experiment or something."

"Do you want to tag along?" Nick asked. "You seem to be pretty pumped up just talking about it."

"Why would you want me to come with you?" Cara asked.

"Why not? I'll just tell them you're a new broker and I'm bringing you with me to show you the ropes. It'll be fun. Besides, it's too nice out to sit inside all day with the newspaper. Come with me! You can practice your sociology experiment on beach houses."

"Won't Sebastian be jealous if I replace him as your sidekick?"

"Nah. He won't mind if I leave him here. He loves Meg and he makes a great guard dog. He'll keep an eye on the place until Meg or Jane gets back."

Cara turned and eyed the affable Lab sitting in the corner with a chew toy, blissfully tossing it up in the air and catching it again and again. "What does he do, lick intruders to death?"

"He's the strong, silent type. Like his owner."

"I see."

"So what do you say?"

Cara thought about it for roughly ten seconds. "I'd love to! Let me go get dressed. Make yourself a bagel."

"Good. I need to meet them in about a half hour, so no primping. I don't want to be late."

Cara ran upstairs to get changed, surprised at how happy she was to pretend she was back at work.

The Stillmans seemed like a lovely couple who Cara knew right off the bat were going to drive their Realtor absolutely bonkers. They had a wish list a mile long and a budget that stretched a few inches at best in one of the priciest real estate markets in the world. Cara had dealt with this kind of buyer before, and almost always had to fight the urge to physically shake them until they understood that what they asked for simply wasn't possible, but Nick was taking it all in stride.

Instead, he asked friendly questions, trying to figure out what kind of home would make sense for them. Mrs. Stillman mentioned that she had a labradoodle whom she adored, but who was getting on in age. Nick added a whole bunch of ranch houses to the list, pointing out how much easier it would be for their dear old dog if she didn't have to climb stairs in her old age. *Genius,* Cara thought. They'd been married for ten years and had two small children, and after years of careful investing and frugal spending, they were finally ready to put a down payment on a little family vacation home. They were amenable to looking at lots of different properties, and while their budget was by no means large—so as a result, Nick's commission wouldn't be, either—she was impressed by how smoothly Nick handled their questions and concerns. She'd met more than a few brokers over the years who thought of themselves as gatekeepers to the town itself; if they didn't like the prospective buyers, they all but drove them away from the property. They didn't want to risk running into them in town, or worse, having their children become friendly and be forced to host play dates. Real estate was like politics in a way, and a good broker was a rare find. Nick was one of the best she had ever seen, and just from listening to him for a few minutes in the car, she realized how much she had to learn. This week had proved that she had a lot to learn about a lot of things.

They arrived at a fixer-upper north of the highway, away from the beach but close to the docks, embedded in lush woods heavily populated with deer. Not the greatest location if you were someone who hoped to have a garden, as the deer would eat just about anything, but otherwise, Cara thought it had a lot of potential. There was a rusted old flagpole in the front yard, and dead plants and bushes lined the broken slate slabs that made a walk from the driveway to the front door. It had absolutely zero curb appeal, but someone with vision and a little creativity could change all of that. Meg was one of those people, she thought, and Cara admired her, and Steve, for undertaking the task of redoing their home instead of looking for one that was move-in ready. Loving anything should require some work. Some things more than others, but still.

Mrs. Stillman couldn't get past the fact that there was carpet (who *would* put carpet in a beach house?), or the fact that the kitchen cabinets were gray (admittedly a strange color for a house by the beach, but how hard was it to paint them?). They didn't like that the house didn't have a pool, despite the fact that Nick had told them over and over that a house with a pool in Montauk was out of their budget. Cara found herself growing impatient just listening to them bitch and moan about all the things the house didn't have, but Nick never did what Cara was fighting the urge to do: remind them that unless they had a million dollars to spend, they weren't going to get million-dollar amenities, chief among them Jacuzzi tubs, acres of land, a heated pool, and top-of-the-line appliances. Nick just encouraged them to see what the house could be if they did a little work on it, and when the couple made it clear that they had no intention of lifting a finger to do anything other than stock the shelves with groceries, he encouraged them to keep an open mind.

"Why aren't we looking at any homes near the beach? I don't know that I want to sit in traffic to get here and then not be able to walk to the beach," Mrs. Stillman griped from the backseat on the way to the next house.

"The inventory of homes for sale near the beach is very low. They don't turn over very often, and when they do, to be frank, they tend to be priced significantly higher than what you're willing to spend."

"That's absurd. Our budget is high enough that we should be able to find something," Mrs. Stillman insisted, as if she knew more than Nick.

An hour later, Cara's patience was worn out. They'd seen house after house and nothing had pleased Mrs. Stillman. Her husband had said about ten words since they had left on this expedition—he was not the one wearing the pants in the relationship. "May I make an observation?" Cara asked, knowing that she was probably overstepping her bounds as a fake Montauk real estate agent in training, but she didn't care. It was either try to find a way to shut this woman up, or push her out of the car into oncoming traffic.

"Sure," Nick said, eyeing her curiously from the driver's seat.

"The problem with houses near the beach, aside from the fact that your insurance will be astronomical, especially after the storms that have plowed through here recently, is that there's very little room for price appreciation."

"I'm not sure I understand what you're saying," Mrs. Stillman admitted, which pleased Cara. Until now, she'd seemed to have an answer for everything.

"Homes in that area are already overpriced. The supply simply doesn't meet the incessant demand for beachfront properties. Even if you did buy a home down there, it won't increase in value. Now, in some of these other sections, near the woods or back in the hills, for example, a lot of homes are still undervalued as the market out here continues to recover from the recession. There are some great bargains that you can get and in a few years should increase tremendously in value. At that point, if you want to take your money out and maybe look to move down by the beach, you'll be able to. From an investment standpoint you really should be considering some of these properties. There are real finds in there that will make you a lot of money over time."

"That's a very good point," Nick said, clearly impressed with Cara's sales pitch. Truth be told, so was she.

"I hadn't thought about that," Mr. Stillman said, finding his voice for the first time since he'd gotten in the car. "I'd rather buy something that can make us some money in a few years. Maybe we should reconsider some of the houses we saw."

"The one in the woods was charming. But the kitchen wasn't updated," Mrs. Stillman pointed out.

"You don't cook," her husband said.

"Maybe I would if I had a nice kitchen."

"Does the oven work?" he asked.

"Yes. Everything is fully functional. Do you want to go back and look at it again?" Nick asked.

A silent nod from both parties in the backseat was all Nick needed to turn left and head back to the cottage nestled deep in the woods.

After they had spent another twenty minutes roaming around the house, Cara decided to further test her powers of persuasion by being a bit more aggressive with her sales pitch. The fact that she didn't work for Nick's firm and had no business pretending she did didn't bother her at all. It felt good for her to regain some confidence in her work. Being self-assured was never something she could manage to do at home, not at her job and not in her marriage, but out here, now, it seemed to come effortlessly. It was as if the salt air had taken over her brain, making her do and say things she had never had the nerve to before. She kind of really liked it.

"The closets are adequate, but if you need more storage you can always get some great wardrobes or bureaus at some of the tag sales. I know a lot of people think tag sales are a waste of time, but out here, where people are constantly refurnishing or moving or selling their second homes altogether, you can really get some great finds. It's a fantastic and inexpensive way to add character to the home, not that this house has any shortage of that. Once you pull up the carpets in the living room I'd bet you'll find original hardwood flooring, the kind that tracks through the rest of the house upstairs. All you'd need to do is refinish them and they'd be really special. Did you notice how quiet it is back here? There's something comforting about waking up surrounded by nature, don't you think? And let's not forget the fantastic windows in the bedrooms upstairs. They're new and fully insulated. The light that comes through them during the day is amazing."

They followed her from room to room, finally beginning to see the possibilities of the property, and by the time Nick dropped the Stillmans back in town an hour later, he had an offer to submit to the seller.

"You were great back there," he said.

"Thanks," Cara said shyly, suddenly feeling silly for shooting her mouth off and hijacking Nick's listing without his permission. "I really hope I didn't overstep. I don't know what came over me."

"What are you apologizing for? I was losing them, and I knew it. You managed to turn that entire appointment around! It was quite impressive. That doesn't mean I have to share the commission with you if the sale goes through, though."

Cara laughed. "Of course not. How do you manage to show people who are so lucky to have the opportunity to live out here house after house and have them shoot them all down because they don't like the carpets or the paint color?"

"People are lazy. These are vacation homes; buyers think of them as a place where they come to relax. Doing any work at all is an added stress in their life. At least, that's how most of my clients see it. Not you, though. You really know how to sell a piece of real estate. Do you do it full-time at home?"

"Not even close. I would never have the nerve at home to act the way I did. The other women would eat me alive. It's very competitive."

"Doesn't seem to me like you have any problem with competition. Why do you let that get in the way?"

"I'm more the invisible type at home."

"If you act like you did today, you couldn't be invisible."

"You'd be surprised."

"Why do I get the feeling that this is about your husband? What, he convinced you that you suck at it, is that it?"

"Something like that."

"Stop listening to him and start listening to yourself. You know way more than you give yourself credit for. And if you don't want to listen to yourself, then listen to me. You were really great."

"Thank you—again!" Cara smiled as she held her hand out the window, letting the wind snake through her fingers as they drove back toward the house. When they got to the turn that would lead them back to Meg's, Nick instead kept his course. "Where arc we going?" she asked.

"To a bar by the docks. You just helped me get their bid, and while that doesn't entitle you to a commission, it does entitle you to a beer. What do you say?"

Cara checked her watch. "It's two o'clock. I should probably gct back to the house sooner rather than later."

"Come on! It's on me. I want to hear more about your life as a real estate agent. I think maybe I could learn a thing or two from you."

Cara felt a feeling she barely remembered, but she was pretty sure it was pride. "Okay. You're on," she said. "I'd love to."

twenty-seven

think we should go out for lunch today," Meg said the following afternoon while Cara filed her nails at the kitchen table and Jane did sit-ups on the rug in the den. "We've spent too much time in the house. Let's go into town."

"I think that's a great idea," Cara replied. "You deserve a break from cooking anyway."

"I'm happy to go to lunch, I just don't know if I can pay for it. Can we go somewhere cheap?" Jane grunted in between crunches.

"I'll treat," Cara offered. "You went and bought Meg stuff from the farm stand and I haven't done anything yet. Let me take both of you to lunch to say thank you."

"Sounds good to me!" Jane yelled. She hopped up from the floor and grabbed her sunglasses from her bag. "I'm ready when you are!"

"Great. Let's go have a nice afternoon in town."

They all piled in Meg's car and drove to East Hampton, grabbing a table at an Italian restaurant with sidewalk seating and an impressive selection of wood-oven pizzas.

Jane had just ordered a bottle of wine from the waitress and a round of waters with lemon when Meg caught sight of Tracey Hines, a woman she typically tried to avoid at all costs. Close on her heels was her crazy toddler, Milo, who had no respect for his parents, other children, or the word *no*, and who Meg was reasonably certain was going to grow into a sociopath. Tracey waved as Milo weaved in between tables, knocking into anything

in sight, waving his hands over his head, and screaming like a
teenage girl at a Katy Perry concert. Much to Meg's horror, Tracey
stopped at their table to make small talk.

"Meg! It's so great to see you. It's been forever, how are you?"
Tracey asked. "I'm sorry to interrupt your lunch."

"It's no problem, it's nice to see you, too. These are my friends
Cara and Jane," Meg said, silently praying that Tracey wouldn't
recognize Jane and make a scene. Tracey was the kind of woman
who went out of her way to talk to you for the sole purpose of
gossip or information gathering.

"Hi," Jane said, as Cara nodded politely. Meg could tell by the
somewhat defensive tone in Jane's voice that while she'd never
met Tracey before, she already knew her type. She watched as
Jane pulled her back a little straighter.

"That over there," Tracey said as she nodded toward her son,
now crawling around on all fours under their table, "is Milo."

"He's a handful," Meg said with a smile.

"Oh, he is! He's just so extraordinary and filled with energy,
you know?" Tracey said with pride, as if it were totally normal
for her child to disrupt the entire restaurant despite the fact that
he was small enough to fit into a garbage can. Meg had a pretty
good feeling that the rest of the people in the restaurant were
dreaming of actually throwing him into one.

Suddenly, Jane screeched and jerked her legs out from under
the table. She grabbed her napkin off her lap and wiped her shin
with it. "Did he just lick my leg? Why is he licking me?" Jane was
disgusted and it was obvious.

"Oh, sorry about that, yeah. It's a phase he's going through.
He'll grow out of it. I think it's adorable."

"A phase? More like a fetish. You better hope he grows out of it before he turns sixteen. I'm sorry, but that's not normal behavior," Jane said, turning her legs sideways to place them out of reach of Milo's serpentine tongue.

"I take it you don't have children?" Tracey asked Jane, clearly more than a little annoyed by the criticism.

"Nope. Can't say I've had the pleasure," Jane shot back.

"What about you, Meg?" Tracey asked, finally grabbing Milo's hand and forcing him up from under the table, probably because she was now concerned that Jane was going to "accidentally" kick him in the head. "I'm sure you'll be chasing one of these around yourself pretty soon, huh? You guys are trying, right? You've been married for a while now and we're not getting any younger!"

Meg's mouth began to water as she fought back her nausea and forced herself to smile. Anyone with any sense at all would know that this particular topic of conversation was off-limits with even the closest of friends. Bringing it up with an acquaintance was inappropriate by any standard. "Well, I guess we'll just see what—" Then, before she could finish her lie, Jane swooped in.

"I'm sorry, on what planet is it okay to interrogate someone about her personal life while she's trying to have lunch?" Jane asked, looking at Tracey with contempt. "And while she's with other people, no less? Is that what's considered normal now? Cara, do you think that's normal?"

"I think it's horrible, actually."

"Tasteless," Jane said.

" 'Moronic' is another word that comes to mind," Cara added, falling right back into the rhythm of their old banter.

"I agree. It's not at all normal to completely invade someone's privacy for no reason other than that you're a gossipy little troll with nothing better to do. Unless, of course, you'd like to have a real heart-to-heart, in which case please pull up a chair because I'd love to hear all about how long you had to try before you got knocked up with your little leg-licker over there. Months? A year? Did your husband shoot blanks the first couple of times before you finally decided to go to a clinic and get pregnant via turkey baster? Seriously, I'm curious . . . since we're all sharing and apparently no topic is off-limits."

Tracey stared at her, mouth agape, seemingly appalled by Jane's outburst, until suddenly her demeanor changed. "Wait a minute, aren't you Jane Logan?"

Cara and Meg froze.

"Oh God," Meg sighed. This was actually going to get worse.

"You bet your ass I am," Jane responded, indignant. Meg felt her heart ache knowing that while the last thing in the world Jane wanted was to be recognized, she was more concerned with protecting Meg than with protecting herself. "Do you have something you want to say to me? Maybe you want to get home and wash your kid's mouth out with disinfectant or something, since his tongue was just all over Doug Logan's wife's leg. I hope being a criminal isn't contagious or he's screwed." Jane turned to Milo and in her best baby voice said, "Can you say 'juvenile detention,' Milo?"

"What is wrong with you?" Traccy screamed as she grabbed Milo and left the restaurant, while Cara started to shake with laughter.

"I can't believe you just said that to her. Even though she totally deserved it," Cara said.

"Whatever. Let her run around the Hamptons gossiping about how I told her off in a restaurant for being a nosy pain in the ass. I'd much prefer she gossip about me than Meg's reproductive organs anyway. Besides, she started it! God, the nerve of some people."

"Thank you," Meg said, still trying to process what had just happened. "Sadly, that's not the first or even the hundredth time something like that has happened to me. I wish I had you around all the time, Jane. Thanks for making it go away." She took a long sip of wine. "I never know how to handle those questions."

"Some women can be bitches," Jane said.

In between bites of her slice, Cara added: "It's not an acceptable topic to just bring up in public like that. People don't think sometimes. I'm sure she didn't mean anything by it, but seriously, use your brain, you know?"

"No, no. Don't give her too much credit. She's a bitch, believe me. I know her type and sniffed her out the second I saw her," Jane said.

"That was one of the hardest things for me to deal with. Comments like that don't hurt all that much anymore, but they nearly killed me when I was doing in vitro. I can't tell you how many times I canceled lunches or avoided going to parties because someone was going to be there who was either pregnant or had just had a new baby and it was too hard for me to be around them. I used to have some really close friends from town who I don't even speak to anymore because of my own stupid issues. No one ever warned me that this type of stress could cause serious divides in your relationships. Maybe if someone had prepared me for it, I would've handled it better. Instead I let it rip apart every relationship that was important to me—even ours, Cara, and you were never anything but supportive and respectful of my privacy. It just overtook my entire life. I felt like I couldn't escape it."

"I understand where you're coming from," Cara said.

"What do you mean?" Meg asked.

"Do you know how many people just assumed that I didn't have children because I was having physical problems? Two different women offered to give me the name of their fertility specialists, unsolicited. I used to just take the info and tuck it away because it was either let them think that I was having problems with my body or admit that what I was really having problems with was my marriage. I felt like I couldn't win either way. What was I supposed to say? 'Actually, I've decided against having kids because my husband and I hate each other. It would be a toxic environment in which to raise a goldfish, never mind a child'? How do you think that'd have gone over at Reed's club?"

"But that drives me crazy!" Jane said, refilling her glass for the third time from the bottle in the silver bucket. "We shouldn't have to feel pressured to answer these questions, or defend the choices we make as grown-ass women. Why is it that we can be our own bosses, run our own households, even run for fucking president, but we have to answer questions about our decisions to have families? Why is that something that needs to be explained? If I don't feel like having kids at this time in my life because I'm not ready to get fat and push a watermelon out of my vag, then that's my decision and I don't have to justify it to anyone. Certainly not over my lunch in the Hamptons."

"Amen," Cara said.

"Is that really why you don't want kids?" Meg asked.

"No," Jane answered. "I think the issue of my husband being

incarcerated is a much bigger problem at the moment, don't you? I mean, logistically that would just be a nightmare. I don't think the warden would be interested in scheduling conjugal visits to coincide with my ovulation dates, you know?" she joked, causing Meg to finally crack a smile.

"I could see how that could be a problem," Cara said.

"No matter what, women are still defined by these labels: wife, mother, grandmother," Meg said. "And if you don't fit the label people make you feel like you're a dragon lady or like . . ."

"Like there's something wrong with you," they said in unison. Children—a strange and surprising intersection to meet at, one that none of them had really ever wanted to talk about . . . until now.

"It's the same bullshit we do to each other in our twenties with getting married, and look how we handled that! Maybe we all let some kind of weird pressure influence the decisions we made there, too. This is the thirties version—fertility. What do we have to look forward to in our forties? Who hits menopause last? *That's exciting*. I look forward to that one," Jane said.

"It makes me angry and it's so hugely unfair. There's nothing wrong with any of us," Cara said.

"Seriously? You're going to say that with a straight face?" Jane asked.

"Okay, fine. That's not entirely true, there's a pretty strong argument to be made that there is something very wrong with all of us, but you know what I mean."

"Cara, if I were you, the next time that someone asked me why I don't have kids, I'd say that I currently sleep in a separate bedroom from my husband, who doesn't like the way I buy groceries, so I figure that adding a kid to the mix would probably not go over well. And Meg, you should just say you tried, and it hasn't worked yet, but you realized that baking muffins like a lunatic has helped soothe your soul so now you're okay with it. See how fast they run away."

Cara burst out laughing. "This is amazing. I don't remember the last time I've felt this good. It's just so nice to finally talk about it with people who get it, with people who don't think I'm a freak."

"Oh, make no mistake, I think you're a freak. But I also get it, so I guess that's okay," Jane added.

"You're right. It feels good to just put it out there. I've been afraid to admit a lot of this because of what people would think of me," Cara agreed.

"Me too," Meg said as she flagged down the waitress and asked for the check. Cara slipped the waitress her credit card while they finished off the rest of the wine, and five minutes later, the waitress returned, holding the card in her hands.

"I'm sorry, ma'am, your card has been declined," the waitress whispered politely so the rest of the diners wouldn't overhear. They'd given them enough of a show for one afternoon.

"What? That's impossible," Cara said.

"It could be our machine. Do you want to try another card?"

"Yeah, maybe the strip is worn," Cara said. Meg knew immediately that the second card wouldn't work, either.

"He canceled my cards," Cara said as soon as the waitress left again, reaching over and grabbing Jane's wineglass to finish off her drink. "I was wondering how long it would take. He lasted longer than I thought he would."

The waitress returned before Meg or Jane had a chance to ask a question. "I'm sorry," she said. "This card isn't working, either."

Cara wondered which one of them was more embarrassed, the waitress for having to say it, or herself for having to hear it.

"Can you give us a minute?" Jane asked the waitress politely. She nodded and walked away. "Okay, this is not that big of a deal! I've been there, and while I can't say that the day when the ATM refuses to give you money because of insufficient funds is fun, exactly, I can tell you that it's not the worst thing in the world. I'd offer to cover you for lunch but I'm broke, too, which means that Meg is now lodging and feeding us both for free. God, we are awful houseguests." She added, "Then again, that's another reason why it's probably a good thing we don't have kids. You and I can't afford them, and Meg is too busy taking care of us at the moment to buy onesies and diaper bags."

"That's true," Meg agreed, stifling a laugh. "You guys do keep me very busy, not to mention, if I had a baby, there'd be no place to put Jane's wine. Babies drink a lot of milk and I don't think I'd have enough room in my fridge." Meg held her credit card up in the air for the waitress and she quickly returned to take it.

"See! There's another bright side," Jane said.

"You guys, seriously, this isn't funny. I have nowhere to go," Cara said, the moment of levity crushed by her realization that Reed's patience had worn out.

"Can we please worry about this tomorrow? We were having such a nice day," Jane said.

"Ignoring your problems won't make them go away. You should know that better than anyone," Cara said.

"That's true. But addressing them now does all but guarantee to ruin our day. Come on. Let it go for now, and we'll deal with it tomorrow. So he took away your credit cards? Big deal."

"I'm so angry I could scream. I am so pissed off at him, and pissed off at myself, and pissed off at the world in general. I want to hit something. I swear to God, I just want to hit something!" Cara said, a little louder than would be considered acceptable for a public lunch conversation.

"Oh, I know!" Jane said. "Want me to find a tennis ball machine? Remember when you were pissed at Mark and we broke into the courts and you nailed tennis balls at the fence? You felt great after that! I will find you one. There has to be a country club out here I can break into."

Cara laughed, which Jane considered a huge victory. "Oh God, I'd forgotten about that. We had fun that night."

"We had a lot of fun nights," Jane added.

"I still think I'm lucky I didn't get tetanus," Meg said, which caused the whole table to giggle. "No one cared that I injured my butt."

"I'm serious. It's been a while since I've wielded bolt cutters. I will do it for you, Cara. Because I love you."

"Thanks. I miss that girl," Cara said. "Teenage me had fire. She had confidence. She knew what she wanted. She'd be so disappointed to meet me now."

"Stop it. We'll figure this out. You still have some money in the bank, right?" Jane asked.

"Just a little," Cara admitted.

"That's all you need. We will figure out the rest," Jane replied.

"Aren't you the optimist today? What happened to you?"

"Rising from the dead has given me a whole new perspective on life. You learn to not sweat the small stuff," Jane said with a smile just as she caught sight of Sheila out of the corner of her eye. The brat from the coffeehouse had her cell phone aimed directly at them and was snapping pictures from two tables away. "Oh, hell no!" Jane screamed as she jumped up, knocking her chair over in the process.

"You want to take pictures of me for cash, huh? It'll be a cold day in hell before anyone makes money off me and my misery, sister!"

Before Sheila knew what was happening, Jane pounced on her and ripped her cell phone from her hand. Before Meg knew what was happening, Jane tossed it to her, like they were playing a grown-up version of monkey-in-the-middle, while Sheila helplessly looked on. Meg wanted nothing to do with the phone, mostly because she was pretty sure that Sheila was stronger than she was and would probably be able to take her down. So she turned and threw it to Cara. If a fight broke out between Cara and Sheila, smart money would bet on Cara every time.

"Catch!" Meg said as the phone went flying through the air. She glanced around at the other ladies having lunch, who were leering at them for the second time in an hour, and made a mental note to never return to this restaurant for lunch. Probably not for dinner either, but definitely not for lunch.

"Give me back my phone, you psycho!" Sheila yelled as she ran toward Cara. Unfortunately for Sheila, she'd picked the wrong day to mess with this particular group of women. Cara calmly dropped the cell phone into the ice bucket that had held their wine bottles for the duration of lunch. They watched as it drowned in the icy water.

"You just destroyed my personal property!" Sheila screamed.

"It's quite annoying when people get in your personal space, isn't it?" Jane said. "Maybe you should think about that next time you want to take a run at me!"

"Listen," Meg said calmly, trying to keep the situation from spiraling into a different level of crazy. "I'm a friend of Nick's, and he told me how you'd already planned to sell photos of Mrs. Logan for your own personal gain, which is not only an invasion of her privacy, but also just plain creepy. Plus, I don't know how the local celebs would feel about a trigger-happy girl working in the coffeehouse where they go in the morning for bagels and caffeine wearing pajamas and no makeup. So assuming you want to keep your job, I suggest you buy a new cell phone and stop bothering people who have nothing to do with you. Otherwise, I'll make sure your boss, your parents, and the editors of the local newspapers know what you're up to in order to make some extra cash, and you can kiss your summer tips good-bye forever."

"Now get out of here before we break more than your cell phone," Cara said.

"I think you just found your fire again," Jane said as Sheila stormed out of the restaurant.

"I'm really sorry for the disruption!" Meg said to the waitress as she quickly signed her name on the credit card receipt.

"Don't say you're sorry. You're not sorry. She started it!" Jane said, still shooting eye darts at Sheila as she hurried down the block.

"I'm a little bit sorry," Meg said, holding her fingers up an inch apart. "Just a little."

"I think we should go now," Cara said, fishing the phone out of the bottom of the bucket and throwing it in her purse. "I'm going to keep this. I don't want to risk her being able to pull something off it."

"Smart. Thank you," Jane said.

"No problem. Now let's go. I need another drink, and I can't afford to have one here," Cara said as she made her way toward the front door.

And that was yet another something they could all agree on.

twenty-eight

t was Tuesday afternoon and Cara hadn't heard from Reed once since she'd left the house four days ago. He'd never called to find out where she went or sent a text asking what prompted her to leave or begged her to come back in a carefully worded e-mail. He wasn't planning on sweet-talking her into coming home; he was planning on humiliating her and forcing her to come back whether she wanted to or not by cutting off her credit and debit cards. When they returned to the house, Cara immediately sprinted upstairs to her room and grabbed her cell phone from the top of the bureau, knowing that she'd have a message. She stared at the text on her phone and her head started to throb. She wondered if Jane had any pills left. She was so going to need them.

> Friday is Neal Booker's birthday party. Cody picking us up at 7. Come home. Now.

Typical, Cara thought. He didn't care that she had run away from home to God knows where with God knows who, but he'd be damned if he was going to have to show up to a social commitment alone. Reed had spent his entire life upholding the legacy of his family's name, and he'd die before he let Cara disgrace that. She didn't know what she was going to do, or how she was going to get out of this, but she knew one thing with absolute certainty: there was no fucking way she was going to that party.

She'd never liked charades and she was done playing along.

She padded downstairs in her socks and found the girls sitting in silence at the kitchen table with mugs of coffee. Cara knew that they didn't know what to say and were waiting for her to speak first. She collapsed in the chair next to Meg and took a sip from Jane's drink. Then she gagged and had to control her urge to spit the coffee back into the mug.

"Oh my God, what is in this?" she asked.

"Whiskey," Jane answered unapologetically. "Today we need the hard stuff."

"Who puts whiskey in their coffee?" Cara asked.

"Irish people. That's why it's called Irish coffee. Though the better question is: Who puts coffee in their whiskey?" Jane asked.

"That's disgusting," Cara said, reaching to take another sip. "Hand it over. You're right, today I need the hard stuff."

"Do you want to talk about it?" Meg asked.

"What's there to talk about? I need to figure out what I'm going to do about going home," Cara said quietly. "I knew this was going to happen eventually. My little mini vacation is over. I got four days of happiness and now I have to face the fact that I can't hide here forever, especially without a line of credit. I'm thirty-seven, not sixteen. I'm too old to just run away from home with absolutely no clue as to what I'm going to do next."

"Okay," Meg said. "What do you want to do? You can't go back there. I can loan you money if you need it."

"I honestly have no idea what I'm going to do! That's the problem. It's not really about what I want anymore. I know I don't want to go back, but I can't keep hiding."

"You're not hiding. You're on vacation from your problems," Jane said.

"It's crazy, isn't it?" Cara asked as she absentmindedly stared out the window.

"What's crazy?" Jane asked.

"That this is even an issue. On paper it should be easy. I'm in a horrible marriage that makes me miserable, I don't have any children—I should be able to just pack up and leave. But he's my husband. I can't just skip out one day and never go back like some angry teenager running away from her parents."

"Why not? What do you have there? Clothes? You can buy new clothes. Get a lawyer, file for divorce, and see him in court," Jane said. "You can send for your stuff."

"It's not that simple. I called the bank. We had a joint checking account and he's transferred almost all of our funds out and into an account he controls. I don't have any money. I let him put everything in his name."

"What about the money from the sale of your mom's house?" Meg asked.

"There wasn't that much. By the time I paid off the mortgage and the taxes and her medical bills it was almost all gone. I put what little there was left into our joint account and now he has that, too. How could I have been so stupid?"

"You weren't stupid. Why would anyone think it was a bad idea to have a joint checking account when they got married? You couldn't have prepared for this and it's not your fault, but you can do something about it now. I know it won't be easy, but you can't go back there," Jane said, surprised at the wisdom in her words. "I know I'm the last person who should be telling anyone how to move on with her life, but for some reason it's always easier to give other people advice than to take it yourself." She paused. "Why is that anyway?"

"My life is completely intertwined with his," Cara said, ignoring the question. "I mean, look at me! I'm living out of a travel bag. I have a few pairs of jeans and some sweaters. I'm not going to pretend like this is some Underground Railroad stop on my way to freedom. What if there is no freedom? My whole life is with that man, in that house, and I can't just leave everything behind. My mother's jewelry is tucked in the top drawer in my bedroom. Every picture I have of her. They're all there." She started to sob.

"In the guest room," Jane pointed out. She was trying to make Cara laugh. It didn't work.

"Whatever. It's all there and I'm not going to pretend like it doesn't mean anything to me. It means everything to me." Cara was shaking. She wasn't someone who was beholden to material things. She didn't care about the cashmere scarves in her closet or the china in the hutch in the dining room. The only things she cared about were the things that reminded her of her mother. They were the only ties to her past and to a time in her life when she felt safe and happy. Those things, and now, thankfully, the women sitting next to her at the table.

"I understand," Meg said. "I get it, and you're right. You've given up enough for him. There has to be a way for you to get your things back and to get some cash. It's not like you lived off his income. You sold real estate. You earned that money yourself. He can't just take it away from you." She added, "Maybe you should go to the police."

"I have an idea," Jane said, which was never a good sign. Cara couldn't remember a situation that started with one of Jane's ideas that ever ended well for anyone. "Screw the police. Cara, how badly do you want out of your marriage? Because if you're serious, I think I know a way."

"What are you talking about? What are you going to do, hire a hit man? Knock him unconscious and throw him in the Long Island Sound?" Cara asked.

"Don't be ridiculous. I've had enough bad press. I don't need to add murder to my résumé. That's exactly the point, though," Jane said, the familiar glint of mischief returning to her eyes. "I've been thinking about a conversation we had the other day and I'm telling you I have a really good idea. Cara, I want you to get pissed. I want you to figure out where your anger went, and I want you to get it back. No more pity, no more regret, just pure, unadulterated fuck-you anger."

"I don't get it," Meg said. "And I don't know if I want to."

"What's Reed's Achilles' heel? The thing that he worries about most in this world? The correct answer, by the way, should be you, but we know it's not, so just play along. If you wanted to do something to really back Reed into a corner, what would you do?" Jane asked.

"I don't know. Ruin his reputation so he'd be exiled from his stupid club? Let the world know that the guy they think is husband of the year is really an asshole?" Cara answered.

"Bingo," Jane said.

"And how do you suppose I do that?" Cara scoffed. "Take out an ad in the newspaper?"

"I have a plan. A good one, and it will work. It will definitely work. I think. I'm fairly certain it will probably work. But you guys have to help me, and you have to be willing to trust me. What do you say? Are you in?"

"I'm sorry, I need more information before I agree to anything," Meg said. "I don't typically like your ideas. I still have a scar on my ass from that fence."

"It was my idea to come here," Jane reminded her.

"Hmm. You have me on that one."

"Reed hates me," Jane said. "I heard him saying he didn't want me staying at your house because he's terrified someone will think he and I are friends or something. What if people think we're *more* than friends? What if we make people think we're having an affair?" Jane asked. "Do you think he'd give you a divorce if the alternative was letting the whole town see him in bed with Jane Logan?"

"I think he'd rather die than have people think you two were having an affair, no offense."

"None taken. In fact, I'm counting on it," Jane said. "Man, I was wondering when Doug being in jail would somehow prove to be a positive in my life, and here we are. I'm going to use my loser husband to get rid of your loser husband. How's that for cosmic intervention?"

"How do you plan on fabricating an affair? It's ridiculous! There's no way," Meg said.

"I know a way. I swear on our friendship I do. But Cara, you have to be ready to leave, for good. And Meg, I'll need your help. I can finally use all the bad things that have happened to me to do some good. But, you have to be willing to trust me."

"Okay," Cara said. "What else do I possibly have to lose?"

"I'm in," Meg agreed.

"Great. The first thing I need you to do is call Nick. Tell him to come over here and to get out a suit and tie. We're going to need a fake lawyer."

Cara grabbed Jane's coffee mug and pulled it in front of her. "I'm going to need this."

"Drink up, buttercup. Are you ready to reclaim your life?"

"Yes," Cara said. "I'm definitely ready."

"Okay, then. Here's what we're going to do . . . ," Jane said.

Meg and Cara hovered over the table and listened intently while Jane told them the single craziest (yet best) idea she'd ever had in her entire life. It might have been misguided, but with Jane and Meg encouraging her, Cara began to feel like she could do anything. She thought about everything she'd been through over the years: her mother's death, explaining grocery receipts, canceled gym memberships, broken friendships, white button-downs and pearls and the guest bedroom, and then one last thought—a surprising one that put her over the edge—her zebra coat.

She loved that thing, and he'd made her throw it away.

And just like that, the anger resurfaced.

She picked up her phone from the kitchen table and responded to his text. *I'll be home tomorrow around noon.*

"I'll be there," she said. Once again she squeezed their hands. "I just won't be arriving alone."

twenty-nine

Early the next morning, Meg climbed into her car with Nick as her passenger, and Jane climbed into her usual seat in the front of Cara's hatchback. Jane had packed all the essentials for their trip: muffins for sustenance, Xanax and Ambien for a lot of reasons, and wine for a celebratory drink when everything was over. Cara couldn't remember a time when she'd been looking forward to something this much and yet dreading it at the same time. She glanced over at Jane and could tell instantly that what they were about to do wasn't fazing her in the slightest. Cara had always envied her courage—now more than ever.

"I thought about this all night, and it's never going to work," Cara said.

"Yes, it will. I want you to know that I was expecting this. Some doubt is totally normal, but I'm not going to let you scare yourself into backing out. You will do this because he deserves it and because the Cara I know is fearless. Plus, we're already in the car. There's no way we're turning around now. Have some faith in me. It will work. I know it will. It's time to man up."

They drove toward Cara's house with little traffic, but that was the least of Cara's worries. She repeatedly checked the rearview mirror to make sure that Meg and Nick were still following them. When they turned onto Cara's block, both cars pulled over so that Jane could hop out and get into the backseat of Meg's car. Before she left, Jane pulled a sandwich-size zip-lock bag from her purse. She handed it to Cara, wrapping her fingers firmly around it. "Are you sure you know what to do? Do you have any questions?"

"I'm pretty sure this is a felony. I could be arrested for this," Cara said.

"I doubt it will come to that. At least I hope it won't."

"That's comforting."

"Just stay calm and do exactly as we planned. I have no doubt that this will work. Zero."

"Really? Zero?"

"Well, maybe not *zero*, but pretty damn close. This is your best shot. Text me when it's show time."

Cara watched Jane amble back to Meg's car and tried to steady her breathing. Something about this felt horribly wrong: morally and ethically. Still, it just might work. It might—as long as she could force herself to go through with it. She pulled her car into the driveway and removed her bag from the trunk. As she suspected, Reed's Jeep was parked by the garage. Once she'd told him she was on her way home, she knew he wouldn't dare miss the chance to make her squirm upon arrival.

She entered through the front door and scanned the foyer for any sign of him. There wasn't any, but that wasn't surprising. Reed wasn't the type of guy who came home from work and slung his jacket over the banister or left his briefcase in the hall. He was meticulous, immediately putting everything away in its proper closet or drawer, and he demanded the same of her. For the first time, she was struck by how cold and sterile her house was. Meg's home in Montauk was smaller than Cara's house, but it was inviting. It was cozy, it was welcoming, and it was filled with loving memories and the smells of freshly baked muffins. Cara's own house looked like a museum. There was no love here. She dropped her bag on the floor and walked into the living room, where she found Reed sitting on the cream-colored sofa, waiting for her.

"Hello, Cara," he said. "I honestly don't even know where to start. Do you have anything to say for yourself?"

Cara reminded herself to stay calm. If she lost her cool, there'd be no reasoning with him, and she needed to make him feel as if he'd won. "I'm sorry. I needed to get away. I'm having a hard time dealing with my mother's death and I needed a time-out."

"A 'time-out'? From what? Did leaving home for almost a week bring your mother back to life?"

"That's not funny." Hearing the callousness with which Reed referred to her mother made the lump return to her throat. How someone could feel no empathy, or sympathy, or sorrow in a situation like this was beyond her. Cara had never really understood the ways in which her husband's emotional circuit board was wired, but she no longer cared.

"Are you honestly going to make me ask where you went?" he asked.

"I went to my aunt's house in the Poconos," Cara lied. She held her breath, knowing full well that her story wouldn't be an easy thing for him to believe. She hadn't been up to her aunt's cabin in years, but still, if she wanted time alone, there'd be no place better for her to go.

"I didn't think you liked the cabin. You always said it smelled like skunk."

"I don't like it, but it was the only place I could go to be alone. I made do."

"And totally forgot about your obligations here? Were you going to be back for the party if I hadn't texted you? How would I have explained your absence? If you have no problem embarrassing yourself in front of the entire town, that's one thing, but you don't have to embarrass me. You know how important this is to me, and that I need Neal's approval if I want to get into the club down south. Do you care at all about what's important to *me*?"

"Of course I do," she lied again, so mind-numbingly tired of pretending to be sorry. "I just needed some time to think, that's all. I'm back in time for the party. No one needs to know I was gone."

"And the letter? Did writing *that* help you to think?"

"I was angry. I said . . . wrote, actually, some things I shouldn't have. I'm sorry."

She choked out her apology. Jane may have dictated the words, but penning that letter was still the first really honest thing she'd done in years. No one would argue that there wasn't a better way to handle this entire situation, but it was too late for what-ifs now. The end result was the only thing that mattered.

"Sorry isn't sufficient. Is that how you're going to handle problems in life? Run from them?"

"No. I can honestly say that I agree with you. Hiding in the woods alone is a really stupid idea." *Hiding in the Hamptons with old friends, however, is not.*

"I mean it, Cara. I won't allow this kind of behavior in my home, and I don't know how, but I'm sure that Jane had something to do with you thinking it was okay to run out of here like that. It's not a coincidence that she shows up and you start acting completely crazy. It's one of the reasons why I told you she wasn't welcome here. She's not good for you. Do you want people in town, or at the club, using our name in the same sentence as hers? Do you know what that would do to our reputation?"

"I know that would ruin you and everything you've worked for. I know your reputation is the foundation of your business and every social connection you have. I shouldn't take them lightly. It won't happen again," Cara said. That much was true.

"Can I expect you to get your head on straight and be a good wife at the party on Friday? Can you do that for me?"

"Yes. Everything will be fine. You have nothing to worry about."

"I don't want to see Jane ever again. Do you understand?"

"Yes. I promise you'll never see her again."

But that doesn't mean she won't see you . . .

There was smug satisfaction in avoiding a lie by actually telling the truth. Cara was tired of doing this little dance, the one where she pretended to be the one in the wrong and let Reed chastise her like she was his daughter instead of his wife. She didn't know how much longer she could trust herself to hold it together before she just blew a fuse and went completely ballistic on him.

"Do you want some tea?" she asked. Reed was habitual to a fault, and he always had a cup of green tea in the afternoon because he stupidly believed the antioxidants would help him stay young. Still, if he said no, she didn't have a plan B. Everything hinged on it.

"Yes, I think I will have a cup. Make sure the water is scalding hot. Half the time you make tea, I feel like I'm drinking dishwater."

Cara went into the kitchen and put the kettle on to boil. She leaned her elbows on the counter and let her head hang while she waited for it to whistle. *Desperate times call for desperate measures, and you are most certainly desperate.* She removed two mugs from the cabinet and dropped tea bags into both. She peeked into the living room and found Reed still sitting on the sofa, talking on his phone. When she was assured that he wasn't going to surprise her in the kitchen, she removed the zip-lock bag from her pocket and placed the two small pills on a cutting board on the counter. With the back of a chef's knife, she began to crush them, reducing them to a powder, and then dusted it into the bottom of his mug. She poured boiling water over it, watching it fizz and bubble and then, as Jane had promised, ultimately disappear.

She calmly picked up the mugs, the one with the crushed-up sleeping pills in her right hand, and carried them into the living room. She handed him his tea, took a sip from her own, and sat quietly on the sofa next to him. Jane had promised her that it wouldn't take long, twenty minutes maybe, for the drugs to kick in. She could think of only one thing that could get her away from him while she waited for him to fall asleep. "I'm going to go upstairs to work out. You're right. I should exercise more."

"It's about time," he said as he took a slug from his drink.

"Do you mind if I use the StairMaster in your room?"

"By all means."

Cara went upstairs and threw on a pair of yoga pants, a T-shirt, and sneakers and pulled her hair into a ponytail. She went into Reed's room and climbed on the machine, not because she gave a shit about exercising but because she had so much nervous energy it was either that or pace the room. When fifteen minutes had passed, she hopped off, and skulked down the hallway. She paused and listened intently, but heard nothing. She must have waited three minutes at the top of the stairs, until she worked up the courage to creep down and check on him in the living room. When she did, she found him snoring on the couch, the empty mug on the table, the white powder now seeping into his bloodstream. She stood over him and clapped her hands loudly three times, but he didn't even flinch. Satisfied that he was out cold, she said a prayer to her mother to help her get through this, then furiously typed two quick messages. The first was to Tabitha:

Something came up and we won't be able to make the party on Friday, so don't worry about picking us up. So sorry to miss it. Have fun!

Then she sent a text message to Jane.

Mission accomplished. You're up.

"I don't know how or why I let you guys talk me into this, but I'm reconsidering my decision. I don't want to play anymore," Nick said from the front seat of Meg's car. "I don't know why I agreed to be a part of this absolutely ridiculous idea."

"I'm sorry you feel that way, but the fact is, you did agree and it's too late to change your mind," Jane said calmly as she stared out the window from the backseat.

"I really don't want anything to do with this! I don't know what I was thinking. I'd like to chalk my momentary lapse in judgment up to extreme boredom or the overabundance of crime drama on cable TV, but now that my common sense has returned I'd like to change my mind."

"Sorry, buddy," Meg said. "You're in. Deal with it."

"Come on, don't let your nerves get the better of you," Jane added.

"Have you lost your mind, Meg? Besides the fact that this is illegal, I will never be able to pull it off. The last time I tested my acting skills I was in grammar school and cast as a dancing bear in *The Nutcracker*. This is way out of my league."

"You can't back out now, Cara's already inside. If you bail on us we'll be screwed! It's time to man up, Nick," Meg said, attempting to be authoritative even though there was nothing authoritative about her.

Nick sighed. "Look, I'm sorry, but I can't! I want to help you, really, I do. But there's no way in hell this guy is going to believe me. Look at me! I don't even look the part."

"That's not true. You look very handsome in your suit. Powerful, commanding, manly," Jane said.

"I've never come across as manly and I've never cared. Know your audience. You'll have to do better than that," Nick joked.

"I was trying to give you a compliment."

"This guy is not an idiot. Why on earth do you think he'll believe me?" Nick asked, panic noticeable in his voice.

"Because there's no reason for him not to," Jane said, as calm as ever. "Just use a bunch of big words and don't get ruffled. He'll be so blindsided by this whole thing he'll believe you. Don't give him too much credit. He's not used to being challenged by anyone, certainly not Cara. He'll be too stunned to really think about the specifics of anything. You can do this. Besides, I'm the one who has the hard job here. At least you get to keep your clothes on."

"That's supposed to make me feel better?"

"We can do this," Meg said. "If Cara can go through with her part, then it's up to us to go through with ours. We aren't leaving a man behind."

"What are you, a navy SEAL?" Nick asked.

"No, just someone who's tired of being a passive player in life. I'm nervous, too. That doesn't mean I'm not going to help. For

Christ's sake, I'm the getaway driver. You know what happens to those people? They're always the first to be busted."

"I'm beginning to understand how all of you guys managed to fuck up your lives so badly before the age of forty, you know that?"

"Yup. And now we're going to drag you down with us," Meg said, nudging him with her elbow.

Jane's phone buzzed on the center console. "Okay. She's ready for us. Are you guys good to go?"

"I am," Meg said.

"Good," Jane said. "Let's do this. Nick, it's time to spice up your life a little."

"I'm a gay man living in the Hamptons. The last thing I need is more spice in my life."

"Just because you think that doesn't mean it's true. Come on, let's have a little adventure," Jane sang.

"An adventure, huh?" Nick said. "You're right. That sounds much better than 'let's commit a felony.' In that case, I guess I'm in." He straightened his tie, smoothed his hair behind his ears, and pulled up his argyle socks. He was as ready as he'd ever be. "Okay, ladies. I agreed to do this and I'm not going to leave you hanging. Is my tie on straight?"

"Yes," Jane said. "But you have time to get into your costume, you realize that, right? Reed won't be up for a while."

"I'm not leaving anything to chance, so I'm going in there fully prepared. If this caper fails, it won't be because I wasn't dressed properly."

Jane leaned over into the front seat and planted a kiss on his cheek. "You, my friend, are a gem. Someday we'll find a way to thank you."

"I doubt that. Let's go."

They climbed out of the car and snuck around to the kitchen door at the back of the house. "How much time do we have?" Meg whispered as soon as they were safely inside and Cara had quietly closed the door behind them.

"A few hours," Jane answered. "He just took two Ambien. That will knock him out until later tonight. How bad was it?" she asked Cara.

"I expected worse, actually," Cara admitted.

"That's not saying much," Jane replied. "Okay, let's get this party started." She pulled her sweater over her head, revealing a synthetic black demi-cup bra that barely covered her synthetic boobs, and dropped her sweater on the floor. Then she removed her shoes and her jeans, tossing them in a ball in the corner. It didn't surprise anyone that before Jane had run from the city, she'd packed matching black lingerie just in case it came in handy. Jane took her mother's warning to never leave the house without clean underwear to the next level. "Ready when you are."

The foursome crept over to where Reed was passed out on the sofa. Cara removed a small mirror from her pocket and held it beneath Reed's nose.

"What are you doing?" Jane asked.

"I'm checking to make sure he's breathing. I'm all for blackmail, but murder is something I'd really like to avoid." Satisfied with his vitals, she undid his belt and unzipped his pants. With Nick's help supporting his dead weight, she was able to slide his pants and his tartan plaid boxers down to his ankles. She unbuttoned his shirt, Nick once again helping to raise him off the couch so she could free his arms from the sleeves. Meg removed his socks and marveled at his feet.

"He has the cleanest man-feet I've ever seen!" Meg exclaimed. "Does he get pedicures?"

"Every two weeks, religiously. The man has better grooming habits than I do," Cara said.

"There's nothing I hate more than men who get pedicures. I refuse to sit next to them in the salon if they're there. It's bad pediquette," Jane said.

"I'm sorry, what word did you just say?" Meg asked.

"Pediquette. Pedicure etiquette."

"I get pedicures," Nick admitted, staring at his toes. "But I don't wax my toes, and I'm pretty sure he does. There's no hair on them! Are you sure he's not gay?"

"You guys!" Cara yelled. "Can we please get on with this? I don't care how long he's unconscious, there's no need to drag this out."

Jane undid her bra and climbed on top of Reed, nestling in the crook of his arm, her leg thrown over his hip. "How's this? Can you see enough of my boobs? These pictures need to be racy or there's no point to doing this."

"Turn to the side more," Meg said. "It'll look better if we can see your nips."

Jane obediently rolled slightly onto her back, exposing an entire boob, and tilted her head so her face could be clearly seen. "I feel like Kate Winslet in *Titanic*. Is that weird?" she asked.

"Oh my God, I love that movie! How many times did we go see that? Like a dozen?" Meg asked.

"Probably more," Jane said. "Wait, do you remember the time that we—"

"You guys!" Cara snapped. "Can you please focus?"

"Sorry. You're right," Jane said. "You know, for the record, this has got to be the first time anyone has ever used naked pictures of themselves to ruin someone *else's* reputation, but I'm doing it because I love you and I think we need to work on building the bonds of sisterhood."

"I love you, too," Cara said.

"Good. Now, are we ready to make it look like I'm banging your husband?"

"Wait. One more thing," Meg said as she grabbed an eight-by-ten wedding photo from a console table by the fireplace. She placed it dead center on the table next to the couch, a clear indication to anyone who ever saw these pictures that they were taken in Reed's home. There'd be no way for him to argue that they were Photoshopped, that the man wasn't him, or that he'd never seen Jane before in his life. There'd be no way for him to explain anything. Now that they were actually doing this, Cara had to admit, this idea was freakin' genius.

Illegal, but genius.

Sadistic, but genius.

Crazy, but genius nonetheless.

"Okay," Nick said as he stepped back and hit the camera app on his phone. "This looks great. Clear as day. Jane, just make sure that we can see your face. There has to be no question it's you."

"I know that! This was my plan, remember?" she answered.

"I just want to make sure I get everything right! It's a lot of pressure being the cameraman," Nick said.

"Just start taking the pictures already. It's cold in here and as much as I want to help Cara, lying on her naked husband isn't exactly fun for me, so can we please move this along?" Jane ordered.

"Just one more second," Cara said before she sprinted up the stairs and down the hall into the master bedroom. As she suspected, the pearl necklace was still lying on the nightstand, exactly where she'd left it. She grabbed it and ran back downstairs, handing the strand to Jane. "Put these on."

"Why? Do you want me to eat them or something? Didn't that look go out in the eighties?"

"No, I don't want you to put them in your mouth. Everyone thinks these pearls are my signature. These pictures will be even better if you're wearing my jewelry in them. How much of a pig do you have to be to let your mistress wear your wife's necklace?"

"You might have a future in this," Jane said. "That's fucking brilliant."

Jane lowered the pearls over her neck, tousled her hair, and adjusted her visible boob one more time. Cara, Meg, and Nick stood back and examined their staging. Everything looked great, exactly how they'd talked about it. Better, in fact. Jane put her hand on Reed's chest, arched her back, and said, "I'm ready for my close-up!"

And with that, Cara and Meg hurried upstairs to pack Cara's things, and Nick began to quietly snap photos with his iPhone.

thirty

Cara sat on the beige chintz couch in her living room and held her breath when Reed began to stir. It was almost comical to watch him wake—confused, disoriented, cold—and downright hysterical to see the look on his face when he realized he was buck naked on the living room couch. He glanced out the window at the blue-and-gray-streaked sky, the orange glow of sunrise bouncing off the crystal lamp on the coffee table, and rubbed his temples. Cara exhaled slowly before she began.

"Good morning," she said coolly, not sure that her tone completely registered. She was shocked that it had taken Reed as long as it did to wake up. Jane had said it would take a few hours, but she'd underestimated the power of Ambien on someone who never took so much as a Tylenol PM. He'd been out for almost eighteen hours. He sat up and rubbed the remnants of sleep from his eyes, then focused on the woman sitting across from him. Cara was sipping a glass of juice, fully dressed, which probably seemed strange to him for this time of the morning. Cara figured he'd find it even stranger that she wasn't alone. Nick sat next to her on the couch, wearing a suit and tie, a briefcase resting on his lap. Reed immediately reached for the blanket on the back of the couch, as if that would somehow make any of this normal.

"Who are you?" Reed asked, his voice still groggy from his chemically induced slumber. Cara stared straight ahead, pretending that this was a business meeting or something—which, when she thought about it, was basically what it was. She watched as Reed tried to clear his head, no doubt wondering if he was hallucinating.

"My name is Nicholas Redmond. I'm Cara's attorney," Nick said calmly. If he was nervous, he wasn't showing it. If anything, he seemed to be enjoying this. She was beginning to wonder if maybe she was, too.

"What? What are you talking about? Get out of my house!" Reed demanded. "What kind of lawyer shows up at someone's home at this hour of the morning? My wife doesn't need a lawyer. I don't know who you are, but get the hell out of here. What time is it?"

"Six thirty," Cara answered. "On Thursday."

"I think you should hear me out. There are a few things that we need to discuss," Nick said flatly. Cara enjoyed watching Reed as the cobwebs cleared and he started to focus on what was going on. She'd never seen such a look of utter bewilderment on his face before.

Actually, she loved it.

"Cara, I don't know what the hell you're doing, but you've exhausted my patience. It's Thursday?" he asked, still groggy, confused, and growing more irate by the second.

"The feeling is mutual. I want a divorce," she said, unflinching, as if this was a decision she'd made a long time ago. Hearing herself say the words made her wonder if maybe she had. Maybe she'd always known this day was coming and just needed Meg and Jane to give her directions to get here. Now that she'd said it out loud she felt lighter, like all of Reed's insults and injuries were melting off her.

"Joke's over. I don't know who you are, but I'll only repeat myself once. Get out of my house before I call the police," Reed said, fumbling around the floor looking for his pants.

Cara held up her cell phone. "I don't think you want to do that. Don't you want to see what's on this first?"

"What are you talking about?" Reed asked again. "Are you drunk?"

Cara tossed him her phone. "Go ahead," she said. "Scroll to the left."

Cara watched as Reed glanced down at the pictures. His hands began to shake, then his ears turned bright red when he processed what he was seeing. He scrolled through shot after shot of him lying naked on the couch with Jane Logan, persona non grata in any circle within a hundred miles of New York City, straddling him, nuzzling his neck, wearing his wife's pearls. Cara had to admit they'd done very, very good work.

"What the hell is this? When did this happen? This doesn't make any sense . . ." He trailed off as he started to piece together the last few things he remembered, exactly the way Cara knew he would. "Oh my God. The tea. You drugged me."

" 'Drugged' is a strong word. I helped you sleep. That's all."

"Have you gone completely crazy? You psychotic bitch!" he screamed.

"Sweet-talking won't get you anywhere," Cara said, knowing full well how much he hated to be antagonized.

"Those are pictures of you cheating on your wife with a well-known but not well-loved woman. I believe you recognize Jane Logan," Nick said effortlessly, keeping in character as Cara's attorney.

"Where is she?" Reed asked, hopping off the couch. He ran

into the kitchen, checked the bathroom, opened the coat closet as if this were some twisted game of hide-and-seek. "Jane!" he screamed. Nick and Cara sat quietly on the couch while Reed scoured the first floor for signs of his nemesis. "Jane, get out here!"

"She's not here," Cara said, feeling icy and calm.

"As you can see," Nick said from his place on his couch, "these pictures are quite incriminating. If you look closely you'll notice your wedding photo is prominently displayed in the pictures. There is no doubt that these photos were taken in your home, and that Mrs. Logan is wearing your wife's necklace. Should these photos surface in the tabloids, your reputation would be irrevocably damaged. From what your wife tells me, you'd rather choose death. I think maybe it's time you sit back down and listen to what we have to say."

Reed grabbed the phone and feverishly began deleting the photos. When he was convinced they'd all been erased from the memory card, he dropped the phone back on the couch. "That's it? That's your big plan? You go through all of this and then you just turn over your cell phone? You're more of an idiot than I thought, Cara. Now what are you going to do?"

"Actually, neither one of us is as stupid as you'd like to believe. I'm sorry to disappoint you, but copies of those photos have been sent to my law offices. Copies have also been placed in a safe deposit box controlled by Jane Logan with instructions that should anything happen to her, they'll be released to a certain tabloid editor who has been quite anxious to get an exclusive interview with her. As you can imagine, she's not all that concerned about these pictures being released. In fact, she couldn't care less. She has bigger things to deal with at the moment."

"This is blackmail," Reed said, the color draining first from his earlobes, and then from his entire face.

"I like to think of it as persuasive reasoning. That sounds much better. Don't you think?" Cara said. "Besides, blackmail is illegal. I would never dream of breaking the law. I'm just a stupid housewife, remember?"

"You're willing to embarrass yourself by making it look like I had an affair with your slut friend?" Reed seethed. "Your pride is worth that little to you?"

"Slut friend? Hmmm. That's interesting. Didn't you tell Cody that neither you nor I knew her? When Tabitha mentioned that she saw her outside our house, didn't you say that it was ridiculous, and that you'd never seen her before in your life? Looks like you're going to have to explain that to the fellows at the club. Do you think they'll believe that li'l ol' me orchestrated this? Or do you think it's more likely that they'll take one look at these photos and figure you were sleeping with her and then lying to cover it up? I'd imagine that will make for some pretty good gossip at the next poker game, don't you?"

"Oh my God. Cody and Tabitha are supposed to pick us up tomorrow for the party," Reed said. "Did you send these to Tabitha?"

"No. Not yet," Cara answered. "I texted her and told her not to pick us up. No one knows anything as of now, but believe me when I tell you that it won't take much for me to make sure that every guy you hang out with sees these pictures. Don't push me."

"I never liked Jane. Not from day one," Reed said, his mind clearly processing the fact that Cara now single-handedly controlled his precious social life.

"She knows, but she doesn't care. Never did, and neither do I," Cara answered, smiling as she echoed Jane's exact thoughts when they'd discussed Reed's opinion of her in the kitchen only a week ago.

"So, what do you want?" he asked. "What's so important to you that you'd go through all this?"

"Cara is filing for divorce," Nick said. "You will not contest the divorce, and you will not make her endure a protracted legal battle. You will provide her with reasonable spousal support, and since you two never entered into a prenuptial agreement, you will sell this house and split the proceeds equitably. Assuming you comply with these conditions, the pictures will disappear and you can go on with your life as a single man without ever worrying that you will one day open the *New York Post* and see these pictures on Page Six. These are your only two options: a quiet divorce with spousal support, or a public divorce with incriminating photos and personal ruin. Your choice. My office will be in touch."

"Cara, if you walk out this door, don't ever think of coming back. Once you start this ball rolling there's no stopping it. You'd better be damn sure you're really ready to come after me," Reed said through gritted teeth.

"Oh, I am. Thanks for giving me the option, though. I appreciate it."

"I had no idea you hated me so much."

"There's a lot you don't know about me," Cara said as she stood to leave. "And you are fucked up way beyond repair. You can keep the pearls. It's been a pleasure doing business with you."

Nick picked up his briefcase—which contained absolutely nothing—and nodded in Reed's direction. "Good day, sir," he said. Cara followed Nick toward the front door and smiled as she stepped onto the walkway and made her way back to the car.

Cara tried as hard as she could to look composed leaving the house. She knew Reed would be watching them from the window as they climbed into her car, Nick carefully placing his fake briefcase in the backseat before buckling himself into the passenger side. She pulled out of the driveway with a white-knuckle grip on the steering wheel, her knees trembling so badly she feared she'd crash the car into the mailbox at the curb. They drove down the street and made a left toward town, and only when her car was safely lost in traffic on the Long Island Expressway did either of them bother to speak. They'd done it.

She'd won.

"I was awesome, wasn't I?" Nick said, so giddy he was literally bouncing up and down in his seat. "I was like a prizefighter, I mean I took him *down*. I was like Tyson. I was like Frazier. I was like Ali. I was like LL Cool J when he sang 'Mama said knock you out!' That was me in there."

"Did you just list every pro athlete you know of?" Cara teased.

"Pretty much! And the only rapper."

Cara chuckled, finding Nick's enthusiasm contagious, and began to feel giddy herself. "You were great in there, really," she said, reaching over and patting his leg. "I don't think I'll ever be able to thank you."

"Do you think he bought it? I think I was convincing, although admittedly I could've done more with my character. I didn't come anywhere near exhausting my legal vocabulary. I didn't use the word 'jurisprudence' even once! Next time someone asks me to pretend to be a lawyer, I'll do much better."

They were returning to the beach, which should have been comforting. The problem was, now that it was done, now that she had forced Reed into a corner, she knew there was no going back. That wasn't an issue. What was an issue was that she had no idea where she was going to go now. She had her entire future ahead of her, and not the first damn clue as to what she would do with it. This was how people were supposed to feel when they graduated from college, not when they were going on forty.

"I don't know," she said. "It will be a while before I know for sure. I think now he's probably too stunned to process much of anything. Jane may have just solved some problems, but she also created a bunch of new ones."

"Well, no one said that things were going to be easy. You may have a new problem, but it's better than still dealing with your life the way it was. Now you can do anything you want. Provided he signs the divorce papers."

"I guess so!" Cara said, though it unnerved her more than a little to know that she had absolutely no idea what to do next. She doubted Jane had a plan for that, either.

"For what it's worth, I think you're doing the right thing by leaving him. You're way too great to deal with someone like that. I wish I had some single friends to set you up with."

"Thanks, but the last thing I need right now is a man. I want to be alone for a while. I need to rebuild myself. More than anything I need a new job in a new place to support my new life far away from Reed. I have to start refurbishing my bank account until the house sells."

"Why didn't you say so? You have a friend who has a real estate firm, and you have sold real estate, have you not?" Nick asked.

"In my hometown, yeah. I don't know the first thing about the market out east. I don't know anything about selling vacation homes."

"You sold one the other day! You have a passion for it, that's clear, and it just so happens that I could use someone in my office.

I don't see why you couldn't work out here, make a little money, and get your feet back under you. It would be mutually beneficial."

"You're serious?" Cara couldn't believe what he was saying.

"Completely. You don't have to tell me now, but think about it. If you really want a fresh start, I think this is a great way to get going. I told you I was impressed with you the other day. You're really very talented."

Cara was stunned. She'd been through a crazy amount of change for one twenty-four-hour period, and this didn't help calm anything down. Still, the offer seemed too good to be true.

"You'd do that for me?" Cara asked.

"Yeah, I would. Like I said, it would help me out, too. But I think you need some stability and something positive in your life right now. I've been there, so I get it. I think it could work out great."

"I don't know what to say," Cara said, feeling a sudden urge to hug him.

"Think about it."

"I will. Thank you, Nick. If someone would've told me that this week would end the way it has, I never would've believed them."

"I didn't think this week would end like this, either. I just spent my night photographing a naked celebrity with a comatose man, and my morning pretending to be a lawyer. How is any of that normal?"

"It's not. But you'd better get used to the abnormal if you're going to be friends with us!"

Two hours later, she drove through East Hampton and onto the stretch of Route 27 that would lead through Amagansett and then to Montauk. What she would do when she got there she wasn't exactly sure, but oddly enough, even though she had just left her husband, her life, and her house, she felt like she was coming home.

thirty-one

I wish I could've seen his face. That might have been my greatest performance yet. He's going to lose his fucking mind!" Jane said. She slapped the dashboard so hard in her excitement that she winced in pain. She had to admit, she was proud of herself. True, maybe her methods weren't ethical by social standards, but this wasn't a normal situation. She'd found a way to solve Cara's problems, to feel like she was useful, and to put her acting skills to good use. If she had to get naked to do it, so be it. Most people in Hollywood stripped for much less.

"Where do you get your courage from? I could never in a million years do what you just did," Meg asked, wondering how girls who grew up as close as they did could be so completely different.

"It has nothing to do with courage. It's spite. He doesn't deserve her, and now, hopefully, he'll let her go. What could be a better reason than that?"

Meg drove east on the highway, staring at Cara's taillights in front of her, but her mind had been wandering for the better part of the ride. She couldn't stop thinking about Reed and how awful he'd been to Cara, and Jane and how her husband had betrayed her and ruined her life because he was selfish and greedy and arrogant. Then she thought about Steve and about how he had done absolutely nothing—not one single thing since the day they'd met—except love her and support her and value her. And she'd thrown it all away. Jane and Cara were alone because that was what was best for them. But what was best for her? Could this really be the way her life was supposed to play out? Did she really toss away everything that mattered to her willingly? She had chosen to be alone this past year, and for some reason, until now, she couldn't see how very, very stupid that was.

"Are you okay?" Jane asked. "You've been quiet, even for you. What's on your mind?"

"Steve, actually," Meg said.

"It's not too late," Jane answered.

"I was so awful to him. He tried so hard and I pushed him away. Why would he even want me back? Nothing has changed. We'll never have kids. Not our own, at least."

"So what? You'll have each other. Why can't that be enough?"

"It's not what we had planned. It's not how things were supposed to happen."

"Meg, you need to adapt. So what if it isn't how things were supposed to happen? Look at the rest of us. You think this is how any of us thought our lives would work out? You have a great guy who loves you. I'm really sorry about your medical issues, I am. But you're not the first woman in the world to have fertility problems, and honestly, if he's okay with it, then that's his decision. He's a big boy. He can decide for himself. Do you think that being separated is the better option? Really?"

"No. I've known that it's not for a long time, but I can't bring myself to call him. I mean, what will I even say? Sorry? Sorry I left you and moved to Montauk and made you worry about me nonstop for a year? Sorry that I can't have kids and because of that I abandoned you? Seriously, what do I say?"

"Nothing. You don't say a word," Jane said. She paused, then added, "You let me do it for you." Jane removed her phone from her bag and scrolled through her contacts.

"What are you doing?" Meg asked.

"Today seems to be my day for solving all of my friends' problems. I'm calling your husband."

"Jane, hang up the phone! Stop it!" Meg yelled, remembering a similar conversation they'd had when Jane had called the boy Meg liked in fifth-period French class and tried to get him to come to a party. That hadn't ended well, either.

"I will do no such thing. I'm taking matters into my own hands. You need my help."

"Please hang up the—"

"Hi, Steve!" Jane said. Meg realized she was holding her breath listening to Jane speak, a vein in her neck pulsing so strongly she could actually hear it. "No, she's fine. Everything is great. Well, I spent last night taking naked pictures with Cara's soon-to-be ex-husband, but other than that things are great. Don't worry, though, Meg was only the getaway driver; she had nothing to do with the pictures, or the drugs, or the blackmail. We've been taking good care of her, as promised!"

Meg unwillingly cracked a smile just picturing Steve's face on the other end of the line as he tried desperately to understand what Jane was talking about.

"Anyway, it's a long story. You know what would be great? Why don't you come out for dinner tonight? We're celebrating and we'll fill you in on everything when you get out here. Meg really wants to see you. I think it's time you guys talk things out. I don't want to overstep here—you know how much I hate to meddle in other people's problems—but in this case, I think it's warranted. It doesn't matter what time, six, seven, whenever. What do you say? It'll be nice."

"Tell him I hope he comes," Meg said. "Tell him . . . tell him I'd like him to come."

"Did you hear that?" Jane asked. "Don't make her ask twice. Please come. Great. We will see you around six!" Jane hung up. "Maybe I should be a relationship counselor."

"What did he say?" Meg asked.

"He's coming. He's looking forward to it. He wants to hear the story. You can still save this. You can still get your life back. I'd kill to be in your position."

"I—I don't know what to do," Meg stammered. Who got this nervous over seeing her own husband?

"I just told you what to do. Meg, please don't make him come all the way out east hoping to reconcile with you and flake on him. That's just cruel."

"No, that's not what I mean. I meant I have nothing to wear."

"Oh, well. That's a different story, then. I don't think he'll care what you wear. I think he only cares about what you have to say. Let's focus on that."

"Do you really think I can do this?"

"I think we can do anything we want to do. You just have to be brave enough to put yourself out there. Do you want me to get naked and straddle him when he gets to the house? I'll do that for you too, if you want."

"Keep your clothes on or I will end you," Meg said, her insides churning at the mere thought of it.

"That's my girl."

There were so many questions bouncing around Meg's brain: What if Steve changed his mind and didn't show? Or worse, what if he drove all the way out there, but then decided that

he didn't want to listen to what she had to say? She knew that
he was running out of patience and she couldn't blame him.
It didn't take a genius to understand that this was probably
going to be her last chance to save her marriage, and that if
she couldn't convince him that she was ready to move on from
everything, he'd probably move on without her. As soon as they
returned home, they headed straight for Meg's room. Cara,
Nick, and Jane sat on her bed for over an hour, watching as she
tore through everything in her closet, ultimately deciding on
nothing. She felt like she was back in college, getting ready to
go on a first date or something, instead of preparing to meet her
husband for the first time in almost a year. She never thought
she'd have these feelings again, the butterflies that overtake you
when you're really excited and nervous and hopeful and scared
all at the same time.

Two hours later, Steve knocked softly on the door. It takes a special kind of man to be willing to knock before entering his own
house, but Meg had always known he was special. She smoothed
her hands over her hair before she opened the door, suddenly
having to resist the urge to cry. Cara, Jane, and Nick had scurried
upstairs to give her some privacy, but she knew they were all
piled on top of each other at the top of the stairs, eavesdropping
without feeling the least bit guilty like only best friends can. Meg
wouldn't have it any other way.

"Hey," Steve said when she opened the door. He held a bottle
of wine in one hand and a bunch of flowers in the other. "I heard
you were having a dinner party. You look great," he added quietly.

"So do you," she answered. There weren't words to say how
sorry she was for everything, so she didn't even try. Instead, she

flung herself on him. "Welcome home," she managed to choke out before she started to cry.

An hour later they sat around her farmhouse kitchen table, Meg and Steve on one side, Cara and Jane on the other, with Nick at the head. They ate tequila-and-chili-spiced chicken and sipped champagne as they celebrated too many things to count. Meg watched Steve eat slowly, savoring the first home-cooked meal she'd made for him in a very long time, and listened to Nick and the girls fill him in on their adventure. Steve waited until the very end before he said a word. Meg knew his brain was swimming with all the details they'd just thrown at him, and that made complete sense. Meg had done more in the past week than she'd done in the past year. Part of her had come back to life.

"You guys did all of this in the last twenty-four hours?" Steve asked.

"Yup," they said in unison.

"Wow. You know, I always knew that you were not women I wanted to mess with. It's too bad that Reed had to learn that lesson the hard way, but screw him. I never liked him anyway."

"Cheers to that!" Jane said, raising her glass. "Now can I say I told you so?"

"Not yet," Cara said with a laugh. "Maybe tomorrow."

"Okay. I've been waiting a long time. One more day won't kill me."

They finished their celebratory dinner and cleared away the plates, then returned to their seats to dig into an apple pie and vanilla ice cream.

"So now what?" Steve asked after finishing his second slice. "What are you guys going to do next? Rob a bank?"

"I haven't gotten that far," Jane admitted. "Now that you mention it, I have absolutely no idea, but bank robbery is not on my to-do list. I'm in enough trouble with the banking industry."

"Nick offered me a job," Cara said, trying in vain to hide her excitement.

"Really?" Jane asked.

"It's true," Nick said.

"You know how much money people spend on summer homes out here? Serious bucks. You might end up making a fortune," Meg pointed out.

"I might end up making nothing," Cara said.

"It would behoove you to show a little optimism as you embark on this new phase of your life," Nick chided.

"Sorry," Cara said. "I'm still trying to process everything."

"I'm positive that I'm completely fucked. How's that for optimism?" Jane asked. "Don't get me wrong, I'm so happy that I have you all back in my life, but I am still totally screwed. I don't know what I'm going to do with myself," she admitted.

"Wait! What about Sheila?" Meg said. She slapped her hand on the table in excitement and Sebastian immediately hopped up from the floor and came scurrying over to her side.

"What about her?" Cara asked.

"She said she was going to sell the pictures she took of you to a tabloid."

"Real gem of a girl, that one," Jane scoffed.

"No. You're missing the point. The point is, there's money to be made by being *you* right now. Everyone wants to know what you're doing, right? Everyone wants to know what's going on with you. Hell, the news is insinuating you're dead."

"They are?" Steve asked. "Why?"

"Don't ask," Jane said. "Yeah, sure. There's money to be made if people want to chase me and sell pictures of me looking miserable. Good for them. They're basically bounty hunters. I hate all of them."

"So don't give them the chance," Meg said. "I think you should tell your story yourself. If people want to know about you so badly, give them what they want. On your terms."

"Are you saying she should write a memoir?" Steve asked.

"Bingo. You can write your story yourself and tell everything you want to tell, the way you want to tell it. Don't let the media spin everything out of control. You're Jane Logan. You tell the Jane Logan story. I'd bet you could sell it for a ton of money. You might be able to afford a new apartment, or at the very least rent one, and the tabloids will back off because the mystery will be gone. No one will care about you anymore once you demystify yourself."

"I don't know why you girls thought up your blackmail scheme, but didn't think of this earlier," Steve said. "It's the much more obvious fix."

"Thanks, guys. I appreciate you trying to come up with something productive for me to do with my time, but I don't think I can write a memoir. If for no other reason than I'd like to try to move on from this phase of my life, and writing about it will only keep it alive longer. It's so pathetic, isn't it? I'm almost forty years old, and I've never really given any thought to what I wanted to do when I grew up. I went from being an unemployed actress to being an unemployed trophy wife. It's not exactly the résumé I hoped to have at this stage of the game."

"So what if you never held a normal job?" Meg asked. "It doesn't mean you can't use this time to figure out what you want to do and go after it. You're smart, dedicated, and talented. You just need to refocus."

"I know. I need to take some time and really figure out what I want to do now, you know? I don't want to make any stupid decisions on a whim. I've made enough of those for one lifetime, and all they've ever done is get me in trouble."

"I think that's one of the smartest decisions you've ever made," Cara said. "You're right. One thing you have going for you right now is that you don't have any obligations. You can do anything you want—once you figure out what that is, exactly."

"Right. I just have to figure that out," Jane said.

"You will. We will help you. You don't have to go through this alone anymore," Meg said.

"What do you say we clean up and then have some after-dinner drinks in the den?" Cara asked.

"Great idea. Steve, will you put a fire on and make a pot of coffee while we get rid of these dessert plates?" Meg said. Steve happily stood to head into the living room. Cara liked knowing that time apart hadn't changed Meg and Steve's connection in the slightest. She had no doubt that they were going to be just fine.

"Actually, I have an idea," Jane said. "Why don't we leave the guys to clean up?"

"Why?" Cara answered. "What do you want to do?"

Jane smiled. "I think we should go for a drive."

Acknowledgments

I want to say thank you to the people who helped make this book possible:

Thank you once again to my agent at William Morris Endeavor, Erin Malone. You're awesome.

Thank you to my editor at HarperCollins, Emily Krump. I'm sorry you had to work on this manuscript while on your maternity leave. I owe you one.

Thank you to my friends and family for supporting me as I wrote this. I love you guys.

About the author

About the book

Read on . . .

Insights,
Interviews
& More . . .

Meet Erin Duffy

Elena Seibert

ERIN DUFFY graduated from
Georgetown University in 2000 with
a B.A. in English and worked on Wall
Street, a career that inspired her first
novel, *Bond Girl*. She lives in New York
with her husband and children. ⌢

Finding Time for Our Friends

I'm just going to come right out and say it: I don't trust girls who don't have girlfriends. I'm sorry. I just don't. If we meet and you tell me that you don't have any girlfriends, you can bet that I'm operating under the assumption that you're either half alien or that there's something seriously wrong with you.

When I was growing up my parents returned from every single parent-teacher conference with the same feedback: Erin talks too much. I did. In fact, most people who know me would argue that I still do. I was the kid who was constantly chatting with my friends about everything and nothing. I remember having a twenty-minute conversation with a friend about where to buy the best leggings, instead of learning how to solve for the hypotenuse of something or other. Fifteen years later, I had a different twenty-minute conversation with the same friend about where to buy the best body shapers. Any woman will tell you that there's no better source for honest information than a girlfriend. I love mine. I cherish them. I don't have any sisters and without my girlfriends I don't know how I'd have made it through junior high, or high school, or college, or my twenties. Now that I think about it, I've needed them desperately throughout my thirties, too. ▶

Finding Time for Our Friends *(continued)*

You get where I'm going with this.

Here's the thing: maintaining adult friendships is not easy. We are busy women. I'll admit that it's sometimes challenging to keep in touch, with so many demands pulling us in a million different directions. I don't know one woman who has an abundance of free time on her hands. Everyone I know is either working like a lunatic, or taking care of lunatic children, or working like a lunatic while also taking care of lunatic children. It's hard to schedule lunches, or dinners, or even phone calls in the middle of the week when 90 percent of the time everyone, this author included, is so tired by seven P.M. that it takes herculean strength not to face-plant into a bowl of pasta before Alex Trebek throws out the final *Jeopardy!* question. It's not easy to keep in touch in a meaningful way, but really good friends will understand that sometimes a few text messages, or pictures on Instagram will have to be enough. We are busy women. We are doing the best that we can.

Those texts will have to be enough until you and your besties are able to steal away for a weekend together for the first time in years and fall right back into the same rhythm you had when you met and became friends freshman year of college—that is what I did this past spring. My college roommates and I hadn't all been together since my wedding three years ago. We spent the first two hours catching up on the basics: jobs, husbands, relationships, kids, and the rest of it pretending like none of those things existed. Forty-eight hours on a beach with them was all I needed to completely recharge my oh-so-very-drained battery and tap into a part of myself I'd forgotten existed. Girlfriends are awesome like that. We made tentative plans to do it again next year, and I hope that we can make that happen. If not, no biggie! We'll get it on the calendar when we can. We all understand that leaving real life isn't easy. We are busy women. We are also best friends.

That's not to say that I haven't had challenging friendships, or that there haven't been some people who've gotten lost along the way. (No plug intended!) A few years ago, I had a difficult conversation with a then-close friend who'd become a major source of stress in my life. Originally, I'd wanted us to work through our problems. I'd wanted her to understand that life had gotten very demanding, and that time together wasn't as easy to come by as it used to be. Then she uttered two little words that all but caused me to choke on my latte: "You've changed."

I've changed? Since when? The nineties? Thank God! I'm proud to say that I'm nowhere near as stupid as I used to be. This is somehow a bad thing? Really? A friendship that expects, or demands, that you never change or grow, is one that you can do without. At ▶

Finding Time for Our Friends *(continued)*

least, that's how I felt about it, and it's why I haven't spoken to her since. It hurt for a while, as breakups do, and I beat myself up over the end of our friendship for a long time. I blamed myself. I wondered if I should've done something differently. Then I realized that it was okay to let her go. Honestly, anyone who wants me to be the exact same person I was in 1998 can bite me. Hard.

We are busy women. We are allowed to decide who we want to be without anyone else's expectations holding us back. I used to shop at Banana Republic with a girlfriend who suddenly decided she only wanted to speak Spanish and dance in underground Dominican clubs in the East Village. Good for her! I hope she has an awesome time and learns to salsa with the best of them, but we probably won't hang out on weekends quite as much because I don't speak Spanish, and I certainly can't dance and have no desire to learn. We now have very different definitions about what makes a fun Saturday and that's totally fine. I miss her, but I'm happy she's happy with her life. I don't think she owes anyone an apology for becoming the woman she wanted to be. She certainly does not owe one to me.

We have to be smart with how we allocate our spare time, and we have to be forgiving of our friends who have very little of it. I don't need to talk to my girlfriends every day, though I certainly wish that I could. I know that if I send a text asking, "Are you free?" I'll get a response. It'll go something like this: "I'm running around like crazy, but I'm here if you need me. Is everything okay?" We are busy women, but we will always make time for our girlfriends.

That's how we know who they are. ～

Reading Group Guide

1. Jane says that one of the reasons she pulled away from her friends was that she felt left behind once Meg and Cara were both married. Do you think that marriage can cause rifts in lifelong friendships? Should it?

2. Having children is a major theme in this book. One of the big issues Meg has is that she finds the social pressure to have a baby overwhelming. Do you think that women intentionally put pressure on each other to marry and have kids? Is there judgment when or if those life events never happen? Why or why not?

3. The girls grew up like sisters, but were unable to maintain their bond into their thirties. Why is it sometimes difficult to maintain friendships from our teens and twenties into our thirties and forties? Do you think the girls should've worked harder to stay together? Would it have been possible? Why or why not?

4. Jealousy is another major topic in this book. Do you think all women envy their friends to some degree? Why or why not?

5. Jane has no idea that Doug is a fraud, and her ignorance causes extreme self-loathing. Do you think she was wrong to never question him, or is it

okay for her to trust him because he was her husband? Should she have known better?

6. Meg and Steve were obviously in love, but Meg decided that Steve was better off without her. Do you think that was her decision to make? Was she trying to do Steve a favor, or was her leaving him a selfish act?

7. Fate helped bring the girls back together after years apart. Do you believe that people come into your life at a particular time and a particular place for a reason? Do you think the girls learned anything about themselves from their eventual reconciliation? Were any (or all) of them free from blame?

8. Cara is trapped in an emotionally abusive marriage, but no one knows. Why do you think women are so reluctant to talk about hardships in their marriages, or to ask for help when they need it? Do you think society pressures women to keep their problems to themselves? Why or why not? Should Cara have behaved differently? If so, what should she have done?

9. At the end of the book, the girls have reconciled, but their futures are still very much up in the air. Do you think they will manage to maintain their friendship into their next decades? Or, once they go on with their lives, do you think they will ▶

drift apart again? What other challenges will they face as they get older? Is it really possible to have friends for a lifetime?

10. Which of the main characters do you identify with the most? Cara is headstrong and a perfectionist. Jane is a free spirit and a bit of a loose cannon. Meg is private and responsible. Why are they so drawn to each other when their personalities are all so different? Do opposites attract in friendship as well as in romance? What role do friendships play in a person's life? ～

Have You Read?
More from Erin Duffy

ON THE ROCKS

Six months ago, Abby's life fell apart for the entire world to see. Her longtime boyfriend-turned-fiancé, Ben, unceremoniously dumped her—on Facebook—while she was trying on dresses for the big day.

When the usual remedies—multiple pints of Ben & Jerry's, sweatpants, and a comfy couch—fail to work their magic, her best friend, Grace, devises a plan to get Abby back on her game. She and Abby are going to escape Boston and its reminders of Ben and head to Newport for the summer. There, in a quaint rented cottage by the sea, the girls will enjoy cool breezes, cocktails, and crowds of gorgeous men.

But no matter where they go, Abby and Grace discover that in this era of social media—when seemingly everyone is preserving every last detail of their lives online—there is no real escape. Dating has never been easy. But now that the rules are more blurred than ever, how will they find true love? And even if they do, can romance stand a chance when a girl's every word and move can go viral with a single click?

"Duffy's second novel [On the Rocks] is tenderly introspective. . . . Abby's attempts to navigate the ever-changing rules of dating are infinitely relatable and will prove to be an ideal beach read for fans of Elin Hilderbrand and Sarah Pekkanen." —*Booklist*

BOND GIRL

While other little girls were fantasizing about becoming doctors or lawyers, Alex Garrett dreamed of conquering the high-powered world of Wall Street. Now she's grown and determined to make it big in bond sales at Cromwell Pierce, one of the Street's most esteemed brokerage firms. Though she's prepared to fight her way into an elitist boys' club, she starts out small, relegated to a kiddie-size folding chair with her new moniker, "Girlie," inscribed in Wite-Out across the back.

Always keeping her eyes on the prize (and ignoring her friends' pleas for her to quit), Alex quickly learns how to roll with the punches, rising from lowly analyst to slightly-less-lowly assistant in no time. Suddenly she's being addressed by her real name, and the boys' club has transformed into forty older brothers . . . and one possible boyfriend. But then the apocalypse hits, and Alex is faced with the most difficult choice of her life: to stick with Cromwell Pierce as it teeters on the brink of disaster . . . or kick off her Jimmy Choos and go running for higher ground.

"I'm crazy about *Bond Girl*. Erin Duffy is a fresh, funny, and fabulous new voice in literature. Her heroine, 'Bond Girl' Alex Garrett, has moxie and drive, her veins are pumped with Red Bull while her heart is full of hope. At long last, thanks to Ms. Duffy, I grasp the world of high finance, and the hearts and minds that drive it. Great story. Delicious debut."

—Adriana Trigiani, author of *Lucia, Lucia* and *Brava, Valentine*